Ednah Walters

SEERESS

Book Three

Ednah Walters

Published by Firetrail Publishing

Firetrail Publishing
P.O. Box 3444 Logan,
UT 84323

Edited by Kelly Hashway
Cover Design by Cora Graphics.
First **Firetrail Publishing** publication: April 2014
www.firetrailpublishing.com

ALSO BY EDNAH WALTERS:

The Runes Series

Runes (book one)
Immortals (book two)
Grimnirs (A Runes book)
Seeress (book three)

The Guardian Legacy Series:

Awakened (prequel)
Betrayed (book one)
Hunted (book two)
Forgotten (coming 2015)

The Fitzgerald Family series
(Writing as E. B. Walters)

Slow Burn (book 1)
Mine Until Dawn (book 2)
Kiss Me Crazy (book 3)
Dangerous Love (book 4)
Forever Hers (book 5)
Surrender to Temptation (book 6)

DEDICATION

This book is dedicated to
my older sisters, Joyce and Meb.
Meb, you introduced me to romance genre
And I haven't stopped reading or writing, thank you.
Joyce, thanks for trading books with me.
You two rock as sisters.

ACKNOWLEDGMENTS

§

Many thanks to people who've supported me over the years:
To my editor, Kelly Bradley Hashway, my beta-readers and
dear friends, Jeannette Whitus and Jeanette A. Conkling,
you ladies are amazing. To my person/virtual assistant,
Julia Hendrix, I'm so lucky to have found you.
To my critique partners, Dawn Brown, Teresa Bellew,
Katherine Warwick/Jennifer Laurens, and Mercy,
thank you for being there when I need to vent.
Our friendship goes beyond writing and publishing.
To my husband and my wonderful children,
thank you for your unwavering love and support.
Love you, guys.
Last, but not least, to my wonderful fans
who have embraced this series thank you for your support,
show of love, and spreading the word about it.
You guys rock!!!!

TRADEMARK LIST

Google
Nikon
Mercedes
Elantra
Sentra
Harley
Chex Mix
Vampire Diary
Supernatural
The Originals
Warner Bros
Cheetos
Coca Cola Company
Poltergeist
The Three Stooges

GLOSSARY

Aesir: A tribe of Norse gods

Asgard: Home of the Aesir gods

Odin: The father and ruler of all gods and men. He is an Aesir god. Half of the dead soldiers/warriors/athletes go to live in his hall Valhalla.

Vanir: Another tribe of Norse gods

Vanaheim: Home of the Vanir gods

Freya: The poetry-loving goddess of love and fertility. She is a Vanir goddess. The other half of the dead warriors/soldiers/athletes go to her hall in Falkvang

Frigg: Odin's wife, the patron of marriage and motherhood

Norns: deities who control destinies of men and gods

Völva: A powerful seeress

Völur: A group of seeresses

Immortals: Humans who stop aging and self-heal because of the magical runes etched on their skin

Valkyries: Immortals who collect fallen warriors/soldiers/fighters/athletes and take them to Valhalla and Falkvang

Bifrost: The rainbow bridge that connects Asgard to Earth

Ragnarok: The end of the world war between the gods and the evil giants

Artavus: Magical knife or dagger used to etch runes

Artavo: Plural of artavus

Stillo: A type of artavus

Grimnirs: Reapers for Hel

Hel: The Goddess Hel in charge of the dead

Hel: Home of Goddess Hel, dead criminals, those dead from illness and old age

Nastraad/Corpse Strand: The island in Hel for criminals

Yggdrasil: The tree of life or tree of knowledge that connects the nine realms of Norse cosmology

Seidr: An old Norse term referring to a magical practice by the Norse, it includes act of divination or prophecy performed while in a trance.

Spákona: A Seidr Seeress

Necromancy: Witchcraft or use of magic and communicating with the dead in order to predict the future

1. A VISION

"Wet, drenched through, and shivering cold, despairing of ship or boat, we lifted up our eyes as the dawn came on," I read. *"The mist still spread over the sea, the empty lantern lay crushed in the bottom..."*

I studied my father's face, and my heart squeezed. *Moby-Dick* by Herman Melville was one of his favorite classics, yet even that couldn't hold his interest anymore.

"You stopped," he said slowly, his voice low and whispery.

"I thought you'd fallen asleep," I said and cleared my throat before adding, "Do you want me to continue?"

His eyelids lifted, and I stared into eyes the color of muddy pond water. The same eyes stared at me in the mirror every morning, except his were lackluster.

"No, pumpkin. I think Captain Ahab will have to wait until tomorrow. Get Femi, okay?"

"Okay." I reached for his hand, but he jerked away, cringing from my touch. His eyes sharpened in reprimand, and for one brief moment, I saw the father I'd known before the cancer ate up his brain. "Dad?" I asked.

"No more, Raine. You cannot keep trying to see my future when there's nothing to see. Accept it."

"I have." I meant to say it matter-of-factly, but my voice came out shaky.

A film of tears brightened his eyes, but his gaze didn't waver from mine. "I love you, sweetheart, but you cannot touch me anymore. The anguish in your eyes every time you do is too much. You must stop."

My hand fisted and fell to my side. I tried to tell myself he was right, but it still hurt. He was my father, the man who'd pushed me on swings, wiped my tears when I fell, and read to me from books about Norse pantheon when I was young and naïve and didn't know the stories were real. Now I couldn't touch or hug him because I was a Seeress. He closed his eyes, long lashes forming a canopy over gaunt, pale cheeks.

"Go," he urged.

An ache spread across my chest. I stood, stepped away from his bed, and placed the book on the table, my hand shaking slightly. Tears weren't far, but I fought them. He wasn't dead yet. I hated crying. Hated that I was a Seeress yet I couldn't see his future. Hated that I knew magical runes yet I couldn't heal him.

What good was magic and abilities when you couldn't help those you loved? The pain my father was enduring was too much. It wasn't natural. Somehow, I knew the Norns were behind it.

"Do you want the TV on?" I asked.

"Not right now. Just get Femi."

I left the room. Femi was in the kitchen looking up something online. Femi Ross wasn't your typical nurse. She was an inked, smart-mouthed Immortal who'd fought more battles than she had amulets and charm bracelets weighing down her arms. Looking at her spiked black hair and smooth brown complexion, you wouldn't guess she was Ancient Egyptian. Half the tats on her arms were hieroglyphs, including the ankh, the symbol of life.

She looked up and smiled. She had the same startling blue eyes as the boy I was madly and unequivocally in love with, except Torin's were brighter and sexier and had the ability to make me go soft and gooey inside. Hers didn't look bad on her either, just unusual for a brown-skinned person. I had no idea where Mom found her, but Valkyries and Immortals seemed to be everywhere these days.

This was the world I lived in now. The world of soul reapers and those they served and helped them: Valkyries, Grimnirs, Immortals, Seers, Norse gods and goddesses. Even my best friend Cora was part of my world, although I doubted she had a title. Soul Whisperer perhaps? She helped souls find closure. I was the Seeress who couldn't see anything. An epic failure as far as I was concerned.

"Are you two done reading?" Femi asked in a voice made raspy from screaming at concerts. She'd attended many, from rock-n-roll to rap. Personally, I think she used to be a smoker before smoking became uncool.

"For now. He wants to see you," I said.

She hopped off the chair and hurried toward me. Something about her often reminded me of Pink, the singer. She had the same rough-around-the-edges look and personality. She touched my arm. "You okay, doll?"

"Yeah."

"If you want to talk, I'll be back once I etch some pain runes on your father."

I shook my head and pushed hair away from my face. "No, I'm good."

"Super, but I'm here if you need me. I'll order something for dinner, so go visit the others." By the others she meant Torin.

She disappeared inside the den, my father's new bedroom. Mom had refurbished the room for him when he became too ill to climb the stairs. She'd be in there with him right now if she hadn't gone to Asgard for her hearing. She'd decided to rejoin the Valkyries after giving up soul reaping for love. For Dad.

Exhaling, I entered the bathroom by the den and closed the door. Lavania, my tutor, had said I could get premonitions by touching items and people. A soft brush with strings of Dad's brown hair, which I'd also inherited from him, begged me to pick it up.

I hesitated, unsure whether I should. Scared of what I'd see. Or not see. Blowing out air, I placed an unsteady hand on the thistles and closed my eyes.

Nothing. No sounds. No images. Just inky darkness.

Frustrated, I left the bathroom. Femi was a coffee addict, so there was always some brewing in the coffeemaker. I poured myself a cup, added creamer, and glanced at Torin's house.

The house next door would always be Torin's even though my childhood friend, Eirik, was the first to live there. The other Valkyries and Immortals had moved to the mansion up the hill, but Torin liked being close to me. It didn't matter that most places were only a portal away. He liked to glance out his kitchen or bedroom window and see me. Cute. I liked catching him watching me.

I caught movement from the corner of my eye and frowned when I saw a tawny-haired guy at the mailbox. What was Blaine doing picking up mail at Torin's?

Blaine Chapman came from a long line of Immortals. He and his family had left town until Torin asked for his help. Immortals were the backup team for Valkyries. They were earthbound and provided Valkyries with anything they needed, including pretend parents.

I carried my mug to the portal mirror in the living room and debated whether to use it. No, I only did that when Torin was home. It still amazed me how much my life had changed in the last seven months.

Last fall, I'd been your average high-school student with a crush on her childhood friend. Nothing exciting was happening in my life, just a looming seventeenth birthday and swim practice. Then a leather-wearing, dark-haired British guy knocked on my door and my life had never been the same.

Sipping my drink, I let myself out of the house. Spring was in the air, but the weather was typical Willamette Valley, Oregon: sunny one minute and rainy the next. It had rained a little in the morning, but the sun was back up again. A non-Oregonian would consider the day cold. To someone like me, born and raised here, it was perfect. I adjusted the hem of my fitted T-shirt.

Mrs. Rutledge, the nosey neighbor across from our cul-de-sac waved when she saw me. Before Dad's illness, she couldn't look at me without judging me. She hated young people. Or resented them. Now she found me tolerable. I was the poor girl whose father was terminally ill. Someone to be pitied.

I crossed the yard just as Blaine disappeared inside the house and closed the door. I should have used a portal. It was faster and private. I glanced over my shoulder and caught Mrs. Rutledge peering at me from behind her curtain.

Get a hobby already, lady.

It felt strange knocking on Torin's door. Usually the portal from my house led straight to the one in his bedroom or living room.

The door was yanked open from inside and Blaine scowled down at me. I was five-seven, taller than average for a girl, but he loomed over me. Most Immortals and Valkyries were tall. I tilted my head back and smiled.

"Oh you," he said as if I was the last person he wanted to see.

I didn't let his attitude get to me. He was in mourning, and my heart ached for him. Three months ago, his girlfriend, Casey Riverside, died during a football game, and he was pissed off at the world.

"Hey, Blaine."

He frowned, glanced over at my house then back at me, and cocked his brow.

"We haven't really talked since you came back. Do you want to come over?" I lifted my cup and grinned. "I have coffee."

He smiled, but it didn't reach his topaz eyes. Girls used to swoon whenever he turned those eyes and his megawatt smile in their direction. Me included. Now he was sullen and broken.

He shook his head, his wavy locks of hair flopping over his eyes. "I have to do some stuff at the mansion."

He sounded impatient to leave. "Oh. Okay. I thought I'd ask. See you." I turned to leave.

"How's your dad?" he asked.

I turned and gave him a tiny smile. "Still hanging in there."

"You know this is *their* fault," he said, voice low and accusatory, his eyes suddenly burning with rage.

"Whose fault?"

"The Valkyries. They have the power to save lives, but they pick and choose who they save."

"No, Blaine. The Norns are the only ones with the power to change destinies. Valkyries get in trouble if they use their artavo on Mortals."

He shook his head as though he didn't like what I was saying and stepped back from the door. I noticed the blade in his hand. Seven months ago, if a guy his size had stared me down with such rage while stroking a blade that sharp, I'd have taken off screaming. But I recognized the dagger for what it was—an artavus. We used them to draw runes on our bodies and on surfaces to create portals. Besides, as an Immortal, a cut might hurt for a second but it self-healed right away.

Blaine's anger was totally misdirected. He needed to talk to someone. "You sure you don't want to come over and talk?"

Topaz eyes met mine, then he looked away, but not before I saw the despair in their depth. "I'm heading back to the mansion then hitting the gym."

They had a fully-equipped gym at the mansion and an Olympic size pool. So unfair. "I could join you if you'd like."

A sad smile touched the corner of his lips. "Nah. I'm good. See you around, Raine. I hope your father… I hope you find him some help."

I didn't know how to respond to that. Dad's cancer had metastasized. Nothing could save him. Not human medicine and not all the runic magic in the world. Only death could set him free, and he was being denied that, too. I hated Norns.

"See you at school tomorrow." I turned and headed home.

TV sounds came through the door to the den, and I wished I was in there with Dad watching a game. I didn't even like football, but I now watched Sunday football religiously. How was that going to work now that I couldn't touch him? We'd probably sit far away from each other with separate bowls of popcorn.

My eyes smarted. I missed Mom. She would make all this bearable.

I glanced at my watch. It was barely after five and Torin wasn't due home for several hours. My best friend Cora hadn't called the whole day. She was probably out with her boyfriend, Echo.

I sent her a text, then grabbed a bag of lettuce from the fridge. I was in the middle of making myself a mean salad when warmth crept up my spine and my heart tripped.

Torin. His eyes on me always had the same effect.

"You're back early," I called out and glanced over my shoulder.

Torin walked away from the mirror portal in the living room. Leather jacket, jeans hugging narrow hips, and windblown hair wrapped in pure deliciousness couldn't begin to describe him. He sauntered to where I stood, his sexy smile melting my insides.

"I had a feeling you needed me," he said, the British lilt stroking my senses. He came to stand behind me and ran his knuckles up and down my arms, his movements slow and sensual. I shivered and leaned against him, welcoming his heat. "Your arms are freezing."

"I went outside to talk to Blaine."

"Blaine visited you?" He cross-crossed his arms around my waist and pulled me closer, curving his body into mine. I closed my eyes and inhaled. He smelled amazing. But when he rubbed his cheek against the side of my head, I tilted my head, so our faces could touch. His skin was hot.

"Freckles?"

"Hmm…"

"You're purring."

I was. "No, I'm not."

"Am I distracting you again?" he whispered.

He always did. "No. Did you ask me something?"

He chuckled. "What was Blaine doing here?"

"Collecting the mail from your mailbox. I invited him over, but he wasn't interested." I zipped up the plastic salad bag and put it aside. "He's a hot mess."

"He needs to get his act together." His breath teased my nape, and I shivered.

I turned in his arms and faced him, the bowl in my hand acting as a barrier. "He needs to talk to someone, Torin."

"Not you." He lifted the bowl out of the way and returned it to the counter. "You have enough on your plate."

"Then you do it."

He scoffed at the idea. "I'm not Dr. Phil."

I cocked my brow. "Do you even know who Dr. Phil is?"

"Nope, but he's the go-to guy when you don't want to face your demons."

"Says who?"

"Andris." Torin ran his knuckles along my cheek as though memorizing its texture. "Blaine can sweat away his problems in the gym like everybody else."

"That's not nice." I leaned back and punched him playfully in the stomach. He smirked. That iron-board stomach of his was all muscle. "He really needs help."

"I'll talk to him." He shrugged off his jacket and held it for me. I shoved my arms in the sleeves. "It is still too cold for you to be walking around without a coat. I don't know how you ever survived before me."

I rolled my eyes. "Yet here I am."

"You got by."

He moved closer until our thighs met and the edge of the counter pressed against my back. His warmth wrapped around me, messing with my senses. He caressed my chin, tilting it up, then sideways as though looking for something on my face.

His eyebrows lifted, his eyes losing their teasing gleam. "What's wrong?"

"Nothing." I turned and reached for my salad. "You want to share?"

"Is that your dinner?"

"Yep." He made a face, and I grinned.

"I can whip up something better if you'd like," he offered.

I studied his beautiful face: the chiseled cheekbones, the kissable lips, and gorgeous eyes. He was good at many things. Cooking, being a "big brother" to Andris, sports, fixing machines no matter how old or intricate. Best of all, he was good at making me happy. The last six months had been rough, but he'd made them bearable. I didn't want him to cook for me. I just wanted his arms around me.

"I'm really not hungry," I said.

He brushed strands of hair away from my face. "Then talk to me."

I hated running to him with my problems. Not that his broad shoulders couldn't carry them. My parents didn't raise a whiner and I didn't want to start being one now.

"Freckles, you know I will eventually know what it is, so you might as well fess up," he whispered, his hands coming to rest on my hips. He pulled me close, our hips locking. Bad idea on so many levels. He had a thing about invading my personal space. He craved contact all the time. "Is it Blaine and his I-hate-Valkyries rant? Because if you want me to shut him up, I will."

"No. Dad cringed from my touch today and told me I shouldn't touch him anymore."

Torin winced as though the words had been directed at him. "He thinks you're trying to see his future."

I nodded. "But I wasn't. I swear. He's so frail that sometimes when I'm reading to him and I can't hear him breathe, I panic." I looked down, feeling foolish. The move created some space between us. Torin up close could be so overwhelming. "I know that sounds insane because on one hand, I hate to watch him suffer this long and on the other, I'm scared he'll die before Mom comes back."

Torin lifted my chin. "It doesn't sound insane. Anyone's feelings would be ambiguous if they were in your shoes." Torin removed the bowl from my hand again, put it on the counter, and picked me up as though I weighed nothing. He headed for the round kitchen table, nudged a chair, and sat with me on his lap. I leaned against his broad chest and sighed.

Usually I hated it when he babied me, but today, I needed to cuddle and feel loved again.

He stroked the hair at my temple. "Did you see anything today?"

"Nah. Same inky nothing."

He rested his chin on my shoulder and reached down to play with my palm, running his fingers from the heel to my fingertips. The movement was stimulating and hypnotic. "How was he today?"

"Same as usual. We read *Moby-Dick*. He drifted a few times, but he knew when I stopped. Have you guys heard anything from Valhalla?"

"No. No one died in the pile-up in Seattle. A few old timers bound for Hel left with Grimnirs, but no healthy souls."

No wonder he'd come home early. I shivered despite his jacket, and his arms tightened around me. Ever since I'd learned that Norse Pantheon was real and Norns wanted me to join them, things had gotten crazy around here. Nothing was what it seemed.

Eirik Seville, my childhood friend and first crush, turned out to be the grandson of Odin, and the couple who'd raised him were merely Immortal guardians. But when my tutor took him home to Asgard, Eirik had rushed right back to help us fight off

Hel's private army sent by his mother, Goddess Hel. Turned out they were really after him.

Eirik being Eirik had made the ultimate sacrifice and headed to Hel to visit his mother on his own terms. Walked through the gates of Hel's Hall as the long lost son returning home, not a kidnapped victim. It took balls to do that.

We haven't heard from him in over three months. We didn't know whether he was okay or not. Worse, in all that time, no one destined for Asgard had died. People were having near-death experiences all over the place.

"Do you think we are responsible for what's happening with the healthy souls?" I asked.

Torin lifted my chin and pushed wisps of hair away from my face, his eyes darkening. "We?"

"Eirik and me. I won't join the Norns and he's in Hel instead of Asgard where they expected him to go."

Torin's eyebrows lowered. "Eirik made a choice. The Norns saw it coming and tried to prevent it, but it backfired on them. They also tried to influence you and that backfired in their faces, too. Don't start taking blame for everything that's wrong in our world."

I couldn't help it. Things started going crazy after I refused to leave with them. Deities, my butt. They were old hags acting like children. If they didn't get their way, they threw tantrums. The last time I saw them, they'd warned me about not choosing them and to be aware of vindictive gods and goddesses. I was supposed to foresee the exact moment the War of the Gods started, the beginning of the end of our world, and they wanted that knowledge. I ought to send them a memo that my visions were non-existent.

Torin pressed a kiss on my nose. "What are you thinking about?"

"Everything and everyone. Do you think Echo could try to find Eirik in Hel?"

"I'll ask him." Torin planted another one on me, his lips soft. The kiss was sweet, a mere whisper, yet I felt it to my core. "Knowing him, he'll say no just to piss me off."

Echo was Cora's boyfriend and Goddess Hel's number one reaper. Every time I thought about them, I smiled. They were an odd couple, but their relationship worked. One of the Immortals had marked Cora with weird runes and given her the ability to connect with souls and hear them. Then she'd fallen for Echo, a soul reaper. I'm talking madly, deeply, and I can't-live-without-you kind of love. Like what I had with Torin. If Echo loved her as much as Torin loved me, he would not refuse her anything.

"It might be better to let Cora do the asking." I angled my head and kissed Torin's jaw.

He smiled and lowered his head for a longer and deeper contact. He started to lift his head, but I cupped his face and held him in place. A shudder rolled through him, his heart beating in perfect sync with mine.

Time lost meaning as we got caught up in the moment. It was the same every time we kissed. He took me to a place where nothing mattered but him. His scent. His touch. The texture of his lips. I forked my fingers through his hair, loving the way the silky strands caressed my sensitive skin. He needed a haircut.

"About that salad," he whispered in a thick voice.

"Not hungry." He had a way of slowing us down when I didn't want us to. Except this time, he didn't put much effort into trying to slow things down. I tilted my head, so he could nibble my jaw.

I braced myself, but I could never be prepared for the shot of hot sensations when he nicked my ear. His hand moved down to rest on my waist, right where my top and pants met. He stroked the bare skin there, and I trembled.

"We really need that salad right about now," he growled in my ear.

He was right. Without my mom around, things could get out of control fast. She had a way of knowing when to interrupt us. Then there were her rules.

I buried my face in the crook of Torin's neck and tried to control my thundering heartbeat. He stroked the side of my face with the tips of his fingers until we calmed down.

I jumped and finished preparing the salad, adding mushrooms and tomatoes, then a liberal amount of dressing. I glanced over at Torin. His eyes were on me. The heated look unmistakable. I grabbed two cans of soda from the fridge. He'd developed a liking for root beer, the one drink I couldn't stand. I placed them on the table, straddled his chair, and sat on his lap again.

He chuckled. "You have a cruel streak in you, Raine Cooper."

"And you are a tease, Torin St. James." I forked some of the salad and was about to give it to him when I noticed the outline of something under his shirt. He never wore jewelry. "What's that around your neck?"

He tugged it from under his shirt. The ornate pendant looked old. "It's the original matrix of my family seal. It belonged to my grandfather, who gave it to my parents. My mother was attached to it. Echo found it at an auction a few weeks ago."

Torin was born during the reign of King Richard the Lion-hearted, when family seals were favored by noble families. The writing on the ornate pendant was a mirror image. I recognized *de Clare* written backward.

I touched the surface, and Torin disappeared.

Or maybe *I* disappeared.

All I knew was one second I was on his lap, the next I was outside, my thoughts jumbled up and my heart pounding. I looked around, not sure what had happened.

I was on top of a building. On the ledge. I looked down, my vision blurry as though I was looking through a smoke screen. Dizziness washed over me and for one second, I thought I'd lost my footing. I screamed. At least, I meant to. But there was no sound.

I tried to move away from the ledge, but my feet stayed cemented to the ground.

This was bad. I was perched precariously on top of a building without knowing how I got there. Could I be having a vision? Finally?

Below, sounds from cars, people, and machines added to the craziness. Above, the sun rode high in the sky. It was early afternoon. To my left was an industrial air vent.

This wasn't Kayville. My town was small and sat on the valley floor with mountains in the background. This town was spread out with tall buildings atop the flat surrounding land. *Then something even weirder happened.*

The clouds sped across the sky as though someone had pressed fast forward. The sun sunk into the horizon and darkness spread across the city. Below, streetlights sprung to life, and people moved at a supersonic speed. Then the voices died down as people went into their homes.

There was a new moon, so darkness clung to the sky. I shivered and tried to move again. No such luck. I squinted at my watch. My sight was still off, but I think my watch had stopped at three. Three am: the witching hour.

Light flickered at the other end of the roof behind the air vent. Shadows shifted on the rooftop as though there were people moving about. I strained to see through the hazy vision. I tried to walk again, tried to reach up and rub my eyes, but I couldn't move my arms either.

I sniffed and frowned. There was a weird scent. Incense or something. A song rose in the air. It was beautiful, yet eerie and seemed to have a lulling effect on me. My eyes closed.

No, no, I couldn't sleep while standing on a ledge. I struggled to stay awake. Then just like it had started, the music stopped. I strained against whatever was gluing me to the ledge.

Damn it. This was my first vision and I couldn't even see anything.

"Do you see them, Seeress?" a voice asked.

My stomach hollowed, and I stopped moving. The British accent was unmistakably British, like Torin's. A woman answered, but I didn't hear what she said. My mind was slow processing everything. Frustrated, I tried to move again and cursed. But like before, no sound came from my mouth.

"What do you see?" the dude with the British accent asked urgently with a tinge of desperation. He still sounded like Torin. This time I heard her.

"What you seek will only bring you pain and loss," the woman said.

"No, we will bring them loss and pain if they try to stop us. Where can I find them? The last Seeress chose not to cooperate, and I had to punish her. So speak the truth or join her."

"Then I choose to join her, you cursed son of a—"

A scream finished her sentence, the sound sending terror through me like a live wire. I landed on all fours on the roof. Finally, I was free. I tiptoed across the roof, my stomach churning, heat racing. I peered around the corner, expecting to find Torin and a dead Seeress at his feet.

There was nothing but an outline of a circle and runes inscribed on the ground. A fire burned in the middle of the circle, sending a strange smoky scent in the air. There were a few feathers on the floor covered with a dark, gooey liquid that could only be blood.

Witches sacrificed chickens, didn't they? These feathers were too big for a chicken. Maybe a giant turkey? I reached down to pick up one without blood but my hand only caught air.

Realization hit me. The stupid things weren't real. The whole set up wasn't real. The runes faded away. The fire flickered and the building disappeared from under my feet, leaving me in total darkness. I opened my mouth to scream.

"She's coming around," Torin said.

Bright lights shone on my eyelids, and I was lying on my back. I opened my eyes and found Torin. His features were taut, eyes shadowed, and hair a mess as though he'd run his fingers through it. The words I'd heard echoed in my head.

Had I witnessed something about to happen? Why would Torin want to visit a Seeress? *Kill* a Seeress?

"You okay?" he asked.

No, I was totally freaking out. I shook my head. Of course, he misunderstood and went into his protective mode. He wrapped his arms around me and lifted me.

I tried to wiggle out of his arms, but they tightened. He sat in the chair we were using earlier and placed me firmly on his lap. I got the message: I wasn't going anywhere.

"What happened?" I asked.

2. OLD RELIGIONS

Torin's eyebrows shot up. "That should be my line. Your eyes glowed, and then you slumped over in a dead faint." His voice was bleak.

"They're still glowing," Andris added.

I looked up and tried not to cringe. They were all here, Valkyries and Immortals—Andris, Ingrid, Femi, and even Blaine. I groaned at the curiosity in their eyes. My first vision and they all had to be here for the humiliating details?

"You had to call them in?" I griped, elbowing Torin.

He didn't even flinch, his jaw set. I hated it when he got that look. It meant nothing I said was going to stop him.

"I had to send someone to get your mother," he said.

"What? She's supposed to be sequestered until the end of her hearing." I looked around. "Where is she?"

"Andris was just about to leave. And FYI, you are more important than a stupid hearing." His eyes dared me to tell him I was wrong.

"The hearing is important, too. She comes back and poof goes her only chance to rejoin the Valkyries." He *would* send for her and damn the consequences. And knowing my mother, she'd ignore the rules and run to my side. "You know what? Forget it. You are impossible and annoyingly stubborn. How long was I out?" I asked.

"About an hour," Torin said. "What happened?"

I shuddered, remembering the scream. "I think I got my first vision."

Torin's eyebrows slammed down. "You think?"

The others left the counter and grabbed chairs around the kitchen table, eager for details. Andris was having a lazy Sunday, which meant pajama day. From his messy hair, he'd probably been having a read-a-thon. He winked when our eyes met.

Ingrid watched him with a hard-to-read expression. She always looked like she'd stepped out of bed ready to wow the world. Perfect hair. Flawless makeup. A body any Victoria's Secret model would kill for wrapped in the latest designer outfit.

Blaine grabbed an apple from the bowl before taking a chair. His expressionless face said he didn't really want to be here, but he was part of the group whether he liked it or not. Femi stayed by the counter, working on her laptop, but I knew she wasn't missing a thing. She might be a housekeeper slash nurse, but I had a feeling Mom had asked her to keep an eye on us.

"Raine," Torin urged, his arms tightening around my waist.

He was tense and edgy, and being this close to him was making me edgy, too.

Gripping his hands, I pulled them away from my waist and moved from his lap to the adjacent empty chair. He leaned forward as I explained what happened.

"It was just so weird," I finished. Torin scowled as though he could see through me to the parts I'd omitted, like the part he, or the man sounding awfully like him, played. "Anyway, that's it," I said. "My pitiful first vision."

"There was no pentagram inside the circle?" Andris asked.

I shook my head. "Just the inscribed runes, the fire, and the feathers."

"That's Seidr," Ingrid murmured from my right.

I glanced at her. "Say-what?"

Ingrid's cheeks grew pink. "Seidr, the magical practice of my people," she said. Ingrid was originally from Norway and still spoke with an accent. Unlike the others, she'd only been an Immortal for about a century.

"You sacrificed chickens?" Andris asked.

Ingrid glared at him.

"Raine mentioned feathers and blood," Andris protested and shot her an apologetic look. "It is not a stretch, right?" Ingrid's face said she wasn't forgiving him. "Tell us about Say-der," he urged, pronouncing it slowly.

Ingrid shrugged. "Maybe I'm wrong."

Ingrid didn't talk much. She'd been used to living in the shadow of her more beautiful and magnetic older sister Maliina. Then when Maliina went psycho and started working for the evil Norns, Ingrid crawled farther into the shadows. She probably felt ashamed of all the mayhem her sister had caused. This was the first time I'd heard her offer an opinion on anything.

I kicked Andris under the temple and gave him the behave-or-else glare. "I don't care if you are wrong or right, Ingrid," I said. "Tell us about this practice."

She glanced at Torin and blushed even harder. Torin, I'd noticed, tended to make her more nervous.

"Pretend they're not here," I urged her. "I do it whenever they act like morons."

She smiled. "It is a trance magic," she said. "We use it for many things, but what you heard was probably a Seeress in a trance seeking guidance from the spirit world."

I wasn't sure I liked that. "Why did she appear to me?"

"I don't know," Ingrid said, but I had a feeling that she did.

"I think it is the other way round," Femi said from the counter. We all looked at her.

"That doesn't make sense," Torin said. "Raine is a Seeress."

News flash, love of my life. I haven't seen anything yet to warrant that title.

"I know, but I think the Seeress reached out to Raine." Femi stepped down from the stool. She was about five-six, the shortest of all the Immortals I'd met so far. But she knew how to command attention with her personality and voice.

She pushed her hands into the pockets of her nurse's tunic and studied our faces. The uniform wasn't really necessary, but she insisted on it. How had she put it? She was covering all bases in case our nosey neighbors wondered why Dad wasn't in a hospital or nursing home.

"How much have you learned about the path of the Valkyries, Raine?" she asked.

"It is a journey and only a select few make it," I said. "Spiritual people are chosen by priestesses and taught about magical incantations, spells, and runic magic. If the high priestess deems them worthy and receptive to the idea of immortality, they are taught about the path to the gods. In olden times, it took years to get to that point. Now?" I shrugged. I was the poster child of high-speed transition to Immortality. "Anyway, from these priests and priestesses, a select few are chosen to become Immortal and given artavo for etching runes. Some stay on earth to serve humans, while others become Valkyries."

Femi nodded. "Those not chosen to become Immortal continue to practice magic. Now, there all types of magical practices out there, but Ingrid is right. What you heard or saw are used in Seidr."

"Whoa, I didn't go through *all that* to become a Valkyrie," Andris interrupted.

"It is a bit different for you boys," Femi said. "You were chosen in the battlefields, but Lavania made sure she chose well." She slanted Torin a look then Andris. "You are both very spiritual."

Torin nodded impatiently.

"Nah," Andris cut in. "I'm not buying this spiritual crap. I didn't learn about the gods and runes until *after* Lavania healed me and turned me into an Immortal. It was a life-or-death situation. In fact, I was in a bathhouse getting my—"

"We don't want to hear about your bathhouse adventures, Andris," Ingrid interrupted sharply. "Let Femi talk."

I was so liking this new Ingrid. She was coming out of her shell and kicking ass. Even Andris gawked at her.

"I wasn't talking about *that*," Andris protested.

"You always do," she said. Then, as though she realized she was once again the center of attention, she blushed. I reached for her hand and squeezed.

"I agree with Ingrid," Torin said and gave Andris a look that said if he opened his mouth one more time, he was going to flatten him, which was like waving a red flag at a bull. I really didn't need their testosterone crap right now.

"Down, boys," I said. "I want to hear this." Silence followed as our attention shifted to Ingrid. She hesitated.

"Tell them, sweetheart," Femi urged her.

Ingrid gave her a small smile. "Seidr is a trance magic because you can only do it when you are in a trance. It can be used for good or evil, so some consider it a dark magic," she said.

She had all our attention. Even Femi pulled out the last chair and sat.

"The Vanir people and gods practice Seidr, but Goddess Freya, a Vanir, is the one who brought it to Asgard and taught it to the Aesir gods. Odin, his wife, Frigga, and even Thor's wife, Sif, now practice Seidr. Odin is known to go into a trance or to appear to be asleep when he's off in different realms. He uses spirit guides to see things, including his birds."

Lavania had mentioned Odin's birds and how they gathered information for him. She never said how Odin used them. Ingrid gestured as she continued to talk, her cheeks flushed. This was the most animated I'd ever seen her.

"But Freya will always remain the goddess of Seidr. She shape shifts into other animals and even owns a magical coat of falcon feathers that turns her into a falcon when she wears it. That's why Seidr Seeresses cover themselves with animal cloaks or sit on cushions made of feathers." She peered at me. "The blood you saw was probably from the Seeress being killed." She glared at Andris. "We don't sacrifice chickens."

He smirked. I wondered if he'd deliberately mentioned sacrificing chickens to get a rise out of her. He was the one who had runed her and Maliina, making them immortal. Surely, he must know about their practices.

"While in a trance state," Ingrid continued, "a person takes spirit journeys. Some use familiars, like Odin's birds. Others use spirit guides. They can conjure images, good or bad, and project them into the minds of others. Deliver spells. Blessings or curses. But the more advanced practitioners and the Seeresses can travel to other realms. Just like Odin and Freya."

"Can they visit Asgard?" Blaine asked.

"Still planning to visit your girlfriend?" Andris teased Blaine.

Blaine sat up, eyes narrowed, but one glance from Torin and he sank back into his seat. But the look he gave Andris could have neutered any grown man. Andris just smirked.

I kicked him under the table again.

Andris glared. "Do that again and you'll be sorry."

Torin smirked. "Really?"

He could convey so much with just a word. This one had whoop-ass written all over it. Andris just shrugged as though saying "whatever."

"Uh, the journeys can take them anywhere, but most of them go to Hel," Ingrid said. "All our ancestors are in Hel's Hall. So when you want to know something, they are the ones you talk to. Some Seeresses communicate with the Norns." Ingrid paused then added slowly, "I think the Seeress probably connected with you, Raine, instead of a Norn."

If she'd reached over and slapped me, I wouldn't have been more surprised. Norns were the bane of my existence. It was my job as a Seeress to see their secrets, damn it. Not become the go-to person for magical people who couldn't communicate with them. I crossed my arms and pressed against my stomach, feeling a little sick.

"Why in Hel's Mist would she connect with Raine?" Torin snapped, and Ingrid jumped. "She's not a bloody Norn." His accent tended to grow stronger when he was pissed. I reached for his hand under the table and interlaced our fingers.

Ingrid threw me an apologetic glance and shrugged. "Maybe the Seeress is a novice and didn't know what she was doing."

"Or maybe she knew exactly what she was doing," Femi said slowly, and we all focused on her. "Maybe she wanted Raine to witness her death. Like Ingrid had said, Seeresses do other things, not just travel to different realms. They roam this realm too and do things, good and bad. Drive people crazy with spells or protect them from harm. Find missing children and dogs. Cheating spouses. Those with powers over the elements can mess with nature. They can cause winds, storms, and drought. Seeresses communicating with each other is something I'd never heard of before, but she may have chosen to connect with Raine instead of a Norn for a reason."

O-kay. She wasn't helping. Torin looked like he wanted to rip something apart. Why would a Seeress want me to witness her death? Everyone was staring at me as though waiting for something.

"My watch said it happened at three in the morning. Maybe I'm supposed to find this Seeress and help her before she is killed," I said.

Femi nodded. "That's possible."

"Do you remember anything about the city, landmarks that could give us a clue about where she lives?" Torin asked.

"No. It's still blurry, but the landscape was flat. No mountains and hills. No water. Lots of tall buildings." Kayville's tallest buildings were only four stories high.

"That could be anywhere," Torin said and leaned back into his chair, but I could tell his mind was racing and searching for a solution. "The death of one Seeress will go unnoticed by the magical world. Several could start a ripple."

"He said another Seeress had sent him, or something along those lines," I said.

"Maybe we should warn witches not to hold a séance for some psycho killer at three in the morning," Andris suggested.

I liked that. "Can't you guys talk to the other Valkyries?" I asked. "So they can warn the Seeresses in their reaping grounds?"

Torin looked like he was about to argue, but then he nodded. Reluctantly. "Valkyries don't socialize with witches, unless they're about to turn them." He glanced at Blaine. "But the Immortals can help spread the word. I'll be back." He squeezed my arm, jumped up, and disappeared toward the portal.

"So what was the purpose of the fire, the runes, and the circle?" Blaine asked.

Ingrid glanced at him, her pale blond hair swinging across her cheeks. She'd recently chopped her long strands into a bob cut. Andris hated it. Personally, I think it suited her. Gave her that polished Upper East Side socialite look.

"The circle contains the energy and magic within that narrow space and protects it," she explained. "Unlike other forms of magical practices, Seidr witches don't have covens. There's no drumming or frenzied dancing. We sing a special song, and that's it."

"The song I heard?" I asked.

She nodded. "A Seeress chooses an elevated place somewhere where there's very little distraction, creates a protective circle around her, and burns recels to purify the space and clear her mind of all things worldly. In most cases, someone sings the Seidr song to relax the Seeress and help her drift into a trance. The runes help her channel her visions."

I was so going to need lots of runes, because even when summoned, everything had been blurry. Not only was I supposed to get visions, I had to worry about other Seeresses contacting me for help. My life couldn't get any weirder.

I glanced toward the portal, wondering where Torin had disappeared to. The conversation around the table revolved around magical practices. Blaine had something to say about Gaelic magic, which his people practiced in Ireland.

"Don't ask me how our magic works because we're sworn to secrecy and any Druid or Druidess worth their salt will keep that to their death. That's why your people came after us." He glared at Andris. "You didn't just hate that the entire Gaulish society depended on us. You hated the fact that we refused to share our knowledge."

"Before my time, Chapman, so put a sock in it." Andris blew him a kiss. He was born in Rome, just before the Ottoman invaded and captured Constantinople. "By the time I arrived, you guys were extinct."

"Gone underground," Blaine retorted.

"Whatever, dude." Andris glanced around the table. "I wish I had cute anecdotes to share. We had pentagrams and covens and witch hunts, the worst time to be a witch." He glanced at Femi. "May I borrow your laptop?"

Femi waved toward the counter, where she'd left her computer. Andris left the table.

"What was your magic like, Femi?" I asked.

She grinned, studying her charm bracelets. "Egyptian magicians were powerful in the old days. They didn't just communicate with the gods; they controlled them. When we wanted to know something, we channeled the powers of a particular god. Say I wanted to know about the harvest, I channeled Hapi, the god of the Nile. We created statues of the gods, which acted as oracles. Or we got visions through incubation," Femi said.

Everyone wore a perplexed expression.

"What is incubation?" I asked.

"Sleeping in a god's temple to get visions through dreams," Femi explained.

Torin returned, and the room became quiet. "It's done. I talked to a few Valkyries, who agreed to pass the info to other Valkyries and Immortals. Others weren't home, but the word is out."

"I'm done, too," Andris said. He turned the laptop around. On the screen were several open windows. "Message boards for witches. I just posted a warning anonymously under Seeresses Beware."

Torin gave Andris a back slap. "Good job, bro. That should cover things for now." He stopped behind me, slid his hands down my arms, and whispered, "Do you want to go for a ride?"

Anything was better than sitting here worrying, talking, and thinking about visions. "Sure. Can I be in charge?"

"Aren't you always?"

Yeah, for about five seconds. "Okay. Let's go."

"But I ordered dinner," Femi said when she realized we were leaving.

"We'll eat when we come back," I said. "Rides tend to make me hungry."

Andris whistled. "Oh, I need that kind of ride."

Torin smacked the back of his head. I just shook my head. Andris always reduced everything to something lewd.

***

I loved the Harley since the first time Torin had offered me a ride to school and showed me what he could do with his runes. It was like hurtling down on *Formula Rossa* without safety straps. Dangerous, but exhilarating.

Torin went to get another leather jacket when we arrived next door. He hadn't changed the décor even though Andris, Ingrid, and Lavania moved to the mansion. The white and gray furniture and framed nature pictures on the walls weren't really him. He was more leather and chrome.

"Are you ever going to move to the mansion?" I asked, adjusting the leather gloves.

He adjusted the collar of my jacket, lifting my hair out of the way. "Do you want me to?"

"No." I adjusted his collar too, my hand lingering on his wide shoulders. "I like looking across the yard and seeing you tinker in the kitchen."

"That's insulting." He lowered his head until his lips were inches from mine and whispered, "I don't tinker." His warm breath teased my lips.

"But you look so adorable doing it."

"Adorable is you chewing your lower lip and looking unsure about what to do next. Adorable is you scolding Andris because he's being a turd again or having one of your heated debates with your... dad."

Dad and I hadn't had one of our debates in weeks. "Okay. You look sexy. Let's go." I pushed open the door to his garage, but he grabbed my hand and pulled me to him. He lifted my chin.

"You'll have to start talking about him, Freckles."

"I know he's dying, but..." I sighed. "I just don't want to talk about him as though he's gone. He might never cook for me or debate or go for runs, but... but he's still here."

"I know."

"And I hate saying 'Dad used to do this or that.' I want him healthy, yet I know it's never going to happen."

"Come here." Torin started to pull me into his arms, but I jumped back.

"You are just trying to get out of letting me take the first seat." I wagged my finger. "Not happening, mister." I ran into the garage with him hot on my tail. When I glanced back, the look on his face said he knew I was bailing.

I wanted to be as far away from here as possible. Put distance between me and my problems. It was irrational. No one could outrun their problems, but I was going to try.

We grabbed helmets and goggles. His hair had grown long. I tucked in a few strands and got rewarded with a kiss on my nose. He pressed the keys in my hand.

"It's all yours," he said.

Grinning, I straddled the bike and turned the key. The purr of the engine filled the garage. I'd never get tired of feeling the power of the modified Harley engine. Or Torin curled onto my back with his masculine arms wrapped tightly around me. I always felt safe when he did that, even though I was the one controlling the machine.

"Where are we going?" he asked.

We only have an hour or so of daylight, but that shouldn't be a problem. "Uh, Portland? It's only an hour away and I can practice weaving between cars in a big city."

"Um, okay," he said slowly.

He was humoring me. I wasn't ready to drive at a super speed in a city. Mrs. Rutledge peered at us as we pulled off. Was she ever going to get tired of spying on us?

"Seriously, where are we going?" Torin asked.

"Don't worry. I'll bring you home in one piece," I teased.

He chuckled, but didn't push for an answer. I grew up in Oregon and knew every landmark, back road, and hidden treasure. Dad often took us on long drives in the backcountry on weekends, camping, biking, and fishing. I could find most places without a map.

We left Kayville behind and headed toward I-5. The traffic was low. Typical Sunday evening. "Ready?" I called out.

"Ready," Torin yelled back.

We engaged our runes at the same time. The effect packed quite a punch, like a shot of dopamine. We shifted to super speed, zipping past cars and dodging oncoming ones. I took corners like an Indy car racer, laughing and woo-hooing. Torin laughed.

We hit I-5 and headed south. I loved that he trusted me enough to let me take the front seat. If only he did it often. Twenty minutes later, I exited the highway and used back roads until we reached the south entrance to Crater Lake National Park.

We parked by the gate and removed our helmets.

Torin looked around. "Where are we?"

"Crater Lake National Park. My family used to come here a lot. We'd camp or stay at one of the cabins." Funny how I left home to get away from thoughts of Dad and we ended up at one of his favorite places. There was still snow on the ground, but in the summer, the place was spectacular. "We should come back here in the summer. The lake is breathtaking."

It was past five and the park was closed, but a few cars dotted the parking lot at the entrance. Some people drove past us and stared. I wasn't sure whether the attraction was Torin or the Harley. It was the same everywhere we went.

"Ready to go back?" Torin asked.

"Not yet." There was really nothing to see unless we went inside the park, but it was a nice resting place. Torin leaned against the bike and pulled me into his arms. I wrapped my arms around his waist and tried to enjoy the moment, but the vision I'd seen came back to haunt me. I lifted my head and studied his face. "Would you visit a Seeress if I disappeared and you didn't know where to look?"

He stiffened. "What?"

"If something bad happened to me—"

"That's not funny." He glowered.

"It's a hypothetical situation, Torin."

"I don't care. Don't say that."

I sighed. "Okay, I won't. But would you visit a Seeress to see the future if a friend was missing and you didn't know where she was?"

"Why is my friend a *she*? I don't have she-friends except you."

I wanted to deck him. He could be so impossible sometimes. "If a *he*-friend was sick, would you visit a Seeress to get some answers?" I said through clenched teeth.

"Nope." He smirked, confirming he was messing with me.

I wiggled out of his arms and gave him a you'd-better-answer-me-truthfully-or-else glare. "Why not?"

"I don't like witches."

My jaw dropped. "How can you say that? I happen to be one. A Seeress."

"Until we confirm your first vision, you," he stroked my nose, "are just a glorified Immortal and… my girlfriend."

I punched his arm. Hard. "Jerk."

"Witch."

I reached for him, but he engaged his runes and slipped past me. Then he had the nerve to laugh. There were no more vehicles left in the parking lot, so I figured no one could see us. I engaged my runes and went after him. I tackled him, or he allowed me to catch him, and we landed on the snow. We rolled a bit until I pinned him down. I had snow in my hair. I shook it, spraying him.

"Cut that out," he growled, a playful light in his eyes.

"What do you have against witches?" I asked.

He cushioned his head on his arms and smirked. "The ones I knew growing up were horrible."

"What did they do to you?"

He pulled me down for a kiss and the conversation was forgotten, until I became aware of cold and wetness on my knees. Torin's pants had to be wet, too.

"Let's take this home," I whispered.

"I like it when you lust after me."

"Shut up."

He studied me in the fading light. "Feel better?"

"Yeah." I got off him and pulled him up.

The drive home was shorter since speed junkie was in charge. The others were gone. Femi was in the laundry room, folding up clothes fresh from the dryer. The TV was on and a quick glance inside the den showed Dad propped up against pillows watching a basketball game.

"Hey, Dad," I said.

He looked up and smiled. "Hey, sweetheart. What happened? We were supposed to read this morning."

I frowned. One, he sounded coherent. Two, we'd read. "Uh, Dad, we—"

Then I remembered my marathon reading on everything brain cancer after I learned about his illness. Memory loss was one of the symptoms of the cancer in his part of the brain. It was probably silly of me, but I was happy he couldn't remember this morning and what he'd said about me not touching him.

"Uh, we can read now," I said.

"After the game," Dad said. "The Grizzlies' in-your-face defense is killing us. Scott should call a time out and come up with a better play. "

Smiling, I closed the door. He sounded like his old self. Didn't know long it would last, but I was watching that game with him.

"He's watching a Blazer game," I told Torin. "I'm going to hang out with him for a while."

"No problem. I'll just grab my food." Two boxes from WOTG—Wok on the Go—and chopsticks were on the counter. He peered inside. "Sweet and sour or beef and broccoli?"

"Either." I got a drink, kissed him, and shooed him out of my kitchen. "Go. Warm yours at your place. I'll see you later."

On a different day, he would have been insulted I was kicking him out. I got my warmed sweet and sour chicken on rice and hurried to Dad's room.

3. BEWITCHING SONG

The next morning my throat felt funny from all the yelling. Last night, Dad had acted like his old self, bringing back memories. He and Eirik used to watch games and yell at the players. Eirik...

I missed him. Worried about him. I tried not to, but I couldn't help myself. I didn't care that he'd chosen to visit his parents in Hel. The fact remained it had been months and we still hadn't heard anything.

But worrying about him wasn't going to bring him back.

I jumped up and walked to the window. Torin was in his kitchen. Shirtless. Those abs. That sculptured, endless chest. There ought to be a law against men like him and sweatpants that hang so low they bordered on indecent. He reached down and scratched his butt.

I giggled. Only Torin could look hot scratching his perfect ass.

He disappeared from the window. Dang it. He was supposed to glance out the window and check on me first. Now I wasn't going to get my morning coffee.

I turned to head to the shower, and he walked through the portal shirtless and barefoot. He had the sexiest feet ever. I ogled him a little. Okay, a lot.

"You continue with that and I'll forget your mom is not here," he warned, putting the cup on my dresser.

I braced myself against his chest, went on my toes, and kissed him. I couldn't help what I did next. I scratched his butt. "Still itchy?"

He chuckled, wrapping an arm around my waist. "I knew you were checking me out, you perv."

"How? Your back was to me."

"I have lustful-eyes-on-me radar." My feet left the floor as his lips claimed mine in a kiss that shot from warm to scorching in warp speed. Then we were rolling on the bed. I did what any sane girl would do when met with a force beyond her control. I soaked it all in and clung.

He tasted amazing. Coffee, vanilla, and stomach-curling goodness. He rolled again so I was on top. He knew how I loved that. My thick hair formed a curtain around us. *He* loved that.

"Good morning, Freckles," Torin whispered against my lips, his hand slipping lower.

"Behave," I warned, grabbing his hand and bringing it back to my waist.

He chuckled, the sound sexy. "You scratch and I scratch back."

Now he was putting ideas in my head. "Sounds fair."

"I love it when you agree with me." He planted a kiss on my nose. "Last night must have been great. You had a smile on your face earlier when I stopped by."

"Watching me sleep is creepy."

"I like creepy, but I hate this new sleeping arrangement."

Me too. We'd agreed on brief goodnight and morning kisses while Mom was gone. No sleepovers. No risking things getting out of hand. Mom was my chastity belt. Her impeccable timing just when things got interesting never failed to amaze me.

In one smooth move, he rolled us over, so he was on top. "Tell me about last night."

Was he serious? I couldn't think. "I, uh… uh…"

"Breathe, Freckles," he whispered.

Stinker. "I had Dad back and it was great, but we lost to the Grizzlies. A win would have made the night perfect."

"I'm sure having you there made it memorable for him." After another long kiss, Torin shifted. Cool air rushed in to replace him, and I shivered. "Come over to the mansion when you're ready. I need to see Blaine about something."

"Is everything okay?"

"He wants to move out, but I want him to stay. We have to stick together, despite our petty differences. He's an asset I don't want to lose." He ran a finger along my nose and stood.

Once he left, I sipped the coffee and smiled. It was scary how he knew what I liked. He paid attention to details. One of his many loveable qualities. The ding of my phone greeted me when I left the shower.

Cora. I texted her back, then got ready as fast as I could.

"Breakfast is on the stove," Femi called from the foot of the stairs when she saw me. She was on her way to Dad's room with a tray.

"Thanks. Is he up?"

"Yes." She pushed the door with her shoulder. "Stop by before you leave."

In other words, he wasn't ready for company. Femi meant well. She was overprotective of Dad and only allowed me to see him when he was at his best. Most of the time, I didn't mind. But after last night, I really wanted to see if he was okay.

I wasn't in the mood for eggs. I dropped frozen waffles in the toaster and finished my drink. Outside, the sun was warming our yard. I wondered how long that was going to last. Six more weeks of school then summer break and my eighteenth birthday. I couldn't wait.

I had a lot planned for my birthday. For now, I was taking it one day at a time. Dealing with Norns had been rough, but hopefully they were gone. For now anyway. I was under the protection of the gods. All because I would foresee the beginning of Ragnarok, the battle between the gods and the giants, the flooding and destruction of the worlds. It sounded all too surreal. I, a mere seventeen year old, would foresee the exact moment the world ended.

"He's ready now," Femi called out, snapping me out of my daydream. I left my bags at the entrance of the portal and went to see Dad. He was listening to an audio book.

"Morning, Daddy. What are you listening to?"

"The book we forgot to read last night."

"We can continue after school." He patted my hand, and I froze. I smiled and turned my hand to grip his.

"Can you run by the shop after school and see how things are going?" he asked.

"Sure."

"And, uh, ask Jared about tax forms and the inventory. I know it's asking a lot—"

"It's okay. I can handle it." I pressed a kiss on his cheek. "Love you."

"Same here, kiddo."

I left his room, grabbed my things, and engaged my runes. The runes on the frame responded and the mirror became grainy. "See you later, Femi."

She blew me a kiss. "Have fun, doll."

While the others could open portals to just about anywhere they'd ever visited, I tended to use people as locators. I visualized Torin and the portal opened to reveal the mansion's hallway. I followed their laughter to the kitchen.

Torin was by the stove while the others sat around the counter eating. The aroma of mouth-watering breakfast wafted in the air. It was cute how he still took care of them despite living elsewhere. That was the kind of guy he was, and the others, consciously or not, always deferred to him.

He'd changed into my favorite blue polo shirt. It made his eyes pop, hugged his masculine arms, and fitted snuggly across his broad chest. He gave me a slow, wicked smile. His eyes said he liked what I was wearing. Warmth crept up my cheeks.

We'd been dating for about five months, give or take a few weeks, and he still took my breath away. He was the only guy with the power to make me blush with a look.

"Is that your breakfast?" he asked.

I glanced at my pitifully dry waffles. "Yep. One hundred and eighty calories of pure goodness."

"Come here," he said and reached up for another plate, his shirt riding up to give me a teasing glimpse of his rock hard abs. He served the remaining sausage and potato breakfast skillet into two plates, and we joined the others.

***

Cora and Echo were making out by her car when we pulled up. The two never failed to make me smile. Psycho Maliina had used her Norn powers to completely mimic Cora and fooled us for weeks. We didn't know Cora had been admitted to a psyche ward during those weeks because Maliina had marked her with some jerked up runes and she could see souls. Like any sane person, Cora had thought she was seeing ghosts and going crazy. Meeting Echo had changed her perception of things.

"Come on," Torin said, wanting us to leave the couple alone.

I dug my heels in. "I want to talk to Cora."

Torin sighed. "I don't want to deal with *him* this early in the morning."

I thought they'd made up, but I supposed a few months of working together couldn't erase centuries of bad blood. Grimnirs like Echo reaped for Hel and had a long history of stealing souls bound for Valhalla.

"You two need to make up. Cora is still my best friend."

"*I* am your best friend," he said firmly, hand slipping around my waist.

I gave him a look over my shoulder and teased, "I don't know. She's my best *girlfriend*, but Eirik... now *he* is best friend material." My voice cracked. "You're just a glorified Valkyrie... my boyfriend."

Blue flames leaped in his eyes. He leaned down and whispered in my ear, "Boyfriend, lover, guinea pig for naughty fantasies, and—"

"Shut up." Just like that, he'd deliberately distracted me from my worries about Eirik. He had an uncanny way of reading me.

"I'm not complaining, you understand," he added. "Just want to make sure you recognize my awesomeness."

"Oh, I recognize alright." I bumped him with my hip. "Your arrogance."

"We were having a moment here, you two," Echo griped, and we looked their way. Cora waved from the confine of his arms. Despite his voice, Echo didn't look angry.

He winked at me. "Hey, *Völva*. Why are you with the Valkyries when you could be running on the wild side with us?"

"I'm neutral, Echo. But if I were to choose, I'd be on the human side."

Echo smirked. "Uh, the losing side?"

Cora stepped from Echo's arms. She looked radiant as usual. Hair perfectly curled. Makeup flawless. We hugged.

"Sorry I was MIA over the weekend. Echo hid my phone."

And she said that while grinning? The girl I knew didn't take crap from any guy, not even one she was nuts about. "And you let him?"

Cora grinned. "He was being protective, and he's adorable when he shifts into a protective mode."

Was she serious? Torin was unbearable when it came to protecting me. Made me want to scream.

"I spent Saturday on soul duty," Cora continued. "I crashed afterwards and didn't wake up until yesterday afternoon. He was pissed I'd overdone it. Mom thought I was coming down with something and insisted I stay in bed." She turned, and I followed her gaze to Echo. "I didn't mind."

I'd bet. Echo and Torin were having an intense conversation by the Harley. Girls walking past turned and stared at them. Seeing the two of them together showed just how different, yet alike they were. They were both tall and in amazing shape. Maybe it was the way they carried themselves, confident and cocky. Whatever it was, it gave them a magnetic aura no woman could resist. But that was where their similarities ended.

Torin had a refinedness or refinement that made him slip in and out of any situation and fool anyone that he was just another pretty face, yet in a fraction of a second, turn feral to protect those he loved. Echo, on the other hand, was the kind of guy you met in a crowded room and warning signals went off to run in the opposite direction. Cora had chosen to run toward him instead.

Today, he almost looked like a normal guy in black jeans and a matching T-shirt under his duster. Usually, he preferred leather pants, a vest, and sailor shirts. So last century. The Druid rings were an on-and-off thing, but the fingerless gloves, like Torin's, were on all the time. I didn't know what that was about.

Torin rocked whatever he wore. The black boots and leather jacket were all kinds of sexy, and I loved the way his jeans hung perfectly. But if I had to choose between jeans and sweats, sweats would win hands down.

"We're lucky, aren't we?" Cora said.

I looped an arm around hers. "Why?"

"Our men have the sexiest asses in the entire universe."

Trust Cora to say something raunchy. "You're not lusting after mine, are you?"

She laughed. "Looking, Raine. I'm in love, not blind, but I leave the puppy-dog drooling to you. And quit pretending you weren't checking out my man, too. I saw you."

I laughed. "Let's go before the bell rings. Torin can be late and get away with it."

"That's because he has no problem runing teachers and anyone else to get his way, while you're chicken."

"Cautious, smarty pants. Not the same thing." We started across the street, but the guys ran to catch up.

"We should let them walk in front of us for a better view," Cora said.

"Better view of what?" Torin asked, coming up behind me and putting an arm around my shoulders.

"Your asses," Cora said, slipping a hand inside Echo's back pocket. "We happen to like them."

My face warmed. Did she have to be so loud? A few girls walking past us giggled.

She threw Torin a glance. "She tries to be subtle, but I know my girl wants you something bad," Cora added, and Echo laughed.

I vowed to smother her when she was asleep and send her soul straight to Hel's Hall. Unfortunately, that was her man's home and he'd probably rescue her.

"You're not subtle, are you, luv?" Torin whispered. "Should I tell her how you—?"

I covered his mouth, left Echo and Cora saying their goodbyes at the entrance, and went inside. A blushing Cora caught up with us in the hall, where Torin's fans waited. He had made history when our football team won state and was considered the golden boy. The darling of Kayville High. I was basking in his glory. The stares from the other students didn't bother me anymore.

I'd never cared about being popular, but I'd be lying if I said I hated it. Now I understood why girls clawed their way to the top of the social ladder in high school. The attention was addictive. I didn't even mind the adoring female fans with envious glances.

Okay, that was a stretch. My fingers tightened on the back of Torin's shirt, and I sunk against his side. His arm tightened around my shoulder.

Yeah, back off, piranhas.

We headed toward the lockers. Cora talked nonstop about the people she'd helped over the weekend, but she was careful not to mention the word "soul". There were rules for Immortals and Valkyries, and number one was anonymity. Mortals were not supposed to know about our world.

Now that the swim season was over, Cora was working a few times a week and Saturdays at hospitals and nursing homes. Six months ago, she'd insisted that working for the Habitat for Humanity was enough community services to impress any college application committees. Nursing homes and hospitals were going to write her glowing recommendations for the time she spent with patients.

Me? I didn't think any college admin would ever know I'd saved lives. I couldn't explain the things I'd done.

Torin disappeared in the direction of his locker, while Cora and I headed toward ours. I was putting my books away when a sliver of awareness shot up my spine. I associated that sizzle with the Norns, except this time it was different.

Someone was humming a tune. The song was familiar, but I couldn't place it. Heart pounding, I turned and searched for the source. I couldn't tell where it came from or explain why the hairs on my neck rose.

Cora slammed the door of her locker and yanked my attention. I grabbed my folder and the books for my morning classes, and followed her. Torin met us in the middle of the hallway.

One look at me and he asked, "What's wrong?"

I squeezed his hand. He knew what that meant: wait.

"See you at lunch," Cora said and took off toward her English class. Torin and I headed upstairs toward the math floor. His jock buddies followed us like he was a magnet. Someone was throwing a party on Friday. Another had a birthday party, or was it a dinner? One wanted him to join lacrosse.

We lost them a door away from my math class, and I heard it again. The same song was being hummed again. This time I recognized the tune from last night during my vision, or whatever it was. I turned and searched the students hurrying past us. The sound rose above the conversations and the laughter. Was I the only one hearing it?

Torin caught my hand. "Hey? What's going on?"

"Can't you hear it?" The person was using words now. Not English.

"Hear what?"

"The song." I didn't understand the words, but the song was sweet and soothing, like a lullaby. I cocked my eyebrows at Torin. "It's beautiful, isn't it?"

Torin shook his head. "I, uh, can't hear anything other than the noise from the students." The first bell rang. "And the bell."

The song disappeared, drowned out by the bell—or the singer had decided to stop. "You didn't hear that haunting music?"

He frowned. "No. You sure you're okay?"

"Yeah, or I'm hallucinating." If I told him it was the song I'd heard last night during my vision, he'd start worrying. "Let's go."

We entered the class just ahead of Mrs. Bates. Torin's seat was right behind mine. When I glanced back, he was still frowning. I shouldn't have mentioned the song.

"I'm fine," I mouthed.

His expression said he didn't believe me. For the rest of the class, my thoughts kept drifting to what I'd heard and what it meant.

***

In-between classes, I cocked my ear to catch the song again. No such luck.

At lunchtime, Torin was waiting outside my class, a group of girls hanging on his every word. One reached up and brushed his shirt. That was crossing the line. I staked my claim when I reached his side, sliding my hand into his. They took off. "Groupies?"

He laughed. "No."

"Next time Leanna Finch touches your chest, I'll break her fingers."

"Who's Leanna?"

I forgave him for not noticing. Girls were always pushing boundaries like damn predators checking for weaknesses. Someone needed to tell them Torin and I were tight. Fortified like Fort Knox. "Have you seen Ingrid?"

"No." He caressed my cheek with his knuckles. "Are we eating here or at home? I can make us something."

I wanted to stay there and let him stroke me. His touch was intoxicating. But first things first. "Okay, but I need to ask Ingrid something before we go."

He went still. "About?"

"Something." I reached up and kissed him. "Go. I'm right behind you."

He didn't look happy leaving me behind, which was sweet.

"I won't take long," I added.

He nodded. With a fingertip brush across my cheek, he disappeared into the men's room to find a portal. I shook my head. Sometimes he could be so possessive. He hadn't had a relationship in centuries and was learning to adjust to ours, which hadn't exactly been smooth. What mattered was we loved each other, knew it, and cherished our time together. Whatever bumps lay ahead—and I was sure the Norns weren't done with us—I was determined to never let them destroy what we had.

I turned the corner and saw Cora at the cafeteria entrance. Her lunch schedule depended on whether or not Echo was around. She waved.

"Please tell me you're eating here. Please. Echo will be gone most of today and this evening," Cora explained. "There was a fire at some nursing home in Seattle."

"I'm heading home, but you can join us. Torin already left to make something."

She sighed melodramatically and looked around the cafeteria. "I don't want to be a third wheel."

"You won't be."

"Nah. Go enjoy your man." She waved, and I turned to see three girls from the swim team, Kicker, Sondra, and Tess. "I'll join the girls and catch up on the latest gossip. See you tonight."

"You want to come and watch *The Originals* online? I missed the last two episodes."

Her eyes widened. "Ohmigod, the poor, damaged, just-needs-to-be-loved Klaus. I have to get my Klaus fix every week. I've even gotten Echo to tolerate him. Okay, I'll watch with you, so we can hate on some witches. I also want your opinion on something."

"Okay."

Ingrid, her cheerleader friends, and their jock boyfriends walked in.

Cora beamed at me and gave me a quick hug. "You're the best."

Everyone at Ingrid's table looked up questioningly when I stopped by. "What?"

"Where's Torin?" a girl asked.

"Around. You know I can actually breathe without him. Ingrid." I indicated outside with a nod and took off.

"What's going on?" she asked, sounding a bit worried.

"I want to pick your brain." Some of the students were hanging out on the deck. Others threw a football in the grassy area along the building. It was still cold, but the sun was up and diehards were already wearing shorts. I found an area away from the others and faced her.

"You're beginning to worry me," Ingrid said. "If this is about Andris—"

"No, this is about me. Do you remember I told you last night that I heard the woman sing during my vision?"

She nodded. "*Varðlokur.*"

"Varo-what?"

"The warding or spirit-summoning song. We sing it before the Seeress goes into a trance. What about it?"

"I thought I heard it this morning."

Her frown deepened. "Where?"

"Here at school. What does that mean?" I saw a movement from the corner of my eyes and turned to look. It was Blaine. He waved.

"It means there's a witch here at school," Ingrid said, drawing my attention.

I shook my head. "The Seeress was older. At least, she sounded older."

"Uh, I'm talking about the singer. A Seeress never does the singing."

Someone working with a Seeress was here at my school. "Is Blaine waiting for you?" He was talking to friends but he kept looking in our direction.

Ingrid waved to him. "No. Do you want me to point her out when I recognize her?"

"You can do that?"

She shrugged. "Oh, yes. It's like, uh, having witch radar. Why do you think Maliina hated you from the moment she saw you?"

"Uh, because Andris was being a total douche?"

She laughed. "That came second. My sister was a powerful Seidr witch, but in you, she saw something else. Something she'd never seen before, and she was jealous. Maliina always wanted to be important and, uh, revered. Back at home, they revered her, but it wasn't enough. Then she met Andris and he turned her. She thought she'd be the most powerful woman in our land, but he took her away from home and her adoring fans. She stopped being important and she didn't like it. That's why she joined the Norns. She was very ambitious."

It didn't excuse what she'd done, but it made sense. "So what did she see in me?"

Ingrid shrugged. "A more powerful witch, I guess. I'm not as strong as Maliina, but I should be able to spot the witch here at school. I'll let you know when I do."

"Thanks." I really liked this new Ingrid. She stopped by the group with Blaine, said something to him, and disappeared inside the building. Blaine followed her. I went to the nearest restroom and headed home to Torin.

***

I pushed the matter of the witch aside for the rest of the day. After school, Torin dropped me off at the back of our shop.

"Text me when you're done," he said.

The back door of the store dinged when I pushed it open. Mirage was our family shop. We did custom framing, but we also sold mirrors. Lots of mirrors. Big. Small. Runed and unruned frames.

Mom had hired an assistant before she left. Hawk. An Immortal. If Dad knew about him, he'd hit the roof. He didn't like Asgardians as he liked to call Immortals and Valkyries, yet he was married to Mom, a Valkyrie, and I was an Immortal. The irony was lost on him.

Hawk didn't seem to be around, but Jared, our regular employee, was with the one person I didn't want to see, his wife Celine. His bubbly blonde wife could drive any sane person crazy with her smothering.

"Raine," Jared said, waving me over. "How's school?"

"Busy. Hey, Celine."

"Oh, you poor dear." Her beefy arms looped around me in a hug. She came up only to my chin, and I had my backpack looped over my shoulder, which made our hug awkward. She stepped back and gripped my hands. "How's your mother doing?"

"Better. She'll be home soon." Mom had left six weeks ago, so we'd come up with a reason for her sudden disappearance. She was officially undergoing treatment at a private institution for a nervous breakdown. Dad's illness had taken a toll on her.

"How are you coping, dear? How is your father doing?"

"Dad's doing much better and, uh…" I tried to wiggle my hand from the woman's, but her grip tightened. "I'm fine, too."

"Oh, how brave you are. First your father's plane crash, then the cancer, and now your mother, it's too much for someone so young to bear." Tears rushed to her eyes.

With my eyes I begged Jared to rescue me. I'd had to deal with her when Dad disappeared, then when she learned he was ill, and now.

"I was just telling Jared we should visit your mother. She's been so good to us. She's at PMI, right?"

"No, she's at a private hospital in Portland and only family is allowed." I finally freed my hands. "I'll let her know you were asking about her."

"Oh, that's nice. As for you, young lady," she peered at me, "I want you to know you can come to the house any time, okay? If you need anything, anything at all, call us. Do you have Jared's cell phone number?"

"Yes, she does." Jared practically dragged her out of the store. He came back with a sheepish expression. He ran his hand through his thinning hair. "Sorry about that. Celine has a big heart, but sometimes she gets carried away. So what can I do for you?"

"Dad wants a copy of this month's inventory and tax forms."

He chuckled. "The person to talk to is Hawk. Come on. He's in the office."

Hawk got to his feet. He was a tall man with a coppery complexion, straight black hair, and brown eyes that seemed to never miss a thing. He also loved black suits. "Ms. Lorraine, this is a nice surprise."

"Dad sent me to get a few things, Mr. Hawk."

"Hawk. Sit, please." He indicated the chair across from his. Jared excused himself.

"How's your father doing?" Hawk asked. He kept the pleasantries short and soon shifted to business. An hour later, he'd explained inventory while I tried to keep up.

"Why are you telling me all this?" I finally asked.

He studied me as though trying to figure me out. I stared right back. Most Immortals I'd met were centuries old, so I tried to figure out how old he was. He could pass for a fifty-something Native American man.

"One day you'll inherit this place, Ms. Cooper, so you should know how things are run. If you'd like, you could come to the shop and I can show you."

Mom never liked me working at the store before. She'd said something about my being clumsy because of a few broken mirrors. Now I knew it had something to do with her customers. She hadn't wanted me around Immortals. Of course, she hadn't known about the Norns' agenda.

"Okay. Until Mom comes back." She'd be surprised. In a good away, I hoped.

He nodded without cracking a smile. "Every day?"

"No." I laughed. "I have school and homework and... a life. Let's start with three days a week. If I can stomach all the business jargons and whatnots, then I'll add a day. If not, then I can say *adios* and convince myself I tried." No, I wasn't going to quit. I was broke. Mom had forgotten to put more money on my debit card before she left. "I get paid, right?"

"Of course. Ten dollars an hour," he said.

Sweet. "When do I start?"

"Tomorrow. I can show you what you'll be doing now."

"Deal. And please call me Raine." I leaned forward and offered him my hand, feeling more grownup than I'd felt an hour ago. I reached down for my backpack and got up. He stood, too. I put the folder with the tax forms and inventory in my backpack and left the office.

My eyes met with Andris'.

4. HATING WITCHES

"What are you doing here?" I asked.

"Picking you up." He bumped fists with Jared.

Okay, that was new. Andris couldn't stand Mortals, unless he was dating them. And Jared wasn't his type. He loved them pretty. "Where's Torin?"

"Up and about."

He didn't seem resentful. Usually Andris hated being saddled with playing bodyguard. Or babysitting me as he often put it. "Give me a few minutes. Hawk is showing me the ropes."

Andris walked toward us. "The ropes?"

"I start work tomorrow," I said.

"You? Working?"

I made a face. "Why do you have to say it like that?"

He shook his head. "Torin won't like it."

I opened my eyes wide. "Really? Oh, I should have asked him first. I can't make decisions without him. What am I going to do now?" Andris shot me a mean look. "Here. Make yourself useful." I pushed my backpack into his arms.

"Why do we need to work?" he asked, still following us.

"There's no *we* in *me*," I said, hoping he'd take the hint and stay back.

"Why?"

I sighed. Hawk pretended not to hear us. "This is my family's shop and one day I'll own it. Now do you mind? Hawk is a busy man and you're in the way. Go and admire yourself in the mirrors until I'm done."

He looked at Hawk, who was now staring at us with an unreadable expression. "Good afternoon, Hawk."

"Andris," the Immortal said.

"I'll leave you two, but you," he gave me a pointed look, "have some explaining to do. You're supposed to work with us."

I didn't want to remind him that souls bound for Asgard were cheating death. No matter what Torin said, I knew it was my fault. If Torin hadn't stopped Echo from reaping my father's soul, he would be dead and the world would be running smoothly. They'd messed with destiny for me.

Hawk went to the customer's service desk and showed me in painstaking details how to answer the phone. I almost fell asleep. He did the custom framing and wasn't to be disturbed unless there was an emergency, he explained. Jared was in charge of sales, and I was to confer with him.

"So I'll answer the phone?" I could do that blindfolded.

"Yes and help customers. Mortals never seem to make up their mind about what they want. They'll want to know about sizes and prices. You have to put them on hold and check with Jared. Then there's the framing side of the business, which is what most of our customers come in here for. They will want to know the types of frames we carry. We have shadowbox frames, float frames, clip frames, and digital frames. What materials the frames are made of: metal, acrylic, or wood. They'll want to know the timeframe if they brought their paintings and portraits, and if we do matting or cropping."

Yikes. "Okay, now that you've broken it down, it does sound like a lot of work," I mumbled. "Can I get a raise?"

He didn't crack a smile or even acknowledge he'd heard me. "You'll get the hang of it. I'll see you tomorrow after school. If your father wants me to mail the tax forms or do anything at all, don't hesitate to call me."

"If we're not busy, am I allowed to do my homework?"

"Sure. You'll be here for a couple of hours, so why not."

A couple of hours could seem like a life sentence if I hated the job. On the other hand, I could always quit. "Okay. See you tomorrow."

Andris led the way out of the shop, my backpack slung over his shoulder, hands deep in the front pockets of his pants. At the back entrance, he stopped suddenly and peered into the alley.

"What is it?"

"Looking for something," he mumbled.

I tried to see over his shoulder, but all I saw were tops of a few cars. The parking lot served several stores, including ours. "You sure it's not some*one*?"

He glanced over his shoulder and scowled. "Someone?"

"A stalker. You broke up with Pretty Boy Roger, didn't you? Is he stalking you?"

"Nope." He pointed the key at the SUV and unlocked it. Then he casually dropped an arm around my shoulder. "Roger and I, Ms. Nosey, had an amicable breakup. He doesn't even know I exist."

"Translate that into Mortal lingo, please."

"I runed him so he'd forget we ever hooked up." He opened the door and practically shoved me into my seat. "And you are no longer part of their world. You are one of us now." He smirked, closed the door, and engaged his runes. Next second, he was behind the wheel. He seemed in an awful hurry to leave. "Besides, Roger is not stalker material."

"You really do have a stalker," I said, watching him peer out the window as though he expected someone to jump out of the shrubberies separating our parking lot from the art center.

He handed me my backpack and started the car. "You live and learn. I should have runed each and every one of them. You have no idea the nutcases I've dated."

I laughed. "I do."

"Other than Maliina. She went the extra mile." He chuckled at his understatement. Wisps of silver strands escaped his perfectly styled hair and fell over his forehead. He was androgynously beautiful—the kind the Biebs' fans would go ga-ga over, until he opened his mouth. He was rude, sexist, and a general ass-hat.

"Do you want to stop somewhere for coffee?" I asked.

He made a face. "Nah."

"Please?" I gave him a sweet smile and fluttered my eyelashes.

He shot me a disgusted look, backed out, and eased into the traffic. "You do know I'm not Torin. The sexy smile doesn't work on me."

"Sexy smile?"

"Borderline sexy, until you open your mouth and I'm reminded you are an annoying teenager with a penchant for getting those around her in trouble. If you tell Torin I said that, I will snap your neck."

I laughed. "You would try. Don't forget I'm Immortal now and a witch to boot. I could make you see things that aren't there."

He threw me an uneasy glance. "You wouldn't dare."

I shifted, so I could see his face while we talked. "Did you know I was different when we first met?"

"Fishing for complements now?"

"No, wondering if you noticed something different about me, smart ass. Ingrid and Maliina did." I faced forward and sighed. "Ingrid said witches can recognize each other."

He shuddered. "Don't talk to me about witches."

"What is it with you guys and witches? Torin reacted the same way." I noticed we were headed east toward my place. "You're really not going to buy me a macchiato?"

"Got that right, but since I'm such a nice guy, I'll go back to town and pick up your favorite. Extra large."

I frowned. "Sounds like you don't want to be seen with me."

"No, I don't. You'll mess with my game. I'm single and on the prowl. Besides, you have papers for your father to sign and you want to catch him lucid."

He was right, dang it. "How did you know about the forms?"

"Vulcan hearing."

I rolled my eyes. He was a serious sci-fi fan. Movies. Books. TV series. He ate it up. Of course, he'd never admit it to anyone but those closest to him. He pulled into our cul-de-sac. My eyes went to Torin's place. The house was closed up.

"Where did you say Torin went?"

"I didn't." Andris pulled up in front of my house. "He'll be back before you know it, so go hug his pillow or something." He ducked when I aimed my backpack at his head.

"Grande caramel latte with extra cream and watch your back," I said. He scowled. "Your stalker, Einstein."

"Oh, that. I'll be okay." He was acting weird.

I disappeared inside the house.

"I'm home," I called out. The door to the den was closed. I pulled out the files from my backpack just as Femi appeared at the top of the stairs.

"Can I see him? I brought the papers he wanted." She hurried downstairs, but something in her eyes sent warning bells off. "What happened? What is it?"

"He didn't do so well today," she said.

"What do you mean?" I started toward the den.

"We went for our daily walk and he became very fatigued. He's been restless since. Go ahead."

My hand was already on the door handle. I entered the room. The TV was on some nature channel, but the volume was muted. I saw Dad and gulped. He had an oxygen tube attached to his nose. He hadn't had that in weeks. I inched closer, my heart pounding with every step.

I eased into a chair and watched his chest rise and fall. His skin was dry to the touch. The light from the screen flickered on his face, giving him a ghostly appearance. I didn't know how long I'd been sitting there when someone knocked on the door.

Andris entered the room, two extra large Starbucks cups in his hands. He didn't speak, which I appreciated. He gave me my drink, squeezed my shoulder, and pulled up the only other empty chair in the room and sat.

Oh, he was staying. He could be so sweet sometimes.

Dad was still asleep when I finished my macchiato. Andris had joined him. I shook him awake, and we slipped out of the room.

"Thanks for staying," I said.

"Don't read anything into it. I'm a self-seeking opportunist, so now you," he pointed at me, "owe me," he jabbed at his chest. "And I'll collect with interest." He sighed. "You look like shit. Crying doesn't suit you."

Laughing, I threw my arms around him. He was no Torin, but he stepped up really nice when his big brother wasn't around.

"Hey. You don't have to choke me." He patted my back, then stopped protesting as his hands started venturing in Torin territory. "I could get used to this."

Self-seeking opportunist of the highest kind. I grabbed his hands before they went too low and pulled them way. I stepped away from him. "You have a death wish."

"What Torin doesn't know won't tick him off."

"I'm not talking about Torin." It wasn't until he was gone that I realized we never discussed why they hated witches. Oh well. Time for homework before Cora came over.

***

I was in my bedroom finishing when my mirror dissolved into a portal. I waited, expecting the warmth that usually accompanied Torin. It was frigid. Eirik?

I got up, my eyes on the mirror.

"Anyone home?"

Cora. Disappointed, I forced myself to sound upbeat. "Yeah."

"Are you decent?"

"No, I'm doing the cha-cha with nothing on but a lei around my neck."

There was laughter followed by, "No, you cannot, you letch. You have a one-track mind. Go. She and I are going to hang out for a while." Silence followed. They were probably kissing. Then Cora stepped into my room looking flustered. She turned to wave.

"Hey, Echo," I called out.

He entered the room, looking dark and dangerous. "Dang! What happened to the lei?"

Cora pushed him out of the room, but she left the portal open. She plopped on my bed and sighed.

"Is that a sigh of happiness or boredom?"

She laughed. "Blissful. I need a junk food fix. Please, tell me you have Cheetos or potato chips for this marathon."

"Two episodes do not equal a marathon. I'll get the junk food and the drinks." I hopped off the bed and went downstairs. Femi was watching something on TV. "What are you watching?"

"*Supernatural.*"

"Ooh, getting your Winchester boys fix." I'd introduced her to the series.

She grinned. "Want to join me?"

"Tomorrow night. I'm watching *The Originals* with Cora upstairs." We were running low on potato chips. Every time Cora came to my place, she pigged out on junk food. Her mother was a health nut. They grew organic fruit and vegetables, and her mother didn't buy processed foods.

I took the last bag of potato chips from the cupboard and cans of soda from the living room wet bar, looked up, and caught Femi watching me. "I hope you don't want something. We are out of chips."

"No, I'm good. I'll go grocery shopping tomorrow. If you need anything else, add it to the list on the fridge door. Is Torin coming later tonight?"

"I think so. Why?"

"The door..."

I rolled my eyes. "Stays open," I said and almost reminded her she wasn't Mom. Torin and I made out often enough without me giving it up, but I still wanted some privacy during those moments. Upstairs, I stopped when I entered the room. Cora lay on her stomach on my bed and the portal was open. "Why is the portal still open?"

"So I can hear my parents if they knock on my door."

"Oh." I threw her the bag of potato chips. She already had my laptop on and the episode up. I slid beside her and opened my soda. "Have you mastered portal runes?"

"I wish." She swept her hair to the side. It tumbled down her shoulder. "Lavania is supposed to teach me, but we didn't start because of you and now she's gone. Do you know when she'll back?"

"Nope. She's one of Mom's supporters, so she's sequestered, too, until the end of the hearing."

"She should have just let Echo teach me. He's brilliant."

We settled on the bed and shared the chips while we watched the original vampires fight witches for dominance in New Orleans.

"Klaus is so..." Cora sighed melodramatically.

"Tortured?"

"Yeah. He reminds me of Echo, but my man is not so messed up like him."

I'd noticed she compared every tortured, cocky character on TV to Echo. No one out there could be compared to Torin. Not the Salvatore brothers, not the Winchester boys, and definitely not the Originals. I glanced out the window, but his place was in darkness.

At the end of the second episode, I closed the laptop. "Wow."

"I know. Don't you just hate those witches?"

Even in a fictitious TV series, witches were portrayed as evil. "Uh, I think they're not all bad."

She bumped me with her shoulder. "You're just supporting your fellow witches."

"Loyalty is priceless."

"I hear you. This has been nice." She jumped up and walked to the window. "How come Torin's place is all dark? Did he move to the mansion?"

"He's around. What is it?" I could always tell when she wanted to say something but wasn't sure how to do it. She got really antsy. When she hesitated, I sighed. "Seriously, you want me to nag it out of you?"

She made a face. "I want to go back to vlogging," she said then added quickly, "not about *Hottie of the Week* or anything that superficial. I want to vblog about real people with real problems."

She was serious. "Okay."

"Dealing with souls has shown me people never have conversations about important things. They hold on to their pain, anger, and resentment until they die. But then it's too late. I want to use the stories the souls tell me, Raine. You know, make each a blog entry, so if there's someone out there who's having the same problems, they can do something about it before it's too late." She stared at me as though she expected me to blow her off. "I know I don't have a degree in psychology, but—"

"It's a brilliant idea. And you don't need a degree. You're learning from listening to people."

She blew out a breath. "Listening to dead people kind of puts things in perspective."

I'd bet. I had yet to see my first soul. "So when do you want to start? Are you going to change their names, the setting?"

Her face crunched as though she was about to cry, and then she hugged me. "Oh, I knew you'd support me." She jumped up and peered into her room through the portal. "Echo doesn't know. I thought I'd run it by you first. I'm going to start this week. I'll need your input before I upload, so expect to watch something in a day or two. Oh, there was something else I meant to ask you, but I can't remember now." She pouted and blew out air. "Phew. Oh well. It will come to me. Gotta go. See you tomorrow."

I smiled. She still got all chatty and her voice developed a high-pitch tone when she was excited. It was one of her endearing qualities.

I got ready for bed and went downstairs to say goodnight to Dad, but he was still asleep. I left the inventory and tax papers behind.

Torin wasn't back when I went back upstairs. I stared at his house. I was tempted to text Andris, but I didn't want to be that girl—needy and clingy and completely useless when her boyfriend wasn't around.

I was in bed when warm air blew into my room and Torin entered.

My heart tripped. He made it so easy for a girl to drool. He'd already changed into his sweatpants and tank shirt that hugged his chest and showcased his sculptured arms. As usual, he was barefoot. I studied him from above my book.

He swaggered to the foot of my bed. "How come you're in bed early?"

I lifted my book without speaking.

"Miss me?"

I pursed my lips and pretended to think about it before shaking my head. Okay, so I was a bit pissed at him because he hadn't bothered to check in. Teleporting took seconds.

He crawled under the blanket from the foot the bed and worked his way up, slowly driving me crazy. Did he ever do anything like a normal guy? I didn't realize I was holding my breath until he wiggled his head between my chest and my book. He gave me the most adoring look ever. "Hi, luv."

The stinker. He knew when to work that British accent to his advantage, and I almost forgave him, but I had standards. "What are you doing?"

"Trying to get your attention. You know I hate to be ignored." He bobbed his head to indicate the book, which was on top of his head. "What are you reading?"

"*Moby-Dick*," I said, forcing my heart to behave. It wasn't easy with his chest pressed against mine and his legs trapping one of mine.

"Isn't that the book you're reading to your father? You're cheating again?"

I put the book face down on his back and ran my fingers through his hair. I tended to get caught up in the stories Torin and I read together and sneaked a read without him, which drove him nuts. This was different. Dad had read *Moby-Dick* to me when I was little, and I had a feeling this time round, we might not finish it. I couldn't even explain why I was reading ahead. I still didn't feel like discussing my father.

"Guilty," I said.

"And you look it." He slid his arms under my shoulders and propped himself on his elbows. His face was inches from mine. "So what did you do while I was gone?"

"After the shop, I came home. Cora visited after dinner. Where were you?"

"Touching base with the other Valkyries."

I frowned. "About the Seeress?"

He nodded. "Most Valkyries are being called back to Asgard."

My stomach hollowed out. If he left… I couldn't even begin to imagine my life without him. "You're not—"

"Not that I've heard. I'm sure they have enough helpers in Valhalla." He stroked my hair. "I'm not going anywhere."

He couldn't promise that. "But if they order you—"

"I'm not going anywhere, Freckles." His voice said he'd defy any orders, which would only land him in trouble. He lowered his head and added, "No one will ever make me leave you." The kiss that followed was sweet and too brief. He shifted and switched our positions, his arms wrapping around me. "So when you said you came home, do you mean you came alone or did Andris pick you up? Because if he didn't, I'm going—"

I pressed a finger to his lips. "Whoa, slow down. Andris did. Poor guy. He has a stalker and acted really fugitive-ish. He also seemed to think you won't approve of my working at the shop after school."

He stiffened. "Why would you want to do that?"

"It's something to do."

"You do me after school," he retorted.

I giggled. "That sounded wrong."

"That's because you have a dirty mind." His tone said he didn't find my comment funny. "You know what I mean. We hang out and do stuff. Now that it's warmer, I plan to teach you how to move faster without hitting someone or something, and I'm not talking about while riding a Harley."

"You should have said something or texted me." He stared at me like I was a ditzy teenager, which I wasn't. He hated texting. "I don't read minds, you know."

"Well, now you know. Then there's creating portals in the air instead of solid surfaces. Portals to places around the world without appearing in someone's bedroom or in the middle of some high society ball in London. That happened to me once, and it wasn't funny. They thought I was a stable boy trying to steal the family silver."

"And the bedroom?"

"The woman believed she'd conjured me. I mean, she was standing naked in front of a mirror talking to herself when I walked through it." He shuddered. "One mistake and it had to be with a bloody witch."

I ignored the comment about the witch. "No one walks blindly through portals. You must have seen her."

He smirked. "I was young and cocky, and she was hot." A wicked twinkle entered his eyes.

"Oh, you were such a man-whore." I tried to slide off him, but his arms tightened and his legs lifted and trapped me.

"That was before I met you. Now, I only lust after one woman." He buried his face in my neck, his breath fanning the sensitive skin. I shivered.

"Tell me again why you hate witches."

"Technically, all Valkyries were once *spiritual Mortals*," he stressed, lifting his head. "Mortals in touch with their inner selves. Mortals sensitive to nature and those around them. Mortals aware that they are part of something bigger than what an average Joe sees. They didn't have to draw circles or chant. No matter how nice or whichever culture they come from, witches can turn vicious and go Carrie on you."

Movie reference? He was picking up stuff from me. I wrapped my arms around his neck. "You think I could hurt you."

"No. You could never hurt anyone." He forked hair away from my face and kissed me again, deeper this time. When he stopped, I had trouble focusing on his next words. "Just promise to stay away from witches. We have runes for everything imaginable, except for fighting witches and their ability to mess with people's heads."

I frowned. "Have you ever been attacked by a witch?"

"No, but I've seen what they can do and it's not pretty. Now, about this job…" He nibbled his way along my jaw to my neck, sending heat through me. His hands slid down my sides, passing over my hips to my thighs. He tugged until I straddled him. Then his lips covered mine, the taste of him going straight to my head. He really didn't play fair. "So you'll tell Hawk you've changed your mind?"

I wasn't ready to be a doormat yet. "You can have Tuesdays, Thursdays, and sometimes Saturdays, but I'll be working on Mondays," I pressed my lips on his cheek, "Wednesdays," then the other, "and Fridays at the Mirage." I kissed him on the lips.

I thought he was going to resist, but he let me in and allowed me to play with him. I loved it when he let me indulge myself. A shudder rolled through him, his arms tightening around me. He was wound tight like a caged tiger. Fighting his natural instinct to take charge.

I lifted my head. "Deal?"

"No. Convince me," he said, his voice husky.

Grinning, I speared my fingers through his hair, gripped, and tilted his head. He watched me from under the canopies of his lashes, waiting to see what I'd do next. Daring me with a half smile. I closed the gap between us and rubbed my nose against his.

"Tease," he whispered.

"You asked for it, so relax and enjoy." I took my time, savoring his responses. He stopped me before I got carried away and tucked me on his side. I buried my face in his neck and inhaled. I could never get enough of his piney scent.

He didn't mention the deal again, but then it wasn't really about the deal. Torin liked to push boundaries to see what he could get away with. Sometimes, I let him. Most of the time, I pushed back.

5. BRITISH BASTARD

Something woke me up. A sound or maybe a feeling that something wasn't right. My room was in total darkness. Darker than usual because I couldn't see my hands. I reached for Torin, but he was gone.

I slipped out of bed and automatically glanced out the window. His house was in total darkness, too. Voices came from downstairs again. They must be the ones who'd woken me up.

I left my room and headed downstairs. The door to my parent's bedroom was open, but it was empty. Where was Femi? She slept there now that Mom was gone. Halfway down the stairs, the voices reached me again. They were coming from outside.

I went to the front door and angled my head to listen. My stomach dropped. Someone was singing. It was the same Seidr song. A witch was outside my house. Or was this a summoning? I unlocked the door and turned the knob, but it didn't move.

Not again.

I ran to the window, jumped on the couch, and pushed aside the curtains. Several people stood in my front yard. I tried to see the faces of the ones facing me, but they were blurry. The glowing circle and runes were visible between their legs, and light flickered in the circle, but I couldn't see the Seeress.

"Why do you need to find them?" a woman's voice asked. Probably the Seeress. Her voice was different from the one from last night. It sounded low and husky, like Femi's.

"We don't need to give you a reason, Seidkona." Dang it, he still sounded like Torin. I tried to see which one of them had spoken. Maybe see his face.

"I cannot help you," the woman said defiantly.

"You will or you will die," he snarled.

"Just like you've killed the others who refused to help you," the woman said with disgust. "Your kind is not supposed to kill."

"We can do whatever we want. This is your last chance," Mr. British warned.

"I will not betray my kind," the woman snapped. "Not for the likes of you."

"Then you seal your fate, too," Mr. Brit said. A scream filled the air, but it was cut short with a telltale crack.

Holy crap! He just snapped her neck.

I let go of the curtains and jumped away from the window. Totally forgetting I was on the couch, I lost my balance and fell backwards.

Arms wrapped around my waist.

"I got you," a voice whispered in my ear. It was the voice of the Seeress killer. I screamed, kicked, and reached up to claw his face. He caught my arms and pinned them down. "Whoa, Freckles. It's me."

The familiar warmth and earthy scent registered first, then his words. Only Torin called me Freckles. I stopped struggling, opened my eyes, and stared into Torin's.

"Is she okay?" Femi asked from the doorway, and my focus flew to her. Everything became confusing fast. Her voice superimposed on that of the Seeress. Torin's voice became that of her killer.

I scrambled from his arms and shot off the bed. My knee connected with my dresser, and I hissed as pain shot up my leg. When Torin reached for me, I dropped on the window seat and scooted back until the hard ledge pressed against my back. I tucked my legs up to my chin and hugged them. My eyes volleyed between him and Femi. The confusion on their faces didn't help, so I focused on my room and familiar things.

According to my alarm clock it was only ten. I'd barely gone to sleep. I heard Torin say something, and then Femi left. Panic still churned in my gut. I stole a glance at him.

Torin stared at me from the bed with a grave expression, his expressive blue eyes shadowed. He was shirtless, yet I couldn't see the shirt he'd worn earlier. The last thing I remembered before falling asleep was the rhythmic motion of his hands as he stroked my hair and the thumpity-thump of his heart.

"What happened?" I asked.

"You fell asleep a few minutes ago and I left. Then I heard you scream."

He got off the bed, his movements slow. Graceful. It was a weird thing to notice, but I was processing things at a weird level. The muscles on his arms flexed and relaxed, the light casting a golden blush on his skin. The entire time, he kept staring as though he knew just how skittish I was.

He sat on the edge of the bed and studied me without speaking, giving me time.

"Was it bad?" he asked.

The killer only sounded like him. That was it. I nodded.

Concern darkened his eyes. "You want to talk about it?"

I shook my head.

He looked ready to push, appeared to change his mind, and raked his fingers through his hair. "Do you want a hug?"

Did I want his arms around me? Like I needed the freaking air. With that thought, sanity bitch slapped me. This was the man I was madly in love with. The man who'd broken rules to heal me without thoughts of consequences. The man whose memories the Norns had erased yet had fallen in love with me again. He knew me in ways I still didn't understand. Knew when I needed to be held or wanted a good fight.

I didn't answer him. I leaped into his arms. He caught me and, without saying another word, shifted against the pillows, pulled the covers over us, and turned off the lights.

I wrapped myself around him and buried my face in his neck. His scent and warmth enveloped me. I listened to his heartbeat until I was ready. "Can you spend the night?" I whispered.

"Uh, sure."

I knew what the hesitation meant. "We can open the door."

He chuckled, the sound rumbling through his chest. "Opened or closed, we are in control. We agreed to take things slow. No matter how hard it is for some of us."

I nudged him with my arm. He made it difficult for a girl to stay sane.

"We have a lifetime ahead of us," he added and pressed a kiss on my forehead. "Go to sleep. I'm not going anywhere."

No wonder I was crazy about him. He could be infuriating, but he was immovable and dependable. "I had another vision."

"I figured as much."

"They killed another Seeress," I said.

"They?"

"I don't know who they are. In my vision, their leader kept asking the Seeress to find them. See where they are. I'm not sure who these killers are after, but they're willing to kill Seeresses. She refused to help them and even said something about not betraying her kind. That's when he snapped her neck."

Torin was quiet, his arms tight around me.

"Like yesterday, I don't know if what I saw happened in real time, like Ingrid had implied, or if it was a vision of what's going to happen. All I know is these people are killing Seeresses."

"I don't know anyone who would want to kill a Seeress, unless it's another witch. The world's changed and people can practice whatever they like, so this is not another inquisition or witch trial."

"Did you hear anything about my first vision?"

"No. Like I said, one dead witch might go unnoticed. Many will send a ripple through the magical world."

Part of me wanted to mention the man who'd sounded like him, but I bit my tongue. I sucked at accents and British people kind of sounded alike. I couldn't tell a British and an Aussie apart, so what did I know?

No, accusing the man I loved of killing Seeresses would be stupid.

***

When I woke up, Torin's side of the bed was empty. Fingers of light filtered through my window and threw shadows on my bedroom wall. Last night's vision returned to haunt me.

Seeresses were being killed and somehow I was seeing their deaths. What was I supposed to do? Stop their deaths? Identify the killers and find them justice?

I sighed, turned, and something metallic pressed against my back. Torin's family heirloom. It must have slipped off of his neck. It had been under his tank top the last time I saw it. Before my vision.

I lifted it up by its chain. The clasp was on, which meant he'd removed it. I couldn't recall him doing that. Placing it by the table, I reached for my laptop and booted it. Keeping an eye on the clock, I Googled murders and witches.

Ritual Child Murder... Teen Charged with Ritual Murder... Santa Muerte Ritualistic Killings... Sick bastards. There was nothing about recent deaths of witches or Seeresses.

Closing the laptop, I went to the window and waved when Torin looked up. He tapped his watch. Grabbing a robe, I went through the portal, appeared in his living room, and came up behind him. He was once again parading around shirtless. His back was just as fascinating as his front.

He turned and offered me a mug. He studied my face as though a lone zit had taken residence on the tip of my nose. "You don't look too hot."

"Ouch."

A smile tugged the corner of his lips. "Maybe you should skip school today."

"Seriously? I didn't miss school because of the Norns, or when Maliina went psycho, or even when a certain neighbor etched runes on me and scared the beegeebees out of me." He grinned. "And now I should because of a few morbid visions? No way." I sipped my coffee. "Besides, I need to find the witch at school and warn her or something."

He stopped in the process of sipping his coffee and cocked his eyebrow. "There's a witch at school?"

"Yep. I heard someone singing the Seidr song. Remember I asked you if you'd heard it? I talked to Ingrid, and she told me a witch was at our school."

His expression turned sour like he'd used stale creamer. "Ingrid?"

"Yeah. What's with the expression?"

He shrugged and turned to walk away. I grabbed his pants and pulled. Yikes. I let go.

"If you want me to take it off, just say so," he threw over my shoulder, smirking.

I rolled my eyes. "If that's an attempt to get out of talking about Ingrid, it's pathetic." He poured more coffee into his mug. "What's your problem with Ingrid?"

"She knows a lot about witchy stuff." He leaned against the counter and sipped his drink.

"That's because Maliina was a powerful witch. Stop hating on witches." I gripped the string of his sweatpants, tugged teasingly, and let go. "See you in a few. Oh, you forgot your family shield pendant thing in my room."

"No, you claimed it and I decided to let you have it."

I frowned. "Claimed it?"

"Clasped it and wouldn't let go, so I removed it. Take good care of it for me."

It looked old, like something he'd want to lock away. "Thanks. I will. I'll hitch a ride with you today, but tomorrow, I'm taking my car."

"Why?"

"I have to work at the Mirage."

He groaned. "I thought we agreed you'd be too busy."

I laughed. "You stated your case and I disagreed."

"You're so… so…"

"Loveable. I know. Thanks for the coffee." I disappeared through the portal, turned, and caught him standing in his living room scowling. He *was so cute when he pouted. I wiggled my fingers as the portal closed. I was still grinning when I raced downstairs for breakfast.*

Dad was asleep, but I still checked on him and made sure he was breathing. It was a stupid habit, but I did it anyway. Sometimes I could hardly see the rise and fall of his chest. One day he'd open his eyes and catch me holding a mirror to his nose.

Torin was waiting in his garage. "We have two minutes before the first bell," he said, raising the garage door.

"Then get us there in one, luv," I said, imitating his British accent.

He chuckled and started the engine. Across the street, Mr. Rutledge waved to us with his newspaper. I wondered if they believed I slept at Torin's whenever we left together without seeing me go to his place first.

We pulled up outside the school at the same time as Blaine's sports car, except he wasn't behind the wheel. Ingrid was. She was laughing at something Blaine said when they stepped out of the car. Andris watched them from the SUV a few feet away. This was an interesting development. The mansion must be full of drama.

"I need to check on something first," Torin said.

"You're not going in?"

"No, but I'll be there before lunch." A quick kiss and he was back on the Harley.

The first bell rang as I entered the building. I took off toward the lockers. I was so going to get a tardy slip. A few slackers were also just arriving and didn't seem worried about making it to class.

I raced upstairs. The hallway was nearly empty, except for two girls giggling over a text message. The second bell rang. Just before I entered the class, I heard the Seidr song again.

The hairs on my arms prickled. The giggling girls entered a classroom at the end of the hallway, leaving me alone. I angled my head, trying to find the source of the song.

It was beautiful. Haunting. Hypnotic.

I thought someone called my name, but I was drawn to the song. I followed it to several doors away. The boys' bathroom? The voice didn't sound like a guy's, but then again I could name a few teen heartthrob singers who sounded like girls. I checked left then right, so undecided about my next move. This was an opportunity I didn't want to miss.

Making sure I was alone again, I pushed the door and yelled, "Hey, you in there. Come outside so we can talk." The singing stopped, but the echo hummed and magic charged the air. "Can you hear me?"

No response. Maybe he was shy.

*"Listen, I just wanted to warn you that your kind is being killed."
Frowning, I let the door swing close, but the singing started again. Getting
pissed, I pushed the door and called out, "This is not funny, okay? Just
remember what I said. Warn your people."*

*I waited for a response, but there was none. I hurried to class. Mrs.
Bates, my über strict calculus teacher, stared at me with narrow eyes.*

*"You know how I feel about tardiness, Miss Cooper," she said.
"See me after class."*

*I should rune her to make her forget. On the other hand, this was
my first tardy, so I was safe from detention. Throughout the class, I kept
waiting to hear the song again or see a witch boy walk past my class, but no
such luck.*

*Mrs. Bates' brown eyes were cold as she watched me walk to the
front of the class. "You've always been a hard-working, responsible student,
Lorraine. I don't want to see that change because you're associating with the
wrong crowd."*

*Seriously? One tardy and I was associating with the wrong crowd?
"I have an A in your class, Mrs. Bates."*

*"This is not about your grades. This is about breaking school rules.
You were outside the classroom when the bell rang, and then you left." She
studied me from the rim of her rhinestone glasses. "What were you doing
outside the boys' bathroom?"*

*Crap! "I, uh, heard someone crying and I went to make sure he was
okay." I gave her a bright Girl Scout smile.*

Mrs. Bates' eyes narrowed. "Was he?"

*"No. I tried talking to him through the door, but he didn't respond.
I even opened the door, but there was no response. I know it's against school
policy for girls to enter boys' bathrooms, so I came to class."*

"Hmm." That meant she didn't believe me. "One tardy check."

*My day basically went downhill from there. It got worse when Torin
was a no show during lunch. He wasn't waiting outside my classroom, and
his Harley was missing in the parking lot. I headed to the cafeteria. Cora
was already seated with Kicker and Sondra.*

"So you got ditched, too?" Cora said.

"Yeah" was all I said.

*Cora scooped the soup and tipped the spoon. Mystery meat and
overcooked veggies dropped in the bowl. "Echo didn't even stop by to tell me
he'd be gone."*

"Torin always makes us lunch." I pushed the lettuce around the table.

"Echo usually has the food delivered before I get home."

A giggle came from Kicker, but Sondra elbowed her. They looked at me expectantly. "What?"

"We are living vicariously through you guys," Kicker said. "It's your turn. What does Torin do?"

Oh crap, I couldn't be that girl. The annoying, whiny, clingy girlfriend. I pinched myself. Ouch. I wasn't dreaming. I was actually indulging in self-pity. Total loser-dom.

"Are you guys going for early decision?" I asked, determined not to think about Torin or dying Seeresses.

Kicker and Sondra groaned.

"We don't want to discuss college," Sondra said. "We want to hear about your love lives. Do you two double date often?"

Funny, I hadn't thought of that. Cora wore a look that said the idea never occurred to her either. "We're planning on one this weekend," I fibbed.

She caught on. "Is it Friday night or Saturday?"

"Saturday. I'm working on Friday."

"Working? Where?" Cora asked.

"At our shop. Three days a week. I'm going to learn how they run things." I put a bit of lettuce in my mouth and munched on it. It tasted like crap. I pushed my tray aside.

"So back to your question about college," Cora said, pushing her soup aside. "Have you guys decided on one yet?"

Kicker was planning to attend the University of Portland. Sondra's mother was a former Husky, so she was planning to apply to the University of Washington in Seattle. With everything happening in my life, college was the last thing on my mind.

"I haven't decided. You?" I asked Cora.

"I thought about going to Florida, but I might just stay closer to home. Eugene or Portland. As long as I study psychology I'm good."

Kicker wanted to know why Florida. Echo had a house in Florida he used when he wasn't escorting souls to Hel.

"Is Echo going with you?" Sondra asked, eying Cora's Druidic ring. Echo had given it to her last month after meeting her parents.

"He'd better. Will Torin go with you to wherever?"

"*Yeah.*" *I hoped so. We hadn't discussed college. There were lots of things we hadn't discussed. Part of me was envious of Cora. She had her life together. With Dad's illness and Mom's uncertain future, I was waiting for something else to go wrong.*

I found myself indulging in a little self-pity after lunch, but I kicked the habit when I realized what I was doing. It was pointless.

Torin, Andris, and Echo were by the Harley when school let out. The three of them being civil to each other was a rarity. Seeing them in a deep conversation set off warning bells all over the place. Torin often knew when I was nearby, but not this time. Whatever they were discussing must be serious.

"*Hey, guys,*" *I said, and they all turned. Maybe I was imagining it, but they looked guilty. Then something the Seeress had said in my vision flashed in my head.*

Your kind is not supposed to kill. Could the killers be Valkyries?

"*What are you three plotting?*" *Andris and Echo took off with mumbled excuses.* "*Okay. Weird. What's going on?*"

Torin chuckled, his hand coming to rest on my arms. "*We need to talk.*"

"*Does it have anything to do with why you've been gone?*"

He pressed a kiss on my forehead. "*Let's talk at home.*"

"*Why? Is this about the Seeresses?*" *Something flashed in his eyes.* "*Are they dead?*" *Again his expression gave him away.* "*How many?*"

"*Raine...*"

"*Do you know who's targeting them and why?*"

His eyes darkened, but his expression said he wasn't going to talk. Anger slammed into me. "*Are they Valkyries or Immortals? Your kind is not supposed to kill Mortals, yet they are killing Seeresses. Mortals. I'm right, aren't I?*"

"*Raine—*"

"*Don't try to hide things from me, Torin. If Seeresses are being targeted by Valkyries, I need to know why. What are they after? Am I next?*"

He closed the gap between us and shut me up the only way he knew how. I tried to fight him, but I lost before I even began. When he lifted his head, I could only stare at him. Blue flames leaped in his eyes. He was furious.

"*We'll talk at home.*" *He lifted me and put me in the seat of the Harley. Then he sat in front of me, taking my arms and wrapping them around his waist.* "*Hold on tight.*"

I obeyed him and hated it. My anger started building up again halfway home. By the time he pulled up in his garage, I was ready to decapitate him.

"I cannot believe you played me like that. I swear, sometimes I want to knock sense into your thick skull, but you won't feel the pain. So I'm left yelling while you look at me like you have no idea what I'm talking about."

"I really have no idea." He crossed his arms and angled his head. "What did I do this time, luv?"

His voice had dropped an octave, all smooth and sexy. I shivered, responding to it even when I was so pissed I wanted to scream. Then he had the gall to smirk at my reaction. Most of the time, I didn't mind that he found my responses to him amusing. This time, it only fanned my anger.

My hands landed on my hips. "You are a bully, you tard. You manipulate me when I ask questions you don't want to answer."

His brows disappeared under the shaggy hair across his forehead. "We kissed, Freckles."

"No, you kissed me and you did it to shut me up. You used my feelings against me. And that means my feelings for you make me weak, and pathetic, and easily manipulated."

The smile left his face, and his eyes turned cold. I took a step back. He followed. "You think your feelings for me make you weak?"

"That's right." I stopped running when I reached the steps leading into the house. There was nowhere else to go except inside. From Torin's expression, he would catch me before I turned around. "And you took advantage, you jackass."

He opened his mouth, but I knew he'd only try to justify his actions and make me see things his way.

"Don't want to hear it. Until you are ready to talk and not treat me like I was born yesterday, stay. Away. From. Me."

Eyebrows came down, until they were slashes. His eyes grew cold, promising retribution, but I wasn't backing down.

"I refuse to be treated like some delicate person that must be babied and shielded from unpleasantness all the time. If you can't see that, then I don't know what's going to happen to this relationship."

I swallowed as his cool eyes suddenly pulled a one-eighty and blazed with something I'd only witnessed once, before the Norns stole his memories. He was furious. "Are you done?"

I hesitated. Had I gone too far? "No." I hated that my voice shook with uncertainty. "Yes, I'm done. For now." I turned, opened the door, and marched to the mirror in his living room. I wanted him to stop me, to beg me to stay.

"Uh, Raine?"

Thank goodness. I turned, so ready to fly into his arms. He stood by the back door, my backpack in his hand. One eyebrow lifted. "Forgetting something?"

My backpack. He called me back for my stupid backpack. I marched back and reached for it. He whipped it behind him. "Apologize first."

Now he wanted to play games? "Give it to me, Torin."

"Apologize for the mean things you just said."

"Mean…? Bite me."

"With pleasure." He dropped the backpack and reached for me.

He was insane. I took off, engaging my runes before I reached the mirror. I didn't hear him behind me, but he moved so quietly like a jungle cat and I didn't dare look.

I went through the portal, expecting him to come charging after me. When I turned, he was in his living room, smirking, my backpack dangling on his finger.

"When you're ready to beg me for forgiveness, come for it." He walked away as the portal closed.

6. APOLOGIES NEEDED

I couldn't explain how I focused, but I managed to read to Dad without drowning in my anger. I was about to leave when he said, "Femi tells me you're going to work at the Mirage."

Did I talk to her about it? I couldn't remember. "Yes. Three days a week. Monday, Wednesday, and Friday. With Mom gone, I figured I might as well learn how things are run."

He smiled. "I think it's a wonderful idea. If I wasn't laid up, I would have come up with it myself." He patted my hand. "I'm proud of you, pumpkin."

I faked a gasp. "Finally, some appreciation."

He chuckled. "So we'll read on Tuesdays and Thursdays?"

"And weekends." He might not say it, but I knew he looked forward to the hours we spent together. "This time I promise not to cry when Ahab harpoons Moby-Dick."

"Or cover your ears?" he asked with another dry chuckle. The only way I'd need to do that was if he read it to me again. Femi had explained that the tumor was pressing on the part of his brain that affected vision. His eyesight was getting worse.

"I know how it ends now, so I'm good," I said. "But I still hate the pompous, egg-head Ahab."

Dad shifted on his pillows, and I reached over to adjust them. "I think you're confusing Patrick Stewart in the movie with Captain Picard in Star Trek."

"Well, despite Captain Picard's stellar performance, I still think Captain Ahab got what he deserved." It was nice to see Dad laugh and go toe-to-toe with me on a subject.

I left him watching TV and went in search of Femi. Singing led me upstairs. She had headphones and was singing along with Bon Jovi while putting away towels in the hallway closet.

"Done, doll?" she called out, removing the ear buds.

"Yeah. He's looking great."

"He had a great day. He signed the papers you brought home and even conferenced with Hawk. Oh, Torin stopped by. He said he'll be at his place."

Yeah, like I was ready to talk to him. My hour with Dad had become almost two hours. Lucid moments with him were so rare I hadn't minded. "Do you need help with the laundry?"

"No, I'm good. Text me if you're not going to be home for dinner, okay?"

"Okay." I touched her arm. "Thanks." A hamper with my laundry sat in the middle of my bed, but I didn't bother to put them away. I stopped telling Femi I could fold my own laundry because she never listened.

I reached for my backpack from where I usually dropped it and realized I'd left it at Torin's. Just my luck. I needed to do my homework, which meant crawling back to that slug.

I grabbed my cell phone and turned to leave when something caught my eye. Torin's family seal. I slipped it on and studied my reflection.

Torin loved to buy me gifts, including a cute tennis bracelet for Valentine's Day last month, which I was sure cost an arm and a leg. The diamonds were real. But this piece was the best yet. As I traced the etched horseman I swore I heard a horse neigh. There was something special about it. It was the only reason that could explain the visions.

Should I show it to Torin? Maybe later. As for begging him for forgiveness, it wasn't happening. Two could play this game. Andris would get my backpack.

Letting the image of Andris fill my head, I engaged my runes and the mirror responded. The portal opened into the mansion's foyer and memories flashed through my head. Unpleasant, nasty images that made me feel queasy.

Instead of the smooth marble floor and walls with works of art I was sure belonged in a museum, slabs of concrete crumbled and floors cracked like a ten-pointer earthquake was ripping it apart. Twice I'd fought Maliina in this room and each time I'd come close to dying and losing someone I loved.

Voices reached me before I changed the destination to the portal in the hallway near the kitchen, and Andris and a middle-aged woman came into view. He saw me and winked. The fact that the woman kept walking without glancing my way told me she was a Mortal. Mortals couldn't see portals.

"See you tomorrow, Mrs. Willow," Andris said when they reached the front door. He shook her hand and closed the door after she left.

"Are you into cougars now?" I asked, entering the room.

"Really? Does she look hot enough to hold my interest?"

I rolled my eyes. And I used to think Torin was full of himself.

"Don't roll your eyes at me, missy. I have taste."

"Sure you do."

"All my cougars have been hot. Mortals and Immortals. Valkyries and even minor goddesses. Variety spices life." He looped his arm around my shoulder. "I'll give you a couple of centuries and your eyes will start wandering, too. Of course, I'm assuming Torin is your first, unless you and golden boy closed the deal."

He'd assumed wrong about Torin being my first because we were waiting, and Eirik and I never went that far. He always called Eirik golden boy and not in a nice way. Poor Eirik. Thinking about him meant worrying about him. Unfortunately, the mansion used to be his home, which was another reason I hated coming here.

"Hey," Andris said and squeezed my shoulder. "You okay?"

"Yeah. And FYI, the idea that I'd ever want anyone other than Torin is beyond absurd." He might act like he invented douchebaggery and piss me off at every turn, but he set the bar so high I couldn't imagine another man reaching it.

"Ah, to be young and naïve again," Andris said and sighed. "I'll make you eat those words someday, sweetheart." We walked past the stairs and entered the hallway connecting the foyer and the other downstairs rooms. Andris stopped suddenly and lifted the pendant from my chest. "The de Clare seal. He gave it to you?"

He sounded surprised. I nodded. Torin's family name was de Clare, but he'd taken up St. James after his older brother James died in the crusade. "It's beautiful, isn't it?"

"It is priceless, and I'm not talking about its value."
Andris frowned and bit his lower lip as though undecided about
something. "It means a lot to Torin, so don't lose it."

He was acting weird, and I hated when he talked down to
me as though I was a child. "Of course I won't lose it." I took it
from his hand and slipped it under my shirt, so it rested on top of
my undershirt. We continued down the hallway. To our right was
another set of stairs leading to the second floor. Beyond it were
several bedrooms, including Eirik's old room and the pool. To
our left were the doors to the dining room, kitchen, and pantry.

"Has he told you about his family?"

"No." Torin didn't talk much about the past, except
about his brother.

Andris' frown deepened. "I'm sure he will when he's
ready. Some things are way too personal and painful to share,
even with those you love." He sounded glum as though reliving
his painful past. "I only found out about a century ago when he
was wasted after... Let's just say he was wasted."

Curses came from the kitchen, and a change came over
Andris. His serious tone disappeared, and the flippant guy I knew
took over. "Lover boy is still venting. He scared four of the six
applicants before we even started interviewing them."

Crap! I didn't want to see him yet. But curiosity won.
"Applicants for what?"

"Cook slash housekeeper slash whatever I want her to do
around the house," he said.

"A Mortal for a housekeeper? You're going to give her a
heart attack if you appear out of nowhere." I waved toward the
hallway mirror portal.

He shrugged indifferently. "We all don't have Immortals
tripping over themselves to work for us. Mrs. Willow only makes
dinners, so she won't be here until we are home from school,
except Fridays and Mondays, when she'll come in the morning
before we leave for housecleaning and laundry. She doesn't get a
house key either. Torin insisted." Andris pushed the kitchen
door, and I smiled when I saw the dishes on the counter. "He
refused to consider the two I liked just because one couldn't cook
and the other was intimidated by the size of the house."

"We were interviewing for a housekeeper, not your next lover," Torin retorted. He looked up and saw me. "Hey, you. Came to apologize?"

"We could have hired one as the cook and the other as a maid," Andris cut in before I could respond."

"And you'd have seduced both by the end of the week." Torin's eyes stayed on me. "I can tell you what to say if you'd like."

Seriously? "I'm not apologizing. I'm not the one who acted like a douche."

"Did I miss something? Did you two fight?" Andris asked with glee. "Your fights are so entertaining and hil—"

"Shut up, Andris," Torin snapped, but his eyes didn't waver from mine.

"Whipped," Andris muttered and snatched a plate of food off the table.

We ignored him. After the seriousness of our discussion outside the kitchen, I'd concluded that Andris was a lot more complex than he let on. He adopted different personas to suit each occasion, faking shallowness when he wasn't. No, change that. He could be shallow, rude, and childish, but he also had depth. He was amazing with electronics, and only those close to him knew he loved books.

Torin still waited, but I wasn't playing. "You made them cook something as part of the interview?" I asked instead.

Surprise flickered across his face. I'm not sure whether it was my calmness or question that caused it. "Just a dish and they couldn't get it right." He dumped the contents of two plates and reached for two more.

He'd shed his jacket, and every time he reached up to put the spices back on the shelf, the shirt rode high and bared his abs. No sane woman could focus on cooking with his intoxicating presence around. I knew I couldn't.

"Most of them thought if you just throw in spices everything would naturally turn out perfect," he continued. "And they called themselves cooks."

"No one can meet your impossible standards, bro," Andris called out from the other end of the counter before cutting something on his plate and putting it in his mouth. He ate with utter enjoyment. "He even had them sample what he'd cooked," he added. Despite his belly aching, Andris loved fine food. "If they couldn't identify at least two spices, they were out the door."

"Mrs. Willow did," Torin said. He dumped the entire content of a pan in the garbage. "She was the only one who understood that cooking is an art." He scooped a piece of something and offered it to me.

Our eyes met, and the moment stretched. The air sizzled with so many emotions it hurt to breathe. If this was an olive branch, I was accepting it. Fighting with him was too emotionally draining. I opened my lips, and he placed the morsel in my mouth. Flames leaped in his sapphire blue eyes.

I wanted to close the gap between us, but my taste buds exploded. "Whoa. That's good. Is that yours or hers?"

"Mrs. Willow's." Torin pointed at the fork-licking Andris. "He's eating mine. She didn't even blink when I told her that sometimes she'll have to cook for twice the number of people. One woman had the nerve to ask if she'd get a bonus for cooking for more people. Another asked if we were interested in a live-in housekeeper since our "mother" was out of town indefinitely. We didn't advertise for a live-in."

"She was perfect," Andris mumbled.

Torin shot him a disgusted look. "Don't you have something better to do?"

Andris pointed at his laptop. "Researching witch stuff. After what we found out..." His eyes went to me and slid away. So they were determined to keep secrets. Great. The olive branch just broke. And I couldn't ask Andris to get my backpack now.

I started out of the kitchen. Behind me, I could hear them argue.

"There's plenty of time for that," Torin said. "You're on kitchen duty, so glove up."

"Again? Why me? Why can't Ingrid or Blaine do it? They're Immortals assigned to us, not the other way round. They are the ones who should be interviewing the housekeeper and doing chores around here. Blaine raids the kitchen after the lights are off and never cleans up after himself."

"One hour then turn off the oven, Andris."

I felt a little sorry for Andris. Blaine had lacrosse, and Ingrid was at cheer practice. It didn't matter that Immortals assigned to Valkyries were supposed to lend them whatever support they needed. Torin wasn't too big on depending on other people.

He stepped into the hallway just before I entered the portal. "Where are you going?"

His place. "Home."

He laughed, mocking me. Was I blowing this out of proportion? Surely, I'd better make sure he understood I wouldn't take crap from him. His place was quiet. He had such a vibrant presence he tended to dominate his surroundings. Without him, his home lacked its usual appeal. Or maybe it was our fight messing with my head.

I checked the living room, then the kitchen, but my backpack wasn't there. I peeked in the garage. Nothing. Sounds came from upstairs. Dang it, he was back. I tiptoed and searched everywhere downstairs and came up empty, which meant he had it upstairs.

Sighing, I headed his way, wracking my brains for solutions. He was going to make me beg. Try to anyway.

His door was open, and I caught him changing. He kicked off his shoes, toed off his socks, and reached for his T-shirt. I usually enjoyed watching him pull his shirt off and on. Not today. I wanted him clothed and focused on what I was about to say. He pulled off his shirt and reached for his belt.

I stopped breathing. He pulled off his belt and unbuttoned his pants. Hel's Mist, he needed to stop.

"Torin!"

He turned and cocked an eyebrow, lips curled in a smirk. "I was sure you'd let me go all the way before stopping me."

My face burned. "You knew I was out here?"

"I knew you were downstairs snooping, Freckles. You make enough noise to wake up the dead. I knew when you made it upstairs." He sauntered toward me. He chuckled, and I dragged my eyes from his washboard six-pack and the fascinating thin line of hair disappearing under his waistband. "I can finish if you'd like."

He needed to stop messing with me. Maybe if I started with what the pendant could do, he might stop. "I need to show you something," I said and reached under my T-shirt for his seal pendant.

"Apologize first."

"Torin, this is not the time for games."

"Who said I'm playing?" He braced himself on the doorframe and lowered his head until he and I were on the same eye level. "You told me to stay away from you. Unforgiveable. You implied our relationship might not survive. Totally wrong and cruel. But the worst part, you said your feelings for me make you weak." His eyebrows shot up. "Weak? Seriously? What in Hel's Mist does that mean?" He was furious.

"Are you forgetting what happened before I said those things?"

"So no apology?"

"No." I was dying to, but he had to understand I wasn't a breakable doll.

He stepped back and slammed the door in my face.

My jaw dropped. No, he didn't. That arrogant man didn't just do that. I turned to walk downstairs so angry I wanted to chuck something. Halfway down the stairs, I stopped and glared at my phone, wishing I could send him a nasty text. Too bad he wouldn't see it.

I stomped back.

When I burst into his room, he was waiting. His eyes said he'd known I'd be back.

"Let me tell you exactly what I think of your tantrum, Valkyrie. It was unforgiveable. You don't slam the door in my face. Ever. You do it again and I'll... I'll..." I took a step back as he closed the gap between us. "What are you—?"

He scooped me up and my cell phone fell from my hand. "I have to be the bigger person and forgive you, Freckles. Now we can make out."

I wanted that, but... "No, we're not." I tried to free myself. "I want to show you something."

His eyebrows rose. "Will I enjoy it?"

"I don't know."

"Will *you* enjoy it?" He wiggled his brows.

"You are a perv." My arms tightened around his neck, so he wouldn't drop me on the bed. "Stop being difficult."

He sighed. "You're no fun."

"I'm fun. Plenty. I mean, I'm plenty of fun." I escaped his arms, picked up his shirt where he'd dropped it, and threw it at him. "Put it back on."

"No." He sprawled on the bed, stretched, and leaned back against the pillows, his eyelids dropping. The look was sexy and irresistible. He knew how to turn up the heat, the snake.

"At least sit on the chair and turn off the sexiness."

He laughed. "Turn it off? That's impossible. I'm the essence of sexiness. The sum of all your fantasies wrapped up and tied with a little… bow." Something on my face must have convinced him that I was serious.

"The things I give up for you. One day…" He got up, pulled up a chair, and sat with his arms crossed and one leg resting on top of the other. He watched me with narrowed impatient eyes as I kicked off my flats and sat in the middle of the bed. When I pulled the pendant from under my shirt, he uncrossed his arms. His leg landed on the floor with a thud.

"What are you doing?" he asked in a voice that was no longer playful.

"Your pendent is magical. Watch this." I closed my hand around it, and everything disappeared.

Next second, I was standing in a forest surrounded by trees stretching up to the dark sky. Stars winked innocently at me while gravel dug into my feet. I looked at my feet, but my blurry sight made it difficult to see much. So I used my other senses.

I was no longer barefoot. Whatever shoes I now wore were furry. My jeans and layered tees were now replaced with a dark, heavy cloak lined with fur, and my gloved hand was closed around a walking stick.

"Move," the same voice I'd heard in my earlier visions snarled from behind me.

I turned to glance at him, but he pushed me and I stumbled forward, almost tripping on the hem of the cloak. "Where are we?" I asked.

"What kind of question is that? You brought us here."

We entered a clearing. The place shimmered like a mirage, but I could tell it was already set for a ceremony. A large tree stump was in the middle of a circle made of dug out earth. There was no soil, so I knew the line wasn't fresh. This was a place of rituals. Runes were carved on the base of the stump, and a smoldering fire sent aromatic smoke into the air.

"Open the circle," the voice commanded.

"She sees us, you know," I said. I wasn't watching this time. I was the Seeress, or at least I was seeing things through her eyes.

"Then she knows we are coming for her," Torin's Doppelganger said. "Get inside the circle and show us where they live."

I used the staff and waved it above a section of the dugout circle. Dirt filled up the section, breaking the circle. Then something weird happened. I appeared to stay behind the circle while the Seeress stepped inside the circle. Now I could see that she wore a lot of furry things: boots, gloves, and a cap. Over her shoulder was a fur pelt. The circle closed and she turned, pressed her hands together, and appeared to look directly at me.

"I will do the warding spell, too," she whispered, "but you must protect the others. You must stop them from hurting our kind."

"Who are you talking to?" the guy with the British accent asked, and I whipped around. Or should I say I floated around and faced him?

My heart stopped. Even through my jacked up eyesight, I recognized the same black hair and brilliant blue eyes. Torin.

"It's okay," Torin said, his arms tightening around me.

My first instinct was to wiggle out of his arms and put some distance between us. He was a killer. I might not have known the people with him, but I'd recognized him. This didn't make sense.

"I'm fine." I sat up and tried to contain my panic, my mind racing. There had to be an explanation for what I'd seen. Torin was many things, but he wasn't a killer. The man I'd come to know wouldn't be. "I, uh, that's what I meant to show you. The amulet is magical. Every time I touch it I get a vision."

Torin sat on his haunches, carefully removed the amulet from my hand, and threw it in the chair he'd sat on. He peered at me, concern in his eyes. "What did you see?"

How did I tell the man I loved that I thought he was a killer? He was innocent. He had to be. I slid off the bed, feeling like a traitor for believing what I saw, for suspecting him even for a second. "First, tell me what happened when I lost consciousness."

"Your eyes glowed golden-yellow then rolled into their sockets and you fell sideways. I tried to wake you, but you were so still. Your face…" He shook his head. "I could tell you were terrified. I hate when I can't reach you or help. I can't take these trances."

I stood in front of the mirror and studied my eyes. They'd stopped glowing and my stomach roiled as I thought about the leader of the people killing the Seeresses. Maybe I'd superimposed Torin's face onto the killer's because of the accent. Or maybe it was because his face was the last thing I saw before I went into a trance.

The latter made sense. Yeah, that was it.

"Freckles?"

I rubbed my arms, suddenly feeling cold. Through the mirror, Torin watched me with an unreadable expression, hands in the front pockets of his pants. Shirt still off. I loved and trusted him. If, and that was a big if, he was the man in my vision and what I just saw was going to happen in the future, someone was going to make him do these things, which meant I had to find him help. Who would he search for in the future? Me? Did that mean we would be separated?

"This time, I saw things through the eyes of the Seeress. At least for a while. But when she entered the circle, we separated. She said she'd do the warding spell, but I must protect the others. What does warding mean?"

"Protecting. Did you see the killers?"

Yes. I shook my head. No, I didn't. It was my mind playing tricks on me. "No, but they were forcing her to hold a séance and find some people. The Seeress mentioned a 'she'. Said *she* was watching them, and the killer seemed pleased. Why is the pendant magical?"

Torin got off the bed and reached for his shirt. He pulled it on, his eyes not meeting mine. I had a feeling he didn't want to discuss this. He reached for his socks and shoved his feet into them.

I moved closer. "Torin?"

"It was my mother's," he said, his jaws tight. "I'm going to find out where Echo found it and why you are reacting to it."

"Whoa." I slid off the bed. "Your mother was a witch?"

He made a sound between a scoff and a chuckle. "No, Freckles. My mother was most definitely not a witch." Seriously, his distrust for witches made no sense whatsoever. But then he reached under him, pulled out the pendant, and said, "She was killed by one." My breath stalled in my chest at the anguish in his voice. "A very bad and evil witch."

The pain in his voice was raw and I reacted to it, our fight forgotten. I walked to him, wanting to touch him and ease his pain. I lifted his hands out of the way, sat on his lap, and wrapped my arms around his shoulders. Even though his arms wound around my waist and his head rested on my chest, his body stayed rigid.

"She used it just before she died. She always kept it in her room. I saw her that night before it happened. She didn't see me because I was an Immortal and couldn't reveal myself. She didn't deserve to die the way she did, a sacrifice to a power-hungry Necromancer. I should have saved her. Would have if it weren't for Lavania and Valkyries' laws."

He went quiet, but I felt his sorrow all the way to my core. Even after centuries, he was still hurting and blaming himself. Torin rarely talked about the past, so this was new, and touching, and sad. I fought tears and gently rubbed circles on his back, trying to absorb his pain. Now I understood why he hated witches.

"I hope you made her pay," I said.

"He. He got what was coming to him," he growled. "He and every last member of his coven."

He? I wanted to ask, but then I remembered that in the eleventh century, before the inquisitions and religious fanatics, magic was practiced by both men and women in England and Europe. "Tell me about her... your mother."

"Freckles—"

"Please." Maybe if he shared more of his past, he'd start to let go of the pain.

Wow, that sounded like something Lavania would say. Before she left with Mom, she'd told me to see Dad's dying as a journey to the next level and appreciate the wonderful moments he and I had together. At the time, I wanted to tell her to shut up. Now it made sense. Torin had been carrying pain and hurt for centuries because of the circumstances of his mother's death. He wasn't given a chance to say goodbye.

"What was she like? Was she nice or mean?"

He gave me a look that said I was pushing it. "She was loving and caring."

"Noble or a commoner?"

He smiled. "Noble. She was Norman, a descendant of the Vikings," he explained when I gave him a blank look. "Norman comes originally from the word *Norseman*."

"So you have Norse blood in your veins after all," I said.

He chuckled. "Viking blood sounds better. Conquerors and marauders' blood, even better."

"Plunderers, pillagers, murderers, and ravishers of women," I piped in.

He laughed. "So a few people got killed along the way, and the women preferred the stronger and manly Vikings. You can't blame them. First they conquered Northern France, then England when William the Conqueror, Duke of Normandy, invaded England and defeated the Anglo-Saxons," he continued.

"Was your father Norman, too?"

Something changed in his voice when he said, "Yes and no. He considered himself an Anglo-Saxon although he was the illegitimate son of an Anglo-Saxon nobleman and a Norman maid."

"How did he meet your mother?"

His jaw tightened. "Do we really need to go into that?"

"Please." I stroked his hair. "You know everything about me, and I know next to nothing about you. Except for your brother and the crusade—"

"Okay. My father's background is where the story becomes murky. King William moved his court and nobles to England after he conquered it, took away land and titles from the Anglo-Saxons, and gave them to the Normans. My grandfather on my father's side lost everything, but my father somehow got them all back. My grandfather never openly acknowledged him as his son, so instead of using the Oakley name, he chose a Norman name, de Clare." Torin frowned as though some of his thoughts bothered him.

"Mom was the daughter of Comtes d'Arques. Her parents and grandparents before them were very prominent in court. By the time my parents met, the king had given my father the earldom and the lands that had once belonged to my grandfather. The illegitimate son had become the Earl of Worthington." He frowned. "But it wasn't enough for my father. He was hard. Ambitious. Cruel. He made those around him miserable."

I could feel him tensing as he talked about his father. I forked my fingers through his hair, pushed back the locks on his forehead, and tilted his face upwards. I kissed him until he relaxed. I stroked his cheek. Kissed his forehead. "Tell me more about your mother."

"I can't focus when you do that," he mumbled in a voice gone smoky.

I stopped messing with him. "There. I won't distract you anymore."

Torin chuckled. "You're sitting on my lap."

"I'll move to the other end of the room." His arms tightened, firmly holding me in place.

"You distract me by being in the same room, Freckles. Your voice. Your laugh." He closed his eyes, inhaled deeply, and exhaled. "Your scent. My essence has a way of finding yours, so no matter where you run, I'll always find you."

Then why was someone who looked like him searching for me in the future? "I'm not sure if that's a threat or a promise, but it sounds stalker-ish and not romantic."

"I can be romantic."

Yes, he could. "What was your mother's name?"

"Adelaide," he said.

I grinned. "Like the city in Australia."

"Yes. She was the best. Noble by birth but a serf at heart, my father used to tell her. She didn't care about court life, fashion, or who was wearing what. She learned to speak English and treated the servants with dignity when her fellow aristocrats spoke French and treated the Anglo serfs like crap. If a villager needed her help, she gave it. If they needed food, she supplied it. Soldiers were welcomed to our home, and she helped treat them with herbs and healing ointments she made. Everyone loved her."

Despite what he'd said, herbs and healing ointments sounded witchy to me. "So you spoke French?"

"Yes and English. After Lavania turned me, it took me three years to learn everything there was to learn about runes, Immortals, and Valkyries. We didn't have a crash course like some people." He squeezed my waist, his fingers caressing my skin. I forced myself to focus. "Lavania had a castle in Normandy and about three hundred Immortals under her care. I'd sneak out to see my mother. I'd watch her, walk beside her, and listen as she talked with the servants or friends about us—her, James, and me." His voice grew gruff. "She took our death hard. We had no children, so we left her nothing. And it was hard being so close to her, yet not tell her that I was still alive and ease her pain." His voice became hoarse.

Tears filled my eyes and flowed down my cheeks onto his hair.

Torin's arms were like vices around my waist. "Yet I couldn't walk away. I tried to so many times, but I always went back. I couldn't give her what she wanted, yet she was there for me. Even if she didn't know she was there." Torin blew out air. "I started to see immortality as a curse. I was alive, yet I was withering from the inside, my connection to those I loved severed."

No wonder he hadn't wanted to turn me. He'd said being an Immortal was worse than death and had begged me not to do it. I didn't know why until now.

My arms tightened around his shoulders.

"Then she died and everything ceased to matter," he whispered in low voice. "I was like the walking dead. I reaped souls, ate, slept, yet felt nothing. Empty. Darkness became my companion. I hated what I had become, but there was nothing I could do to change it. Perhaps I didn't want to change it. Most Valkyries reaped in groups. I preferred to be alone. I didn't want to connect with another person, Mortal or Immortal. By the time I was paired with Andris, I hated being a Valkyrie. His carefree attitude pissed me off. When he turned Maliina and Ingrid without thinking about the consequences, I snapped his neck and threw him out. He stayed away for a while, but he came back. It didn't matter how often I told him to get lost or stay away; he always came back. Then I met you."

Silence followed. Like me, I was sure he was reliving our first month together, how he'd been drawn to me against his will, how he'd fought healing me and making me Immortal.

"So when you say that your feelings make you weak, I wonder what mine make me, because you are my existence. The reason I breathe. Smile. Laugh. Live. You've taught me to feel again, to love and to trust. You give me a reason to wake up in the morning." He chuckled, though he didn't sound amused. "But if you ever decide this relationship is not right for you, I will let you go, because above all, above my pain and needs, your happiness is the most important thing to me."

I stopped breathing when he reached up and touched the side of my face with the tips of his fingers, leaving behind heated flesh. For one brief moment, I closed my eyes and savored his touch, tears burning my eyes. But I opened them just as quickly because I needed to take him in with all my senses.

"Every night when I leave you and crawl in my cold bed, it hurts. I'm not talking about sexual frustration. I need to hold you in my arms. Feel you. Breathe you. Every moment you look into my eyes and whisper you love me, I give you a piece of myself. Yet loving you feeds my soul. Kissing you reaffirms what I believe deep down in my core—that you and I are meant to be together." He wiped a tear from my cheek. "Do you know that when I wake up every morning and don't see you by your window I break out in a cold sweat? The thought of losing you to the Norns or stupid Mortals who use magic frivolously is my worst nightmare. I'd do anything, fight anyone to keep you safe, so don't ever think I don't listen to anything you say. Everything you do and say is important to me. If it takes a lifetime to convince you of that—"

I cut him off with my lips, poured every drop of love in my heart into the kiss, showing what I couldn't say. When we pulled apart, he chuckled, the sexy sound rolling over my sensitized senses.

"I should tell you how I feel more often," he teased.

I hugged him tight. "You do with every look and smile, with every touch and kiss."

"Okay. Can I breathe now?" he mumbled, and I realized I had pressed his face to my chest. I eased up, leaned back, and studied his beautifully sculptured face—the chiseled cheekbones and those kissable lips. He studied me lazily, his brilliant blue eyes glittering under those incredibly long lashes.

"I know I can be difficult sometimes."

He grinned. "Understatement there."

"Okay, I can be a real pain."

"True." I could tell he was fighting laughter.

"And I'm not good at telling you how I feel."

His eyebrows shot up. "Yeah, you kind of yell it. A lot. But you're really good at showing."

He was teasing me now. I was going to get better at telling him. "And I can be really mean to you sometimes."

"Nah, I love your feistiness. If you haven't noticed, we burn a lot hotter after we fight. Wouldn't trade that for anything. You turn into a doormat and I promise you right here and now that I'll make your life miserable. I'm very insufferable when I get my way all the time." He kissed my nose. "You get me."

His eyes glowed with the intensity of his feelings, and I felt silly, stupid even, for my earlier reaction. This man adored me. I didn't know what I'd done in my seventeen-and-a-half years to deserve him, but I was so damn lucky.

We just sat there, my arms around his shoulders, his around my waist. I still had questions. So many of them I didn't know where to start. I hated bringing up his father, but I had to know.

"Where were we before you distracted me?" I asked.

"We were done." He lifted me up and threw me onto the bed. I smothered a scream, my legs and arms flailing. "Now I have places to go, witch. Things to do."

I gawked at him as he reached for his socks. "Did your father die before your mother?"

"No." He shoved a foot in a sock and reached for the second one.

"Where was he when she was grieving?"

"With his mistresses in Aquitaine, or was it London? My mother was alone at the manor with the serfs most of the time."

"The bastard."

Torin chuckled. "I think she preferred being alone."

"Did she know about you? I mean did you, you know, reap her?"

He stopped in the process of putting on his boot, and I thought he wouldn't answer. "I wanted to, but I couldn't. I wanted to tell her about me and the time we spent together even though she didn't know I was there. She was very ill towards the end."

Oh no. That meant his mother's soul was in Hel's Hall. I scooted to the edge of the bed. "Have you ever seen her soul?"

He shook his head, his eyes sliding from mine. One booted leg done. "I searched for her. When Andris turned Maliina and Ingrid, we both got tour duty in Hel for about a decade. I searched for her there too, but Hel is huge. The souls there are not like the ones in Valhalla who trained for Ragnarok during the day and partied at night. Souls of the sick and the elderly in Hel's Hall are at peace. They go there to rest. The evil ones are herded to Corpse Strand, the island of the damned, where they meet their fate."

Tortured for eternity, Cora had told me. I shivered. "I hope the Necromancer who killed her is rotting on that island."

Torin chuckled. "I knew you were a vengeful witch."

"He deserved it." I didn't think it was possible to love him more. I did now more than ever.

The smile disappeared from his lips. "I wish I'd told him that I knew what he'd done, but the journey to the island is dangerous and it's easy to be trapped there. In fact, Goddess Hel sends Grimnirs she punishes to Corpse Strand." Torin stood. "Okay, Freckles. Story time is over. I need to talk to Echo about the amulet."

"*We* need to talk to Echo," I corrected.

He rolled his eyes.

"And we haven't discussed what you found out today," I whined. "I need to know what's going on, Torin. You can't keep me in the dark and claim you're protecting me."

He pondered my statement while studying my face with unnerving intensity. I started to feel uneasy.

"What? Do I have a zit?"

He chuckled. "Counting your imperfections."

"What?"

"Your eyes are too close together. Weird I never noticed that before. And your lips…"

"Jerk." I grabbed a pillow and chucked it at his head. He ducked and came up laughing.

"We're going to Echo's, so stop goofing around and put on your shoes," he ordered.

I thought of ways to make him sorry. I couldn't find anything insulting about him physically to throw at him. "My eyes are not close together," I said. "And if you think for one second we are leaving without you telling me about what the three of you were plotting outside the school and why you disappeared this morning, then think again. You guys could be the ones knocking off Seeresses for all I know." There, I'd said it.

He laughed. "You wouldn't find me anywhere near a witch if my life depended on it. Come on. We'll talk later."

I lifted the blanket and crawled in his bed.

His brows lifted. "What are you doing?"

"Getting comfortable," I shot back the same words he'd told me earlier. "Start talking. And FYI, I'm a witch."

A glint appeared in his eyes. When he started around the bed, I scooted to the other side. He paused, eyes promising retribution. "You are being a brat," he said. "We need to find out why the pendant is making you see visions. That's more important right now."

"And I say that your refusal to tell me where you three went today is more important."

He angled his head and gave me a slow, naughty smile. I hated that smile. It said he was about to do something I wouldn't like. Like grab me and carry me caveman-style out of his room. If he dared…

He pocketed the pendant, grabbed his jacket, and started for the mirror portal.

"Where are you going?" I yelled.

"To Echo's." The runes flickered on his skin and blazed. The portal responded. He disappeared through it while I sputtered. I was sure my face was beet red. He was such a...

"Jerk," I called out. Blowing out air, I counted slowly from ten, imagining all sorts of medieval tortures raining on his arrogant head. Then I heard him.

"You home, Echo?"

"Get lost, Valkyrie," Echo said rudely. I grinned.

Cora said something that sounded like "be nice."

"He's invading our privacy, the one place we find peace and quiet."

"Peace and quiet?" Cora laughed.

"Okay, St. James. What do you want?"

Instead of answering Echo, Torin said, "Hi, Cora. Can you make sure he's dressed? I'll be back in a few."

"We're going for a swim..." The rest of Echo's words disappeared with a door closing.

I grabbed my phone, turned away from the portal, and faked an interest in my phone. I knew the moment Torin entered the bedroom. The bed shifted when he sat.

"Still sulking?" he asked.

"Nope. Texting, Femi." I did, asking her when dinner was going to be ready and what we were watching tonight. I knew both answers, but Torin didn't know that. "Let me know what Echo says."

Torin gave a long-suffering sigh designed to make me feel guilty, but it wasn't working. "I'm sorry for being a jerk."

An apology from the mighty Torin? The realms just became one giant blob of goo. I turned and eyed him suspiciously. "Really, really sorry?"

His eyes smoldered. "I'm going to regret this."

"I could make you grovel," I warned.

"Not in this lifetime." He finger combed my hair, cupped my face, and added, "There's absolutely nothing I'd change on your face. I love your eyes. Your freckles," he touched my nose, "and these," he touched my lips, "are a work of art. Your face is perfection."

It wasn't. My brown eyes weren't poetry-worthy and even though I've grown to love my freckles because of him, I still hated when new ones popped up. "You don't play fair."

"I never do. Now, I didn't want to tell you what we found out because you'd feel bad and blame yourself, and I'd feel like a total shithead."

"Torin—"

"Then you'd want to visit them or attend their funerals and give eulogies while crying." I scowled, but he pretended not to see. "Which would piss me off because I hate to see you cry. Of course, I'd want to console you in the only way I know how and become even more frustrated because I can't fully make love—"

I covered his mouth. Seriously? He could drive a saint crazy. "First, Mr. Smarty Pants, I gave a eulogy at Kate's funeral because no one else volunteered and I'd known her, like, forever. Second..." I groaned. "I can't believe it you're doing it again."

He pulled my hand down and gave me a fake innocent smile. "What?"

"Distracting me instead of answering my question, you faker. What did you find out about the Seeresses?" He hesitated. "I can handle it, Torin. Please. Just tell me."

He sighed. "The visions you've been having are real. They happened at the exact moment you saw them, so these are not premonitions. The Seeresses are reaching out to you. Talking to you."

Instead of a Norn. Freaking great! Then something occurred to me. If they were happening in real time, the person I'd seen couldn't have been Torin. He was here with me at the time.

"But the time kept changing," I protested, but inside I was celebrating.

"It was three in the morning where it happened. There were other attacks before that and more since."

"Yikes."

"There's more." The change in his voice should have warned me. "The reason they are after the Seeresses is... you."

7. DEAD SEERESSES

My breath got caught in my lungs. I listened to the pounding of my heart, which seemed loud and heavy. I should have seen this coming. I swallowed a sob.

She's watching us, the last Seeress had said. *You must protect the others. You must stop them from hurting our kind.*

She'd been communicating with me. She'd known I could see them. It always came back to me. I'd bet it had something to do with the Norns too, bitter old hags.

When I could speak without sounding like a banshee, I asked, "Why?"

Torin scowled as though my calmness surprised him. What had he expected? Tears and a why-me pity party? I might not blame myself for what happened at the swimming pool months ago when a lot of my teammates died, but everything that had happened since then had been my fault. Ever since I met the Norns in charge of my destiny, I saw things with amazing clarity.

The love of my life still watched me as though he expected me to, I don't know, throw a fit, or summon the Norns. I might do that later. Right now I needed answers.

"Torin?"

His eyes narrowed. "We don't know. We talked to the relatives of the Seeresses. One texted a boyfriend before she left with them. Another sent a vision to her twin. These people wanted the location of the young *Völva* who could talk directly with the Norns. The Seeresses did what they could to protect you and led them on a wild goose chase. The first one happened at three o'clock in Amsterdam. They are nine hours ahead of us. That's why your clock stopped at three. The next one was in Australia, then Italy, West Africa, Dominican Republic, New Orleans, and Maine. All of them practice trance magic."

Seven dead in two days. How many more before? Then what he'd said registered. "Practice? Does that mean they're not... dead?"

He shook his head. "No. Remember, we haven't been able to reap. These are good witches. Unfortunately, they are in comas. All of them."

They were not dead. The relief was sweet. I laughed and hugged Torin. Then I remembered the coma part. "Will they be okay?"

"I don't know. Two of them are brain dead."

Yikes. "Can't we heal one and—?"

"No." He shot me a censuring glance. "You know the rules. We either catch these people in the act or hope they use an evil Seeress Echo can reap. You started to blame yourself, didn't you?" Torin said. I gave him an innocent smile. Didn't fool him one little bit. "I tried to lighten things up by mentioning your eulogy."

I elbowed him. "*That* is what made me think they were dead. Does anyone know who these people are?"

"No."

"What do they want from me?"

Torin shook his head. "If we can help you get a clear vision, we could catch them in the act and either ID them or their location. Blaine already mobilized more Immortals, so the word is out. No Seeresses are to hold a séance without our say so."

"They were forcing the last one. We should talk to Ingrid. Maybe she knows a way I can sharpen my visions and get a future reading."

Torin's eyebrows slammed down.

"What?"

"Echo will tell us all we need to know." He seriously needed to chill.

"Listen, I get it. Your reasons for disliking witches are valid. I'd feel the same if I was in your shoes, but you shouldn't hold Ingrid's past against her. Even though she practiced Seidr, Maliina was the one who was powerful and evil." His expression was unrelenting. "Can't you see what a hypocrite you are? If you dislike her just because she's a witch, you should dislike me, too. Seeresses are witches, and I happen to be one."

"I don't dislike her."

I studied his shadowed eyes. "Then what is it?"

He shot me an unreadable glance. "We don't know anything about Ingrid except that she's Maliina's little sister. Andris never bothered to find out. I didn't care before because I assumed she and her sister were Andris' problem. But then Maliina targeted you and she became my problem. Anyone that hangs around you must be vetted as far as I'm concerned. She has not been vetted."

Seriously? He was beginning to sound like the freaking head of the Secret Service. "Then talk to her, get to know her, ask her about her past or whatever you need to know so we can get past this. She is the only one around here who knows about trance magic."

"I can't talk to her. She clams up whenever I'm around."

"Then turn on the charm." He gave me an annoyed look. "Fine. Get someone else to talk to her or something. You're Mr. Solutions." A thought occurred to me. "What about Femi? We could talk to her. She seemed to know something about magic."

"We shouldn't involve her yet. *Echo* will answer our questions for now. Druids knowledge of magic surpasses anyone's."

"Femi is from Ancient Egypt. The magic there is older than the Druids. No one could be wiser."

"Yet their gods disappeared. Never to be heard of again. That should tell you something. Norse gods rule. Druidism is the oldest religion, so Echo it is." Torin stood and pulled me up. Then it hit me.

"You don't trust Femi."

Torin made a face. "I wouldn't go as far as to say that. She is an open book with tattoos and pictures to prove it. She also yaps non-stop about her colorful past, so it's easy to confirm everything she says. I just don't trust her to put *your* interest first."

I pouted. "That's an insult to my mother's judgment. She hired Femi."

He dropped a kiss on my lips. "And she chose well, but Femi's first priority is your father. Anyone who doesn't put you and your interest first cannot be trusted." There was no hesitation or apology in his voice.

"That's ridiculous."

He shrugged. "Works for me."

"Other than you, me, and my parents, I don't think anyone cares about me or—"

"Andris does. He's like the annoying little brother I never had, hot-headed, shallow, gets bored easily, and does something every couple of decades that makes me want to disown him or beat the crap out of him, but I can count on him. He's loyal, smart, and in a fight, once he's resigned to it, he watches my back. He'd go to Hel's Hall and back for you."

Was he talking about the same Andris? The one who whined and complained every time he had to keep me company? "If you say so."

"The other is Eirik," Torin added softly.

The fight drained out of me. Eirik was a painful subject. He could kick some serious ass. I wished he were back. I wished I could see him even just to make sure he was okay. Echo hadn't seen him, but then again, Hel's Hall is humongous.

I shifted focus.

Seeresses were willing to die to protect me. But protect me from whom? What? I needed to know how to communicate with them while in a trance, so we could stop this craziness. It was obvious now that the person I had seen wasn't Torin.

"Okay," I said. "Let's talk to Echo."

***

Echo didn't look too thrilled to see us. "Let's make this quick," he said.

"Yeah, that's not going to happen, so chill," Torin said. "Andris needs to be here." He touched my arm and left through the portal.

Seated on a stool by the wet bar, a drink in hand, Echo studied me with a tiny smile. He looked like a normal guy in a black tank top and jeans, instead of his usual leather pants. Of course, he was barefooted. What was it with these people and bare feet? Or maybe I had a foot fetish because my eyes kept drifting to them.

"How's the *Völva* doing?" Echo asked.

"The *Völva* has a name, Echo. Use it."

He chuckled. "The Seeress has claws. Want a drink?"

"No, thanks." I looked around. The décor was contemporary, done in silver and slate, but I could see Cora's influence. The colorful pillows and vases had her name written all over them. "Where's Cora?"

Echo moved away from the stool and sauntered toward me while sipping his drink. The Druidic rings looked dark against his skin. He had an aura around him that was both menacing and fascinating. I forced myself to stand my ground when I wanted to take a step back.

"Cora?" I called out.

Echo grinned as though he sensed my unease. "I sent her home."

I scoffed at the idea. "Right. Is she in the bedroom?"

He stopped in front of me and studied me. "Are you as powerful as the Norns think you are, or are we wasting our time protecting just another ordinary Seeress?"

"*You* are protecting me?"

"Somehow, I've been forced to be part of your little group of whatever you call yourselves." He stepped away just before the portal opened. Torin and Andris stepped into the room. "Okay, the cavalry is here. Let's get started."

Andris made a beeline for the bar and poured himself a drink. Torin angled his head, walked to the bedroom door, and opened it, almost hitting Cora, who was obviously listening through the door. "Want to join us?"

Face red, she looked at Echo, then me, and finally Torin. "Okay."

We all found seats. Andris sipped his drink by the bar. Echo took a side chair and pulled Cora down on his lap. She had a gauzy cover over her swimsuit. Torin sat on the arm of my chair, and I sunk against his side.

"Did Echo tell you what's going on?" Torin asked, looking at Cora.

"No." The look she shot Echo said he'd refused to tell her.

I told her everything that had been going on the last couple of days. She left Echo's lap and came to sit beside me. "Why didn't you tell me last night when I was at your place? We watched a stupid TV show, for pity's sake."

"I like doing normal things once in a while. Yesterday was normal."

"Ooh, me too," she whispered then glanced at Echo. "We should do the date thing we discussed at school."

"I agree." Torin cleared his throat. I patted his thigh. "We're not ignoring you. You can come, too."

He gave me a look that said there was not going to be a double date. "We need answers, Echo. What Raine forgot to say is that she gets the vision every time she touches this." He dangled the seal.

Echo stared at me and rotated one of his rings. "And you're coming to me because...?"

Torin studied him with narrowed eyes, and I could imagine his thoughts. He barely tolerated Echo. "You are a Druid. This pendent has Druidic symbols. Unless of course, you're a poser and those rings your wear are just for show."

Silence followed as they seized each other up. I'd bet on Torin any day. Echo might look like Hel swallowed him and spit him out, but Torin was the calm and collected type, until he turned into a raging tornado mowing down everything in his path.

Echo must have decided not to take the bait. "People have signature energies, which they leave on things they touch. You know, like the scent dogs follow after sniffing someone's clothes. Certain Seers and Seeresses, the rarest of them, can touch people or their personal things and connect with that person's soul. Raine is connecting with that energy." He slanted Torin a glance. "You told me the pendant belonged to your family when I came across it."

"My mother," Torin said.

"That makes sense. Magical energies are a lot more powerful. Like this. Catch!" Echo threw his ring at me. I caught it, and everything around me faded to black.

The next second, I was in a forest. Like my visions before, everything was blurry. People in long robes and hooded cloaks hurried past me. Some carried satchels; others had wooden staffs. I didn't understand the language they were speaking, but I sensed their fear. The men weren't many, but they flanked the women and children, who appeared to be the majority.

Then the ground shook, and screams filled the air as everyone started to run. My heart pounded, panic surging through me. Behind us came men in medieval skirts and armor, wielding swords. Without hesitation or remorse, they cut down the people. Men. Women. Children.

"No!" I screamed as a mother went down, leaving behind a defenseless child. "Run. Someone help her." I tried to run to the child, but I couldn't move. A sword swung down on her head. I screamed.

I was still screaming and kicking when I came to. Everyone was yelling at once. "I'm going to break every damn bone in your body, you bastard," Torin vowed.

"I needed proof," Echo protested.

"Stop it, you two," Cora yelled. "She's coming around."

Silence followed. I opened my eyes and wish I hadn't. Torin looked ready to rip something or someone apart. "Are you okay?"

After the vision I'd just seen, I didn't think so. I was still shaking. I knew it happened in the past, but still... To be hunted like that? Slaughtered mercilessly? It was gruesome. Inhumane.

Cora reached out from my other side and wiped the tears from my cheek. I gripped her hand. Did she know about Echo's past? He kept his distance. I wanted to kick him into the next century for making me see that, yet something in his eyes told me he'd known firsthand what I'd just seen.

"I'm okay." I pushed Cora's hand away and tried to sit up. Torin's arms eased up, but he didn't let me go. "I didn't need to witness that, Echo. No one should ever go through that."

"What did you see?" Andris asked. "A threesome?"

That would have been preferable. "Roman soldiers hunting down Druids. Old men. Women. Children. It was horrifying." Too late, I realized this was the wrong thing to say.

Torin was gone from my side before I could blink. The next second, he rammed into Echo. The force of his attack catapulted them across the room. The two of them crashed through the glass door to the pool deck. Shards of glass flew everywhere.

Cora screamed. Andris laughed.

Of all the supernatural bullshit I had to deal with, testosterone-driven soul reapers were not on the list. Not today. "Andris, are you just going to just stand there and do nothing?"

"Yep." He poured himself a shot and went to stand by the window to watch them. "Best fight I've since the Grimnir showdown at the mansion."

Cora yelled Echo's name and issued threats I didn't bother to listen to. I'd had it. I engaged my runes and went after them. Torin and Echo were nowhere in sight. The pool deck had giant cracks like someone had taken a giant sledgehammer to it.

A giant splash came from the pool, and then a glowing Echo shot out of the water, rolled on the deck, and sprung to his feet. The look on his face said he was enjoying himself.

I pinned him with a glare. "Don't even think of going back into that pool, Echo."

"He started it," Echo said.

"No, *you* did." Lucky for him, his neighbors were too far to have seen the sudden cracks on the deck and water splashing when no one was in the pool. I walked to the edge of the pool just as Torin's head broke the surface. "No more, Torin. I don't need this from you."

"He's an ass…" He glared at Echo, who appeared beside me. He'd removed his drenched shirt and was putting on a thick, terry robe. He offered another one to Torin, but I didn't think he'd take it.

Torin pulled himself out of the pool. He looked like a drowned rat. A gorgeous rat with flames leaping in the depth of his blue eyes. I planted myself between them, snatched the robe from Echo's hand, and shoved it in Torin's chest.

"You two are going to play nice from now on," I said. "You pull this crap again and I'll flatten both of you myself. No, I'll use my witch powers and screw with your heads so badly you won't want to leave your houses for weeks. And that's a promise." I turned and started for the house. "Now fix this…"

The shards of glass and cracks were gone, remnants of glowing runes on their surfaces. Andris waved an artavus from the other side of the door. *Now he steps up.*

No one spoke as we walked back into the house. Torin's wet boots made sloshy and squeaky sounds with each step. He disappeared through the portal while Echo headed to his bedroom.

"I wish they wouldn't do that," Cora said.

"Nah, it's good for them," Andris said.

"How come you don't go punching people and things when you're pissed?" I asked.

"I'm a lover, sweetheart. Besides, things have been building up between them since forever."

Torin was first to arrive. He'd changed into my favorite sweatpants and a T-shirt. He walked straight to me. "Do I need to apologize again?"

His tone said he would, but he wasn't going to like it. I shook my head.

"Good because I'm not sorry for kicking his ass." He glared at Echo, who'd just entered the room.

Echo smirked and whispered something to Cora. I didn't know what he'd told her, but she jumped up and said, "I have to go home, guys. Fill me in later." She disappeared into the bedroom.

Echo joined Andris at the bar and poured himself another drink. "So, where were we before the Earl of Worthington rudely interrupted me?"

"Your ring," I said and tossed it back to him.

He caught it and slipped it on his finger. "This was my older sister's ring and—"

"Are you forgetting something?" Torin asked in a hard voice, arms crossed and feet apart. He stood beside me, but I knew he could close the gap between him and Echo in a fraction of a second.

Echo glanced at him then me and smirked. "Sorry about the ring, Raine. I meant to give you a different one." He cocked his eyebrow at Torin, who growled. "I was going to give you this one," Echo added and pulled off another ring. "It belonged to my baby sister's. The vision would have been of singing, happy Druids."

Torin didn't seem happy with that either. Guess he wasn't buying Echo's B.S. He really was pissed. I reached up and took his hand. Echo watched us and grinned.

"Okay, uh, we now know you not only see things as they happen, but you can also see the past and hopefully the future. With time, you'll just need to touch or look at someone or something to have a vision. Chances are you can control the elements, too. Now I understand why the Norns want you, why these people are after you. You are the real deal. A true shaman."

He had my attention. Heck, he had everyone's attention. Torin's grip on my hand tightened. "Does that mean I don't have to sketch circles like a Seidr witch?"

"Technically, you could never be considered a witch or merely a Seeress. Your kind doesn't draw protective circles, listen to special songs, chant, or drum to enter the trance state like other Seeresses," he said. "You walk in the land of the living and the dead. You can move in and out of realms at a whim, touch anything and connect with its energy and know where it's been and where it's going. That kind of power only comes to those who've tasted death. You know, died, crossed over, and came back. Anything like that ever happen to you, sweetheart?"

"I was born premature, so I might have," I said. "The Norns made sure I survived." Echo cocked his eyebrows in question. "Long story. Is there a way I can see clearly? My visions are really blurry. We were hoping I could catch the people after me in the act."

Echo glanced at Torin. "Do you want to hear the rest, or are you going to go ape again?"

"Just say it," Torin snapped, his hand tightening around mine.

"There's magical energy imbedded in that seal," Echo continued, and Torin stiffened. "Magical energy responds faster than ordinary energy. The magic belongs to either your mother or her killer. The good part is the energy is responding to Raine and leading her to these people. Next time you connect with it—"

"There won't be a next time," Torin said firmly. "We'll find a way to stop the bastards without Raine watching them hurt another Seeress."

"No." I eased my hand from Torin's. We always knocked heads when he went all protective of me and acted like I was someone that needed to be rescued. "I want to hear this. The last

Seeress looked straight at me and told me to help the others. What should I do differently next time?"

Echo drained his drink. "Focus on what you want without panicking or second guessing yourself. You must be comfortable with yourself, Raine. Completely accepting of what you are. You are more than a Seeress. You are a living, breathing, earth-bound Norn."

My stomach dropped. Torin growled again. Every time someone mentioned Norns, he went ballistic. The implication was too painful to bear. Accepting that I was a Norn meant I belonged with them, not him. The way he felt after losing his mother would be nothing compared to what he'd feel if he lost me. It would destroy him.

"How do we catch these people before they hurt another Seeress?" I asked.

"I think you should be more concerned with how to protect yourself when they get here," Echo said. "Now that the word is out about you, more wackos are going to come out of the woodworks to claim you."

"*We* will protect her," Torin said.

"Not on your own, St. James. You need help. People to claim her. Magical people. All kind of crazies will claim she's theirs. My Druids brothers and sisters can offer her the best protection against any coven."

"Nice try, Echo," Torin said. "Thanks for the help, but we'll take it from here."

***

"Well?" I said when we went back to Torin's.

"I don't want to think or talk," he said, rubbing my arms. "I want to hold you and block out the world."

Andris cleared his throat. "Do you need help?"

Torin glanced at him and smiled. "I'll catch up with you later. Oh, get the info on the auction house from Echo and do what you do best. I need to know who, when, and where A.S.A.P."

Andris saluted him and left.

Wow, that was weird. "Why are you guys being super polite to each other?"

"It's been a long day." He tucked wisps of hair away from my forehead, planted a kiss on my temple, and sat on the bed. Slowly, he ran his knuckles down my arm. The hairs on my skin stood as though I was cold, yet heat surged underneath. I shivered. Usually, he'd smile at my reaction. Today, he threaded our fingers, his eyes not leaving mine. His intensity could be unnerving sometimes.

"Are you worried about me?" I asked.

He chuckled. "No, Freckles. I got your back. Whoever these bastards are, they won't know what hit them if they come near you."

"You're not thinking of going after them, are you?"

He let go of my hands, wrapped his arms around my waist, and pressed his face against my stomach. My fingers sunk into his hair and played with it. His hair was so silky. My breath stalled when his hands slipped under my tank top to stroke my skin.

He ran a finger along the waistband of my jeggings, and my body responded. It was always the same with him. He took my breath away with a touch. Sometimes, all it took was a look. He pulled me down to his lap and nuzzled my neck.

I started to feel dizzy, and I realized why. I was still holding my breath. I fed my starving lungs with gulps of air. This time, he chuckled.

"No, I'm not going after them," he whispered in a husky voice, his breath warm on my nape. "I want to know where the pendant came from." He kissed along my jaw. "Your visions say I must." He rubbed his cheek against mine. "In the meantime, focus on your abilities," he kissed my temple, "and school," planted another on my nose, "and your father," our lips almost touched, "and us."

He rubbed his lips across mine in a gentle exploration, one hand palming my face, the other stroking my arm. The kiss was sweet. I needed more. I threw my arms around his neck and gave as much as I took.

"When do you need to be home?" he whispered.

"Six-ish." The clock by his bed had said five-thirty something. "I texted Femi earlier." I didn't want us to stop. Today had been so stressful

Torin rolled us across the bed and reached for my cell. Kill joy.

I read Femi's text while he did his best to distract me. "Six-thirty."

Making out with Torin was like drifting in a sea of sensations, away from reality and the mundane. His hands and mouth were gifted, and being with him was beautiful, intense, and mind-blowing. Times like this, I hated that we'd agreed to wait before I could give myself to him. Each time, it got just a little harder to stop. It was so frustrating.

Sighing, he wrapped his legs around mine like a pretzel and held me so there was no space between us, as though he was scared someone would rip me from his arms.

We stayed like that for a while, until I couldn't stand it anymore. I kissed his chest. "You want to tell me what's bothering you?"

"Nothing is bothering me." He spoke against my forehead.

I didn't believe him. We had faced some jacked up situations together, but I'd never seen him like this. I was the one who always got twisted on the inside. He was often my rock. My anchor. Something had shaken him to the core, and I wanted to know what it was.

"Torin?"

"Hmm," he mumbled.

"Talk to me."

Silence.

I waited. The silence stretched. "I'm here for you if you need to talk."

His arms tightened around me. "I know."

"Do you want to join us for dinner," I suggested.

He sighed and leaned back against the pillow with me on his chest. "I can't. I need to check on a few things. Andris might have something for me."

"Do you think the person who put the pendant up for auction stole it or is a relative of yours?" I lifted my head and braced myself on his chest. "Do you have any relatives left? Second cousin or third? A Comte d'Arques?"

He smiled and ran a finger down my nose. "I have a few here and there. One of them must have stolen the seal from Mom's tomb." He swatted my butt. "Come on. Time for you to head home. I'll see you in a couple of hours. What do you have planned for the evening?"

"Dinner, a movie with Femi, and homework. Not necessarily in that order." Reluctantly, I rolled off him and stood.

He watched me lazily as I adjusted my top and fluffed my hair. "What are you going to watch?"

"Sam and Dean Winchester." He groaned, but I just laughed. We had a system that worked. I watched his motorcycle races, and he watched my favorite TV series. "Can we have dinner with Cora and Echo on Saturday?"

"No."

"Oh." I pouted. "You didn't even think about it."

"Let's see." His expression grew pensive. "I have something planned in the morning, afternoon, and evening. The answer is still no."

"Why?"

"Echo and I don't mix."

That much was true. "Cora really wants us to try."

He made a face. "Why?"

"Because she's my best friend." His eyes narrowed. "Best *girlfriend* and this is something couples do. It's called a double date. You might not have had it during King Richard's time, but it's a perfectly normal thing to do in this century."

He grabbed a pillow and chucked it at me. "I'm going to get you for that."

"At least think about it. And junior prom, too." He groaned. "You'll enjoy it. I promise."

"I'll think about it."

"And the prom?"

"Will you make it up to me afterwards?" He wiggled his brows.

My face warmed. "Only if you promise to make it up to me after the senior prom."

He laughed. "We're making booty call dates already. Perfectly normal."

I grabbed my cell phone and blew him a kiss. He pretended to catch it.

***

"You know you don't have to do that," Femi said, entering the kitchen with a tray from Dad's room.

"I don't mind." I put the last pan in the rack to dry and reached for a dishcloth to wipe the counter down. "You do everything else around here."

"Half the day, I sit and talk to your father. He loves to hear my version of history as opposed to what Mortals write. Today we were discussing the misinterpretation of my people's history."

I listened to Femi as I rinsed the dishes in the tray and put them in the dishwasher. Once I wiped down the tray and put it in the cupboard under the sink, I turned to face her.

"There's something that keeps bothering me. You are from Ancient Egypt. Hawk is a Blackfoot Native American. Both of you have no ties to the Norse Pantheon. How did you end up in Asgard?"

She chuckled. "If I could tell you the number of times we've been asked that question… We'll need something to drink for this."

"Not me. I'm good." I watched her measure ground coffee into a filter and start the coffeemaker. Torin was big on vetting everyone around me, but I was sure Mom would not have hired Femi if she didn't completely trust her.

Femi waved me over to a chair. "Immortals and Valkyries come from every continent and every corner of the globe. No pantheon is better or more powerful than the other. Norse, Egyptian, Vodun, Greek, Roman, Incan, Mayan, Hindu, Chinese, Slavic, Sumerian, and many more. The problem with gods and goddesses is that they are proud and selfish. They stay involved in our lives and listen to our needs if, and only if, we still revere them and ask them for help. You ignore them and they get angry and retreat to their realm. My gods rest in the Duat, a realm of the dead, the gods, and everything supernatural. It's pretty much similar to this world, except it's magical. My people stopped revering their gods, so the gods retreated. The same thing happened with the other old religions. Just a minute."

She got up to pour the coffee. She must have forgotten I didn't want any and brought back two steaming mugs. She drank hers black, but I liked mine sweetened and creamed. I got a creamer and sat.

"For awhile there, the Greek pantheon was strong because of the heroic deeds of the demigods, but the Norse Pantheon outgrew them because of Valkyries, Grimnirs, and Immortals. The fact that they recruit priests and priestesses regardless of race or continent works in their favor. We connect the gods and the Mortals. Valkyries and Grimnirs with their daily trips to the realm of the gods. We, Immortals, by working here on earth to make sure Mortals don't destroy each other."

I forgot about the movie we were going to watch as she regaled me with tales from around the world. The wars she'd fought in, causes she'd taken on, and the Valkyries she'd been assigned to.

"It is an honor to serve your family. One day, I can boast that I served you when you were just a young, fledgling Immortal."

I winced. "That sounds bad."

She laughed. "No. We were all young once, but we can't escape our destinies. Watching over you is mine." She leaned forward and added, "And that's despite being considered hot-tempered and impossible to get along with. A rebel among Immortals."

"Really? I would never have guessed." She laughed. But I reached a decision. Mom trusted Femi, so I should trust her, too. "Talking of destinies, I had more visions."

Her eyes lit up. "When?"

"Last night and this afternoon. They happen when I touch magical objects."

"Soon, it won't matter whether they are magical or not. You'll connect with the *ka* of things and people."

"*Ka?*"

"The soul. My people believe everything—people, plants, animals, even inanimate objects—has a soul. Did you black out again?"

I grimaced. "Yeah. I forgot that I was having a vision and panicked."

She gripped my hands. "Then we'll work on helping you stay in control and remembering it is just an illusion. We'll start with magical objects. Their *kas* are much more powerful, which is why they are the first ones you've connected with. Next, we'll use inanimate things around the house, then plants and animals, and finally Mortals." She reached under her nurse's tunic and gripped the *ankh* amulet she wore around her neck.

"I also know that the people killing Seeresses are really after me," I added.

She sighed. "I'd suspected it, but I was hoping you wouldn't come to that realization yet. We have much work to do before they get here. And make no mistake, they will. I need to talk to that boyfriend of yours and Andris. Hawk must also be in the loop since you'll be working at the shop." She looked up and groaned. "Look at the time. I need to get your father ready for the night."

It was only eight-thirty. After I wished Dad goodnight, I headed upstairs and booted up my computer. It was time to learn more about Torin's family. I settled in bed and Googled the de Clare family.

Alexander Paul d'Arques, the twentieth Earl of Worthington, was elected to the House of Lords in two thousand. The earldom had passed down from one generation to another. A few times they lost it due to treason or sons being disinherited, some even forfeiting the title to distant relatives. One line caught and held my attention.

Adelaide d'Arques was executed of heresy in twelve-ten. Her accuser was her pious husband and a close friend of the king, William de Clare, Lord of Oakley and Earl of Worthington.

Yikes. This was different from the version Torin had told me.

There were very few photographs of the d'Arques online, except for the present earl and his family. I studied him and his three sons and daughter. None of them had black hair and blue eyes like Torin. Since they didn't look like Torin, who the heck was after me?

8. FRESH RUNES

There were fresh protection runes on my car. Just when I was getting used to the old ones that Mom had scribbled on my car months ago, which had faded. I really, really hated runes on my personal things. Torin knew that. I glanced at my house and groaned.

Seriously?

The man I plan to slowly kill sauntered across the lawn. I forgot about the runes as my heart tripped. He wore a white tee under his leather jacket. He rarely wore white, but it looked great against his black hair and leather jacket. Was it always going to be like this with him? The excitement of his presence? The anticipation and flutter of my heart even when I wanted to scream at him?

"Is this really necessary?" I waved to indicate my car.

"Absolutely." He wrapped an arm around my waist, lowered his head, and planted a kiss on my nose. "Come on. Time for school."

He was in such a chipper mood I was sure he had more unpleasant surprises in store for me. He half-jogged around the hood of my car and gave me a what-are-you-waiting-for look across the hood as he opened the passenger seat.

"What did you do?" I asked.

"What are you talking about?"

"You seem pretty pleased with yourself. So what did you do, other than etch these on my car and house?"

His innocent smile didn't fool me. I put my backpack and oboe in the back of the car and slid behind the wheel. The trees around our homes and the neighbors' all had runes. More runes on trees along the road, buildings, around the school's parking lot, and on the school building.

"When did you have time to do all this?" I asked, touched despite my unease.

"Last night."

"You do know you can't wrap me in a cocoon in the name of keeping me safe."

"We decided it was the right thing to do now."

"We?" I asked, parking in the lot across from school.

"Me, Andris, Femi, and Blaine. Oh, and Hawk. Femi contacted him. When you engage your runes, nearby runes respond and start a dominoes effect. We'll feel the ripple wherever we are and pinpoint your location." He stroked my hair, tucking a lock behind my ear. "For the best part, you start training today. You'll work on speed, engaging your runes while on your feet, and evasive maneuvers. I know the perfect place for practice. After dinner, you can work with Femi on channeling your energy."

This was good. I leaned over and kissed him. "You are amazing."

"I know."

"You should have asked me to help with the runes," I added.

Torin grinned. "You would have slowed us down."

"Hey!" I protested, but he got out of the car before I could act.

He was still laughing when I joined him. "This is why you need to train. Your reflexes are slow. You think and act like a Mortal. That jab should have caught me in the ribs. If you'd engaged your strength runes, you would have cracked a few."

I'd never knowingly hurt him like that. I gave a dramatic sigh. "There goes my belief that being a *Völva* meant I'd be pampered and revered and never have to lift a finger."

"That was then. You have to think and act like a Valkyrie. You have to be fast and strong."

"Oh gee. I thought all Valkyries did was reap souls," I teased. Cora waved to us from the school entrance. "Cora says souls are defenseless and scared like newborn babies."

Torin snickered. "She deals with lost souls. We pluck them from the middle of battlefields, avalanches, hurricanes, earthquakes..." He stopped and scowled. "Why am I telling you what you already know? The Valkyries in Valhalla and Falkvang train with the warriors. During Ragnarok, *everyone* will go to war. Everyone. Even you."

"What?" I screeched.

"Yo, St. James," Heath Kincaid, running back, called from behind us. As usual, he was with his three sidekicks—Sloane Menken, Pete Cavanaugh, and Drew Cavanaugh, the annoying guy who'd dated Maliina during the weeks she'd impersonated Cora.

"We are having a birthday party for my boy here," Heath slanted his head to indicate Sloane, "on Friday at L.A. Connection. He's getting a full ride to U of O, thanks to our stellar performance at state. All the guys are coming, so we hope you," Heath pressed a fist in his palm and bowed toward Torin, "and Raine will make it."

"When does it start?" Torin asked.

"Eight o'clock. The whole team is invited." Heath high-fived Sloane.

I developed selective hearing when they mentioned L. A. Connection and barely heard the rest of their discussion. I'd avoided that club since my seventeenth birthday party when a swim team member died.

"Raine?" Cora yelled. She was getting impatient.

I touched Torin's arm, indicated Cora, and mouthed, "I'll see you in class."

He took my arm and led me away from the others. "I'm following a lead, so I'm not coming in, but I'll drive you to the shop at three."

"You don't have to. I'll be fine."

"I won't. Wait for me after school."

"Torin, I can take care of my—"

He kissed me. When we moved apart, I had completely forgotten why I was arguing with him. Warmth flooded my cheeks when I realized we had an audience. Flustered, I hurried toward the entrance.

"Damn, you two sure know how to stop traffic," Cora said. "So what's with the runes?"

"Protection. You know how Torin gets."

"Yeah, the guy is crazy about you."

He also had an annoying habit of kissing me when we were in the middle of an argument just to shut me up. So not cool. I followed Cora into the building.

Cora glanced at me and sighed. "Sometimes I wish Echo was a student here."

I couldn't see Echo as a fake student. "Have you asked him?"

"No, but he hates it. He doesn't understand how Torin and Andris can stand it." She took my arm. "He told me you are the real deal."

"Define the real deal," I hedged.

"An all-powerful Seeress. Can you read me?"

I gripped her hand and closed my eyes. "Hmm, you'll have a big, glamorous wedding with Valkyries and Grimnirs in attendance, live on an island, and have two adorable kids."

She stopped walking. "Really? Did you really see—?"

I laughed.

"Oh, I hate you." She bumped me with her shoulder.

"Would you really want to know your future?"

She opened her locker, paused, and pursed her lips. "No. Echo has taught me to appreciate surprises, embrace the unknown." She cradled her folder. "Would you?"

"No." Even the thought of being privy to other people's futures bothered me. I elbowed my locker door and followed her. Kicker and Sondra waved frantically from their lockers.

"See you guys at lunch," Kicker said. "We want to ask you something."

"About the junior prom," Sondra added.

Cora groaned. "Looks like I'll be on makeup duty. We're going, right?"

I shrugged.

"We *are* going if I have to drag you there." She switched topics. "Can I stop by tonight with my first vlog entry? I want to know what you think."

"Sure. I should be home by six-thirty." I was sure I could squeeze her in between dinner and Seeress training. She took off toward her class while I headed upstairs.

"Raine, wait up," Ingrid called from behind me.

I stood aside to let the other students walk past, Torin's words flashing in my head. Ingrid had not been vetted. I shook my head. I shouldn't let his paranoia get to me.

"I didn't see you at the mansion yesterday," she said.

"Busy with homework."

"Torin and Andris were hunched over the computer for hours. Then they disappeared."

She was fishing for info. "I came over while you were at practice, right after Torin and Andris finished interviewing your new housekeeper."

"I haven't met her, but if Andris chose her, she's probably very beautiful."

The jealousy in her voice surprised me. "You have nothing to worry about."

She laughed uneasily. "I'm not worried. I mean, I'm not interested in him that way. He'll always be Maliina's. Anyway, see you later." She and Andris were quite the pair.

Twice in between classes, I heard the haunting Seidr song, and each time I ignored it. Now that I knew someone out there was after me, I wasn't taking chances.

I texted Femi at lunchtime to check on Dad. Her reply had me racing toward my car. I fished for the key and came up empty. Weird, I had put the key in the back pocket of my jeans. I searched the front. Nothing.

No, he didn't. That conniving...

I couldn't believe he'd taken it. I was so going to annihilate him.

I found the nearest bathroom, pulled out my artavus, and etched runes on the mirror. Just as the portal started to open, the door opened and two giggling girls entered the room. A Goth and a brunette who looked sickly. They both stopped and looked around as though they felt my presence. What a thought. Humans couldn't see us when we engaged our runes.

Carefully, I pressed against the wall to let them pass. Torin was right. I had to be fast. Etching runes on the mirror should have taken me a fraction of a second.

"Do you feel the magic, Gina?" the pale brunette said with a heavy accent.

I froze.

"Yeah." Gina the Goth sounded surprised. "The air is buzzing with it. If I can feel it, it must be strong."

The brunette one gave Gina an unworldly smile. "It is. She's powerful. She must have done a spell in here before she left. That makes two of them. Now that I recognize their energies, I can find them." She disappeared into one of the stalls.

Gina walked to the mirror and studied her reflection. She was striking. She had black hair with red locks near her forehead, dark lipstick, and dark green eyes. She wore black nail polish, and she had multiple piercing on her ears and nose.

"Hey, Rita," she called out. "Can you stop singing that awful song now?"

"I can't. Remember what Mom said? I can't stop until someone contacts us. We must know who we are dealing with."

Gina sighed. "What if it makes everyone fall asleep?"

Rita left the stall, looking paler than before. "Remember the spell Mom added to it? Only powerful witches can hear it."

She stopped in front of the sink and rinsed her hands. She had the same facial structure as Gina, but her hair was a long single braid and she looked frail. Like she'd been sick.

They had to be new at school or I would have noticed them before. They stood out. Throw in the foreign accent and they'd be hard to miss.

I waited until they left the bathroom before I went through the portal.

"Is everything okay?" Femi asked. "I heard voices."

"Just listening to gossips. Thanks." I took the tray with my lunch from her hand. "Is he still burning up?"

"Yes. I etched runes on him and he has an IV."

I entered the den.

"Svana," Dad whispered, and tears rushed to my eyes. I never thought I sounded like Mom until the first time Dad had a fever and became delirious. He'd kept calling me Svana, and my voice had calmed him down. I put the tray down—my appetite gone—pulled up a chair, and sat by his bed.

"I'm here now." I stroked his brow. "It's okay. Everything will be okay." When he calmed down, I picked up the book we'd been reading and started where we'd left off.

***

I spent the afternoon searching for the two girls I'd seen in the bathroom. They weren't in my classes or the hallways.

"We're going to watch a short documentary," Mr. Finney said, lowering the screen. "Pay attention to details, folks, because you're going to give me your input."

He usually started class with a challenging question and a heated debate. When he switched off the lights, I debated whether I should engage my runes, become invisible, and search each class for the two witches. The problem was I'd have to open a portal through the door or a wall. The runes for those portals were super tricky.

Resigned to waiting until after school, I watched the documentary on the Vietnam War and even had a thing or two to say about America's attitude after the war. But I couldn't wait for school to be over.

"Missed you at lunch," Cora said as we headed outside at three.

"Dad had a fever and I had to go home. He gets agitated."

She frowned. "Is he okay?"

"I calmed him."

"Good. Let's talk junior prom."

"Let's not. Torin wants us to go to the senior one and he hasn't decided about the junior. Until he says yes, don't include me in your plans."

"Oh, don't say that. You have to convince him. We could go on a shopping spree together. We could use the portal and shop anywhere around the world. Maybe take the guys along."

Like she needed an excuse to shop. She loved fashion. Loved to shop. Me, not so much. We left the building. Students were everywhere. A few were throwing a Frisbee on the lawn to our left. Torin leaned against my car while talking to Andris. He looked like a fallen angel. I was still pissed at him.

"Please. I barely convinced Echo. If Torin is not there, he will be bored out of his mind."

I sighed. "What are they supposed to do? Pound on each other."

Cora flipped her hair to one side and hoisted her backpack on her shoulder. "That's how they bond. It's a Grimnir-Valkyrie thing. They're not happy unless they are fighting or solving problems. They came together to protect me and now you."

"They came to blows."

Cora stuck out her lower lip in a pout.

"Fine, jeez. I'll work on Torin."

She hugged me. "You're the best. Are we still on for Saturday?"

"He's doing something during the day, but he should be free by evening." We reached her car first. She'd parked at the curb.

"Echo is busy, too." She unlocked the car and threw her backpack inside. "He said he might be gone the rest of the week, so convince your man to stay at school for lunch. I sat with Kicker and the girls, and all they talked about were books." Cora rolled her eyes. "Which reminds me, I promised to help Dad with his blog. He hates blogging. Can you believe it? The problem is I don't read his books. What do I tell his fans?"

I laughed. Her father wrote amazing books. I owned all of them. I even got to review advanced copies.

"It's not funny. Why does he write science fiction? It's, like, the worst genre ever. Can you help me? You've read all his books."

My life was a hot mess right now. "I can't. Talk to Andris. He's read all your father's books, too."

Cora thumped her forehead. "How could I forget him? Love you. See you tonight."

I waved and started across the street. Rita and Gina hurried passed me, talking in whispers. I made eye contact with Rita, but she smiled shyly and looked away. I noticed something I'd missed earlier. They both wore pendants. Part of me wanted to follow them, but I couldn't do it with Torin and Andris watching me. Talking to them would have to take place away from here. Away from the Valkyries.

"Hey, Andris? What's cookin'?" I said when I joined them.

He made a face. "Let's see. I spent half of last night runing the whole damn town for you, then gallivanted all over the world looking for your faceless, nameless nemesis. I need a caramel frappé."

Sheesh, it was a rhetoric question. "Will a thank you and a hug do for now?"

"Um…" he glanced at Torin.

What? I couldn't hug other guys without the Earl of Worthington's permission? I hugged Andris, taking him by surprise. He hesitated for a beat, and then he patted my back awkwardly.

"I'll buy you a frappé after work." I turned and studied my boyfriend. He didn't look too thrilled. He hated being ignored, and I planned to ignore him. I extended my hand. "My keys."

"Don't I get a hug, too?"

He smirked, but I saw through it to the Valkyrie he once was before we met. The guy who'd hated himself, his life, and what he'd become. He'd come close to losing his soul. Of course, I couldn't deny him a simple hug.

I walked into his arms, wrapped my arms around his mid-section, and squeezed. A shudder went through him, reminding me once again that, despite his cockiness and annoying habits, I meant the world to him. Everything that happened to me affected him in ways a regular person wouldn't understand.

Still, he wasn't getting off easily. I wiggled out of his arms and pinned him with a glare. "What you did was not cool."

His brow shot up. "Now you lecture me."

"Next time I'll start with the tongue lashing. You don't take my things without my permission. My father had a fever and needed to be calmed down. What if I couldn't remember the runes to open a portal?"

He groaned and rubbed my arms. "I'm a jerk."

"First class." I extended my hand. "My keys."

He handed them over, held the car door for me without saying a word, and hurried to the passenger seat. He didn't say anything and neither did I, although I saw the runes on trees along the road. This was the route I often used to get to the store.

Torin kept glancing at me as though to say, "I did these trees too; aren't I awesome?" What if there was an accident and I had to take another route? What if there was construction? He couldn't foresee everything. I had to start training A.S.A.P.

There were a few more cars in the alley behind our store than usual. I parked and grimaced at the runed building, trees, and wooden fence separating our parking lot from the adjacent art center. When he did something, he went all out.

"Try to see this from my point of view, Freckles," he said.

I studied his handsome face. I was everything to him. I understood that. He meant the world to me, too, but my father was equally important. No one was allowed to mess with my time with him. "I do, but you went too far."

"I have my reasons. First, I gave your mother my word that nothing would happen to you while she was gone."

Whatever sympathy I'd felt for him disappeared. "What?"

"Your mother told me to keep an eye on you and vowed to scalp me if anything happened to you while she was gone. I may not know what it feels like to be scalped, but Hawk turned pale when she said it so I believed her."

Sounded like something Mom would say, but that didn't mean I liked it.

"Second, think of the mayhem I'd cause to get my revenge if you were hurt. Mortals who'd get caught in the crossfire. This was my way of making sure that didn't happen." He reached out and twirled a lock of my hair around his finger. "How about this? I promise never to pull a fast one on you if you promise to work with me. The sooner you can take care of yourself when I'm not around, the better I'll feel."

Part of me wanted to hang on to the anger, but another part knew he had a reason to be worried. There are people out there after me, and there was so much I needed to learn to defend myself.

"Maybe I should just use portals. You know, home to school, school to the shop, and shop to home."

Torin's eyes narrowed. "No. I don't want you acting like a prisoner or scared of your shadow because of these bastards. We are all going to act normal, like we don't know they are after you. The element of surprise will be ours, not theirs."

Good looks and brilliance, a winning combo in my book. When he jumped out of the car and came to open my door, I hugged him again. He cradled my head.

"I thought you were going to be mad at me the entire evening."

"It crossed my mind."

"But you couldn't resist me for long." The teasing twinkle in his eyes was cute, but I wasn't stroking his ego.

"You can't keep skating on your charm. One day it won't be enough." He gave a look that said that would never happen. I made a face. "Let's go."

Hawk was waiting inside with a folder in his arms like some supervisor. Seriously, the man needed to smile more. "Hey, Hawk. I'm ready to rock-n'-roll."

He didn't even crack a smile. He nodded to Torin as though they were passing acquaintances. "Good afternoon, Raine."

I waved to Jared, who was with a customer. Several more were browsing. Hopefully no one needed my help. Maybe I should wear a "New Employee" tag, so customers wouldn't think I was a complete dud when I couldn't help them.

Hawk set me up at the customer's service desk with the file, which turned out to be a catalogue of all the items we carried. I texted Cora and got to work. I read about frame styles and colors, framing styles, and quotes for custom framing. I memorized terminologies I'd never heard before like aspect ratio, rabbet, and corrugated backing.

My nose was buried in the file when Torin returned with a caramel macchiato and pastries from Café Nikos, Dad's favorite destination for all things baklava.

He placed them on my desk with a wink. "See you at six." Then he disappeared in Hawk's office. No matter how arrogant and aggravating he was, he was one heck of a boyfriend.

After an hour, I got up, walked along the aisles, and checked if I could recognize different frames. When customers glanced my way, I took a detour or pretended to be a browser. One woman, however, wasn't fooled. But she just wanted to know if we had a public bathroom.

When Torin came back at a quarter to six, I had a serious drool moment. He'd changed into running clothes. Tights. Yummy. The pants hugged his thighs and calves. The light jacket was unzipped, and the thin shirt underneath showed his washboard abs and wide chest.

"Quit undressing me with your eyes," he teased.

"Quit showing off," I retorted. Then I remembered where I was and glanced around. Luckily, Jared was busy and Hawk was in the framing room.

"How was it?" he asked as we drove home.

"Great!" I said, faking enthusiasm.

"Liar. Want to quit?" he asked.

I threw him a reprimanding glance. "You don't have to say it with such glee."

"Just kidding. You're not a quitter."

The man knew me too well. "Damn right. I learned a lot though. We have over twenty frame styles, from traditional to vintage-inspired..." I prattled on until I pulled outside our cul-de-sac.

"You have ten minutes," Torin said. "Change into running gear."

***

I checked on Dad first. He was asleep, his fever down. He looked so frail. He used to be a triathlete, and the two of us would run in the summer and do five and ten-K races at local events. Kayville and neighboring towns were big on outdoor events. Tears rushed to my eyes as memories whipped through my head, and I wanted to slap myself.

No more self-pity.

Cora hadn't responded to my text earlier. She wasn't in her bedroom when I peeked in, so I sent her another message, changed into running pants, a tank top, and a jacket, and raced downstairs.

"We should be back in an hour," I said when Femi looked up.

Torin already had the engine running. I didn't ask where we were going. He seemed impatient to leave, so I hopped on the Harley and we took off.

Instead of going into town, he used back roads. We didn't go far before we hit SW Whitfield Hill Road. Tillamook Forest was on the west side of town. It was hilly with nature trails and rivers The sun was still up, but a chill was settling on the valley floor.

The road forked to the Whitfield Vineyard to the north and a dead end to the right. We headed toward the dead end. There was nothing but trees and patches of grass.

I removed my helmet and looked around. "Where exactly are we running?"

"Uphill and through the forest, where we can't be seen."

"Except by the coyotes, black bears, and the wildcats," I mumbled.

He chuckled. "That's the idea."

My jaw dropped. "Seriously?"

"I'm just kidding. But you can outrun them. Or you should be able to." He shrugged off his jacket and threw it on top of the bike. The shirt hugged his chest like it was painted on. Add the running tights and he was a man worthy of sports magazine cover. "Did you hear what I just said?"

"Yes." I gave him a sweet smile. "Something about crashing."

He shook his head. "Once you engage your speed runes, you must think fast or you'll crash into a tree. Remember, the tree won't be the only thing going down if you do."

"Couldn't we just run in a grassy area today?"

"We could, but I want you to hit the ground running. You won't need your jacket."

"Nah, I'll keep it on." I rubbed my arms, though the sun was still up.

Torin led the way. "Okay. If you fall—"

"You'll catch me."

He shot me an amused glance. "No, I won't. You engage your protection and pain runes, roll, jump up, and keep going."

Was he serious? His expression said he was. Okay, I was officially in love with a sadist.

We entered the trees, and he engaged his invisibility runes. "Remember, the faster you want to go, the more speed runes you engage," he said.

I nodded. The zing that accompanied the runes would never get old.

"Catch me if you can." Torin took off. He started slow, going at a jogger's pace, but boy, did he move gracefully. Like a cat. Every muscle in perfect condition.

Yep, I was perfectly happy following him and enjoying the view. The ground wasn't rocky and there was more grass than trees, so no worries about crashing into one yet.

"Pick up speed, slowpoke," he called out. "Engage your vision runes."

My eyesight sharpened. I focused on him, where his feet landed. The trees in my periphery blurred as we picked up speed. We left the grassy terrain behind as more trees replaced them. Still the area wasn't dense or thick with vegetation. Torin whipped around trees as though he knew the terrain, but he stayed on the trails.

We headed up the hill, moving through patches of grass and shrubbery, then more trees. The sun bathed the vegetation with rays of gold and orange. We had forty-five minutes of light left before sundown, but the sun wasn't the reason I was sweating. No wonder Torin had left his jacket behind. Covering distance faster than a Nascar racer was freaking hard. My heart pounded and sweat trickled down my back, yet I'd never felt so euphoric.

When Torin called out and slowed down, I didn't want to stop. I was in the zone. I shot past him, went on for a minute or two, and then looped back. He grinned, closing the gap between us. He wasn't even sweating or breathing hard.

"How was that?" Torin asked.

"Amazing." I pulled off my jacket. "How often do you come out here?"

"Once a week. I'd like to make it every other day. That won't stay," he added, nodding at my jacket, which I was tying around my waist. "I can carry it for you."

"No, I'm good. It's beautiful up here." The trees to our left were even denser, but I got my bearings fast. "Is Snake Creek down there?"

Torin nodded. "Tomorrow, we'll go all the way down to the creek and back up. Ready to head back?"

"Yep. I'll lead this time." I didn't wait for his response. "Eat my dust," I yelled, engaging my endurance and speed runes.

I was good with directions, always had been. Even as a child, Mom would watch me with amazement as I gave directions to people. Torin was gaining on me, and I made the mistake of glancing back at him. I didn't see the tree, but he did and shot forward like a bullet, grabbed me, and pulled me out of harm's way. At a freaking full run.

He put me down. "Later, slowpoke."

I pushed to catch up with him with little result. When I burst out of the trees, he was sitting on the bike chugging water. He reached inside the saddle, pulled out another bottled water, and tossed it to me.

"You were just humoring me. You are fast." I guzzled my water. "I mean, really, really fast."

"I try." He pushed the hair from my sweaty forehead. Then he handed me my jacket. "You dropped this, too."

"I did?" He was always right, which could be so annoying sometimes. "Tomorrow, don't hold back. I want to see how fast I can go."

9. ALTERED FUTURE

I sat in the middle of my bed and watched Femi remove rings from her jewelry box. I was still pumped after our run, despite the fact that I'd showered, eaten, and even spent a few minutes with Dad. His fever was under control, but he was still lethargic.

"These are mementos from tours, so nothing scary. Every concert I attend, I always visit local shops run by witches and buy something. Some people buy concert T-shirts and hats; I collect charm bracelets, amulets, and rings." She placed three bracelets, two pendants, and several rings in front of me. "Remember, these are visions. They are not real even though they might feel like it." She sat back. "When you're ready, pick up one."

I took a deep breath and exhaled slowly. *Please, let the visions be clear this time.* I reached forward, lifted a charm bracelet, and closed my hand around it. Femi gave me an encouraging smile. Then her face faded to black.

The screaming fans filled my ears, and bodies appeared to press against me. Next to me was Femi waving and jumping to the beat of Michael Jackson. The King of Pop was on stage, but my blurry vision wouldn't let me see him properly. I swear, once my vision cleared, I was so touching this bracelet again. I looked at my hand and realized I still clutched the bracelet.

I opened my palm, and the bracelet dropped. The concert scene disappeared, and my eyes met Femi's. I grinned. "I didn't fall over."

"No, you didn't." She grabbed a hand mirror and held it in front of my face.

My hazel eyes were golden.

"Your eyes didn't roll into the back of your head," she added. "They glowed and stayed transfixed on me."

"That's good, right?"

She nodded.

"So you were a Michael Jackson fan?"

"I still am. If you ever visit me at my house, you'll see. I probably attended more of his concerts than any other musician. The Beatles and Elvis come second and third. Was your vision still blurry?"

I nodded. My eyes fell on the picture of me that Eirik had taken and given me on my seventeenth birthday. It wasn't the best or the worst of his work, but it meant the world to me.

"They were like some pictures Eirik used to take whenever he used the wrong lens. Oh, and I could control my return. I just let go of the bracelet."

"You want to try another?"

I nodded and palmed the ring, which took me to a Bon Jovi concert. I lingered. Torin loved Bon Jovi. Another bracelet took me to a performance by The Beatles, then other bands with familiar songs I couldn't name.

"I think that's enough for tonight," Femi said. "We'll do more tomorrow."

Femi collected her things while I studied my reflection. My eyes still had the golden glow. As I watched, the color faded to hazel, the brown dominating the green.

Once Femi left, I texted Cora before opening the portal to her bedroom. She waved from her desk. "Almost done editing," she said.

Echo wasn't around, and her door was closed. I stood beside her and read the links she was adding at the end of her video. "That's nice."

"Isn't it? I had no idea how many organizations out there help people deal with grief. I thought I'd add them in case they can't talk to a friend or relative."

When she was done, we watched the recording. She'd named it Entry A. "What's going to happen when you reach Z?"

She frowned. "I don't know. I haven't thought that far. I'll do one every other week. If the response is great, then I can do weekly." She got up and stretched. "What's the verdict?"

"It's great, Cora. You said it was a hypothetical situation and didn't use real names. You focused on the power of forgiveness. Anyone should relate to that."

Cora leaned on her desk and quickly changed the title to The Power of Forgiveness. "Now it's perfect."

A knock at the door made us both jump back. I engaged my runes before her mother entered with a hamper. "Hey, hun. Was that Raine?"

"W-what?" Cora asked.

"I heard Raine's voice."

Cora glanced at me and made a face. I pointed frantically at her cell phone.

"Yeah, we were talking on the cell phone. I put her on speaker while I worked on my new vlog."

"Oh. I didn't know you were back to vlogging." Her mother's voice said she didn't like the news. She might change her tune once she saw it.

I pointed at the portal and Cora nodded.

"We don't see her anymore, the poor dear," her mother said, entering Cora's closet. "Does she mention Svana and how she's doing?"

Cora got up. "No."

I glared at her. We'd talked about this. She had to stay true to our story.

"I mean yes, she's talked about it, but no, Mrs. Cooper is not doing well," Cora corrected. She made a face at me as though to say "sorry" and followed her mother. "Mom, I'll take care of my laundry."

Her mother patted her arm and kissed her temple. Watching them, I fought the urge to cry. I missed Mom. Missed her voice. Her hugs. Mom loved hugs. She would embarrass me with long hugs when she'd drop me off in middle school. That was why I'd preferred Dad driving me to school. Now I would kill for one of her hugs.

"Don't stay up too late," Cora's mother said. "Remember it's a school night."

"Kay, Mom."

I waited until the door closed behind her and then rounded on Cora. "Seriously?"

"Oh, come on. I panicked and blanked out." She went to the door and peered outside. "She's gone."

"Stick to the answer we agreed on, please."

"Okay. Your mother is at a private institution in Portland. You visit her every weekend, but you don't like talking about her.

One of these days, she'll ask for the name of the hospital and why I don't go with you."

"Tell her only family members are allowed and it's a name you can't pronounce. See you tomorrow." I paused by the portal. "Show her your vlog. She'll love it."

She grinned. "I know. She hated my old vlog."

I waved and disappeared through the portal. I brushed my teeth and crawled under the covers. Something fell from my bed and rolled onto the floor. I turned on the lights and searched for it. It was one of Femi's rings.

Without thinking about my abilities, I palmed it. The room started to fade. I quickly sat and scooted back until my back pressed against the bed.

I'd expected another band and screaming fans. Instead I was inside a shop. Must be where Femi had bought the ring. A woman dressed like Mom stood behind the counter. Mom was into Boho chic—belted maxi skirts and cute embroidered tops, hair down, head accessories, and lots of handmade jewelry. The woman's image was a little clearer.

I strained to see her properly.

The door dinged, and two men and a woman entered the room. "We are looking for a friend and a regular customer of yours," the woman said.

"I have many customers," the witch said.

"Her name is Femi. Short, brown skin, and blue eyes," the female of the trio said.

"Femi only comes here when there's a concert. I haven't seen her since last year when Bon Jovi was in town."

"Do you have her contact or last known address?"

"No, I'm sorry," the witch said. "I don't give out customer information."

"She's hiding something," a male voice said.

My stomach dropped. It was the same British accent. I turned as the man drew closer to the trio by the counter. Same long dark hair. His face was still blurry, but I couldn't miss the blue eyes if I tried. Who was this man that looked so much like Torin? His brother? Maybe he never died.

The others stepped aside to let him pass. "You know where she is, luv, don't you?" He lifted his hand and did something I couldn't see. "Tell me, witch."

"Ylvis is coming to town next week for a performance," the woman said in a flat voice. "She will be here."

"What is Ylvis?" the Brit asked.

"Two Norwegian brothers talk show hosts and comedy duo, my Lord," one of the men said. "Their song went viral last year."

My Lord? Maybe it was not Torin's brother leading this band of killers. Maybe Torin had a long lost relative who looked just like him.

"Thank you, Keegan." The head honcho lowered is hand and the witch crumbled behind the counter. I let go of the ring.

My eyes opened and met familiar sapphire eyes. Torin was seated opposite me on the floor, legs stretched out on either side of me, elbows resting on his knees.

I couldn't think of anything else to say except, "Hey."

"Hey. You okay? You had that Bambi look going."

I smiled. "Yes. It's called being in a trance without blacking out, something I worked on tonight. Are my eyes still golden?"

"Yes. They're kind of… disturbing."

"They're beautiful," I retorted, reaching for the mirror on my bedside drawers and studying my reflection. Color me vain, but I loved them golden. I looked exotic and powerful.

"I love your hazel eyes. They're beautiful. I love how they change color under different lighting or with the color of your dresses."

I lowered the mirror and glared at him. "You don't like my witchy eyes?"

"No." He got up and offered me his hand.

"Tough. I love them." I grabbed his hand and let him pull me up. I took a tissue from a box and picked up Femi's ring. "I need to talk to Femi about my vision." I started to leave my room but remembered I needed my laptop. I turned and bumped into Torin. He always took too much space.

"Slow down." He gripped my arms. "What is this about?"

I squirmed out of his hands and went for my computer. "This evening, I touched Femi's magical jewelry and saw visions of concert after concert she's attended. The visions were blurry, the concerts loud, and the fans crazy." I left the room, and he followed. "Then just now, I found a ring she left behind."

Sounds came from downstairs, so I knew Femi was still up. "I picked it up and got a new vision. Do you know the two brothers who sing *What Does the Fox Say?*"

He groaned. "I hate that song."

"Seriously? It's fun and catchy." Femi was watching TV in the living room and looked up when we stepped off the stairs. I gave her the ring. "It must have dropped from your box." I explained what I'd seen. "He did something to her."

"That's Rosalinda. She owns a shop in Philly." Femi shook her head. "But *Ylvis'* tour of America doesn't start until next week. They don't come to Philly for two more weeks."

"So I just saw something that hasn't happened?"

She nodded, her excitement matching mine. She reached for her phone and tapped in numbers. I sat, opened my laptop, and booted it.

"What are you looking for?" Torin asked from behind me.

I glanced over my shoulder. "Confirming that the duo is coming to Philly in two weeks and not next week. Concert dates change." He sat beside me, but there was an edginess about him tonight. He was restless. "Have you found out anything about your seal?"

"No." He slouched lower, propped his arm along the top of the chair, closed his eyes, and played with my hair. "Someone gave them to the auction house with a bunch of family heirlooms we thought were lost years ago. Even the present Earl of Worthington didn't know about them. They weren't listed in the family heirlooms, so they must have been stolen centuries ago."

Echo once said that Torin's family had lost their fortune in a humiliating way. The online articles didn't mention it. "Have they always been wealthy?"

Torin grimaced. "No. They've been hit by hard times like everyone else, but I always help."

Typical Torin. Noble and protective. "How? I mean, you can't write them a check or drop off a gold bars?"

He chuckled softly and tugged a lock of my hair. "Cute. Sometimes a mysterious, long lost uncle dies and leaves his fortune to the family."

"And *you* are the mysterious uncle," I said.

"You'd be amazed what you can do with the names of dead people without family ties. They get a 'Descendant of Willian de Clare, Earl of Worthington' added on their grave to the amazement of their friends while a few members of my family get a fortune. Other times, they just get money from an anonymous benefactor."

"And they just accept it, questions unasked? I'd want to know."

He shrugged. "A few have tried and gotten nowhere. Andris is very good with computers and creating dummy companies behind dummy companies. We haven't found the person who stole these items, but Andris is tracking down the buyers and getting them back. The things they sold meant a lot to my, uh, parents."

"Do any of your relatives look like you?"

He cocked an eyebrow. "I told you, no one looks like me."

That was arrogance speaking. "So no black-haired and blue-eyed cousins or uncles?"

He sat up. "What is this about? Are you trying to replace me?"

As if that would ever happen. "Maybe. I'm partial to black hair and blue sapphire eyes, and if something happened to you…"

He laughed. "I'm not going anywhere, and if someone somehow chops off my head, I'll be the headless Valkyrie hanging around you and haunting the both of you. I'm going to bed, luv." He planted a quick kiss on my lips and got up. I watched him until he disappeared through the portal. He was in a strange mood.

Femi finished with her call and came back to the living room with a broad grin on her face. I had the schedule of *Ylvis'* tour. "How is she?"

"She's fine, but I've warned her about the visitors. She has a sister in New Orleans and will stay with her for a few weeks."

One life saved. "That's great."

"Yes, you did good, doll. Your vision saved someone tonight. You just altered a future."

Yay for me, but it sounded too Nornish. "How am I ever going to know whether what I'm seeing is the future, the past, or the present?"

"I wish I could answer that. I think it's one of those things that comes with experience or you are taught by someone better at this sort of thing."

By the Norns, no doubt. "So *Ylvis* is really coming to Philly in two weeks. Are you going?"

"I was planning to, but I'm needed here now."

"I can watch Dad. It's only for one evening."

"Oh, you're sweet, doll, but no. I can see them some other time." She took the remote from the coffee table and switched off the TV. "Come on, it's getting late."

"I still think you should go," I repeated as we headed upstairs. "I won't watch Dad alone. Torin is next door and a portal away. If you haven't noticed, there's nothing he can't do."

Femi chuckled. "I've noticed. I'll think about it. Goodnight." She disappeared into my parents' bedroom while I headed to mine.

Torin wasn't there. I looked out the window, but his home was in total darkness. Maybe he was at the mansion. I crawled in bed, but I couldn't get rid of the feeling that something wasn't right with Torin. He'd seemed so, I don't know, sad.

***

Torin wasn't around in the morning. I missed my morning coffee and kiss. Voices filtered upstairs from the kitchen. Smiling, I flew downstairs expecting him. But when I cleared the last step, I recognized Andris' voice. He was already dressed for school, though he looked like he was off to a photo shoot for some hipster magazine.

"Morning, sleepy head," Andris said. "I was about to wake you up with a cup of coffee."

I glanced out the window at Torin's. Where was he? "So are you riding shotgun with me to school?"

Andris scoffed at the idea. "Nope. *You* ride shotgun. Come to the mansion when you're ready." He kissed Femi on the cheek. "Thanks for the coffee." He disappeared through the portal.

I got a bowl, poured myself some cereal, and munched on it without tasting it, my mind on the two girls at school. How was I going to get close to them without scaring them? If Ingrid was right, they must have recognized me as a witch.

"Hey," Femi said, and I looked up. "You okay?"

I wasn't. Where was Torin? It wasn't like him to disappear when I needed protecting. Not that I needed him now. He'd runed everything, and Andris was pretty capable. And from Femi's stories, she was a one-woman army. "Yeah. I'll see you at lunch."

Upstairs, I grabbed my stuff and left for the mansion. The others were waiting in the foyer. Ingrid looked amazing as usual in a high-low dress, cute cashmere sweater, tights, and boots. I really liked the bob haircut on her. Very high fashion.

Blaine had that preppy thing going. He came from a loaded family and his clothes screamed it. I looked like Orphan Annie beside them in my jeans and red sweater. Good thing I didn't let clothes define me, and the others never pointed out my penchant for jeans.

"Come on, Seeress. Time to go," Andris said. He moved fast and grabbed my backpack before I realized his intention. "Since I'm on bodyguard duty I get do everything Torin does. Maybe I'll get a hot kiss before math class."

I laughed. I waited until we left the house, engaged my speed runes, and moved just as fast as he'd done. I grabbed my backpack back from him. "Haha, I did it."

"Working on your reflexes?" Ingrid asked, watching me with a weird smile. I could tell she wished she were the one goofing around with Andris.

"Yeah. I'm a bit slow engaging my runes, so Torin is helping me get better. We worked on it yesterday and we'll probably continue today."

"I don't think so," Andris said as he opened the SUV. He disappeared inside.

I yanked the door and hopped in the back passenger seat. "What do you mean?"

"Torin is chasing a shadow that doesn't want to be found," Andris said and started the engine.

"What shadow? Is it about the pendant or the Seeresses?"

"Yeah, what are you talking about?" Ingrid asked, getting in the front passenger seat. She closed the door and turned to face Andris.

"Long story, girls." He left the driveway, following Blaine. "Don't bother to question me because my lips are sealed."

He sucked at keeping secrets. I'd wait until it was just the two of us. "Ignore him."

"I always do." Ingrid said. "Hey, I'm close to finding the witch at school."

"Me too," I said.

"What witch?" Andris asked.

"Long story," I said, repeating his words.

"And our lips are sealed, too," Ingrid said.

"Really, Ingrid?" He glanced at her. "I can understand Raine being difficult, because that's who she is. You know better. We don't keep secrets from each other."

Ingrid lifted her chin. "How come you're not teaching me to engage my speed runes like Torin is helping Raine?"

Andris groaned. "She needs them, sweetheart, and you don't."

"Why?"

"Because you're sweet, and nice, and harmless. There're no bad guys coming after you. Your life is perfect."

"You mean boring," Ingrid retorted. "Nothing fun or exciting ever happens to me."

"You are an Immortal, sweetheart. Make fun happen. Find a hobby."

Poor Ingrid. She really needed to stop wanting Mr. Pigheaded here to take her seriously. She had money and could be whatever she liked. I tuned them out and texted Torin. Chances were he hadn't taken his cell phone. He'd only bought it to shut me up after I'd nagged him.

We pulled up outside the school. The spot on the curb where Torin usually parked his bike was empty. It wasn't official, but everyone considered it his spot. Seeing it only reminded me he was out there, probably doing something dangerous.

Andris and Ingrid were still arguing when we left the SUV. Ingrid took off in a huff and joined her friends. Andris watched her with narrowed eyes.

"She's becoming so mouthy," he griped.

"That's because you ignore her. She likes you. Why won't you give her a chance?" I asked. "It's obvious you like her."

"As cute and adorable as Ingrid is, I don't have the urge to kiss her. She doesn't make me lose sleep, and she's definitely not the person I think about when I—"

"I don't want to know," I said. He could become crass in the blink of an eye.

"You have a dirty mind."

"Yours is twisted."

"Don't insult my mind. You want to have lunch at home or school?" he asked as we entered the school building.

He was being really sweet. Normally he'd tell me where we were having lunch and try to bully me into agreeing. "School, unless I'm needed at home."

"Okay, we'll meet in the cafeteria unless I get a text from you." He took off with a bunch of his hipster friends. I went toward my locker and kept an eye out for the two witch sisters. I did that a lot during the day, even heard their Seidr song a couple of times.

***

Andris and Blaine were waiting by the SUV when I left the building at three. Usually, they couldn't stand each other. Today they were chatting like old buds. No, they were laughing.

"Okay, Seeress, we've decided to pick up where Torin left off," Andris said.

I frowned. "Pick up what?"

"Your lessons," Blaine said. "Where did you two train yesterday?"

When I finished explaining, they were staring at me as though I was an escapee from PMI. "What?"

"There are no trails to speak of up there, and the place is crawling with wild animals," Andris said with a shudder.

"There are plenty of trails and you can outrun wild animals," I said and threw my backpack and oboe in the back of the car. "So is the offer still on, or do I run alone?"

They looked at each other.

"Chickens," I teased them, getting inside the car.

"She has a point," Blaine said. "We can run faster than any animal, and if she trains in such an environment, anything else will be a piece of cake."

"I don't care if she's right or wrong. We are not running through some damn jungle like a pack of wild animals. We'll take the back roads and race cars. You two have lived here long enough. Find us a route that's not busy this time of the day. I'll show you who is chicken."

"See you guys at home," Blaine said and hopped into his seat. He was already driving his sports car with the top down.

"Tell me about this witch at school?" Andris asked as we took off.

"I think there are two of them. Sisters. And they are new because I've never seen them before."

"Why didn't you tell Ingrid this morning?"

Torin's words rang in my ears. "I don't know. I want to see if we find the same girls. There could be more."

Andris shuddered. "Witches."

"I understand Torin's aversion to witches. What's yours?"

"None of you beeswax," he said rudely.

He entered our cul-de-sac, and my eyes went to Torin's place. It was still locked up. "Where is he, Andris?"

"Searching for the person that put his stuff up for auction," he said.

"Why is it so important?"

Andris brought the car to a stop at the curb by Torin's mailbox. "I never question why your man does the things he does. I just go with the flow."

"Should I worry about him yet?"

"Nope. Out of the car. Be at the mansion in ten minutes or I'm coming for you."

"Can you promise me something?"

He gave a long-suffering sigh. "What?"

"Promise to tell me the truth if he's in danger, okay?"

"Okay." He rolled down the window and watched me walk away.

I turned and cocked my eyebrows. "Go. I'm at home now."

"Did I ever mention you have a sexy walk?"

I kissed my fingers and patted my butt.

He laughed and took off. I entered the house. "Femi, I'm home."

"In here," she called out from Dad's room. I peeked in. She was changing the sheets on his bed. She must have seen the concern in my eyes because she said, "He's having a bath."

I made a face. The bath had a contraption to keep him in place. "I'm running with Andris and Blaine. I should be back in an hour or so."

She paused in the process of fluffing a pillow and pursed her lips. For one second I thought she'd object, but Andris outranked her. "Make sure you take your cell phone with you."

"I know." I grabbed an apple in the kitchen before heading upstairs. In less than ten minutes, I was in the mansion.

Blaine was pacing in the foyer. He wore running tights and a shirt like Torin had yesterday, but the impact of all that hotness was wasted on me. "Where's Andris?"

"I don't know." He looked up at the second floor. "Hey, Andris, move it."

"So how are we going to do this?"

"I have no idea what he has in mind. He's calling the shots, as he put it." Blaine made a face. It was obvious he wasn't used to taking orders from someone who looked around his age.

"Have you worked with a lot of Valkyries?"

He nodded. "My parents have helped quite a few. I tend to work with Mortals. You know, wars, law enforcement, and private detective stuff."

"You've worked with the police? You look like any high schooler."

He grinned, topaz eyes twinkling. "I can look older when I want to."

"Do you see your parents often? I heard they're in Rio."

"A couple of times a week." He chuckled. "Rio is a portal away." He glanced up again. "Andris!"

"Hold your horses," Andris said from the top of the stairs. His outfit had to be just right. Unlike Blaine's black and gray outfit, his had neon green stripes that matched his shoes and jacket. Since he wasn't sporty, he was probably breaking them in.

"Nice outfit," I said.

"You'll thank me when it gets dark. Blaine, lead until we are out of town. We leave the compound with our runes engaged."

10. MISSING

Cora dropped her tray next to mine, and I dragged my eyes from Gina and Rita. "What do you mean we can't have a double date tomorrow?"

"Torin is out of town. He's been gone since Wednesday." I picked up the biscuit and took a bite. It was the only appetizing thing on my tray.

"Gone where?"

"I don't know." That little fact was beginning to worry me.

"Did you two fight?" She took a bite of her pizza.

Whatever issues Torin was struggling with, I wish he would just talk to me instead of pulling a disappearing act. We'd tackled our share of issues since we met, but he'd never just disappeared. What if he was in trouble and needed help?

"Raine? Did you two fight?" Cora asked again.

I shook my head, my eyes drifting to Rita and her sister. For the last couple of days, I'd studied them. Rita was pale and timid, yet she seemed to be the more powerful of the two. I got stronger vibes from her. The few times our eyes had met, she always smiled. Gina was the poster child of teen angst: dark clothes and black nail polish, multiple ear and nose piercings. She looked like she could kick some serious ass. And she acted protective of her sister.

"Does it have anything to do with his seal?" Cora said. "Echo said he's obsessed with finding the person who had it auctioned."

I didn't want to discuss Torin, so I forced a casual shrug. "I don't know."

"Could this food get any more unappetizing?" Andris asked, sliding beside Cora. He bumped her with his shoulder. "Hey, gorgeous."

Cora grinned and glanced at his styled silver hair. "Right back at ya."

"What are you two plotting?" Andris asked.

Cora sighed. "I was just asking Raine—"

"If we can get our men to get along on a double date tomorrow," I finished. Cora studied me questioningly. "You do want that, don't you?"

"Yeah, but Torin is MIA."

"Oh, he'll be back," Andris said. "He's playing Lord of the Manor right now."

I frowned. Could Torin really reveal his true identity to his relatives? The way he was big on rules, I doubted it.

Across the room, Rita walked away from her sister. Finally. It seemed like forever waiting to see them apart. They were always together. Gina was having a deep conversation with their new friends and probably didn't know her sister had left.

"I'll be back," I said and got up.

"Where are you going?" Andris asked.

"Restroom." I hurried after Rita, not caring if he believed me. He didn't have to worry about me leaving the school grounds without him. With Torin MIA and someone out there after me, I wasn't taking chances.

Rita was disappearing around the corner. I ducked into a doorway, engaged my runes, and rejoined the students in the hallway. She was a few students ahead.

"Not bad," Blaine said from behind me. His runes blazed, too. "Where are you going in such a hurry and fully cloaked?"

"Andris sent you to follow me?"

"Nope. I was talking to some girl when you zipped past. Nice move using a doorway to engage your runes."

"You guys drummed that in me the last two days." Rita disappeared inside the library. "I need to pick up a book. See ya."

I ducked past students, almost bumping into a couple, and entered the room, but Rita had disappeared. Damn! I searched the aisles, aware that Blaine had followed me inside. I was close to giving up when I spotted her at the end of an aisle. She was chanting.

I entered the aisle behind her, made sure no one could see me, and willed the runes away. She whipped around, her eyes wide. She took a step back.

"Hey." I wiggled my fingers. "It's Rita, right?"

"Yes. How do you know my name?"

"You and Gina are new and you both wear the same pendant, which makes you stand out." I paused before adding in a lower voice, "I know *what* you are."

She swallowed and took another step back. "I don't know what you're talking about."

I raised my hands. "It's okay, Rita. My name is Raine Cooper. I'm like you. I heard your Seidr song. You sing beautifully."

She laughed nervously. "Thank you. We knew there were witches in the school, but Mom couldn't find you by scrying."

That was because we weren't really witches. "We can hide our powers."

She smiled, color seeping in her pale cheeks. "I knew it. I told Gina, but she said I was being ridiculous. She said no witch could hide from Mom's scrying. Mom said there was a powerful magical core here. Did you answer the Call, too?"

"The Call?"

"You know, when witches are summoned to help one of our own."

"Oh, yeah. That Call."

"Gina and I didn't go to the meeting, but our mother did." She checked my chest and frowned. "You don't wear an amulet of your coven?"

She was a talker. "I don't belong to a coven. Do you?"

"No. We are just novices. Mom is a Seidr rep. We come from Ireland. What branch are you representing?"

She also asked way too many questions. Good thing I was good at making up stories. It was the way I'd survived high school as an Immortal in love with a Valkyrie. "My mother is local witch, and I'm still a novice, too."

"You're powerful for a novice."

"Why do you say that?"

"I felt your energy the moment you entered the library. I recognized it from the bathroom a few days ago. How many of you are here? Have you met the others?"

"There're just a few of us, and no, I haven't met the new arrivals except you and Gina. Have you?"

"Mom won't allow us to attend the meetings, but we've seen them around town. Each group wears a special amulet." She pulled out a necklace from under her top and rubbed the white surface as though drawing strength from it. It was pretty with an intricate Celtic triquetra knot and a green agate core.

I could learn a lot about her family and the Call by touching it.

"Your amulet is pretty," I said.

"Thank you." She turned it. "It's for good luck. I've worn it for as far back as I can remember."

I leaned in for a closer look. "Is it made of rock?"

"No. Ivory. It's much smoother than a rock."

"Step away from her," a voice growled from behind me.

Gina had arrived. I turned and smiled. Blaine was behind her. "Hi, Gina. I'm Raine—"

"Step back," she snapped.

I pressed against the shelf and Rita scurried past me to her sister's side. They reminded me too much of Maliina and Ingrid. The sweet sister and the aggressive one. The Irish accent didn't help either.

"She's one of us, Gee," Rita said. "I mean, her mother is a local witch."

Gina moved closer, her eyes narrowed. Blaine gave me a thumbs up, then propped his arm on one of the shelves and dislodged a few books. The sisters glanced over their shoulder and frowned. Blaine was still invisible. Grinning, he moved a few books. What was he doing?

"Did you do that?" Gina asked.

Blaine nodded, and I went with it. "Yes."

"You can move things without incantation?"

"Can't you?" I asked.

Instead of answering, Gina asked, "Why have you been watching us?"

"Oh, you noticed that. I wanted to confirm you were the ones singing the Seidr song," I lied again.

Gina frowned. "The friends you hang out with, are they witches, too?"

"No, but you know what? You can meet them any time. They are cool with all this witch stuff." Big lie.

"Well, nice to meet you, Raine Cooper." Gina stuck out her my hand.

Our hands connected, and she started to chant. Her voice grew faint. Gina, Rita, and the bookshelves disappeared. Oh, crap. Another vision.

I was at a clearing in the middle of a forest with a ring of people. It was dark, except for the light from a fire smoldering in the center. No one moved or said anything. The silence was kind of spooky.

I grinned as something else registered. I could see clearly. The faces. The trees. The fire. For the first time, my vision was clear, and I knew it had something to do with these witches.

I moved until I was close to the ring. There was an old woman in the middle of the ring. She represented everything I'd read about witches. She was old, wore a hooded cloak, and carried a long staff. The top of her staff had a green jade stone like the one on Rita's amulet.

"Thank you for coming, daughters and sons of old religions," the old woman said. She spoke with a heavy Irish accent. "It's not often we come together, but then again, it is not often we all receive the same vision, a Call from one of our own. The Call has been received by our people across the globe, not just Europe. I stand before you, not as your leader, but as the oldest practitioner of the Old Religion of the land. Madam Svietlanova is holding a meeting in Kiev, Shaman Istaqa in New Orleans, Hsu Cheng in Shanghai, Sangoma Ziga in Lesotho, Machi Mariella in Santiago, Karadji Yallan in Brisbane..." She continued to list names and places. "We must answer the Call."

"What if it is a trap?" a man called out.

"That is why we are sending a few of us to see if we support the Call or not. As usual, we'll use people they cannot suspect. People who can blend in." She looked at a woman standing to her right. There was something familiar about her. "Stefania, your daughters speak English. You will go with them to America. People rarely suspect a mother with children, and your girls are powerful. A change of scene might be good for your Rita."

My hand was still clenched. Even though I couldn't see Gina's hand in the vision, I knew I still gripped it. All I had to do was let it go and the vision would disappear. It was the one thing I'd practiced every night in the last two days. Control over whether I saw the past, present, or future was something I still needed to work on.

I let go of Gina's hand and the scene faded. Two faces came into focus. Gina and Rita. Arms were around me. I turned my head and smiled at Blaine, who was no longer cloaked.

"I'm okay," I reassured him.

"But your eyes are still..." he said.

"Glowing," Gina and Rita said at the same time. There was awe in their voice.

"They do that when I get a vision," I said and glanced at my watch. "We're going to be late for class. Nice to meet you two. I hope we get to talk later."

"You are... not just a witch," Rita whispered.

"She's a *Spákona*," Gina said.

I wasn't sure what that meant, but I went with it. "Yes." I grabbed Blaine's arm. "Let's go." But even though I was thrilled I'd finally seen a clear vision, one worry nagged me. Who had called the witches to Kayville?

"Do you want to borrow my sunglasses?" Blaine asked, dangling a pair.

I stared at him blankly. "What?"

"Your eyes. People are staring."

Oh crap. "Thanks." I took his sunglasses and slapped them on. If anyone did see my golden eyes and asked about them later, I could always say I was wearing contacts.

***

Mr. Zakowsky was talking about the upcoming concerts and performances at Kearns Theater and Walkersville University we should attend to get extra credit, while all I could think about was witch and Seeress stuff. A few months ago, I'd been worried about Norns and Valkyries. It was always something.

"Cooper!"

I looked up. Everyone in class was staring at me. "Yes?"

"You'll be first chair next Thursday at the performance."

I nodded. We had only three oboe players in the band, me included. I'd stopped taking private lessons last summer, but I was still ahead of the other two when it came to technique and mastering new pieces.

As we put our instruments away, my thoughts went back to my brief meeting with the Irish witches. Who could have issued the Call? And why?

"Raine, wait up," Heath called across the room. In addition to playing football, he also played sax in the band.

"I heard Torin's not around."

"He went home. Family emergency." That excuse was getting old. Every time Torin disappeared, I always used it. I picked up my Oboe case, and we left the class. "He should be back today."

"I hope he makes it to the club tonight. It's not really Sloane's birthday party. The cheerleaders are throwing us a party for winning state, and it won't be the same without the QB. It's supposed to be a surprise."

I smiled. "How come you know about it?"

He grinned. "My girl is a cheerleader. If he makes it tonight, bring him to the club. We won't be done until the club closes at one."

While he headed toward the front entrance, I went to get my backpack. Andris was charming a girl by my locker. Not just any girl. Sarah Lee Jepson, the co-captain of the volleyball team. She braced herself against his chest, reached up, and whispered something in his ear before walking away. He stared after her.

"Another conquest?"

"They can't get enough of this." He indicated his body. For someone who didn't like sports, he tended to go for sporty girls. I put my folder and books in the backpack and locked my locker. "Why the long face? Missing Torin?"

With every breath. "No. I've got a lot on my mind."

He peered at me. "Liar. I told you, think of me as his substitute. I'm good for hugs, kisses, booty calls, crying, and chucking things at when you're pissed. And not necessarily in that order."

I smiled. He was a hoot and a half.

"That's better." He dropped his arm around my shoulders, turned his head, and whispered, "He'll be back. You're too important to him for him to do something stupid."

"What do you mean?" I wiggled out of his embrace. "You keep dropping hints without giving me real information. Is he meeting his cousin as himself?"

"Maybe."

"You're enjoying this, aren't you?"

He pressed a hand on his chest. "You wound me." Then he smirked. "Let's just say he looks nothing like the present Earl of Worthington or his predecessors, so they'll never suspect anything."

So Torin was meeting his relatives. That seal must really be important. We headed toward the foyer. Ever since I saw the guy in my vision, I'd scoured the Internet for everything on the Earl of Worthington. Alexander Sinclair d'Arques looked nothing like Torin, and neither did the previous earls, whose pictures were online. There were a few blue eyes here and there in the family, but nothing like Torin's sapphire blue. Sandy hair to various shades of brown seemed common among them. No pitch-black wavy and silky hair like Torin's, which sort of made sense. Torin and James never had children, and their father had been illegitimate.

Andris stopped making goo-goo eyes at some girl and said, "You are stressing again."

I rolled my eyes. "Since when did you become Mr. Perceptive?"

"You bite your lower lip and a weird line appears between your eyebrows. If you were Mortal, you'd grow facial lines by age thirty."

I laughed. With Andris, either you take him seriously and get offended or you shrug him off. "What do you do? Watch my every action?"

He shrugged. "You forget I was interested in you once upon a time."

"Seems like a long time ago."

"I remember it like it was yesterday. What did Heath want?" Andris asked as we left the building. "If he's hitting on you, I'll have to rearrange his face."

What an idea. Students were everywhere. Some headed to the school buses while others hopped in their cars with friends or on their bikes. Those who lived closer walked away in groups.

Oregon was a green state. We took recycling and keeping the environment clean seriously. When the weather was good, we had more bikers than drivers on the road. Gina and Rita stood under a tree as though waiting for something or someone.

"Hey, did you hear what I just said?" Andris asked.

"Rearranging Heath's face? I heard. You hate fighting, Andris. Besides, you'd have an unfair advantage. Isn't that why you don't play sports?"

"I don't play sports because I hate sports. Doesn't mean I can't teach him a lesson for poaching. If I hit like a girl, I bet I would only break his jaw and nose, and maybe knock out a few teeth."

I didn't need the visuals. And why was he such a misogynist? I punched his arm.

"What's that for?" he griped.

"You're an idiot." He smirked as though I'd complimented him, and I knew he was only trying to cheer me up. I missed Torin and was really worried. To take my mind off him, I explained about tonight's party.

Andris pressed the remote and unlocked the SUV. "Torin already knows about it, but he wasn't planning on going."

"Why not?"

"Because the love of his life hates the place." He shuddered. "This is why I'm never falling in love again. You become a total idiot, co-dependent, and sappy." He threw our backpacks in the back. "Heath kept texting him. Unfortunately—"

"He left his cell phone at the mansion," I finished. I shouldn't have pushed the impossible man to get a cell phone in the first place. The only machines he liked were those he could pull apart, alter, and put together again. "I'm worried about him, Andris."

Andris' expression grew serious. "I know. He should be back tonight."

Something in his voice said he was worried, too. He'd never admit it though. It was like a guy code or something.

"I'm going to look for him if he's not back tonight," I said.

"Starting where?"

"London at his, uh, whatever the earl is, uncle's or cousin's."

"I'll tag along." He was definitely worried. "To keep an eye on you, of course."

He was sweet and very transparent. "Thanks."

Across the parking lot, Rita and Gina entered a blue car. They didn't drive away. Instead, they watched us. Were they seriously considering tailing us?

"Have you talked to Blaine?" I asked.

"I try not to talk to the guy. In fact, I often pretend he doesn't exist."

Drama queen. "Didn't you send him after me during lunch?"

"No." Andris gunned the engine.

I patted his shoulder. "You're sweet."

"I know." He backed out of the parking spot. Gina pulled out, too. They stayed behind us.

No matter how hard I tried to act indifferent to Torin's disappearance, I couldn't stop my thoughts and feelings. What if he was hurt or was in trouble? Once again, I tried to distract myself. "We have witches at school."

Andris shuddered. "I was hoping Ingrid was wrong. She said someone's been singing witchy songs."

"They're not just at our school. They've come from all over the world to meet right here in Kayville. They supposedly answered a Call."

Andris groaned. "Crap."

"You know what that means?"

"Oh yeah. When a Call is issued, witches come out in droves. It takes something big for that to happen. The first time I saw it was at the beginning of the witch-hunt. There's, like, a secret council of Old Religion elders, and each region is represented. They hold meetings and warn their people if something big is going down. Most went underground after the meeting about the witch-hunts and kept their practices hidden. The defiant ones didn't and were busted, tortured, and burned."

"There's no inquisition right now, but they're here waiting for, I don't know, orders or something. Who could have summoned them and why?"

"In my lifetime, I've heard of only several Calls, and in each case witches' lives and their practices were threatened. It's obvious why they're here." He pulled up in the parking lot behind the Mirage, parked, and turned to face me. His expression was serious. "You. You are about the most unusual witch to ever walk this earth and someone somewhere told them about you. Either they're here to see you and pay their respects, or they know you're in danger and have come to protect you. Either case, we should beat the crap out of the witch who issued the Call."

My eyes followed the blue car as it pulled into the parking lot by the art center. "We don't know any witches."

"No, we don't. Thank goodness." He grimaced.

I guessed it was not the time to tell him about the two keeping tabs on us from the neighboring parking lot. He stepped out of the SUV and looked around. "Are you still being stalked?"

He laughed. "Yeah, I am."

That derisive laugh told me he wasn't. "So if you're not, why the cloak and dagger?"

He peered at me. "The perks of being friends with you. Did you really think witches would come to town without us knowing about it? We sensed them and went on full alert. We just didn't know what we were dealing with. Could have been Grimnirs. Actually, I would rather have Grimnirs than witches."

I gawked at him. "You knew and didn't say anything?"

He shrugged. "You didn't need to know."

I made a face. "Yeah. Whatever. See you at six."

"I'll leave when you are safe behind the desk and under Hawk's watchful eyes." He followed me inside. While he chatted with Hawk, I followed Jared who'd come out of the storage room pushing a box on a flatbed pushcart.

"What's that?" I asked.

"New merchandize. I'll show you." He lifted the box from the cart, cut off the tape, and reached inside for a bubble-wrapped item.

"Oh, that's so pretty," I said, when he removed a gilded vintage vanity mirror.

"The free-standing ones go to the right, but ones like this one can be unsnapped so it sits on its handle." He showed me the hinge at the base of the mirror, which transformed it from a hand-held to a standing mirror. "You want to put them behind the glass display case while I get the second box?"

"Sure." Each mirror was bubble-wrapped, each frame exquisitely crafted. I knelt on the floor and checked the descriptions. Gothic cryptograph inlays. Classic Baroque. Vintage handle princess. I wanted one.

"What are you doing?" Andris asked.

"Putting mirrors away. Look at this. Isn't it beautiful?" I showed him the back. "The handle bends at an angle, so it stands. I want to buy all of them."

"Yeah. Whatever. You're supposed to be learning how the business is run, not doing menial work. What's next? Cleaning the floor?"

I hoped not. "Go away, Andris, before I tell Mr. Hawk." Andris made a face as if to say "go ahead." "Please, go. And you don't have to pick me up. I can use the portal in the office and go directly home."

"And deprive me the pleasure of your charming company? I don't think so. I'll be back at six, and you'd better not be cleaning the floor or Hawk and I will have a long chat."

I sighed. I didn't know where he got the idea that I shouldn't do normal things like an average person. "You know what, wise guy? I can do whatever I want to do and you have no say whatsoever." He opened his mouth. "Not another word. Bye." I went back to work.

The back door dinged when he left. Minutes later, it dinged again. Then I felt a presence behind me. "Forgot something, Andris, or are you here to complain about my work?"

"You work here?" a familiar voice said.

Ah, the Irish sisters. "Yes."

"But you are a powerful…" Rita glanced around and whispered, "Seeress."

"You should be practicing your powers, not wasting time doing something so…" Gina waved her hand to indicate the store.

"Normal," I said. "I like normal. What are you doing here?"

"I want to apologize for testing you with the talisman," Gina said. "Our mother gave it to me to test any witches we met."

From my vision, some of the witches weren't sure whether the Call was a trap or not. I studied the circular disk between her thumb and fingers. It had the tree of life on the front and the back had Celtic knots.

"What does it do?" I asked.

"It burns when anyone evil touches it."

"That's okay. It doesn't hurt to be cautious." I put the last mirror away and gathered up the bubble wrap. Rita bent down to help.

"We texted Mom about you and she'd really like to meet you," Gina said.

"Sure." I caught Hawk watching us. "I have to get back to work before my boss fires me. Coming, boss," I added louder and picked up the box with the bubble wrap.

"Hey," Rita said and touched my arm. "Do you want to go out for a cup of coffee?"

"Rita," Gina protested.

Rita shrugged, her cheeks reddening. "It's okay. She can always say no."

I could, but I wanted to know why my vision had been so clear when I touched their talisman. "Sure. I know just the place." I pulled out my cell phone, asked her for her number, and sent her a text. "Now you have my number."

11. PARTY TIME OR NOT

An hour later, the back door dinged and Cora entered the shop. We'd eaten lunch together and she never mentioned stopping by.

"What are you doing here?" I asked, stepping out from behind the counter.

"Coming to pick you up." She looked around. "So what do you do around here?"

"Everything. I help with the displays, customers, inventory... Whatever Jared wants."

"When do you get done?"

"In half an hour. Come on. I want to show you something." I led the way to the display cases where I'd put the hand-held mirrors. A kid at a candy shop wouldn't have reacted like she did.

She chose two. "Mom's birthday is coming up and she'd love this."

"You and Echo got plans for tonight?"

"Nope. He's reaping." She sighed. "I don't know what to do. No boyfriend. No plans. Worse, I don't volunteer at the nursing home on Fridays. You and yours have plans?"

I imagined staying at home and stressing over Torin. The idea didn't appeal to me. I might hate L.A. Connection, but it was the most popular club in town.

"Torin is out of town, so we have two choices. We can hang out at my place, watch one of our favorite series, and pig out on junk food, or dress up and go partying. The cheerleaders are throwing the football team a party tonight. Torin and I were invited, but he's not here. We are."

Cora squealed and hugged me. "I knew you'd come up with something. This could be fun. I can't remember the last time we did something so normal."

It was just like old times. Pre-Torin. I'd missed the squealing Cora. Just a little. Actually, I was beginning to get pissed, too. There was a reason for portals. What was stopping him from using one?

"Now all we have to do is convince Andris to come with us."

She wrinkled her nose. "Andris? Why?"

"Torin left him in charge." When Cora cocked her eyebrows, I glanced around to make sure Jared wasn't within hearing distance. "Remember, the Seeress attacks?"

"Oh crappola. I'd completely forgotten about that." A thoughtful expression settled on her face. "Maybe we shouldn't go out tonight. We could do the marathon and pig out. Oh, and read the responses I've gotten on my vlog. I've gotten hundreds of hits. Two people gave video responses. I'd be so stroked if it went viral."

"The party doesn't start until eight. We have time."

She studied me. "You really want to go?"

"Keep asking and I'll develop cold feet. The last few days I've done nothing but work, run, and worry. I want to unload." Plus, I hated to let fear paralyze me even though deep inside I shook with it whenever I thought about the people willing to hurt others to find me. Like Torin had said, we must act like we didn't know or care. Besides, I'd be conquering another thing tonight—the nasty memories I associated with L. A. Connection.

Six o'clock arrived and Andris was a no show. Instead, the door dinged and a customer walked in from the back. Very few customers used the back door. A woman wearing a hooded poncho walked past, and warning bells went off in my head.

Witch!

No, I was being paranoid now. It was still cold, and people around here liked hoodies. Besides, it rained a lot in Kayville so rain ponchos were very common. A few minutes later, I was helping a man choose a frame for a custom job when she walked past the counter on her way out and I saw her face.

My stomach dropped. I recognized her right away. What name had the old woman in my vision called her? Stefania. And this wasn't the first time I'd seen her in the shop. She'd asked to use our bathroom before.

"Excuse me?" I called out, but she kept going. "Could you hold on a minute?" I asked the man I was helping. I didn't wait for his response, just took off after the woman. The back door didn't ding, and she wasn't in the back parking lot. Could witches disappear in thin air?

"What's going on? Did someone steal something?" Cora asked. Behind her stood Jared, and the customer I'd left inside. Of course, I couldn't tell them I just saw a woman from my vision and she'd disappeared.

"I thought I saw her pocket something, but I could be wrong." Back inside, I offered a brochure to the man I'd been serving. "Take this home and see which one is perfect for the background on your photograph. Or bring in the photograph tomorrow and you and I can find the perfect frame for you."

"Thank you, dear." He patted my hand, and that was when I noticed the ornate ring on his pinkie. Another witch, or was I becoming paranoid?

"Is it always this exciting?" Cora asked.

"No." I glanced at my watch again. It was a quarter past six. "Let's go. I'll text Andris on our way." I grabbed my phone and poked my head into the office. "I'm leaving now, Hawk."

"Is Andris or Torin here?" he asked.

"No. I'm leaving with Cora." A spasm crossed his face. Could that be concern for me? "I'll be fine."

He stood and walked to the door. He glanced at Jared and lowered his voice. "Is she the one who helps souls?"

"Yes."

He didn't seem relieved. "Maybe you two should use the portal in my office, and she could pick up her car later."

"We'll go directly home from here and use the roads with the runes. If anything seems off, I'll call. I can create a portal on the car door." I'd never done it and my runes for non-reflective surfaces were iffy, but I didn't want everyone in my life worrying about me.

He nodded. "Okay. See you in the morning."

"Ten, right?"

He nodded. "That sounds good."

I gave him a tiny wave and high-fived Jared on our way out. Cora was already behind the wheel of her Sentra when I left the building. My eyes automatically went to where I'd last seen Gina and Rita. Their car was gone.

Andris pulled into the parking lot before we pulled out and raced toward the back door. I rolled down my window and yelled, "Over here."

He stopped, turned, and sauntered to our car. He finger combed his silver hair. "I thought I missed you." He leaned down and peered at Cora from above his sunglasses. "Hey, blondie."

"Hi-Yo, Silver," she shot right back. "You didn't have to run down here. I got our girl's back."

"I'm here now. Run along and play house with your reaper boyfriend." He opened the car door.

"Just follow us," I said, sighing.

"We're going by The Hub to get lattes then home," Cora said.

Lattes hadn't been part of our plan. Andris shot me an annoyed look. "That was not in your text."

"It's in the one I was just about to send," I said. "Oh, and tonight we're going to L.A. Connection for the party."

He lowered his sunglasses and peered at me over the top rim. "No, you're not."

"Come on. You and Blaine can come with us."

"Let me think about it." He stepped away from Cora's car and smirked. "Okay. I thought about it and the answer is still no." Then he headed to his car.

Cora slapped my arm.

I slapped her right back. "Cut that out. I swear you're still the same girl I found bawling her eyes out in the bathroom in junior high. Use words."

"Bite me. Are you going to let him," she jerked a finger at Andris' SUV, "talk to you like that?"

"No. You don't argue with Andris. He expects it, and he'll have all sorts of reasons why he's right and you're wrong and make you feel immature and stupid. I just ignore him and do what I want to do. He always comes around."

Andris followed us to The Hub As we stepped out of the car, the hairs on the back of my neck rose. We were being watched. As though he felt it, too, Andris looked around.

The parking lot was packed with people walking to and from the building. Inside, no single table or chair was unoccupied. The feeling of being watched persisted. The bookstore slush café was frequented by high schoolers and college students, but a few stay-at-home mothers with their kids browsed, too.

No one appeared to be staring at us. In fact, most of the customers had their noses buried in books or computers. The free wi-fi here was a big draw.

Andris winked at the cashier as he handed her his credit card. "I'll pay for theirs too, Jessie."

She blushed. "You remembered my name."

"And your eyes. They're unforgettable. Did my sister's books come in?"

What a flirt. And a pathetic liar. Cora and I looked at each other and rolled our eyes. Andris preferred shopping online, but he was drawn to books and often frequented The Hub. He claimed he didn't want anyone at school to know he was a geek, yet every time he visited the place, he left with a pile of sci-fi books. Using Ingrid was a nice touch.

"So when is this party?"

"Eight," I said. I shot Cora an I-told-you-he'd-cave smile.

"When you get home, stay put. We'll pick you up at eight-ish."

I saluted him. "Aye, aye, sir."

He shot me an annoyed look. Cora and I didn't start laughing until we got to the car.

***

Two hours later, we were dressed and ready to party.

The printed black and white jeggings, flirty white top, black jacket, and knee-high boots were perfect for the evening. Cora chose a white dress with uneven hem and ankle-level, high-heeled boots. The back of her dress had a huge chunk of it missing.

She checked her butt and did a model twirl, the dress frothing around her calves. "What do you think?"

"It's you."

She flipped her hair and studied me suspiciously. "What is that supposed to mean?"

"The dress is perfect on you and you know it." Male voices came from downstairs. "They're here." I grabbed my debit card and cell phone and followed her downstairs.

"Oh, I showed Mom my vlog entry," Cora said. "She loved it. How did she put it? 'My baby's grown.'"

"Definitely a giant leap from *Hottie of the Week*," I teased.

"Shut up. Oh, wow, look at you, guys." She studied Andris and Blaine from the foot of the stairs and then walked toward them in a slow gait. "I think we are going to be the envy of every girl at the party."

I studied the guys and grinned. Not bad. The hipster and the trendsetter were in their element tonight. Still, I missed Torin and his earthiness. He didn't conform or let fashion dictate what he wore, yet these two guys couldn't touch him in the sexiness scale.

"That's okay," Blaine said. "We're ditching you ladies as soon as we get to the club."

Cora hugged his arm and pouted. "Come on, Blaine."

"Last time I danced with you, Echo went ape on me, so no thanks." Blaine managed to peel her arms off him.

I didn't blame Blaine for being wary. Echo could be scary possessive where Cora was concerned. She rolled her eyes. "Echo has learned to tame his jealous side. Come on. I want to dance." She went toward the portal.

I hugged Femi and whispered, "I have my cell. If you need me, text."

She chuckled. "Go have fun."

I planned to. Then I was going on a rescue mission. Midnight here would be eight in the morning in London. The Earl of Worthington was going to get a visit from one irate American teenager before he finished his morning tea.

I followed the others through the portal to the mansion and out the door to the SUV. Cora was already in the back seat checking her makeup.

"A few ground rules, Raine," Andris said before I joined her.

"Seriously, Andris? Stop worrying. Let's just go, dance, drink, and have fun."

"You don't drink," he snapped.

"I was kidding. Lighten up already." I hopped in the back seat.

Andris' eyes narrowed menacingly. "Back to the ground rules. You don't leave my sight or the club without telling me. If anyone bothers you, you tell me. It's spring break for colleges, and a lot of local guys are back in town, so no flirting with frat boys. That includes you, Cora. I don't need Echo acting like a Neanderthal."

Blaine chuckled from the front passenger seat. Echo nearly snapped his neck one night because Blaine had flirted with Cora. I never actually got the whole story, but Torin's presence had stopped him.

"It was a misunderstanding," Cora said, reapplying gloss. She pressed and popped her lips. "And leave my man out of this. These rules only apply to Raine."

"No alcohol for either of you," Andris continued, "but if you need anything, I'll keep a tab running at the bar."

"How I wish I was twenty-one," Cora mumbled, snapping shut her compact.

In five minutes, we were outside L.A. Connection. For a brief moment, scenes from my birthday party flashed in my head—ambulances, people lying on the grass, parents calling out their children's names...

I pushed the past aside and got in the moment as we joined the other students inside the club. Ingrid had reserved a table for us. We left our jackets on our seats, ordered drinks, and hit the dance floor. Blaine and Andris stayed behind surrounded by cheerleaders. I tried not to remember the last time I'd danced in this club and got lost in the music.

Cora and I were taking a breather by the bar sipping mockartinis when I felt the telltale warmth at the back of my neck.

Torin.

Nothing could duplicate the effect of his eyes on me. Our eyes met through the mirror behind the bar, and air got sucked out of the room.

The smoldering gleam in his eyes sent a shiver of heat up my spine, and I became an ad for every cliché—my heart skipped a beat, my breath caught in my throat, and little frogs started doing jumping jacks in my stomach. The urge to fly across the room and jump into his arms followed. Eyes followed him, but his stayed locked with mine.

Then he smirked. Jackass. Okay, so I had missed him like crazy, but his smug smile just rubbed me the wrong way. For two days, I'd worried about him, and he sauntered in here without remorse, looking like every girl's dream man. No, I was not throwing myself at him, or kissing him, or welcoming him home.

Despite my thoughts, I wanted to throw myself at him, kiss him senseless, scold him for making me worry, and never let him go.

I dragged my eyes away from his, picked up my drink, and angled the straw. I took a long sip. Behind me, someone called out, "Over here, St. James."

"You made it," another shouted.

"How was London?"

"Okay, I'm super impressed by your calmness," Cora whispered and stirred her drink with a straw. Her back was to the bar. "If Echo gave me a heated look like that, you'd have to peel me off the floor."

If only she knew. The only thing holding me up was the counter.

"He's coming this way. He just brushed off some girls. Seriously, some bitches don't respect boundaries," Cora said.

My hand tightened around my drink.

"He keeps looking at you. Turn around and welcome him already, or I'll do it."

"Don't you dare," I whispered. I knew the moment he entered my personal space. His warmth and scent swirled around me. I closed my eyes and soaked him in. Two days. How could he do that to me?

He slid next to me, his arm brushing against mine. Heat shot up my spine, and I shuddered. My eyes flew open and met his in the mirror. Of course, he noticed my reaction. The corners of his lips tilted into the sexy smile I adored. Not so adorable at the moment.

"Hey, Torin," Cora purred. "Nice to have you home."

"Thanks, Cora. Where's Echo?"

"Busy, but you'll see him tomorrow night."

"What's happening tomorrow night?" he asked.

"The double date we talked about. The four of us."

Torin bumped me with his shoulder. I pushed back. He turned his head and studied me. "Are we going?"

I shrugged. "Are we?"

He glanced at Cora. "I guess we're in." He ordered a drink and angled his head to study me as though searching for something. "Love what you've done with your hair."

I hadn't expected that. "Thanks."

"Love the outfit too," he added.

Okay, he was buttering me up. "This old thing?"

"Too bad the boys you dressed up for won't enjoy it," he said and chugged his drink.

I couldn't have heard him right. "I don't dress up for anyone."

"And coming here, I assume it was your brilliant idea? A place where you have absolutely no protection. What happened? You got bored playing it safe?"

The nerve. I wanted to dump the entire contents of my drink on his head. "You've been gone for two days without a word and this is how you greet me?"

"I did say I loved your outfit and hair." He ran a finger down my arm and drew imaginary lines up and down my palm. Heat raced under my skin, and my breath lodged in my chest. "So, are you coming home with me, or do I have to carry you out of here?"

If looks could kill, he'd be a pile of ashes. "You wouldn't dare."

He turned and glanced around the room, the sexy smirk I usually loved on his lips. Today it was infuriating. "You think I give a rat's tail about what these people think?"

"You humiliate me in front of our friends, Torin, and I'll never forgive you."

"I guess you're coming home with me."

"No, I'm not. I came here to have fun, and I'm not going to allow you to spoil it for me." I stepped around him, my eyes connecting with Cora's. They were wide. "Let's dance."

Cora glanced behind me. "Are you sure?"

My back tingled, which meant Torin's eyes were on me. It took all my effort not to look back. Who did he think he was? Cora, thankfully, didn't desert me.

I got lost in song after song, yet I knew the moment Torin came to the dance side of the club. Sure enough, I found him bonding with Heath and another ballplayer by the curtains separating the dance floor from the lounge. His eyes were on me. I waved and grinned.

He didn't come to the dance floor. I didn't want him to. One of guys we were dancing with was from our school and knew about me and Torin. His friend was familiar, but I couldn't place him. Probably a student from another high school. Torin sized them up, then dismissed them and went back to his conversation.

"We can't stay on the floor forever," Cora yelled in my ear. "I need a drink."

"Then get one," I yelled back.

"Please, go make up already. I keep expecting him to flatten the guys we're dancing with."

He didn't consider them a threat. "Let's go."

We excused ourselves and headed for the lounge. I was surprised when Torin didn't stop me from leaving the dance floor. Back at the bar, someone had put our jackets on the stools we'd been using. We got drinks. My eyes met Andris. He cocked his eyebrows questioningly. I smiled and saluted him.

"Hey, why did you guys leave?" the guy we'd been dancing with asked, easing beside me. A weird chill went through me, and I blamed his sudden appearance. He had the Latin thing going for him, though he spoke with no accent.

"Oh brother," Cora murmured. "She has a boyfriend, Don Juan," she added louder.

The guy glanced at her. "I haven't asked her out." He smiled into my eyes. "Yet."

"Yes, Cora. He hasn't. Would you like a drink?" I asked, aware that Torin was back in the room. He didn't join us. Instead, he and his friends went to their table. Our eyes met, and he winked. He was amused by my behavior. He couldn't even give me the satisfaction of making him jealous.

"Are you buying?" the guy asked. He was really cute with intense dark eyes, naturally tan skin, and confidence that said he was an older student. But he was no match whatsoever for Torin. Not in looks or *cojones*.

I nodded at the bartender. "Put it on our tab."

"I'm Sebastian Reyes," Don Juan said and waved to someone behind me. "And these are my cousins, Alejandro and Matias Torres." Twins. Tall, dark, and handsome.

I glanced behind me and grimaced. The entire room was staring at us. Only Torin didn't seem particularly bothered. He smirked and raised his glass. Stinker.

"I'm Raine Cooper," I said and pointed at Cora, "She's Cora Jemison."

"So you're in high school?" Sebastian asked.

"And in a relationship," Cora added. "Both of us."

Sebastian grinned. "I think you protest too much, Cora Jemison. Raine doesn't mind getting to know us. In fact, we're having a private party at our hotel. Would you guys like to join us? You can invite some of your friends." He smiled at some of the girls.

Okay. Maybe I had started something that could backfire badly and fast. Cora must have thought so, too, because she reached for my hand.

"Excuse us." She practically dragged me away from the bar, past tables, and into the hallway leading to the restrooms. "What the hey?"

"Torin pissed me off," I protested.

"Then smack him or something, not flirt with some loser college boy."

"I hardly flirted. I was just warming up. Besides, they are cute." She pushed me toward the bathroom. "I don't need to go."

"Then stay. I'll be right back."

I studied my reflection. What was I doing? Cora was right. Flirting with other guys was so not me. Torin didn't seem to care. Or he was hiding it well. He even seemed to enjoy my rebellion.

The door opened, and Cora entered. "I cannot believe that a-hole Sebastian. He refused to give me your jacket. Go get it."

"Yeah. This whole experiment is over." I marched into the room, my eyes going to Torin. As though he felt my eyes on him, he glanced over his shoulder, eyes following me.

Sebastian had taken my stool and was holding my jacket on his lap.

"Can I have that?"

"You're not thinking of leaving, are you?"

"Yes, I am." I reached for my jacket, but he moved out of the way.

"How about another dance, sweetheart?" he asked, grabbing my hand.

"Let go, Sebastian," I warned.

"You are a tease, Raine. You led me on and now you want to walk?" His friends crowded me from behind. "Just one dance." He stood, my jacket clenched in his hand.

I'd bet that once we were on the dance floor, he'd do something stupid and bring Torin's wrath on his head. If my debit card wasn't in my jacket pocket, I would have walked.

"Sorry, boys, but I'm done for the night." I reached for my jacket. He hid it behind his back. We were drawing attention. Most of ball players seemed ready to leap across tables and rip apart these three idiots. The only thing stopping them was Torin.

Our eyes met. He smirked, tapped his watch, and gestured with a finger that I should wrap it up. It amazed me how well he understood me. I swear, he had to be a mind reader. This was a battle, and I didn't need him or his boys to come to my rescue.

My attention shifted to Pinhead.

"Listen, Sebastian."

"Call me Bash." Something about his smile was familiar. Cold fingers crept up my spine.

"I was nice, Bash. I bought you a drink, and now you are trying to bully me into doing something I obviously don't want to do. You have ten seconds to give me back my property before someone gets hurt."

The twins chuckled while Bash leaned against the counter and shifted closer. "A sweet little thing like you wouldn't hurt me over a dance."

"Eight... seven... six..."

He smirked.

"Three..."

"Come on, Raine."

"Time's up." I engaged my strength and speed runes, grabbed the jacket, and yanked it from his hand with such force his elbow slipped from the counter. He lost his balance, his face a mask of surprise.

I took advantage and nudged him with my foot. It was a gentle nudge. Nothing to make anyone think I was using super powers. He went flying across the floor. People laughed. Those nearby looked down at him.

I turned and faced the twins. "You want to join him?"

They shook their heads and stepped back.

"Good." I slipped on my jacket and waved to Cora who was standing a few feet away with Echo. He must have arrived while I was having my little showdown.

She closed the gap between us and we hugged. "You are so crazy."

"He was being a douche." We both glanced at Sebastian and his friends. They were whispering and glaring at us. "I gotta go. I'll see you tomorrow." I ignored the whispers following me, walked to where Torin sat, and offered him my hand.

He got up, slipped an arm around my waist, and pulled me to his side. "You're pretty scary when you're pissed, Freckles."

I sank against his side. No more playing games with other guys. Torin and I would knock heads from now on without involving anyone else.

"What happened to you carrying me out of the club?" I teased.

"Who said we're leaving." He led me toward the dance floor. "I owe you a dance or two. And you owe me an apology."

"For what?"

"Implying I'm no fun." As though he'd planned it, the DJ started a slow song. He pulled me into his arms.

12. A SPECIAL BREW

"I brought the picture," the gray-haired customer from yesterday said. My eyes went to his gothic ring first. It had unique symbols on it. If he noticed my interest, he didn't show it.

I dragged my eyes from his finger and smiled. "Did you see anything in the catalogue you like?"

"Hmm, no. I'm undecided. I was hoping you'd help me." He pulled out a portrait of a woman from a large envelope.

The woman was dressed in a leotard and striking a ballerina-pose. She was graceful, her face striking. "She's beautiful. Who is she?"

"My wife. She passed away five years ago. She was a prima ballerina, the toast of Argentina for over ten years. The ballet world remembers her as a very talented and graceful dancer, but to my boys, she will always be their mother." He pulled out two more copies of the same picture. These were smaller—five-by-sevens. "I'd like these framed for my boys."

I spent half an hour working with him. When we finished, he'd selected the perfect frames. He was replaced by another customer. It seemed like there was an endless stream of them. Saturday must be a busy day at the shop.

By noon, they'd trickled down to nothing. I was exhausted, and my mouth was dry from talking nonstop. "Is it always this busy?"

Jared glanced over from where he stood behind the cashier. "Not like this. I think having you here is the draw."

"What?" What if the customers had all been witches? Most of them had bought something, but every time I'd looked up, I always found eyes on me.

"Pretty girls always draw more customers."

Okay. So maybe I was being paranoid. "Most of them were old, Jared."

"Even old people like pretty faces."

The back door dinged. "Incoming," I said.

Instead of new customers, Rita and Gina entered the store. I waved to them. Gina whispered something to her sister and walked to the counter. Today she was dressed in a black lacey dress top, striped tights, and canvas boots. The sister just wore a simple maxi dress.

"Raine, we don't want to bother you, but can we talk?" she asked. She sounded serious. No, scared.

"Yeah. What's going on?"

Gina glanced at Jared and lowered her voice. "Privately?"

The store offered no privacy. "Just a second." I left my throne behind the desk, knocked on the office door, and peered inside the room. "Can I take a break?"

He scowled. Seriously, didn't he ever smile? "Sure. Where are you going?"

"To Café Nikos."

"Oh. That's okay."

That was too easy. "You guys took care of it."

"Of course. St. James knows you visit it when you're at the shop."

And whatever Torin says goes. "Okay. I'll just pop over there for a minute. If you need me, I have my cell."

"I'm sure Jared can take care of things until you return."

Back on the main floor, Gina and Rita were conferencing. "My boss said I can take off for a few minutes. There's a café a few doors from here."

The front of the stores all the way to Café Nikos were runed. Thank goodness no one could see them; otherwise the storeowners would go ballistic. Nikolaus saw me and hurried over.

"*Koreetsi mou!*" He kissed my cheeks one at a time. It was über awkward because he was shorter than I and I had to lean down. "How are you doing?"

"Fine, Nikolaus."

"And your father?"

"Still hanging in there," I said.

Nikolaus shook his head. "He's a strong man, your father. Always has been. He'll pull through this. Just wait and see."

I couldn't bring myself to correct him. I pulled out my credit card. "We want some of your yummy baklavas."

"Put that away," he said, waving at my credit card. "Order anything you want for you and your friends." He smiled at the two witches, his eyes lingering on Gina. I could just imagine what he was thinking: Dad was sick, Mom was in mental home, and I was hanging out with a Goth girl. Intervention anyone?

Once we got our drinks and the pastries, we found a corner table. Just vacated, too. The place was packed with the lunch crowd, and since it was a Saturday, there was a constant flow of customers. I sipped on my caramel frappe and studied the two girls. Gina stared right back, her drink untouched. Rita played with her straw, her head down. She talked a lot more when her sister wasn't around.

"Your father is sick?"

I nodded. "He has cancer."

"Is he going to be okay?" Rita asked, speaking softly.

I shook my head, pushing down the sudden urge to cry. Every time someone asked about him and showed sympathy, tears rushed to my eyes. "So what's going on?"

They looked at each other and communicated with their eyes. I hated when people did that. It usually meant secrets.

"What is it?" I asked impatiently.

"I feel bad asking you now that I know about your father," Gina said hesitantly. Rita sucked on her drink and refused to meet my eyes.

"Ask me what?"

Rita looked at her sister and shook her head. Okay, this was ridiculous. I didn't know these two girls from Adam, but I'd gotten my first clear vision when I was with them and I wanted to know why. "Is this about a vision?"

Gina nodded. "Rita is ill. The doctors can't find anything wrong with her, yet she grows weaker and weaker every day. She wants..." Her voice trailed off, and she glared at her drink. I could swear she was fighting tears. Rita reached for her sister's hand and squeezed.

"I want to know when I'm going to die," Rita whispered, glancing at the people at the neighboring tables. "Mom won't let us see the Seeress in our area. It cost too much money." She reached into her purse, pulled out several ten and twenty dollar bills, and placed them on the table between us. "We have one hundred dollars between the two of us."

"It's our lunch money for school, but this is more important," Gina added.

"I know it's not much, but could you?" Rita asked. "Please."

This was jacked up. I couldn't see my father's future no matter how often I tried, yet here were these two, giving me all their lunch money to get a reading. I pushed the money back to Rita. "Put that away. I would never charge anyone for something that's both a gift and a curse."

"A curse?" they asked at the same time, not masking their horror.

"Yes. Well, you have no idea what it's like to be me." They still wore shocked expressions. "Anyway, my visions are unpredictable. I'm never sure whether I'll see the past, present, or future, and most times things are blurry."

"We don't care," Gina said and pushed the money toward me. "Try, please."

"Please," Rita added.

Dang it! They were drawing attention. This was the worst place and day to hold a séance. But I couldn't invite them to my house or go to theirs. The office was out of the question because Hawk would tell Torin.

"Okay." I planted my finger on the bills and pushed them toward Rita. "Only if you put this away." I watched her take the money and put it back in her purse. "Okay. Um, let's trade places, Gina." I didn't want anyone at the restaurant seeing my glowing eyes.

Once we traded places, I pointed at her amulet. "I need that or something that's personal and magical. Do not panic when my eyes glow, or if I faint."

Gina frowned. "Do you faint?"

"Sometimes." I slid my hand along the table. Rita removed the amulet from around her neck and placed it in my palm. The power of protection in the object was strong.

Okay. *Here goes nothing.* I closed my palm.

Scene after scene played out, but the best part was they were clear. I was the fly on the wall looking at Rita's life. The birth, which I really didn't need to see, totally ruined OB/Gyn as a possible profession for me.

She received the amulet on her sixth birthday. From the party decorations in her backyard, her parents had gone all out. Scene after scene, her life unfolded. She was around fourteen when she started working with an older woman, grinding herbs, learning spells, and making some liquids of various colors. Something about the woman teased my memories, but I didn't try to chase it because things became downright bizarre.

The old woman sneaked into Rita's room while she slept and cut off a lock of her hair. Then she added it to a bubbling pot, causing smoke and a strange green fire to erupt from the pot. Then she did something even weirder, she poured some of the potion into a cup and drank it. The rest, she kept in a cupboard in her bedroom.

She systematically stole locks of Rita's hair and made more brew. Rita appeared to change. She stopped being the bubbly girl who'd laughed as she made potions. She became listless and sickly. It became too painful to watch her. The last scene was heart wrenching, but I didn't stop watching until I didn't need to anymore.

I opened my palm, and the amulet dropped on the table. Rita and Gina watched me with wide eyes, and I realized why. Tears were racing down my face. I swiped at my cheeks. I was definitely not cut out for this Seeress business.

"Are you okay?" Gina asked.

I nodded, glanced around, and wasn't surprised to see more customers had arrived. "How long was I out?"

"Almost an hour," Gina said. From her voice, she wanted answers yesterday.

My watch said it was ten to one. I blew out a breath. How the heck did you tell someone you saw her die a horrible death? Tread in slowly? She didn't just die quietly in her sleep. Someone would body slam her, breaking every bone in her body like a twig. It was the kind of move I'd seen Torin pull, except Valkyries were forbidden to kill Mortals. My eyes volleyed between them, then stopped on Rita. She looked as bad as my father did after the plane crash.

"Your mother gave you the amulet on your sixth birthday. She threw you a big party in your backyard with a bouncy castle."

They both nodded, but I could see in their eyes that they knew I had bad news.

"You, Rita, played violin."

"I still do whenever I can," she said sadly.

"Gina, you play soccer."

"You only saw our childhood?" Gina asked impatiently. "Then why were you crying?"

Because I'm a wimp. "I cry when I'm happy or sad. I haven't had a clear vision until I met you two. So that's kind of great." They gave me uncertain smiles as though they had no idea why I was complaining. "Anyway, when did Rita start studying herb and potions under the woman?"

"She was fourteen. Madam Bosvilles is the most powerful Seeress in our sector," Gina said. "She only works with the most gifted witches. My mother worked with her too, but her gift wasn't that strong. Her abilities faded."

I glanced around. Her voice tended to rise. Once again, a few people were looking at us. "Keep your voice down, Gina. What do you mean abilities?"

"Communicating with the spirit world and seeing the future," Gina said. At least she lowered her voice. "My sister was as strong as you, but during a séance, she'd go into a trance with Madam Bosvilles and journey with her to the spirit world. It started when she turned fifteen."

"How long were you with her before you started feeling sick, Rita?"

Rita frowned. "The summer I stayed at her home. Why?"

"How long was your mother with Madam Bosvilles before her abilities faded?"

They shook their heads. "We don't know," Gina added.

"Madam Bosvilles has been cutting locks of your hair and making a potion with it, which she drinks."

Silence followed. Their eyes were wide with disbelief. Rita spoke first.

"No, that's not possible." She shook her head. "That's evil magic. Madam Bosvilles told me to never listen to anyone who talks or mentions evil magic. Evil." She glared at me then pushed back her chair and stumbled away from our table, muttering under her breath.

Gina's eyes volleyed between me and her fleeing sister. Something weird began to happen. The chairs and tables rattled as though they were trying to jet off the ground. Not all the chairs, just those closest to Rita as she staggered toward the entrance of the car. It was a Magneto moment. I expected her to lift her hands and float everything metal.

Customers didn't seem bothered. Some gripped their chairs while others reached for their drinks and plates.

"It's another one," someone said at a table a few feet away.

"Feels like a five pointer," another added.

"More like a three-point-five," someone yelled at the other end of the café.

Earthquakes were a dime a dozen in Oregon. We got one a day. This month alone, we'd had about twenty reports. Since they were usually about three-point-zero magnitude, except the six pointer off the coast two weeks ago, people just waited for them to pass and then continued with their business. This time the epicenter followed a muttering witch.

Gina jumped up. "I have to calm her down." Then she leaned down and added, "I don't believe you're evil. I never liked Madam Bosvilles, and she doesn't like me visiting Rita at her estate. I should have known she was stealing my sister's powers." She started to leave, then pivoted on her heel, and came back to the table. "Will she die?"

I winced. "If you don't stop Madam Bosvilles."

"I plan to. Thanks." She took after her sister. The rattling stopped. Torin appeared just as Gina went through the door. Andris, Ingrid, and Blaine were right behind him.

Everything was normal inside the restaurant, but they still spread out around the room while Torin came to my table. My eyes fell on the protective amulet. In her haste to get away from "evil" me, Rita had forgotten it. I covered it with a plate of Gina's half-eaten baklava just before my ready-to-kiss-ass boyfriend reached my table.

"Hey," I said lamely.

His eyes roamed my face. "You okay?"

"Yep. I came for some baklava and time just flew by." I stood and pretended to notice the others. "Oh, are you guys here for lunch?" I reached under the plate and pulled out the amulet by its chain.

Torin frowned, still searching for an invisible enemy. "No. I sensed you were in danger and thought you were being attacked."

The runes must have reacted to the magic, and he did have a way of knowing when I was in trouble. "It was just an earthquake."

"A minor one," Nikos' server said from behind him. "We had a few rattling of chairs, but no one was hurt."

"True." I took Torin's arm and led him away from the table. He glanced back and frowned.

"Hawk said you were with friends."

"Yeah, from school." The others headed outside, too. Andris was on his cell phone. "I didn't need rescuing, guys, but thanks for coming. It was just an earthquake."

"They haven't reported it yet," Andris said.

The problem with geeks was they looked up every bloody, freaking thing. "Yeah. Well. It just happened, duh." Thankfully, Rita and Gina were gone. "Let's go home."

***

I was still reading to Dad when I heard the doorbell. Then voices followed. People who came to my house rarely used the door, let alone the doorbell. I angled my head to listen as I continued to read. Multi-tasking was my middle name. The voice grew stronger and then faded. I hoped it wasn't Rita and the witches coming to burn me at the stake.

My cell phone dinged. I angled the screen and read the text message.

"Your father has visitors," Femi said.

"Who?" I texted back.

"The Jemisons."

Cora's parents. "Give us ten min."

"Why did you stop?" Dad asked, his voice low, his eyes closed.

"You have visitors. Cora's parents. Let's finish the chapter first."

He chuckled. At least it sounded like a chuckle. "It's okay, bumpkin. We can finish it some other time. I'm not ready to check out yet."

"I should hope not." It was nice to hear him crack a joke. A sucky one, but a joke nevertheless. I debated kissing him, but fear of rejection kept me from trying. The only time I did that was when he was asleep or feverish. I still didn't get visions when I touched him. "Okay, Daddy. I'll see you later."

"Go out and do something fun, sweetheart," he said.

"I did. Yesterday. We went to L.A. Connection for a party some girls threw, and tonight I'm going out to dinner with Cora."

"Good. Send Femi in first. I need to look my best."

We exchanged a grin. His best would still look sickly and emaciated. I closed the door behind me and saw the Jemisons in the kitchen talking to Femi. The scent of freshly baked pie filled in the air.

"Is that still warm?" I asked when I saw the two pies on the counter.

"One is," Cora's mother said and gave me a hug. "I thought you might want a piece, so I brought a cooled one, too."

"Femi told us you were reading to your father," Mr. Jemison said.

"Yeah." I got a plate and a knife. "Oh, Femi, he needs you." I cut a huge slice. When I looked up, Femi was gone and the Jemisons were looking at me expectantly. What were we discussing? Oh, yeah, the whale. "We're reading *Moby-Dick*. It's one of his favorite books. That and *The Hobbit*. We finished *The Hobbit* last month and watched the movie. Now it's Captain Evil Ahab and then the movie." My father always insisted I read the books before watching movies based on them.

We kept discussing books and movies until Femi came out to get them. I carried my pie upstairs. Torin had been gone since he picked me up from the Mirage. He'd taken Blaine with him.

We didn't get a chance to talk last night, but the explanation he'd given me for his disappearance for two days had seemed sketchy at best. He'd been checking on leads to whoever had robbed his mother's tomb and even got to interview his relatives. Like that would stop him from popping in and out of my room. He'd done it at the hospital, right under my mother's nose and the nurses' watchful eyes. He was up to something, and his obsession didn't make sense.

I finished my homework and practiced the oboe pieces for the upcoming concert. I'd stopped my daily practice after the Norns started messing with me and even fudged the entries on my practice chart a few times. I didn't feel guilty then, or now. It was the Norns' fault.

Downstairs, Femi was watching something on her laptop while working on dinner. Dad ate mainly soft or pureed foods. Cora's mother had left. Probably went shopping. She often did that while her husband visited with Dad.

"Heading to the mansion for a bit," I told her.

"When is your dinner date?"

"Six." I had a couple of hours to kill. I started for the portal, but then I remembered something. "What kind of potion involves using someone's hair?"

Femi froze in the process of chopping a celery stick. "The bad kind. Where did that come from?"

"Just something I saw."

"Where?" Her voice was harsh.

I shrugged. "Does it matter? What happens to the person?"

She stopped cutting the veggies all together and came toward me. The look in her eyes said she didn't like what she was hearing. The way she held the knife was unsettling. "The person practicing *bad* magic or the victim?"

"Both."

"It depends on what the *evil* witch is after or what the person they made the potion for wants. They could control the victim. Make them sick or even kill them. Where did you see this?"

"A vision." She stopped and frowned. "The person making the potion is an old Seeress. The hair is from a young girl, a powerful witch."

Femi pursed her lips. "Poor defenseless thing. That's the kind of magic you find in old grimoires. The hag's magical powers must be waning, so she's using the girl's hair to link with her energy and steal it. If not stopped, the girl will not have any magic left in her. What's going on, Raine?"

"Can the damage be reversed?"

"I don't know. People who own grimoires keep them hidden. Whoever the witch is, she will not want the spell reversed. She's probably destroyed the page with the spell. Whose future did you see, Raine?"

"A girl from my school. She's sick. In fact, she's convinced she's dying. Can you use your contacts to see if we can reverse the curse?"

"Not you. *I* will deal with this. You must not get involved. This is evil stuff. Spells and potions." She shuddered.

"But you just said she was like me," I protested.

"She probably doesn't know it yet. Please, stay away from this girl, whoever she is, until I find out what to do." She shook her head and smiled. "What are the odds of the two of you in one place?"

Part of me wanted to tell her about the witches, but I had to talk to Torin first. "Okay. I'll see you later." I opened the portal to the mansion and entered the grand foyer. It was quiet.

"Is anybody home? Andris?" Thuds came from upstairs and the dining room, which was across from the living room. Mrs. Willow must still be around. I assumed she came on Saturdays.

I peered inside the dining room, but it was empty. The door connecting it to the kitchen was slightly open. My watch said it was almost seven, a bit too late for the cook to be around.

Voices came from upstairs. I stopped at the foot of the stairs and called out again. Andris had a room upstairs by the library. Even when he wasn't feeding his inner geek with some sci-fi book or a gadget, he loved to be surrounded by books.

Maybe he had his latest conquest up there or was deep in some science fiction world and didn't want to be disturbed. I turned to leave.

"Hey," came from upstairs, and I looked up. Ingrid stood at the rail with a sheet around her. Her boyfriend must be around, which might explain why Andris was gone.

"Where's Andris?"

"With Torin."

"Oh. Torin said he was leaving him in charge."

She shrugged. "Uh, about earlier," she added. "You weren't just meeting with ordinary friends from school, were you?"

I frowned. "Why do you say that?"

She started downstairs, the sheet dragging behind her. I wondered if she was naked underneath it. What if she stepped on it? Stupid thing to think about now, but she tended to walk around the house half-naked. I often wondered if it was an attempt to draw Andris' attention or because she was a cheerleader and comfortable in her body.

She glanced upstairs when she reached me and whispered, "I felt the magic, Raine. You found the sister witches, didn't you?"

So she knew. "I did. At school. They came to see me at the shop, so I took them to Nikos to talk."

She pouted. "Oh, phew. I was going to impress you guys with my news. You know, call a meeting and tell everyone about them."

I grimaced, feeling bad for her. The others were just starting to see her as a useful member of the group. "Sorry."

"It's not your fault." She gathered her sheet, which was starting to slip.

"We can pretend I don't know about them if you'd like," I said. "Call the gang and wow them. I'll act surprised."

A weird expression crossed her face. "You would do that for me?"

I shrugged. "Sure. That's what friends are for, right?"

She smiled. "Thanks, Raine. Happy to know you have my back, but you don't have to. I'll be okay." Her cheeks grew pink. "Oh, uh, you can be the first to know my secret. I've decided to leave at the end of the school year. Femi has contacts in the fashion industry, and she made a call for me." She grinned. "I did an interview last month with a market editor at A-la Mode last week. She loved that I know so much about the fashion industry and market. I'm going to intern for her in New York."

"That's great, Ingrid. I'm happy for you." Andris had wanted her to have a hobby. This one was taking her far away. A portal away, but still… Oh, he was so going to hate this.

"Don't tell anyone yet, including Torin," she warned.

I pretended to zip my lips, which made her chuckle. Another sound came from the dining room, and the hairs on my nape rose. "Is Mrs. Willow working late today?"

Ingrid shook her head. "No. She left already. Why?"

"I keep hearing sounds from the kitchen. I don't want her to see me use the portal."

Frowning, Ingrid angled her head. "I don't hear anything. Blaine left with the others, and Echo doesn't come here unless Torin is around."

She gathered the sheet tighter around her, engaged her runes, and zipped down the stairs past me and into the dining room. Within seconds, she was back.

"There's no one there, but one of the guys left a mess in the kitchen again. I'm not cleaning it." She muttered something in her language. Sounded like a curse. "They never admit it."

"Maybe you have a ghost in the house," I teased as I headed toward the foyer portal.

"Don't joke about that, Raine." She shivered. "I don't like souls. I used blocking runes so I don't have to deal with them."

Most Immortals did. I was the opposite. I wanted to see souls. I couldn't be a Valkyrie and work with Torin unless I saw them. I waved to her.

Lavania had insisted that I didn't need to escort souls or do anything because I was a Seeress. The gods would take care of me, whatever that meant. She didn't understand. I didn't want to be a pampered Seeress just because I could see when Ragnarok started. I wanted my life to have a purpose. Like Torin, Andris, and Echo reaping souls. Even Cora had found a way to use her abilities.

Just before I entered the portal, I stopped. I had a weird feeling that I was being watched. I turned and studied the foyer. Ingrid was gone and there was no one but me. A chill filled the air, making me shiver. Weird. Shaking my head, I engaged my runes and went home.

13. DOUBLE TROUBLE

The lights in the bedroom across the yard from mine were the first sign that Torin was home. He didn't come to the window. The stinker.

I found the perfect outfit. I wasn't a dress person, but this was going to be a one-time DD. Two alpha males just didn't mix. They'd knock heads over everything—who drove us, the bill, where to go. The whole evening was bound to be a disaster.

I was putting the final touches on my makeup when the portal opened. Torin. Finally. I turned, expecting to see him saunter into the room.

"Can I come in?" Cora called out.

Disappointed, I sighed.

"Sure." I got up and went to close my bedroom door. "Your dad's still here, so keep your voice low." I turned and caught her studying my outfit. "What do you think?"

"It's perfect. Simple but elegant. Love the accessories, too."

"I raided Mom's jewelry box." The dark-blue dress with white zigzag across the chest flared down from my rib cage. It was flirty and girlish without being over the top. The navy-blue, three-quarter sleeve cardigan was the same length as the dress. The stacks of bracelets, dangling earrings, and necklace had lots of red and matched my heeled boots. I grinned at Cora. "You're rocking a bathrobe tonight?"

"I can't seem to decide on anything, but seeing your outfit helps. I think we're going somewhere private tonight."

"Really? In Kayville?" We had national restaurant branches galore, and they were usually packed on Saturdays.

"They actually got together this morning to discuss the details without starting World War III."

"No way."

She laughed. "Oh yeah. See you in a few."

She disappeared through the portal, and I headed downstairs. Sounds came from behind Dad's door. Femi was preparing two dinner trays. She stopped fussing with the tray and beamed.

"Look at you. You look amazing. You should wear dresses more often."

"You sound just like Mom," I said and wished I hadn't. I missed her. "Do you need me to carry anything?"

She gave me one of the trays.

Inside the room, Dad and Cora's dad were watching ESPN. Dad was propped against the pillow while Mr. Jemison sat on the chair at the head of the bed. Dad usually perked up whenever Cora's dad visited. I stayed with them for a few minutes.

At five to six, Torin entered our living room, and my heart trembled. He looked amazing in a dress shirt and a dinner jacket.

His eyes narrowed on me, a slow smile curling his lips. Hel's Mist. That grin was downright sinful. Warmth infused my body. He had no business looking at me like that. Not when my father was in the next room.

"Keep drooling and we'll skip dinner," he warned in a voice as smooth as satin.

"That should be my line, dufus. Where are we going?"

"It's a surprise." He closed the gap between us, bringing all that pure deliciousness my way. My breath caught. He smelled amazing. "Can you handle that?"

"I can handle anything you dish out." He chuckled, and I realized how that sounded. Like a challenge. He loved challenges. I bit down on my lower lip and wrapped my arms around his. "Am I going to like this surprise?"

"What's not to like? I'm part of the package."

I rolled my eyes. "Bring that arrogance down a notch, pal, or this evening will be a disaster."

He turned his head and pressed a kiss on my temple. "Did I mention how amazing you look tonight?"

"No, but that's a start."

He laughed, then glanced over my head and said, "See you later, Femi."

"You kids have fun." There was laughter in her voice, and I knew she hadn't heard every word we'd exchanged. She might be laid back, but Mom had left her in charge of me.

We entered the portal and appeared in Echo's living room. Now I was confused, but I refused to give Torin the satisfaction of asking again. Then Cora and Echo entered the room. She looked preppy in black shorts, a striped blue shirt with matching high-heeled shoes, and a white dinner jacket. Echo wore his usual duster, but he traded his leather for a black dress shirt and matching pants.

He led us to the front of the house where a limo waited. Cora and I exchanged glances. I was sure I wore a bemused grin on my face. A date with these guys was out there. I'd never been inside a limo or a city like Miami, except at Echo's.

The nightlife was in full swing, people crossing from their cars to restaurants and clubs, some like us rolling in limos. This was an upscale neighborhood, and it showed in the clothes the people were rocking. I was happy I'd worn a dress.

Torin drew my attention when he chuckled. The sound sent a warm shiver down my spine. As though he felt my response, he shot me a half a smile. I had no idea what he and Echo were discussing. He ran the tips of his fingers up and down my bare skin, from my elbow to my palm.

Sensations turned me into a puddle of goo. I couldn't remember accepting a drink, yet I held a sparkling something in a chute. I sipped. Non-alcoholic. Cora stared at her man with a love-struck grin.

I forced myself to focus on Torin and the words coming out of his mouth, but I got distracted again by the sensual curve of his lips and the way the blue lights inside the limo made his sapphire blues glow with an unearthly brilliance. The shadows under his high cheekbones were just as fascinating.

He bumped me with his shoulder, and I gave him a broad grin.

"Would you like some music?"

Wasn't there music already playing? No, that was the pounding adrenaline hurtling through my veins and fantasies I was weaving. "No, I'm good."

We pulled up outside a building. Going by the name, it was an Italian restaurant. Someone opened the limo door from outside, and the guys ushered us toward the entrance. I overheard a hostess on the phone say, "We are booked solid for the rest of the night. We do have a few openings for tomorrow night."

The club must be popular, except it was empty when we entered.

Nice interior. Very upscale. Candles graced every table, but the focus was on the one in the middle of the room. They'd even pushed the other tables and chairs back to create space for our table. The setting was for four, and four servers waited with napkins draped over their arms.

It was surreal. Our servers were super nice and polite. The female with a cart of drinks lost her train of thought a couple of times. I couldn't blame her. Torin had that effect on most of the female population. Throw in Echo and the entire female population didn't stand a chance.

I got ginger-lemongrass soda. The menu listed ten dishes, and they all looked so good.

"Is there something you don't like?" Torin asked.

"Shouldn't that be 'I *do* like'?"

"Nope. We're going to sample all of the dishes listed. If you want Chef Vincenzo to make anything else," he lifted his hand and a hovering waiter whipped out a notepad and pen, "he can add it to our menu."

"This is good," I said. I couldn't believe they'd arranged all this.

"I agree," Cora seconded.

"I'm reserving judgment until I eat this carefully planned menu." He gave Torin a mocking smirk.

"Don't start, limo man."

Listening to their exchange, everything fell into place. Echo had been in charge of transportation, and Torin had been in charge of our diner. I was sure the evening would be a disaster, but we all found a common ground. First was the great food by an enthusiastic chef who came out to personally check on us. Second were horror movies. Who knew reapers would like a zombie apocalypse.

"Everyone dies in the series," Cora complained. "What's so great about that?"

"That's the fun part of it," Echo said. "Now if only something like that could happen in real life."

Cora punched his arm and murmured something I didn't catch.

"Dead Mortals means more reaping for you, Echo?" I teased.

Echo smirked. "No, it means Ragnarok is around the corner."

I frowned. "How do you figure that?"

He leaned forward. "Best way to kill zombies is by chopping off their heads. Best weapon for that is a sword. No more guns, just machete-wielding Mortals trying to avoid the inevitable."

From what I recalled, the first signs preceding Ragnarok was "sword age," a period of violence and battles followed by three years of nonstop winter when families would turn on each other. Then Ragnarok itself would be next, the death of the gods and destruction of the world to make way for a new world.

"Don't be so bloody literal," Torin said.

"Or talk about chopping people's heads off during dinner," Cora added.

Echo rolled his eyes. "Okay. What should we discuss? *Supernatural?*"

"Now that's a series worth discussing," Cora said.

Torin and Echo groaned. Cora and I just laughed.

"Stop hating," Cora said. "I would not have known how to disperse souls with iron if it weren't for the Winchester boys."

"So that's where you got that crazy idea," Echo murmured.

"Brilliant idea," Cora whispered and kissed him.

"Have you guys set a date yet?" I asked.

Cora exchanged a look with Echo. "Don't say it," she warned.

The smile he gave her was downright sinful. "I asked her to elope with me when she turned eighteen, but she wants to go to college first." He shuddered. "I hate college as much as I hate high school."

"Nobody asked you to go," Cora said. "Just plan on being there between my classes and in the evening, or I'll hook up with my R.A."

Echo scowled. "What in Hel's Mist is an R.A.?"

"Older college guys who prey on freshmen," Torin said and smirked.

Echo didn't look too happy. He glared at Torin. "Why are you so happy? Raine is going to college too, isn't she?"

The smile disappeared from Torin's face. I held my breath and waited for him to say something. Anything. We hadn't discussed college and now wasn't the time.

Echo chuckled. "Let me guess. You two are going to the same college."

"Not that it's any of your business, but I plan to be her R.A. and T.A.," Torin said. "Then we'll start working on the basketball team."

"Basketball team?" Cora asked.

Torin gave me a slow grin. I knew that smile too well. He was about to say something naughty. "The number of children I want," he said.

I choked on my drink. Where the heck did that come from? He had the nerve to pat my back and whisper, "You okay, luv?"

I wanted to neuter him. We hadn't even talked about college, let alone marriage and kids. I assumed he planned to propose and wait for my response before I started popping out those babies. Babies. With Torin. The thought was mind-boggling.

"Don't worry, we'll have a couple of centuries to practice and fulfill all my other fantasies before we start," he added.

My face, I was sure, was as red as the jewelry I'd borrowed from Mom's jewelry box. I couldn't come up with a response, so I stared at the flickering candlelight and plotted his slow demise. Would he haunt me if I decapitated him? Probably.

He reached for my hand and interlocked our fingers. He tugged, forcing me to look at him. Glared was more like it. He was always pushing my buttons. Deliberately keeping me off balance.

"I hate you," I mouthed.

"You adore me," he whispered back. He brought my hand to his lips. My heart trembled, heat racing under my skin from where his lips touched. He didn't play fair.

My "not at this moment, pal," sounded forced.

"But I made *this*," he waved his hand to indicate the restaurant, "happen."

He could be such a baby. "It was nice."

He rolled his eyes and glanced at Cora. "Was dinner nice or *awesome*, Cora?"

"Awesome."

Torin slid me a grin. "Dinner was awesome, ergo, your man delivered."

"I chose the restaurant and rented the limo," Echo said.

Pissing contest before dessert. Great! I hated to be around when the bill arrived. Cora showered Echo with praises; then silence followed as the servers cleared the table. One came with the dessert cart. She rattled off the treats and lingered, her eyes volleying between Echo and Torin. Cora and I might as well be invisible.

Andris chose that moment to swagger into the room. The hostess tried to detain him, but he waved toward us. "I'm with them, sweetheart."

Torin was already on his feet by the time Andris reached us. "What is it?"

"We're back," Andris said.

"Are you kidding?"

"Would I?" Andris glanced at me. "Thank you."

I tried to understand their conversation and failed miserably. "Back from where? Why are you thanking me?"

"Someone caused the Norns to remove the death block, and only one person can do that. You. We need to go."

Torin glanced at me.

I shrugged. "I didn't do anything." Or had I? I could tell he wanted to leave. "Go. I'll be fine."

"No. Let's finish here."

Andris rolled his eyes. "Seriously? The Seeresses will not wait and most of them are not in our sector. We need to go question them before they die." The hovering servers gasped. He smirked at them.

"She's coming with us." Torin reached for my hand.

I practically leaped from the chair. He chuckled and shot Echo a glance. "The bill is taken care of so we're good."

"You paid my half?" Echo asked, sounding insulted.

"Tip them, Echo. It's no big deal. Oh, and rune everyone. We were never here. They can remember this was a private party, but that's it." He headed for the restrooms and mirrors.

One of the servers was leaving the restroom and gave us a strange look. I could just imagine his thoughts. A girl entering the men's room with a guy. Two guys since Andris led the way. My face warmed.

Torin gave the man a folded note and touched his lips. "We don't want to be interrupted."

He was horrible. I couldn't think up something snarky. Then I saw the way the guy checked them out. He shot me an envious look and a wink. I laughed.

"What?" Torin asked.

"Thanks for turning me into a freak."

He kissed me. "As long as you are my freak."

I groaned. "That's twisted."

"I know. Listen, this is your first time reaping with us, so watch and learn. Engage your invisibility runes and follow Andris. I'll take the rear. We'll start with the furthest Seeress. Brisbane."

***

The portal opened into a bathroom several floors up. It was eerily quiet, and that weird sterile scent hospitals had lingered in the air. Kind of reminded me of the week I'd spent in the hospital after my surgery.

"Raine?"

I closed my eyes and felt the magic. It was faint, but we were on the right floor. I pointed. "That way."

We walked past the nurses' station. They didn't even look up, but a chill spread across my skin. "Are there souls here?" I asked.

"A few," Torin said. "You still can't see them?"

I shook my head, hating that I still couldn't. How the heck was I going to reap what I couldn't see? Damn the Norns. Seeress or not, I was going to be a Valkyrie.

Andris stopped outside a door and pulled out his artavus. I shivered. A telltale chill crawled its way up my spine. This time, it was stronger and familiar. I caught Andris' hand before he could create a portal.

"She's not alone," I whispered.

Torin scowled. "How do you know?"

Andris already created a portal through the door and peered inside. He stepped back. "There are three nurses with her."

Torin pulled me away from the door. "How did you know she wasn't alone, Raine?"

"Those are Norns with her."

He grimaced. "That's our sign to scat. Let's go to the next one and come back once they heal her."

"No. I don't think they're here to heal her."

Torin and Andris gawked. I saw the question in their eyes.

I shrugged. "I can't explain it. They're too happy. I want to talk to them."

"No, Raine. The last people—"

"I have to, Torin. My own Norns deserted me after I refused to listen to them. The ones in there are not in charge of my destiny. We need answers."

"Raine—"

"I need to do this, Torin."

"Then we're going in with you," he said. He crossed his arms and tried to intimidate me into submission. Was he serious? I wasn't the girl he'd met last year.

I lifted my chin and glared right back at him. "No, you're not," I snapped.

"You piss off Norns every time you open your mouth," he said.

Meanie. "And you piss them off by just being in the same room."

He smirked. "It's a gift."

"It's not funny. You remind them you are the reason I'll never be one of them." The smile disappeared. Blue flames leaped in the depth of his eyes. Oh, so that was the problem. "I'm going to *talk* to them, Torin. Not join them. Eavesdrop on our conversation if you want, but I'm going in."

"I don't like it," he said.

"Just go," Andris snapped. "I swear you two are like a toothache."

I moved closer to Torin, propped myself against his arm, and leaned in to kiss his chin. "Well, I happen to love this particular toothache."

He growled, cupped my face again, and kissed me. He pressed his forehead against mine. "You drive me crazy."

I grinned, turned, and walked to the door. Andris and Torin stared at me with worried expressions. I gave them thumbs up and pushed open the door.

Three nurses looked up. One ginger-haired with freckles, another exotic Hawaiian, and the third had pitch-black hair and porcelain skin. Nice disguises, but they were Norns all right. Just not my Norns.

"What are you doing here, Lorraine Cooper?" the ginger-haired one asked.

How did she know my name? "Checking on the Seeress. How is she doing?" I stayed by the door and peered at the woman on the bed. She was so still.

"She will be okay," Ginger said again. She must be the spokesperson of the trio. "Should you be here, considering what's going on?"

Of course they knew what was happening to me. Probably chuckled over it during dinner at Norns' Hall. "Who's after me?"

"You know we can't tell you that," Ginger said again.

"Maybe I should let them take me."

They stared at me in shock, and I knew they didn't want this to happen.

I grinned. "Why don't you stop them?"

"You chose to follow a path we hadn't set for you, Lorraine. Dealing with him is the consequence of that choice. If you let him win, you'll lose everything." Ginger glanced at the other two. Silent communication followed, but I didn't bother to listen to it. "Leave now, Lorraine. We've said more than enough. All the Seeresses will be fine. We made sure of that."

I frowned as things clicked into place. "You knew this man was going to come after me, and you stopped Valkyries from reaping to save them."

"Leave!" Ginger ordered.

I didn't move. "Admit it. You knew. You set events in motion to save them."

"We took precautions, set paths," Ms. Hawaii said. "Whether they followed it or not depended on them. These Seeresses proved they were worthy when they risked death to save you."

"Worthy of what?"

Silence.

"Worthy to become one of you?" Ms. Porcelain's eyes gave them away. The Seeresses were being recruited to become Norns. "So why save them and not me?"

"They faced him. Why shouldn't you?" Ms. Hawaii asked. I didn't like her tone.

"So if I face him and win, I become one of you? And if I don't, I lose everything?"

Ginger lifted her hand and pointed at me. "Go!"

The door flew open behind me and something pushed me out of the room. The door slammed shut with a bang.

Old farts! I wished I could get in their heads and know all their stupid secrets.

Silly girl, she doesn't stand a chance this time. I recognized Ginger's voice.

I could hear her. Cool. Torin appeared by my side, his mouth opening and closing, but I couldn't hear what he was saying. My mind was linked with the Norns. Next second, I was floating away. I think. It felt that way.

She's not silly, Ms. Hawaii said. *She's smart and annoyingly stubborn. No matter what path they set for her, she always takes one that leads to that Valkyrie.*

That's because she's more powerful than us and she loves him. I didn't recognize that voice. Must be Ms. Porcelain, the third Norn.

She is a child, snapped Ms. Hawaii. *We can still force her to see things our way.*

Force me? Okay. It was official. I hated Ms. Hawaii.

We'll keep creating new paths until she gives up and joins us, Ginger vowed.

Ginger just joined my most hated Norn list, too.

Why can't we just leave her alone? She's made her choice. Ms. Porcelain was nice. She reminded me of Jeanette, my nice Norn.

Don't ever say that, Ginger snapped.

I'm not the only one who feels this way, Ms. Porcelain shot back. *Quite a number of us believe we should leave her alone. She might refuse to offer us shelter during Ragnarok for doing this to her and those she loves.*

Shelter? How the heck was I going to do that? I thought I was going to predict when Ragnarok was to start.

It is a chance we have to take to ensure our kind survives, Ginger said. *Until her choice is official, she is a fair game. Even the gods protecting her know that. That's why they're using her mother. We have the boy. We will not fail this time. His need to protect her will drive her straight to us.*

Don't underestimate them, Ms. Porcelain said. *Together they're unstoppable.*

That's why we're doing things differently this time, Ginger said. *Let's finish here and move on to the next target.*

Silence followed, and I became aware of two things: The floating sensation had stopped, and I was lying on my back. Torin's face appeared in my periphery. Tension shot from him. He was worried. Or maybe pissed. How were the Norns using him?

"How long has she been like this?" I heard Femi ask.

"Since the meeting with the Norns. I should not have let her talk to them."

I was home? The floating sensation must have been Torin carrying me to the portal. I'd eavesdropped on the Norns through space. How had I done that?

"We have to go," I said, sitting up.

"No. You're not going anywhere," Torin said. He nudged me back until I rested against the pillows.

His need to protect her will drive her straight to us.

I slapped his hand. "Stop it." I pushed his hand out of the way and sat up. "The Seeresses are being recruited to become Norns. That's why they didn't let you reap. They were waiting to save them. We have to get to at least one of them before they take them all. They wanted to finish before someone arrived." I scooted to the edge of my bed and looked around for my shoes.

The heels I'd worn to dinner were nowhere to be seen. I reached for the ballet flats I'd left by my bed. "I had a feeling they were talking about the people after us. They know about the man after me but won't do anything about him. If I face him and lose, I will lose everything. If I win, I kind of become a Norn. I think."

Three pairs of eyes stared at me with different expressions. Torin looked pissed. His eyebrows were flat lines above his smoldering eyes. Andris and Femi watched me like I'd just told them I was dying.

"They told you all this?" Torin asked

"About recruiting, but I overheard the rest here." I tapped my head.

"You linked with them telepathically," Femi whispered.

"Is that good?" Andris asked, looking at Femi.

Femi shrugged. "I don't know."

"What is this about winning and becoming a Norn?" Torin asked, his voice a low growl.

"Something that we will never let happen," I said. "We need to get at least one Seeress who can ID the people after us."

Torin's lips pulled back. "I don't care. You're not going out there."

"I do and I am. They are using you. I heard them. They're using you to push me to their side. Something about you being overprotective."

He stared at me in disbelief, his eyes a stormy pool of emotions. I could just imagine what he was feeling. Not protecting me went against his nature. He'd already started training me to be strong and fast.

"You're making that up—"

"No, I'm not," I said.

He thrust his hand through his messy hair. From the looks of it, it wasn't the first time he'd done it. "I want to know everything they said. But right now, I need you to find the Seeresses."

***

We appeared in the hospital hallway we'd visited earlier. I couldn't feel the Norns, just remnants of their energy. "They're gone."

"On to the next one," Andris said, turning to re-enter the nurses' bathroom.

"No. Just a second." Torin switched off his runes and sauntered over to the nurse's desk. The nurse behind the desk looked up, and her eyes glazed over before he even opened his mouth.

"Hey, luv. I'm looking for my aunt who's been in a coma the last couple of days." He gave her the name, his seductive smile at full throttle. The flustered woman hunched over her computer in a matter of seconds.

"I'm so sorry," she said. "She died a few minutes ago. They just took her body to the morgue. Are you the next of kin?"

"No. A distant cousin. Thank you. You've been most helpful." He moved so fast, beyond the perception of human eyes, and etched runes on her cheeks. Then he engaged his runes.

"She can't be dead," I protested as we moved away from the desk.

Torin looked around, his face harsh under the bright hospital light, frustration churning in his eyes. "Norns and Valkyries cover their tracks in two ways. They erase memories or switch bodies. My mother was given a Saracen body disguised as me to bury. Let's find the morgue."

"Should we be going after the other Seeresses?" Andris asked, standing his ground.

Torin threw him an annoyed look. "We need to confirm the MO they're using."

Andris' eyes narrowed. "What purpose is knowing this going to serve?"

"It will confirm what Raine overheard," Torin growled. "If the Norns are recruiting, this entire mess with the Seeresses is a ruse to reel her in. And I'm not letting that happen."

We found the morgue. A single attendant was filling out the paperwork. There were a few bodies by the door. With his back to us, he didn't see tags move as we checked them. He happened to turn just after Torin exposed the Seeress' face.

The attendant jumped up and walked to the gurney. "Hmm, how did you do that, pretty lady?" He studied the dead woman. "Poor thing. So young to be dead."

"Is that what you guys are seeing? A young woman?"

Torin and Andris nodded.

"With runes all over her," Andris added.

"What do you see?" Torin asked.

"An old woman covered with runes."

We left the morgue and followed Andris to several other hospitals. All had Seeresses replaced by dead bodies. Some of the bodies were men. The Norns I'd met weren't working alone. The energies in each hospital felt different. A lot of Norns were out tonight.

"Let's find the Seeress' personal effect," I suggested after the last stop.

Torin and Andris stared at each other. They didn't look too happy. I shifted from foot to foot. When their gazes shifted to something behind me, I turned to look, but there was no one there.

Torin took a step back and shook his head. "No," he said firmly.

"Then how do you plan on finding the people after me? The Seeresses have been taken. And I'm sure the killers won't go after more, or the Norns would know about them. The only connection to them are their personal belongings and what I can see when I touch them."

"I don't like what it does to you when you go all golden eyes." The emotions in his eyes were raw. "You go to places I can't go, see horrible things, and I'm helpless to help you."

"It's not real, Torin. I know that now."

He lowered his head until we were eye level. "But I'm the one who hears you scream and feels you shake."

That sounded gruesome. "Listen, if I can stand it, so can you. It's not real." I moved closer to him. "You are real. What you feel for me and I feel for you is real. And I want our lives free of evil people chasing me and Norns using you to get to me. We stop these people now and deal with the Norns later." Once I figured out what they meant by officially making a choice.

He sighed. "I'm taking you home right now. Then I'll—"

"You know what? I don't need your permission to find out the identity of the person after me. You're not the only one who can smile and lie and make people do your bidding." I turned off my runes and started toward the entrance of the morgue. Personal belongings were sent to the morgue with the bodies.

The next second, my feet were in the air as arms snatched me up and brought me against a solid body. "Engage your runes, Freckles."

"No. I will not let them use you to get to me."

He laughed. "Do you know how ridiculous you look floating and kicking in mid-air?"

"Let them think I'm a ghost—"

"Hel's Mist! I'll get them." Andris marched toward the morgue entrance. "When she starts reaping, you two are on your own," he threw over his shoulder.

I re-engaged my runes. "Thanks, Andris. As for you..." I wiggled out of Torin's arms and turned to face him. "You're such a douche. I'm doing this for you. For us."

He chuckled. "I don't recall asking you to be my guardian angel."

"Neither did I ask you to be mine, you jerk. Yet here you are. You were gone for two days trying to find the person after me and came up empty-handed. We've spent hours chasing hags all over the globe, and they still bested us. Why are you so afraid to let me use my gift to identify the people after me?" I planted my hands on my hips and cocked my head. "What? Only you get to play the hero and do all the rescuing? Would it put a dent in that humongous ego of yours if I rescued you once?"

He pretended to think about it, head tilted to the side. "I took care of myself for centuries before you came along, and I'm really good at it. So yeah, the day I let a young woman rescue me is the day I stop being a man."

I flinched, the hurt swift and precise. "You're not a man, Torin St. James. You're an idiot, too pigheaded to appreciate anything, too blind to see beyond your bulbous aristocratic nose, and too arrogant..." My voice cracked.

His eyebrows shot up. "Bulbous?"

"You know what? Forget you." I started toward the bathroom, fighting hard to contain the tears burning my eyes and the ache in my chest.

I pushed the door open, but he zipped past me and had the portal to my room open by the time I reached the mirror. I couldn't believe he wanted me gone that badly.

I walked right past him, hating that I didn't have a door to slam in his arrogant face. I turned to give him an evil look, but the portal was closing. Then I saw the smug smile and realized he'd just played me. He'd wanted me out of the way and played me like a fine-tuned instrument. Why?

"Jackass!"

14. RUNNING WILD

The aroma of coffee teased my senses. It faded and then became stronger. "Wake up, Freckles."

"Go away." I turned my head the other way.

"Is there a water hose around here?"

He wouldn't dare. Yes, he would. I flung the covers aside and found him at the foot of my bed ready to yank the covers off me. I gave him a look that would have stopped a lesser man cold in his tracks. Not Torin. He smirked. And he just had to be shirtless. From the sweat glistening on his chest and the scent of clean sweat, he'd been working out.

I threw a pillow at him. He ducked sideways, and it sailed past him.

"What do you want?" I asked in the meanest voice I could master when all I wanted to do was ogle him.

"Nice pajamas. Sexy."

"Shut up." I was wearing an oversized T-shirt with a right angle and *I'm Always Right* plastered across it.

"It's eleven, Freckles."

"So?"

He gave me a look that said he was losing his patience. "So what are you still doing in bed?"

"It's Sunday, and if I want to lounge—"

He pulled the covers off me. "We've got places to go. I left a note." He sauntered to the bedside drawers and lifted a piece of paper. His eyebrows shot up. "How fast can you get dressed?"

I snatched the paper from his hand and read the scribbled words. It didn't say he was sorry. "You didn't apologize for last night."

"How does kicking my ass sound for making it up to you?"

Now that was more like it. I grinned. "Okay."

He chuckled and handed me the coffee. "Bloodthirsty witch."

"Douchebag Valkyrie."

He laughed. "Five minutes. Get your running gear; then come find me."

I took my time finishing the coffee and found my running things. After a brief chat with Femi, I left for Torin's.

He was seated on the couch in his living room, feet up on the coffee table, and looked up when I walked in. He gave me a slow perusal. My stomach clenched. He seriously needed to stop with the smoldering looks. I was mad at him.

"Nice outfit," he said.

It was the same as the one I'd worn days ago. Except it was black and hot pink. Nothing spectacular. "Are we going running or what?"

"Woke up on the wrong side of the bed?" He put something down and reached for his sneakers. Then I saw what he'd put down and blinked. His cell phone. The instrument he refused to use no matter how often I begged him.

"You were using your phone."

He cocked his eyebrow. "Yes."

"You know *how*?"

He rolled his eyes. "Engage your runes instead of poking fun at me. I'm not a total Neanderthal."

He *was* a Neanderthal. "I was sure you'd either ditched it or remodeled it."

"I like big things, not puny things that fall apart when I touch them." He gave me a slow perusal that said he wasn't talking about engines. Confirmed it when he smacked my butt as he walked past. "Come on. Catch up, slowpoke." He took off.

Show off. The Rutledges were coming back from Church, and I decided to pull the move Andris had taught me. The threat of death was a big motivator when it came to engaging runes and moving fast.

I stood right in the middle of the cul-de-sac entrance and waited until the car was a few seconds away then—

Torin snatched me and ducked to the sidewalk, almost wrapping us around a tree. "What in Hel's Mist was that?"

I pushed him away. "Something Andris taught me. You should try it. It's all about engaging your runes quickly and exercising your reflexes. It packs quite a punch, too."

His lips pulled back in a snarl. "I'm going to kill him."

"No, you're not. Andris believes in me. He trusts me to protect myself. Try it sometime." I backhanded him on the chest and took off toward Orchard Road.

Torin raced past me and ran backwards. "I trust you."

"Doesn't seem so. Where are we headed?"

"Follow me."

We took back roads, racing past cars. He leaped over oncoming cars, making Andris look like an amateur. But then again, what did I expect from an adrenaline junkie? A few times, I was sure he'd knock his perfect teeth on the road, but he rolled as he dropped and sprung to his feet.

My heart trembled every time he jumped. Who did he think he was? Invincible Spiderman? I almost snatched him from the path of an oncoming truck. I was shaking by the time we reached the edge of the trees.

"Ready for phase two?" he asked.

I blew out a breath, my heart pounding, while all he had to show for his stunt on the road were smears of dirt on his clothes.

"Freckles?"

"Don't do that again," I said.

He frowned, and then it dawned on him. "Nothing is going to happen to me. I've pulled that stunt a gazillion times."

The smirk that curled his sculptured lips only further infuriated me. "I don't care. I will not..." My voice broke. "I cannot watch you do that again, Torin. Just promise. It's stupid and dangerous, and I know you can self-heal, but you just *cannot* do that."

"Whoa, okay." He raised his arms. "I won't. Ever. And you won't listen to Andris' stupid ideas."

If he'd felt half of what I did watching him, then never again. "I promise."

"Good. Ready now."

I nodded. He plunged into the forest, shooting past trees like he expected them to move aside for him. At least I knew the trees would lose if he hit them.

I engaged my speed and sight runes. When the terrain became difficult, I added endurance ones. It didn't matter which ones I chose, the effect added to the rush. I felt alive, energized.

It was too early for hikers, except for a few die-hards, but Torin still chose less popular trails and unchartered territories. I was right behind him. Trails were everywhere, some popular and beaten-down, others with undergrowth due to lack of use.

He started slow as though giving me time to catch my breath. Then he picked up speed. He pushed me hard, going faster and faster. A few times I wanted to beg him to slow down, but I couldn't give him the satisfaction. I might not be able to beat him, but I could bloody well keep up.

Bloody well. Ha. I was even beginning to talk like him.

I lost sense of direction after a while. The creeks and campgrounds were starting to look the same. I knew we were south of Oregon 6 because of the ATV trails. Luckily, the season for all terrain campgrounds didn't start until the end of the month.

I shot past Torin as we neared the top of a hill.

"Slow down!" he yelled.

Oh, he thought he was slick. I had the lead. "Sour loser."

I kept going, until I burst through the trees into a clearing and something red caught my eyes. I slowed down and stopped when I recognized the picnic basket and the neatly-folded blanket on top of it. We'd used them before in his living room during winter.

My watch said we'd been running for over an hour, which meant he'd made this run earlier. One way with a basket of food and drinks. That alone was enough to steal my thunder. For about a second.

"I beat you fair and square," I called out when he appeared in the clearing.

"Show off." He pulled off his shirt and wiped his neck, his movements graceful.

"Except you were here earlier," I added, dragging my eyes away from his abs. I removed my top too, leaving my sports bra. Cool air kissed my bare torso. I dropped the shirt, reached down, and stretched my legs.

"I knew how far we'd go before you started to wilt," he said, stopping behind me.

"I don't wilt. I can handle anything you dish out. If you didn't notice, I kept up with you until you slowed down."

He ran a finger along my sweaty back. Since we still had our runes engaged, sparks exploded under my skin and shot every which way. I moaned. Or maybe he did. I couldn't tell.

This was the problem with runes. When engaged, they heightened our senses. It was as though energy bubbled on the surface of our skin, needing to be released. We engage speed runes, we run faster. Strength runes? Flatten something. Endurance? Climb a freaking rock. Standing next to a man that pushed our buttons with just a look, we might go ape.

It took all my willpower to straighten and move away from him, disengaging my runes when he did his. Slanting me a smirk that could be hot one second and infuriating the next, he opened the basket, removed two bottles of water, and threw one my way.

As I chugged mine, I found myself watching him lift the bottle to his lips, guzzle, and swallow. When he poured the rest on his head, droplets flowing down his face to his chest, our eyes met. Time slowed down to a halt.

Twigs snapped, and I whipped around, expecting to see some wild animal. Instead two hikers invaded our little slice of Oregon Tillamook Forest. While Torin smoothly switched accents from British to American and chatted with the couple, I tried to control my thumping heart. It wasn't the first time he'd pulled a switcheroo. How had he put it? People asked him less questions about his background.

I found the perfect picnic spot by a tree stump and spread out the blanket. When I looked up, the hikers were gone. Torin placed the basket on the blanket and sat on the tree stump. I dropped on the blanket and studied him.

"What are we eating?"

"Beef and turkey sandwiches and chips." He opened the basket and handed me a wrapped sandwich, then dangled a big bag of spicy baked chips. My favorite. Torin hated spicy chips. How did he put it? They numbed his taste buds, while he liked to savor different flavors in each chip.

He moved the basket aside and slid next to me, so we lay on our stomachs, our shoulders touching. We ate in silence. He'd cut the sandwiches into tiny triangles. When he dipped his hand inside the bag and removed a chip, I stared. He didn't hide his grimace.

"How's this for an apology?" Torin asked.

"Great! But do you have to torture your taste buds, too?"

He slanted me a look. "You noticed." He wiped his fingers on the blanket. "This is awful."

I bumped him with my shoulder. "Don't be a food snob. So why last night's douchebaggery?"

He rolled on to his back and studied me. "I told you. I don't like your visions."

"That's a lame reason. I'm a Seeress. Deal with it."

He squinted at me, those ridiculously long lashes fanning his cheekbones. "I liked you better as just my girlfriend."

I put a potato chip against his lips. "I was never *just* your girlfriend. I was me, before you, before us. A person with goals and dreams. Every time you say something idiotic, I feed you a chip. Open up," I ordered.

He ate it, his eyes twinkling. "I love it when you're bossy."

"The Norns said your protectiveness will push me to them," I reminded him.

He stopped smiling. "Bitter old hags. Why do you have to link with them? No chips. How did you link with them?"

"I don't know." The events from last night flashed through my head. "I wished it."

He propped himself on his elbow, eyes sharpening. "Are you saying if you want to eavesdrop on them all you have to do is wish it?"

I nodded.

He laughed. "Brilliant. You can kick them out of your head anytime." He munched on his sandwich. "I like it. I can live with that."

I grinned. "Thank you."

He ran a finger down my nose. He had a thing about my freckles. "Just like I *will* accept your visions."

"Without head butting the person I'm helping like you did with Echo."

"You weren't helping him. He was being a shithead." He tilted his head, eyes narrowed. "You are planning on helping other people?"

Torin didn't sound too happy, but what I'd done for Rita and her mother flashed through my head. "Uh, yeah. My visions are becoming clearer, so if anyone needs my help, I'd like to help. Any objections?"

His eyebrows slammed down fast. "That's a trick question."

"No, it's not. So?"

"Plenty of objections, but I'll keep them to myself." He went back to his sandwich.

Progress. I shifted and rested my head on his chest. His skin was hot. He rested his head on his arm and one hand played with my hair. "So what are we going to do about this guy after me?"

"You don't have to do a thing. I've got it covered."

I pushed him with my head. "OP, Torin. Not cool."

"OP? Oh. I get it." He chuckled, the sound rumbling through me. "Overprotective. Remember I was texting someone just before we left our place?"

Our place. I liked it. I turned my head to see his face. The sun danced over his features. He had such a beautiful complexion. No blemishes. No freckles like me. "What about it?"

"I was texting a woman." He wiggled his eyebrows.

He'd better not. "Ooh, I'm jealous."

He saw right through my BS. "Femi's witch friend. She's in New Orleans, but we have people in her store. A woman who looks like the witch, and her 'cousin' from out of town. Both are Immortal. According to your vision, the guy and his goons will visit the store next week. When they do, we'll get them."

Wow. "So my vision helped."

"Yep." He stroked my cheek.

I grinned. "Sweet. I'm officially a Seeress. A good witch."

"Thank goodness," he mumbled, his hand moving to stroke my bare mid-section.

This hatred of witches had to stop. I caught his hand and sat up. "I have a confession to make."

"Shoot."

He wasn't going to like this, and I wasn't sure where to start.

He sat and lifted my chin. "What is it?"

Okay, here goes nothing. "We have witches at our school. Rita and Gina, uh, something. I don't know their last name. They're here with their mother, who's also a witch. In fact, there are lots of witches in Kayville. I touched Rita's amulet and saw her entire life. Clearly." I grimaced. "She's been living with an evil witch—"

"Whoa. Slow down. Start from the beginning."

Even though he tried to hide it, Torin was pissed. He got up and paced. He was such a drama queen. He stopped, kicked a rock, and continued pacing.

"What part of what I said pisses you off?" I asked.

He stopped, opened his mouth, and closed it. Not a good sign.

I waited. The silence continued. Really not a good sign. "I'll paraphrase. Are you mad that there are witches? That someone told the supernatural world I was in trouble, or that I found the cause of Rita's illness?"

"I don't know. I thought all we had to deal with was this bastard after you. Now a coven of witches is living in our backyard and you've become chummy with them. We don't associate with witches, Freckles. Like Mortals, they're not supposed to know about us."

That hadn't occurred to me. I was an idiot. "I completely forgot."

He rushed to my side, cupped my face, and pressed his forehead to mine. "No, don't feel bad. As long as you didn't tell them who you are."

"Of course not."

He smiled. "Good. We don't know if they're here to protect you or support the other guy. Why? We don't know what he wants or even what he is." He pressed a kiss on my forehead then went for his shirt.

I wanted to say "he looks like you" but until I saw his face clearly, I was keeping my mouth shut. I got up and threw the bottles and wrappers in the basket. He grabbed the blanket, rolled it, and threw it in the basket.

"We'll know next week, right?" I asked.

"Yes." He picked up the basket and extended a hand to me. We walked hand-in-hand. "So this girl caused a mini earthquake at Nikos?"

"The people thought—"

He tugged my hand. "I got it the first time. I was just teasing."

He didn't sound amused. "Oh. Okay. Ha-ha, good one, Torin."

He bumped me with his shoulder. "So can you move things yet?"

"I don't know. I haven't tried."

"Do you want to?"

"I'm barely getting used to visions, so no. Are we walking home?"

"No. But I want to savor this moment. Just the two of us doing something normal couples do. Walking hand-in-hand. Enjoying nature."

Like he could ever be normal. I grinned. "Okay."

We walked, kissed, and acted like a normal couple out in the woods. We even stopped by University Falls and frolicked in the water like a couple of carefree kids before going home.

***

Once again, the gang was meeting at my place. Andris sat at his usual place at the kitchen counter, stuffing his face. I was sure the pies Cora's mother had brought would be gone by the end of the meeting. I wondered if Ingrid had told him about New York. Femi sat by his side. The rest of us were around the kitchen table.

Torin, seated to my right, had told everyone what was going with an expressionless face. Something was off about him. I couldn't put my finger on it. It was just a feeling that all wasn't right with him.

"So who made the Call?" Andris glanced around. "I know I didn't and neither did Torin. Valkyries and Mortals don't mix, which leaves one of you Immortals. Ingrid?"

She shook her head. Her eyes were bruised and red, like she'd been crying, and her usually perfect hair was a bit tousled. I hope the New York plan didn't fall through.

Blaine slanted Andris a look. "I wouldn't, so don't ask."

Femi chuckled. "I know plenty of witches, Andris, but I wouldn't and couldn't have made the Call. Despite what you might think, we Immortals stay away from witches' affairs."

"No one suspects you, Femi, Blaine, or Ingrid." I shot Andris a censuring look. "Seriously?"

"Maybe it's you, Seeress," Andris said, giving me a pointed look. "You probably sent a magical distress signal without knowing it."

"We're not playing the blame game, Andris," Torin said in a hard voice.

"I can defend myself, Torin." I narrowed my eyes at Andris. "Are you forgetting I'm new at this, Andris? I don't know any witches, except the two at our school. I don't even know what a Call is or how it is done."

"If you're in distress, you contact the Old Religion Council representative in your area," Ingrid explained. "That's usually the oldest high priest or priestess or witch or shaman. Then he or she contacts the other council members and they spread the word."

Thank goodness for Ingrid. "Thanks, Ingrid."

"It's not my job to educate you or give you information," she practically snarled.

I blinked, completely blindsided by her attack. "Excuse me?"

"Why is it you screw up and no one says anything? You really think you're above the law just because you're special?" she said.

My stomach dropped. Okay. Not exactly what I'd been expecting from her. "What are you talking about?"

"Laws, Raine. Rules you don't break, or you pay the consequences. He," she pointed at Andris, "drilled them into me. You just ignore them, and everyone is perfectly fine with it because you have a boyfriend who protects you and Immortals ready to do things for you and a mother—"

"That's enough, Ingrid," Torin said.

"Ingrid, what in Hel's Mist?" Andris snapped at the same time.

"I'm tired of everyone bending over backward for *her*. She knows the laws. Why can't she follow them? Think before she acts?" She jumped to her feet and glowered. "Mortals are not supposed to know about our existence. You expose who you are, you expose all of us."

The silence that followed showed just how unexpected her attack was. I tried to swallow, but my mouth felt like sandpaper.

"Ingrid," Torin said gently. "We understand how you feel, but you can't—"

"You don't understand. No one does. I'm tired of being ignored. For once, I want someone to take my side. See things from my point of view." She paced, her eyes darting from face to face. "I'm going to say what all of you are thinking, but won't say because you don't want to hurt her feelings. What if the two witches are speculating about us right now? What if they're asking questions or telling others? We don't know how many people they've told about her because she had the urge to show off her new abilities."

The barb hit hard and sucked the breath out of me. I'd told her about the witches yesterday. She'd seem okay with it. What happened between then and now?

"I didn't tell them anything, Ingrid," I said. "What I did, any Mortal Seeress would have done. I'm not an idiot."

"No, you're not. What you are is a novice, and you shouldn't be out reaping souls with the guys while we stay at home or—"

"That's enough." Torin's eyes glowed with fury. "Whatever issues you have, take them up with Andris or Lavania when she comes back. Leave Raine out of it."

Her chin trembled, tears rolling down her cheeks. "Do you know what it feels like to act normal for centuries? To be a part of a group who treats you like you don't matter, but you can't complain? I've kept quiet even though I've wanted to say something. I've lived with guilt when someone I've known for months got hurt and I couldn't help them. I've lived with nightmares of seeing friends die when I could have stopped it. I don't reap, so I don't have the luxury of escorting them to Asgard or saying goodbye, so excuse me if I want to vent." She stomped her feet.

Andris got to his feet and approached her as one would a wild animal. "Listen, sweetheart—"

"Don't!" She marched away from the kitchen and disappeared through the portal, leaving behind a heavy silence.

I cringed as I looked at the others. How many of them thought I got away with things because of Torin and my mom?

"I'm sorry," I whispered, feeling so small.

"Don't. You owe no one an apology." Torin's eyebrows were slashes above arctic eyes. He stared at the remaining three, daring them to contradict him. "Just so we are on the same page, Raine didn't expose us. She did what any Mortal witch or Seeress would have done."

Did he really believe that or was he just supporting me?

"What are we supposed to do now?" Blaine asked.

"Stay away from them." Torin glanced at me, something flashing in the depth of his eyes. I'd say fear, but Torin didn't spook easily. "In fact, we should all be vigilant because this could be a trap. I'm sure everyone in the supernatural world knows where the witches are. If the bastard after Raine made the Call, all he has to do is follow one of them here."

That never crossed my mind. "Maybe we should ask the ones at our school if various covens are represented and if more are coming."

Torin shook his head. "No. We don't want them to know about us, or even suspect we know why they're here. I'll make sure they don't remember your interaction with them."

"You're going to rune them?" Femi asked.

Torin nodded.

"What if they told their mother or other witches about Raine?" Femi asked. "I can find out more without arousing suspicion since I'm not a student at your school. They won't see me coming, and when I'm done, they won't remember a thing."

"We'll see." Torin slanted Andris a glance. "Do you know if Ingrid has spoken to them?"

He shook his head. "No. They don't know who she is, but she knows who they are."

Torin scowled. "Keep an eye on her. I don't know what's going on, but—"

"I'll find out. She's been acting weird for weeks."

"Blaine, have you talked to them?"

"Other than the moment at the library, no."

Torin didn't even look at me. That hurt. I was the screw-up who'd become chummy with the witches without considering the consequences. "I can rune them."

Torin shook his head. "No. I don't want you anywhere near those two."

"I made this mess; I should be the one to fix it."

He cracked a smile, but it didn't reach his eyes. "Freckles—"

"Please." His jaws tensed, and blue flames leaped in his eyes. A flutter of nervous energy licked my stomach.

There was nothing left to discuss, so Andris and Blaine left, leaving Femi, Torin, and me in the kitchen. His eyes were locked on me with unnerving intensity.

"Anyone wants to watch *Supernatural*?" Femi asked, leaving her stool and walking toward the pantry. "I'm making caramel popcorn."

I didn't respond, and neither did Torin. Flashing a sweet smile, I waited for him to smirk and say something smart-alecky. Instead, he leaned closer, sliding his arm along the table, and took my hands, eyes narrowed.

"You okay?" he asked.

I started to nod then shook my head.

"Ingrid shouldn't have attacked you the way she did. I'll talk to her."

"No, don't. She was right about some things. I shouldn't have followed Rita to the library and exposed what I can do. It was stupid and... just stupid," I whispered, feeling like crying and hating myself for it.

His grip tightened. "It's not your fault. Lavania should not have left you when she did. The first thing I'm going to do when I get to Valhalla is demand she gets back here and finish your training."

I blinked at him, my eyes burning with unshed tears. "She's a witness at my mother's hearing."

"So?" He pushed back his chair and stood.

So? What kind of shitty attitude was that? "Anything that affects Mom affects me. It is her future being decided in that court."

"I know, but she can find other witnesses." He lowered his head so we were eye to eye. "Try to keep a low profile at school until *I* fix this mess."

"But I thought that I was—"

"No, Freckles. I will fix this, okay?"

Anger threatened to swallow me. It didn't matter that I understood where he was coming from. He shouldn't disregard things that were important to me. I opened my mouth to tell him, but I couldn't speak. My chest hurt, and my throat burned. I closed my mouth and nodded.

"And do not go anywhere near those two witches," he added.

I stared back at him without moving.

"I mean it, Raine. Disobey me and you will not like the consequences." He straightened, turned, and walked away. I expected him to, I don't know, look back. Show remorse for the way he just spoke to me. He didn't.

Instead, he walked straight to the portal and disappeared without a backward glance. Tears threatened to fall, but I held them back. Crying would have been too much.

I stood, pressed my hand across my stomach to contain the pain, and scurried upstairs.

15. THE THREE STOOGES

The alarm beeped me out of a dreamless sleep. I rolled onto my back and stared at my ceiling, the events from last night flashing in my head. Torin hadn't returned last night, and this morning there was no coffee to wake me up.

Today was going to be a sucky day.

Rolling out of the bed, I refused to look outside my window. Didn't want to catch a glimpse of Torin. Downstairs, I ate breakfast without tasting it.

"Morning," Femi said, walking into the room.

"Mmm," I mumbled.

"Are you going to the store after school?" she asked.

I nodded, rinsed my bowl, and smiled in her general direction without looking at her.

"See you this evening," I said before heading outside. I couldn't help glancing at Torin's as I drove past. The garage door was open, which meant he was home. Maybe he was avoiding me, too. He'd said I should keep a low profile. Did that mean not being seen with him and the others?

The thought hurt.

I stepped on the gas pedal and left our cul-de-sac. No Harley followed me to school. That was disappointing. Someone called my name as I hurried toward the school's entrance, but I ignored them. I didn't feel like talking to anyone.

I turned the corner, and my heart dropped. Three familiar guys were coming toward me. The three guys from the club. My day just took a nosedive to crap town.

"Your lockers are right here," the office assistant told them, but their eyes were on me. I stared right back.

New students this late in the year? Mondo suspicious. Their eyes drilled into my back as I continued to my locker to put my backpack away.

"Didn't you hear me call your name, woman?" Cora asked, planting herself in front of me.

"No, I didn't," I lied and placed my calculus book on top of my folder. Then I noticed Cora's hair. It was held back with a clip. "What's with your hair?"

"Bad hair day, so stop staring," she admonished, shoving her backpack away.

I couldn't help it. She was a hair person. She spent hours treating and pampering hers. I reached out to touch her hair clip, and she slapped my hand.

"Stop it. Was that double date amazing or what?" she said.

"Give us the deets," Kicker said from across the hallway and several heads turned. She moved closer, and Sondra followed.

"Where did you go?" Sondra asked, finger-combing her hair.

"What did you eat?" Kicker added.

"You are on your own," I whispered and took off. She grabbed my arm, eyes promising retribution if I left.

"You'll get the details at lunch." Cora waved to them and allowed me to pull her along. "Gah, I'm an idiot. Next time I open my mouth after a date, slap me. For now, come up with something. Where, what, and how?"

"Why me? I didn't scream 'double date' in front of the dynamic duo."

She scowled. "What's wrong with you? You sound weird. You know, like you're not too thrilled about something."

I rolled my eyes and eased my arm from her grip. "Nothing is wrong with me. See you at lunch. You go that way," I pointed toward the English hallway, "while I head up." I nodded at the stairs.

"What do we have here?" a familiar voice asked, and I stiffened.

Cora whipped around. "Look, Raine," she said. "The Three Stooges from the club. They allow your kind at our school? Maybe we should transfer."

The guys sneered. What were their names again? There was Sebastian, the one I'd cleaned the floor with. I remembered his name because of the anime about a demon butler. I ignored them and focused on Cora.

"See you at lunch," I said and started for the stairs.

"Hey, witch," hit me from behind halfway up the stairs, and my stomach dropped. I kept walking even though icy panic crawled under my skin.

"I hear you can tell our future, Seeress," Sebastian continued. "That you're powerful."

They were part of the group in Kayville for the Call. Rita and Gina must have told them about me. I kept going upstairs, my heart pounding hard. Behind me, they kept goading me.

"We're talking to you, witch."

"Do people here know about you?"

"Can you tell me my future?"

I reached the top of the stairs and turned to face them. They were right behind me, but several students were coming up the stairs, too. Some whispering. Others pointing or videotaping with their cell phones. This was last year all over again. By lunchtime, the entire school would know about me and these idiots. So much for keeping a low profile.

"If you know what's good for you, you will shut up," I warned.

"We're not scared of you," Sebastian said. "You attacked me. That makes you a bad *witch* in my book."

"And calling people names…" a familiar deep voice said from behind me.

Then several jocks walked past me. "Gets you a serious ass-whopping around here, *boy*," linebacker Tim "Tiny" Launders said and pushed Sebastian against the wall. His buddies, Ruby "Beef" Dunlop and Taine "Junior" Alesana—a Samoan built like a Sumo warrior—grabbed the twins.

"That girl," Tiny Tim pointed at me, "is beyond your radar. You don't ever use the 'W' word around her and you don't look at her wrong."

"Yeah!" Beef and Junior shouted, their faces inches from the twins.

"In fact," Tiny Tim continued, "if you see her coming, you turn your pointy heads around and go the other way. Because no one," he pressed a finger on Sebastian's forehead, "and I mean no one messes with her when we are around. You mess with her, and you mess with us."

"YEAH!" came from the crowd that had gathered around us, most of them members of the football team. I searched the faces for Torin, scared of what he might do. He wasn't among them.

I was touched by what they were doing, but at the same time, scared of what the witches would do to retaliate.

"Tim," I said.

"Don't worry, Raine. These a-holes will not bother you again." He pressed Sebastian against the wall and bared his teeth in a snarl.

"What's going on here?" Officer Randolph, the school security officer, asked, and the non-jocks moved back. "Clear the hallway."

The linebackers backed off and pretended to straighten the shirts of the three witches.

"Nothing, Officer Randolph," Tiny Tim said, smirking. "These morons were making fun of some girls."

"We were just telling them it's not cool," Junior added, putting his arm around Twin One. He squeezed his shoulders. "But now we're buds."

"Yeah," Beef snarled and ruffled the hair of his captive. He was probably the scariest of them. He had to be three hundred pounds.

"Go to class, guys," Officer Randolph ordered everyone. Then he pointed at the three new students, "You three, stay behind."

Since the football team won the championship, the players were treated like royalty, so I wasn't surprised the guard had let them go without a reprimand.

"Thanks, guys," I told Tim and the others.

"No one messes with you, Raine," he said.

"And no one believes that witch crap either," Junior added.

"I know. Thanks anyway." I entered my math class and went to my seat. Torin was still missing. Were they back to reaping? I opened my calculus book and tried to focus on Mrs. Bates and her parametric equations.

Torin was still a no show. I put my books away before heading to lunch. The hallway was nearly empty when I started toward the cafeteria.

"We should teach those bastards a lesson," I heard Sebastian say just before I turned the corner. Without thinking, I camouflaged and pressed against the wall. They walked right past me.

"I hate jocks," Twin One said.

"They're not different from the buffoons at our school," Twin Two said.

Without thinking, I turned and followed them. This was probably the wrong idea, but I'd rather know what they had planned than wait in fear. Besides, this was keeping a low profile.

"I say we punish them," Sebastian insisted. "Humiliate them in front of the whole school."

"Football season is over, Bash," Twin One said.

They stopped by their lockers and put their books away. They didn't seem to care that people were staring at them. New students always drew attention. Three of them, all guys, all good looking, were like magnets to girls.

"I don't care," Sebastian snapped. "We put some serious mojo on them." What a douche.

"Zits or warts?" Twin One asked.

"Think big, Alejandro," Sebastian snapped.

These guys needed to be taught a lesson. I debated whether to be the one to do it. I wanted to so badly. If only Torin's threat wasn't hanging over my head. I couldn't afford to be rash.

I followed them toward the cafeteria. What if this was what the Norns had meant by Torin's protectiveness pushing me to them? Was I being timid instead of decisive because of Torin's threat? Argh, I hated second-guessing myself.

"What if they are all witches?" the other twin asked. "The girls said she's powerful, and they could all be part of her coven."

"Then we'll show her what we can do," Sabastian said.

"Dude, you're talking like you're trying to impress this witch," Alejandro said. "We are here for the Call."

We were almost at the cafeteria, and I couldn't eavesdrop on them forever. I ducked in the last room, made sure it was empty, and de-cloaked.

Cora waved at me from our table, which seemed to have been invaded by jocks. Blaine was one with them. I searched the room for Torin and Andris. They were missing. Ingrid was at the cheerleaders' table. I tried to catch her eyes. I felt so bad for her after her little lecture.

Sabastian and the twins turned and studied me. They were ahead of me in line. I stared right back at them. If only I knew what else I could do with my powers. Witches were supposed to master elements. Rita could move things. I was still wading in unchartered territory, yet I was this powerful Seeress. Maybe being a powerful Seeress didn't necessarily mean I was great at other things.

I got my food and headed to the table. Today was burger day—hamburgers and spicy chicken burgers—but being late meant all I got was PB&J. The spicy sweet potato looked overcooked, and the bean soup was unappetizing as ever. Torin was turning me into a food snob.

"Are those guys bothering you again?" Tiny Tim asked as soon as I sat.

I smiled at the linebacker. "Nope."

"What guys?" Cora and Blaine asked at the same time.

"The three pube-warts over there," Tiny Tim said, and the entire table turned to watch Sabastian and his friends. They were seated with Gina, Tina, and a bunch of fresh faces. I'd bet they were all witches. Tina looked less deathly today.

"Isn't that the dude Raine kicked at the club on Friday?" one of the students said, and the table laughed. They were making things worse. Time for damage control.

"Guys, just ignore them," I said.

Blaine's eyes narrowed as he continued to study the guy. Chances were he knew what they were because of Rita and Gina. "What happened this morning?"

While the guys went into exaggerated details, I squirmed. Lunch was too long.

As soon as I could, I escaped. But not before I indicated for Blaine to follow me. We entered the first empty room.

"We have a situation." I quickly told him what I'd overheard. "Torin gave me a long lecture yesterday about staying low and not exposing us to the Mortal world, so I don't know what we should do."

Blaine cracked a smile. "He thinks like a Valkyrie, so he's overly cautious. I've fought with Mortals without giving away my identity. We're good at it. Ask Femi." He hesitated then added, "I'll see if Ingrid wants to be involved."

I grinned. He was so nice. "She might enjoy it."

He texted her, and within minutes, she entered the room. She wouldn't meet my eyes. Blaine explained what was going on.

"I want in," she said when I finished.

"Are you sure? We're doing this as witches."

"I was a witch before I became Immortal, Blaine."

Blaine's topaz eyes narrowed. "Do you remember your spells?"

Ingrid grinned, her light-blue eyes twinkling. "Oh yeah. Do you?"

He grinned. "Like you, I was a witch before I became Immortal."

Okay, enough with the love fest. I was feeling left out. "Can I come with?"

"No," they said at the same time. "Torin wants you out of this, so stay out," Blaine added.

"I was just kidding. See you guys later." I expected Ingrid to, I don't know, apologize for the mean things she'd said yesterday, but she didn't. I left them in the room and was halfway to my class when Blaine caught up with me.

"Ironed out the plans?"

He nodded. "I'll walk you to class."

I cocked my brow. "Why?"

"Just following orders."

"What orders?" I asked, but I already knew the answer.

"Torin asked me to keep an eye on things while they're gone. You didn't respond to my text and you were gone when I stopped by your place this morning."

No wonder he'd eaten at our table. I decided to play nice and let him walk me to class.

***

"We should go shopping for junior prom next weekend," Cora said as we left the building. The Harley was still missing at the curb, but Blaine and Cora were by his car. They were watching the school entrance, but I knew I wasn't their target.

"Sure. Why not." I had to talk to Dad about adding money to my debit account. Or maybe Hawk was the person to talk to.

"We should use a portal and shop wherever we want." Cora grinned and flipped her hair. "I'm so loving the perks of being a freak."

"Who said you were one?"

"Me. I was seeing things no one else could. It became worse at PMI."

I glanced at her and frowned. Provident Mental Institute was the place local parents sent their sociopaths, which was why I wasn't using it to explain Mom's disappearance. "You never actually talked about your stay at PMI."

She shuddered. "And I will never. Oh, there's my man." Echo just stepped out of her car. "See you tomorrow. Oh, I'm working on the next vlog entry. I'll need your input later in the week."

The way she flew into Echo's arms made me wish Torin was around. I opened my car and put my things away. My eyes met Blaine's, and he walked over.

"Heading to the shop?" he said.

"Yep. You want to follow me and make sure I do?"

He cocked his eyebrows. "Do you want me to?"

I grimaced. "No."

He chuckled. "I didn't think so. You are a lot tougher than you look."

"Finally, someone that sees the real me." The real me when I wasn't screwing up and feeling like crap. I slid behind the wheel and started to close the car door, but he caught it.

He studied me with a weird expression. "You know, I've spent a couple of centuries fighting alongside women, and I don't necessarily mean in combat. I'm talking about women fighting to be seen and heard. Women fighting for survival as their world fell apart. Women sheltering children and the elderly from men mad with power."

He had my full attention. Andris and Torin tended to dominate everyone, so whenever we all got together Blaine often disappeared in the background. Yet, as an Immortal, he must have led an interesting and colorful life, just like the Valkyries.

"What I'm trying to say is Mortal women are a lot tougher than they look. Theirs is a quiet but resilient strength. Like bamboo. They can bend and get bruised, but they don't break. You may look like a china doll, but you're not that fragile. He'll get it. Just give him time." His eyes narrowed, and I turned to follow his gaze. Sebastian and the twins just left the building. "Drive safely. If you need me, you have my number."

"Happy hunting," I said. He laughed. Blaine Chapman was full of surprises.

I gunned the engine and took off. I didn't check to see what he and Ingrid were doing. Whatever it was, they'd be fine. They were Immortals, and Blaine sounded like he'd seen it all.

I paused at the stop sign and noticed a familiar blue coupe pull up behind me. Rita and Gina. What did they want? After they broadcasted what I'd seen, they were the last people I wanted to talk to. In fact, I was so over witches.

I kept an eye on them all the way to the back parking lot of the Mirage. When they pulled up behind me, I jumped out of the car, dug inside my jean's back pocket for Rita's amulet, and dangled it on its chain. Her face was red by the time they reached me. She took it.

"I want to apologize for the way I reacted on Saturday," she said.

"Yeah. Whatever." I turned and started for the shop.

"You were right," Gina said, following me. "My mother made a call and members of our coven raided Madam Bosvilles' villa. They found jars of potion made with my sister's hair, my mother's, and hundreds more. She's been stealing powers for hundreds of years. Moving from place to place, staying young."

I slowed down. Only an Immortal could live that long. I'd never heard of an evil Immortal. Not from the stories Femi shared or Blaine's accounts. I tucked that away for later.

I turned near the back entrance to the shop and faced them. Up close, Rita looked a lot better. Her eyes weren't so haunted, and her cheeks had more color.

"I'm already feeling better because of you, Raine," she said. "Thank you. Madam Bosvilles killed so many witches and took power from even more, including our mother. Her powers are returning, too."

"She's done this all over the world, in Europe, America, Australia, Asia, even South Africa," Gina chimed in. "Word spread fast, and those whose powers she stole are slowly recovering their abilities."

I forced a shrug, faking indifference, but inside, I was dancing to *Gangnam Style*. Of course, Torin would say I'd exposed an Immortal to the Mortals, but damn it, it felt good. I'd discovered an evil Immortal Seeress.

Hoping my face didn't show my emotion, I said, "You shouldn't have told the others about me."

They exchanged a puzzled look. "What do you mean?" Gina asked.

"Three new boys at school followed me around, calling me a witch."

"Sebastian and the twins?" Rita asked.

I crossed my arms and glared without saying a thing.

"But we didn't tell them," Rita protested.

"We only told our mother, who called home," Gina added.

"I swear, we never told," Rita said again.

"Yeah. Well. They know, so excuse me if I don't celebrate with you. I've gone through being ridiculed by students at school—"

"We heard about that," Rita said.

"What we don't understand is why you didn't just put a spell on the entire school or town to make them forget," Gina added.

I stared at her, blanking out. Of course, as a powerful Seeress, they expected me to know such spells. I racked my brain for an answer.

"I don't believe in messing with people's heads, so if you don't mind, don't tell anyone else about me and, uh, just leave me alone." I turned and entered the store, locking the back door behind me. Yeah, I know. It was petty and childish, and really counterproductive, but I was making a point. I wasn't one of them.

The store wasn't busy, so I went back to the car for my backpack and even got some homework done between talking to customers. When there were no more customers, I went in search of Mr. Hawk.

"Could I get an advance?" I asked.

He stared at me as though I was crazy. "I don't understand."

Warmth crept up my neck. "Mom forgot to put more money on my debit card, so I'm kind of broke. I need to buy a prom dress. Two prom dresses, actually, but I don't have the money."

"Please, sit." He pointed at the chair across from his, pulled out his phone, and punched in numbers. Within seconds, the full mirror in his office churned and dissolved into a portal. My eyes widened when I saw part of my living room. Then Femi entered the office.

"Hey, sweetie. How is it hanging, Hawk?"

I almost laughed out loud at her informal greeting. Hawk glared at her, but she didn't seem bothered by it. In his suit and tie, Hawk had an air of grimness around him that was downright intimidating. Femi was opposite him in every way. She dressed in army fatigues and T-shirts when out of her nurse's uniform. Today she sported her least favorite—a floral tunic and light-blue pants. Her black hair was spiked, and her ageless face makeup free.

"You're scaring the poor child with your glowering, Hawk. What's going on?"

"Ms. Raine tells me she doesn't have money for personal use. Were you not supposed to inform me when she needed an allowance?" Hawk demanded, staring down at the shorter Femi.

Femi's slapped her forehead. "Oh crap! I'm so sorry, doll." She walked to where I sat and squeezed my shoulder. "With everything that's been going on, I completely forgot your mother's orders."

"I repeated it several times, too," Hawk said.

"Oh, don't get your undies in a wad, big guy. I'll make it up to her. So sorry, sweetie." She rubbed my back.

I tried not to laugh at her colorful language. "That's okay. You've been so busy with Dad; it's understandable."

Hawk shot me a disapproving stare. "No, it's not okay." He sat and tapped on the keyboard of his laptop. "I can add some money to your card right now." He glanced at me from above his computer. "You said you need two prom dresses, so we are talking about how much?"

"Four hundred—"

"To six hundred a dress," Femi cut in, her hand firm on my shoulders.

Six hundred dollars a dress? Was she crazy?

"She'll also need accessories," she continued. "Shoes to go with each dress, a clutch for her cell phone and artavo, and of course, earrings, bracelets, and a necklace."

Hawk studied her, then me. I bet he could see through her extortion scheme and my guilty expression. I would never pay six large ones for a dress I planned to wear only once.

"They only have one junior prom, so of course she must look her best. But the senior prom, ah... that's going to be spectacular this year. Torin is a shoo-in for the prom king after his stellar performance at the state championship, and Raine, as his girlfriend, will be crowned the prom queen. You don't want her looking cheap in knock-offs. The best for our girl here."

Ohmigod, she was terrible. Hawk had that look Torin sometimes wore when he wanted to throttle me. Usually, he ended up kissing me. I didn't see Hawk doing it. I had a feeling he didn't approve of Femi much.

"Two thousand?" Hawk said.

"Really, Hawk," Femi said. "There's no need to be so tight-fisted."

I opened my mouth to tell him I'd be happy with a quarter of that when a knock resounded on the door. We all froze. Femi wasn't supposed to be in the shop and the portal was still open. Of course, Jared wouldn't see it, but still...

"I better go," Femi said.

I jumped as she started toward the portal. Jared must have assumed someone had said, "come in" because he opened the door and peered into the room. Energy pulsed into the office like a giant tsunami. It was familiar yet different. Whoever was out there was powerful. Femi must have felt it, too, because she turned, a frown on her face.

"Sorry to interrupt, but there are people here to see you, Raine," he said. "Hello, Ms. Femi."

"Hey, Jared. How're things?" she said, smiling so hard I was sure her teeth would pop from her gums, and she kept craning her neck to see behind him. She moved toward the door as though drawn to whoever was out there. Hawk was also on his feet, an expression I couldn't define on his face.

Jared looked over his shoulder and then closed the door. "I don't know what's going on, but there's a crowd out there asking for Raine, and I don't think they're customers."

Witches.

Panic must have shown on my face because Hawk indicated I stay behind. He waved Jared aside, opened the door, and disappeared inside the shop.

"Yes, may I help you?" We heard him ask.

"We are Raine's friends from school," Gina said.

"All of you?" Hawk asked. There was disbelief in his voice.

"No, sir. This is my mother, Stefania Donohue. I'm Gina, and this is my sister, Rita. My mother would like to apologize to your daughter, sir."

Daughter? Femi and I exchanged a smile. They must have learned that the Mirage was family owned. I angled my head to catch Hawk's response.

"My sons and nephew would like to apologize to your daughter as well, sir," a man said. "They behaved terribly toward her."

I recognized the voice of the gray-haired man who'd come to the store last week with a picture of his wife. He'd mentioned framing the smaller pictures for his sons. Must be Sebastian's sidekicks.

"I'm afraid Lorraine is busy at the moment, but I will let her know that you came."

This was stupid. I wasn't a coward, and the sooner they apologized, the faster they'd leave. I didn't want them cornering me when I was alone. I started for the door.

"Raine, let Hawk handle this," Femi warned and gripped my arm.

I shook my head. "No, I started this when I agreed to help those girls. I have to finish it."

"What are you going to tell them? Remember, your identity... *our* identity must be kept a secret at all cost."

"Even when one of us is evil?"

She blinked as though I'd slapped her. "We don't hurt people, Raine. The Valkyries are very particular about who they select to make Immortal."

If only she knew. There was Maliina and now Madam Bosvilles. "I'll explain later. Right now, I'll tell the witches in there that I'm a novice and their presence is interfering with my training." I rubbed my arms. "Can you feel that?"

"Powerful magical energy. Is the girl you told me about out there?"

I nodded.

"Okay, go." She indicated the door.

"I'm here," I called out as I pushed the door open. My jaw dropped. I'd expected Rita, Gina, their mother, the old man, his twin sons, and a sulky Sebastian in tow. Instead thirty or so pair of eyes stared at me. No wonder the air sizzled with magical energy.

16. BAD WITCHES

They watched us with varying expressions. Curiosity. Gratitude. Anger. No, actually, only Sebastian looked pissed. What did he have to be angry about? Had Blaine and Ingrid smacked him around a bit? I hoped so.

I returned smiles and nods. My eyes widened when I spied a shaman in full regalia in the back by a black woman in a big ceremonial hat. I didn't know what to think or say. It was as though people of different ages and from various parts of the world had walked into my shop at the same time.

The robes. Long, white beards and hair. Wooden staffs. One of them was so old that he leaned heavily on his crooked wooden staff. It was a wonder people weren't gawking at them through the store window.

I focused on the familiar. Rita and Gina.

Their uncertain smiles said they weren't sure how I'd react. The twins looked genuinely contrite, while Bash still glowered. Unlike the old geezers, most young people in the group were dressed like me, in jeans and T-shirts.

I glanced at Hawk to see how he was taking all this. He wore a disapproving expression. No wonder the people were focusing on me and not him. He really needed to smile more. Something changed when I faced the witches again. The traditional and witchy clothing were gone. No long hair or beards, and they held regular walking sticks and umbrellas instead of staffs.

How was that possible? Were they using magic to hide who they really were? I didn't realize Femi had moved to my side until she took my hand. I squeezed it.

Color me a coward, but I felt a whole lot better having her by my side.

The man who'd brought his wife's portrait cleared his throat and said, "Seeress, my sons and nephew—"

"Uncle Ignacio, the Noma," Sebastian interrupted.

What the heck was a Noma?

The man mumbled some words and pointed his fake walking stick at something to my right. I whipped around just as poor Jared's head lolled to the side. Ignacio gently lowered him to the floor.

"I beg your pardon, Seeress," Ignacio said. "In my haste to apologize for my sons' and nephew's deplorable behavior, I forgot there was a non-magical person in the room. We try to shield ourselves from people until we know they are practitioners of the Old Religion. He will not remember seeing us here." He glanced at the twins. "Come on, boys. The Seeress doesn't have all day."

The twins apologized and sounded sincere. Sulky Sebastian didn't. His uncle added a long-winded speech about showing respect to someone of my caliber, which was totally embarrassing. I even started to feel bad for the twins.

Rita's mother stepped forward with Rita and Gina. "I want to thank you for what you did. You exposed an evil witch and saved my daughter's life." Her voice broke. "I was a student of Madam Bosvilles', and she stole my powers, too. They are coming back." Her chin trembled.

"I'm happy I could help." Then I did what any compassionate person would. I reached out and gripped her hand.

Bad idea.

Scenes flashed in my head. A younger Stefania with the same Madam Bosvilles cooking potions. The older woman looked younger. She had to be an Immortal. She probably faked aging using makeup and disguises.

Standing in the shadows was a man. All I managed to glimpse was long black hair and his broad back before he disappeared. I shivered. Something about him was so familiar. I let go of her hand and stepped back.

Silence followed. The stares said my eyes were glowing.

"This is no time to cry, Stefania," a voice cracked like a whip from behind her, and she stepped aside to reveal one of the wizened men. He was the one with the crooked staff.

"My name is Carlos Alberto De Los Parlotes De Vaca. For thirty years, my son couldn't practice magic because of what that woman did to him. Today, he called me with the good news. His magic is coming back. May I shake your hand?"

"No," Hawk barked. "The child is a novice and is still learning to control what she sees. The visions might be overwhelming."

The old man's crestfallen face had me saying, "It is okay. I can handle it."

Someone should definitely slap duct tape on my mouth because that was the wrong thing to say. He clasped my hands and visions followed. The old man was going to die a violent death. I'd barely let his hand go when someone else took my hand. Another grabbed my arm. Scene after scene flashed in my head. People's pasts and futures. So many deaths it wasn't normal. I became overwhelmed quickly.

"That's enough," I thought I heard Hawk say.

I tried to move toward the office, but the crowd followed. Since they weren't asking questions, I assumed they just wanted to touch me, which was really creepy.

I was so focused on escaping I almost missed a vision taking place in my bedroom. I'd never had a vision of me before.

I stood near my bed laughing. A male voice came from the bathroom, but it wasn't Torin's. Then a man wearing a duster came into view. At first, the vision wasn't clear. The duster was like Echo's, long, black, and heavy, but he wasn't Echo. The dirty blond hair was like Eirik's, but he didn't sound like him. His voice was deeper, his shoulders broader and more buff. He stopped in front of me, reached out, and stroked my hair and cheek.

Please, let it be Eirik.

Panicking, I tried to see his face. As though my thoughts controlled the vision, the scene changed angles and I saw his face. Eirik. He looked different. Older. More handsome. But his eyes were cold, like a guy who'd been to hell and back. I couldn't tell whether he was happy or not.

Eirik pulled me up and wrapped his arms around me. I wound my arms around his neck. Okay. He was going to come home in the near future and I'd be happy to see him. That was good news.

Then he kissed me. Not a peck or I've-missed-you kind of kiss. He pressed his lips against mine in a deep, tongue-in-the-mouth, soul-blending kiss. Even worse, I grabbed his head and kissed him back.

"No!" I yelled, my eyes focusing on the faces around me. None of them was Eirik's. I pulled back, frantic to get away. Why was I kissing Eirik? I mean, why would I kiss him in the future?

Someone grabbed me from behind. I looked over my shoulder, expecting to see Eirik. Relief was sweet when my eyes met Hawk's. He was furious. I hoped it wasn't with me.

"Are you okay?" he asked, his voice flat.

I shook my head.

"Get her out of here," he said, practically shoving me into Femi's arms.

"Leave now," Hawk told the gathered witches. "The child is tired and needs to rest."

"Why did the young Seeress summons us here, sir?" Ignacio asked. He seemed to be the spokesperson of the group.

"I didn't," I called out without stopping. The vision of me and Eirik was my top priority now. Where in Hel's Mist would Torin be for me to kiss Eirik?

"Did you make the Call, sir?" Ignacio asked.

"No, I did not," Hawk snapped. "And we most certainly don't need your help."

"You may not need our help, but someone wants us here," Ignacio said. "There've been a dozen dead Seeresses across the globe, and your daughter might be next."

Thoughts of Eirik became secondary, and I ignored Femi's attempts to pull me into the office. I couldn't tell these people the Seeresses weren't really dead, but Ignacio's "someone wants us here" had me thinking of last night's meeting with Torin and the gang.

What if the person after me had summoned the witches? To what end? No, that didn't make sense. They would have to know who I was and where I lived to do that. Whoever made the Call lived here in Kayville and either was trying to help me or was working with the people after me. The fact that the killings had stopped kind of confirmed it.

"Miss Lorraine is not my daughter," Hawk said. "We," he waved to indicate Femi, "are her guardians. I'll say it again. We didn't make the Call and we don't need your help."

I turned to face the witches, and Femi groaned. My head was pounding, and even worse, the scenes I'd seen when the witches had touched me were on a loop inside my head. "Has anyone seen the people killing these Seeresses?"

There were murmurs and headshakes.

"He has a British accent and long black hair," I added.

That generated some excitement but no takers, until Stefania asked, "Does he have blue eyes?"

I frowned. "I think so. Why?"

"Madam Bosvilles has a friend, who looks like the man you just described. He kept in the background when I was her student."

"I've never seen him either," Rita said. "He comes and goes at night."

"My son mentioned a man, too," the old man with the crooked staff said. "He never described him. How do you know him?"

"I've seen this man and his friends in my visions," I said. "He was the one hurting the Seeresses. Where can we find Madam Bosvilles? Maybe she can lead us to him."

"She was gone by the time my coven went to her villa," Stefania said. "She's a powerful witch and probably knew they were coming."

"We'll stay until we know for sure she and this brother of hers are not headed this way," Ignacio added, and the others nodded.

Torin was so not going to like this. From Femi's expression, she didn't either. As they filed out, she planted herself in front of me, neatly blocking them from my line of vision. "They can't stay."

"What if we need? We're dealing with evil witches, possibly evil Immortals."

"Immortals are *never* evil," she practically snarled. She jerked her head to indicate the witches. "*They* can be. You can't trust them."

I sighed, the effect of the séance—if what just happened with the witches could be called that—still messing with my head. "What do you want me to do? I don't have power over them."

"But they'll listen to you. We must come up with a reason to send them home. Even though we were once part of their community, we don't mix with them. They're powerful enough to tell we are different. We have to send them packing, or we leave."

Leaving was out of the question. It was time to consult the Norns. Surely, they must know what to do in a situation like this. Heck, they could even erase minds.

"Can I just go home now?"

Hawk was staring at the still-unconscious Jared. They'd forgotten to wake him up.

"He'll be okay," Hawk said when he saw me stare at Jared. "He'll come out of it soon enough. It was a simple sleeping spell. And yes, you can go home."

"Use the portal," Femi said. "I'll bring your car home."

In other words, she wanted me safe at home. I didn't understand how she could mistrust witches when she was once a witch. I grabbed my things and headed to the office.

***

The house was quiet, but my head still buzzed with all the visions I had seen at the shop. I was putting that in the never-to-be-repeated category. I was mentally and physically drained. Then there was the vision of Eirik. That didn't make sense. He wasn't even there, so how could I have connected with him?

I dropped my backpack by the mirror and went to the kitchen to get a snack. Femi must have shopped because the fruit bowl was full. I grabbed a Pink Lady apple and rubbed it against my jacket. Transferring it to my left hand, I grabbed the knob to Dad's room and turned.

My eyes widened at the scene. Dad wasn't alone. He was asleep, but Torin stood by the head of the bed, peering at him. Andris stood on the other side of the bed while Echo rested his arms on top of the headboard.

They didn't hear me open or close the door. It was so sweet of them to check on Dad. That was one thing about these guys. They might deal with the dead, but they were very loyal and respectful to the living.

I started across the room, intending to hug Torin from behind.

"Can't we just snap his head?" Andris asked. "All our problems would be solved."

I froze, my jaw hitting the ground. What? He wouldn't dare. I'd kill him first. I opened my mouth to rip Andris a new one, but Torin spoke.

"You are right," Torin said, smirking. "I should never have healed him or talked Echo out of reaping his soul. He's been nothing but a burden ever since. The Norns wouldn't be punishing us if it weren't for him. Raine will never know we did it."

My breath got lodged in my throat, tears rushing to my eyes. "Torin," I whispered, but I didn't think he heard me.

"As long as I take his soul straight to Hel's Hall, she won't know," Echo chimed in. "Do it, or I will. I don't have time."

"No, guys. You can't do this. He is mine. I'll finish this." Torin reached down and grabbed Dad's head.

"Torin, no!" I engaged my runes and dashed across the room, twisting sideways to body slam Torin. I flew across the room and landed on the bookshelf. My shoulder rammed into something hard and white-hot pain ricocheted through me.

I jumped to my feet, but they were gone.

The bastards. I raced to Dad's side and touched his forehead. It was warm. I placed a finger under his nostrils. He was still breathing. Shaking, I backed away and looked around. I was going to rip their hearts out. All the three of them.

I picked up the books I'd dropped from the shelf with shaking hands, then used the mirror portal and went straight next door.

"Torin?" I yelled.

There was no one in the living room, but the water was running. What kind of a monster claimed to love me and then tried to kill my father behind my back. I burst into his room. At the back of my mind, I knew something was off about his room, but I didn't bother to check. He was in the shower.

"Come out right now, you piece—" I yanked opened the bathroom door just as he stepped out of the shower. Except it wasn't Torin. "Eirik?"

"Hey, babe," he said, flashing his famous boyish smile.

It was the older, more buff Eirik. He had some serious tattoos across his chest and on his arms—and they weren't runes. I recognized a few Celtic symbols including a triskelion.

"Were you coming to join me?" he asked.

I blinked. "Wh… how… what are you doing here?"

"What do you mean? I live here." He pulled me into his arms and lowered his head.

This was not right. This could not possibly be right. I brought my leg up to knee him and lost my balance. I landed on the tiled floor, pain shooting through my tailbone.

A full-blown panic hit. There was no one in the bathroom with me. The shower was dry, which meant no one was in there a second ago.

I was going crazy. I backed out of the room and into the bedroom. It was Torin's room, his framed motorcycle paintings on the walls. Seconds ago, I could have sworn I'd seen a table with cameras and photographs where the paintings were.

Something was wrong with me.

I glanced out the window and saw Femi pull up in my car. I called out her name, and she looked at me and waved. I raced downstairs and yanked open Torin's front door only to be met by a throng of people. Neighbors. People from my school. The witches from the shop. I realized the light came from the porch and the sky was dark and starless.

This made no sense. Seconds ago, the sun was still up.

"So sorry for your loss, Raine," Mrs. Rutledge said, touching my arm.

Loss? Who died? I looked for a familiar face.

"Isn't it terrible about Torin and his friends?" a familiar voice said from my left. I recognized Kicker and other girls from the swim team.

"Poor Raine," Sondra said. "Her father killed by her boyfriend."

Kicker saw me and left the group to give me a hug. "So sorry, Raine."

My teeth were beginning to chatter. "Have you seen Cora?"

"She was with Eirik in the house."

Eirik again? Hysteria bubbled to my throat. I was going mad. There was no other explanation. I tried to push past the people and go to my house, but the crowd seemed to grow bigger.

I backpedaled, staggering into Torin's house. More people stared at me with pitying expressions. I swallowed, but my throat was too tight with fear. My chest hurt with each breath, and my head felt stuffed with horrid images.

This is not real... this is not real... It can't be real.

I repeated it over and over again. I was having visions, one after another. How was that possible when I wasn't touching anyone or anything? Someone was screwing with my head. The mirror portal in Torin's living room was open. I walked through it without caring that the people at the wake could see me.

Cool air slapped my face, and I sucked in a breath. I was on top of a roof. Just like in my first vision. It was still dark, but I recognized the buildings around it and the forests and mountains in the background.

Torin, Echo, and Andris stood on the roof, their heads bowed. No, not bowed. They were staring at something and talking in low tones. I moved closer, but I still couldn't see what they were looking at. I was getting calmer now that I knew I was having visions, but I wished I knew how to get out of them.

"Torin?" I whispered.

He looked up and straight at me as though he'd heard me, but when his attention shifted, I saw what they were staring at on the roof. Celtic symbols drawn with chalk. They were like the ones on Eirik's body. Once again, I recognized the triskelion.

"That's the last one," a familiar voice said from behind me, and I whipped around.

Buff Eirik walked toward me. He winked as he passed me. I turned and followed him with my eyes. Now the group with Torin had grown larger to about a dozen men and women. Torin's back was to me, but I recognized the broad shoulders and the shaggy black hair. Where were Echo and Andris?

The moonlight created shadows on the faces of the men and women, but I recognized the triskelion on the back of their hands and on their foreheads. What did this mean? Rita and Gina's protection amulets also had Celtic symbols.

"Look who decided to join us," Eirik said, and I followed his eyes to a woman dressed in all black. I couldn't guess her age, but she had long dark hair and pale skin. She was gorgeous. Her eyes glowed under the moonlight. The group on the roof parted for her, and she went straight to Torin and slipped her arms around his waist.

The next second, they were kissing.

What? I was so going to kill him. Not just him. Her, too. I engaged my strength runes, marched across the roof past the men and women watching them, and raised my fist.

"This is for you, you jackass," I yelled.

Just before my hand connected with his face, he looked up. I barely stopped before rearranging his nose. It was Torin, yet it wasn't. Same eyes, same facial structure, same lips, but he was older. Gray peppered the hair at his temples.

I closed my eyes tight, praying for this nightmare to end. Voices reached me, as though from afar, and I cringed. *They're not real... not real... not real...*

"What happened?" Torin asked.

"I don't know. I came back from the store and found her like this," Femi said. She kept talking, but I tuned her out.

Nothing is real. It's just a vision.

"I told her to use the portal while I brought her car home," Femi was saying.

I opened my eyes. Torin squatted beside me. The younger Torin. Was he real or a figment of my imagination? I was on the floor outside my father's bedroom. My back to the door.

"Raine," Torin said.

"You're not real," I whispered. Torin would have called me Freckles.

He touched his face and his chest. "I'm real and I'm here now," he said softly. He sat across from me and crossed his legs. He peered at me. "You're going to be okay."

"I won't let you kill my father," I whispered, my voice breaking. My throat burned and my chest hurt. "I know he's sick and dying, but it's not his fault you healed him. I will not let you kill him now."

"I'd never, ever hurt him. I saved him for you and would do it again if I could," Torin murmured.

I wanted to believe him so badly. "You were kissing someone else."

"Feel free to decapitate me if I touch another woman, or man." He smirked as though laughing at his own joke. I didn't think it was funny. "There's no one for me but you, Raine Cooper. And you know it." He reached out and brushed my cheek. Only then did I realize I'd started to cry. "I love you, Freckles."

Freckles. "You... called me Freckles."

"Yes, luv. I called you Freckles." His voice was velvety soft.

I flung myself into his arms, causing him to lose his balance. He rolled with me on the floor, chuckling.

"Now I know what to say when your visions turn you into a nutcase," he said, planting a kiss on my nose.

I knew I should take offense to being called a nutcase, but for now, I just wanted him to hold me. I wound my arms around his shoulders, burrowed my face in the crock of his neck, and cried.

I felt him shift as he sat up and then stood. Without breaking his stride, he carried me upstairs. He carefully lowered me onto the bed, his movements gentle. For what seemed like forever, we spooned, his arms wrapped around my waist.

When I stopped crying and shifted to look at him, he grinned. "So I was kissing another woman?"

And I was kissing Eirik. I needed to talk about these visions or I was going to go crazy. "You were older with graying hair."

He frowned. "I'm never going to gray or grow old, unless I stop using runes."

"The guy in my vision looks exactly like you, except he's older. The visions I had of the Seeresses—he was always there. He was like the leader. I couldn't see his face properly, but I heard his voice. He has a British accent."

Torin sat up, his jaw tense. "Why didn't you say something before?"

"Because I wasn't sure. Remember, my visions were blurry? He was just a shadowy guy with a British accent. Then I saw his eyes and hair, and he looked so much like you I thought he was a relative of yours."

His eyelids lowered, but I still saw the flash in the depth of his eyes. He didn't like that. "That's why you kept asking me if I had relatives who looked like me. You should have told me, Raine."

"I know, but I wasn't sure if what I was seeing was real or not. The first clear vision I got was when I touched Rita's amulet."

"The witch." He said it like Rita was some vile creature that had crawled from a sewer.

"Yes. Being around them unlocked something. The visions I've had since have all been clear. I saw his face clearly for the first time this evening when I was having that vision meltdown. He might look like you, but he's older. Much older."

Torin rolled off the bed and disappeared through the portal. Not sure, where he was headed, I went to wash my face. I looked up and my eyes widened. Not again.

A shirtless, smirking Eirik winked at me in the mirror.

I closed my eyes tight, my heart racing. When I opened them, he was gone. Why was I getting visions of him? Why now? I grabbed a towel to dry my face and hands.

"Is this the man you saw?" Torin asked, appearing in the bathroom doorway with an old portrait. It was the same man in my vision, although the painting was not very accurate or well done.

"Yes, that's him. Who is he?"

Torin walked to my window and stared outside. From the tautness of his shoulders and the way he clenched the portrait, I was sure he wanted to hurl it.

"Torin?"

"I was hoping my mother's amulet had been stolen, but he must have kept it. The bastard."

I reacted to the pain in his voice and closed the gap between us. I rubbed his back, everything he'd told me about his mother's death flashing in my head. "He's the necromancer who killed your mother."

He turned and faced me. His eyes shocked me. There was so much rage and torment in them. "Yes, he's the necromancer who killed my mother."

"Why is he still al—? Oh. He's an Immortal," I whispered.

"And my father," he finished.

17. EVIL IMMORTAL

I slipped my arms around him and squeezed hard. It was my turn to ease his pain. His crazy obsession with finding the person who sold his family's things made sense now. I stepped back and studied his face. "Do you want to talk about it?"

"No. I'd rather find out which one of the witches was playing mind games with your head so I can snap their scrawny neck," he ground out.

"You think someone was deliberately projecting images… No, impossible." I shook my head.

"Yes. It's the only explanation. They find out your weaknesses and use them against you. Typical witch M.O."

Whoever did it knew about my fear, my father, and my relationship with Eirik. "You're right. It makes perfect sense now, but who? Bash? His father? Why would anyone do that to me? I mean, I helped them."

Torin shuddered. "Damn ungrateful witches. I'm going to—"

"No, you stay away from them. I wouldn't wish on anyone what they did to me. It was horrible."

"The more reason to hunt them down."

"No, Torin. And we're *not* talking about me after you dropped that bomb about your father. Sit." I pushed him onto the bed. "I want to know everything, because if he's really the one after me, some of the witches know one of his cohorts. A woman by the name of Madam Bosvilles."

"Is she the one Femi is pissed off about?"

"Yes. She's been stealing powers from younger witches and…" I slapped his thigh. "You're doing it again. Deliberately distracting me. We're talking about you, not me."

Sighing, he leaned back against the headboard and crossed his legs. From his expression, he'd rather pull out his nails with pliers than talk. I curled my legs under me and waited. Silence followed. He really wasn't going to talk until I pushed and nagged him.

"Did you know he was Immortal?" I asked.

"No."

"And?"

"Come here."

I shook my head. I wanted to study his face while he talked.

"I feel better when I hold you. This is *very* personal." He faked a lost puppy look.

Such a drama queen. I crawled over to him and let him pull me to his side. His chest was the best pillow, and after my vision of a certain half-naked dirty blond, I needed to surround myself with everything Torin. When he pressed a kiss on my temple, I patted his chest. "Okay, you got me. Start talking."

"My father and his clergy friends always had secret meetings. I didn't think much of it when I was young. Most necromancers were clergymen anyway. This was three centuries before the witch trials. Mom found out what they were doing, and they killed her. I watched my father die three months later. He and his friends were having a meeting when the house caught fire. No one could have survived that fire."

I wondered if he'd started it. Didn't he once say the necromancer who'd killed his mother and his friends had gotten what they deserved? "Did you—?"

"No, but I didn't stop it either. Not after what they did to my mother. So when the amulet resurfaced, I thought someone had robbed her tomb. I checked and found her body missing. Remember when you asked me if she was a witch?"

"Yes." He'd nearly bit off my head.

"I might not have liked it, but you got me thinking. I wanted you to be right. I hoped she wasn't dead. That she was an Immortal." He frowned. "So I searched. The days I was gone, I followed trails of a powerful witch that seemed to appear every two or three decades then disappear."

"Madam Bosvilles?"

"Possibly. Not many Immortals make their presence known to Mortals. As for my mother's body, it turned out one of the earls had moved her. That's when I realized whoever had auctioned the amulet, this portrait, and others trinkets did it to draw me out. The Norns confirmed it when they told you they were using me. They are using my father to come after you."

I lifted my head. "What do you think he wants?"

"I don't know. He's obviously an evil Immortal." He had that look in his eyes. Like he couldn't wait for the showdown with his father.

I shuddered. "When were you planning on telling me all this?"

Torin traced my nose, stroking my freckles. "When were you planning on telling me about your visions of him?"

My face warmed under his narrowed gaze. "You don't answer a question with a question."

"Yet you do it all the time. You weren't trying to protect me, were you?"

"Oh no." I swept a hand along his shoulder. "These big shoulders can carry all the weight of the world." And he had for so long. First, the mess with watching his mother grieve and not being able to help her. Then knowing the person responsible was his evil Immortal father. "You shouldn't try to shield me from things, no matter how unpleasant."

His lips turned up. "Like how I told you not to hang out with the witches because they screw with people's heads and you went ahead and did it?"

I burrowed under his chin. Telling me not to do something was like waving a red flag at a bull. I barreled ahead at full speed. "They're not all bad."

He stroked my arm and continued down to my jeggings-clad hips. He lifted my leg across his waist. "So what happened at the shop?"

Did he really think I could concentrate now? I trapped his roving hand with mine and threaded our fingers. "Um, I saved several people and restored their magic."

He chuckled, the sound rumbling through his chest. "You only see the positive in the mayhem. Start from the beginning."

"Disclaimer first. I didn't go to the witches. I listened to you and laid low. I was good. I was better than good." He chuckled. "I was a model Seeress. Then they came to see me and thank me and touch me." I shivered. "It got weird fast." I went into details and finished with, "They also thought we'd called for help and insisted on staying, which means—"

"We have a snitch. Whoever summoned them knows we are here and is working with my father."

Eirik. But until I could confirm it, I was not mentioning him. I focused on what happened at school with Sebastian and the twins, then the store. By the time I finished talking, Torin was sitting up. "Can you recognize the building in your vision?"

"Yeah. It's the old Grits Mill on Fulton Street and 10th North."

"Show me." He rolled off the bed.

"Just a second." I raced downstairs. Femi was with Dad. I waved her over. "I need to show Torin something from my one of my visions."

She peered at me. "You okay?"

I nodded. "I'm okay now. The visions were crazy."

"Not visions. An evil witch was messing with your head."

"I know. Torin and I reached that conclusion, too. I just don't know who would want to hurt me like that after I helped them."

"Stay away from them until we figure out what's going on, okay?"

I nodded. "I'll be home to read to Dad."

Upstairs, I grabbed the nearest shoes and followed Torin through the portal to the top of Founders Hall, the tallest building in Kayville. Founders Hall was the oldest and the main administrative building at Walkersville University. The top had a dome and spire, the perfect place for viewing the entire town. I pointed out the Grits Mill building.

"If he's marking buildings to create a magical circle around the city, he's going to etch runes or magical symbols on rooftops around town," Torin said. "Go that way while I go this way."

I went to the right, searching everywhere for the triskelion. Below, students walked across the quad and into buildings. The university was already preparing for spring Aggie Day.

"Got it," Torin called out.

The drawing wasn't on the flat rooftop. It was on the town-facing side of the dome. Torin removed his artavus from the inner pocket of his leather jacket and pulled a Jackie Chan move—jumping off the roof and running up the drum and the dome. Only he did it better. At a Valkyrie speed. He etched a block-and-protect bind rune over the witch symbol.

He landed gracefully beside me, like a cat, and flashed a smug grin. "Let's see who will win this battle. Next stop, Grist Mill."

Father and son rivalry had just taken on a new meaning.

***

"You've got some nerve demanding my presence, St. James," Echo said, entering the kitchen at the mansion with Cora in tow. "I was in the middle of something, so this had better be good."

"My father is coming to town," Torin announced.

Andris choked on his drink. Blaine and Ingrid traded puzzled looks. Ingrid was still acting like I didn't exist. I wasn't even going to stress about it.

Echo laughed. "Now that's definitely worth my time."

Andris stopped sputtering long enough to say, "Your dad is dead, Torin."

"He's very much alive and possibly an Immortal. An evil Immortal. He killed my mother to hide his necromancer activities and is now coming for Raine. We are going to stop him."

If he was going for shock factor, he nailed it. Jaws dropped. But once again, Echo didn't seem surprised.

"Someone here is working with him," he continued, eyes narrowed as he glanced at faces around the room. We looked at each other as though trying to figure out which one of us was guilty.

He was getting some weird kicks out of keeping everyone on edge. I walked to where he stood with his arms crossed and legs apart, clearly using his stance to try to intimidate the guilty party.

"Seriously? This is how you're going about this?" I asked.

He cocked his brow as though surprised I was challenging him. "They need to know how dire the situation is. Someone here is working with my father."

"But we agreed yesterday that none of us is guilty," I said. I glanced at the others. "Sorry, guys. He can be a bit melodramatic. The bottom line is someone here in the valley sent out a witch-in-trouble alert or the Call, as they refer to it. We don't know if the witches are here to help us or to support his father."

"Do Hawk and Femi know what's going on?" Cora asked.

"Yes, but they're not guilty," I said.

Torin grabbed me around the waist, when I could have walked away, and pinned me to his side. "Quit hijacking my meeting," he growled in my ear.

"Then quit behaving like a douche." I tried to wiggle out of his arms, but his grip tightened.

"I vetted Femi and Hawk, Cora," Torin said. "They are loyal to Raine's family. I believe that whoever made the call did it knowing my father would find out about it and follow the witches here. It might explain why they stopped going after Seeresses. We even set a trap in a witch's shop in Philly, but so far nothing's happened there either. He knows where we are."

"Just one question, St. James," Echo interrupted. "What makes you trust me? My first loyalty is to mine." He pressed a kiss on Cora's temple. "Then to my goddess."

I expected Torin to lose it. Instead he smirked. "I don't trust you, Grimnir, but I'm counting on Cora and your feelings for her. You wouldn't do anything to hurt her best friend and screw up what you have going with Cora."

"He's right," Cora said, glancing up at Echo. "You betray my best friend and I'll hurt you in ways you couldn't possibly imagine."

Echo actually winced. Then he slanted Torin an annoyed glance. "What do you want from me? Like I said, I could be reaping or…" He winced when Cora elbowed him. "Woman, you jab me again…"

Cora grinned.

Andris watched them and shook his head. "How are we going to find out who is working with your father?"

"We'll draw them out. They've already started drawing their witchcraft symbols on rooftops. I think they're creating a magical circle around the city to contain whatever mayhem they're planning. I want to know what they mean and that's where Echo, Ingrid, and Blaine come in. You all practiced the Old Religion at different periods and should be able to figure out what we're dealing with."

"Can we see them?" Ingrid said.

Torin pulled out his artavus and etched the symbols on the counter. He stepped aside and allowed the three to study them.

Ingrid shook her head. "I recognize the triskelion, but it looks like things are growing on its legs."

Blaine traced part of it. "It is a combination of symbols."

"Move aside, Immortals," Echo said. He removed his artavus and drew four different symbols, one on top of the other. When he was done, he'd drawn the exact symbol from the Walkersville dome. "They used the triskelion to hide the *Ogham* writing underneath it."

Ohm? "What is that?" I asked.

Echo glanced at Blaine. "Want to tell them, Immortal?"

Blaine ignored him.

Echo smirked. "They're Druidic and ancient Irish Celtic alphabet, something Pretty Eyes here should know. You know what this one means?" He pointed at the symbol.

Blaine shrugged. "Before my time, Grimnir."

Echo chuckled. "But you must have seen them on stones in Ireland, or Scotland, or wherever it is you're originally from."

Fire flashed in Blaine's eyes. "Grave stones and cairns. They are also used to mark boundaries."

"Utter, boy. I knew there was a brain behind those pretty eyes." Echo glanced at Torin, oblivious to the fact that Blaine wanted to rip into him. "They've probably used *Ogham* to create a magical circle. We'll need to find all the symbols to see how wide their circle is. It might cover the whole town or just Raine's neighborhood to contain her within the circle."

I shivered.

"There could be several messages hidden in the symbols, too," Blaine said. "One using *Ogham* and another using the Celtic symbols. We should decipher both."

"Good. Let's do that. Whatever my father is planning is not going to work," Torin vowed. "Not in this town. We're going to check every roof, until we find all the symbols. Then we'll replace them with bind runes to protect the city and block runes to stop them from entering it. If they come into town, they'll be forced to camp outside the residential areas. I'm talking about the forests and farmlands. Use your phones to take pictures of the symbols and the house. Andris, can you monitor which houses we've marked?"

Andris got out his tablet and showed off his Holy Grail of software, an interactive map with satellite imaging. Once he explained how it worked, he handed it to Cora.

"You don't have an artavus, so make yourself useful," he said.

"Hey, don't talk to her like that," Echo warned.

"Easy, big guy," Cora said, patting Echo's arm. "You don't fight my battles." Then she glanced at Andris and cocked an eyebrow. "What's in it for me?"

"I'll help you with your dad's blog."

Cora grinned. "Really?"

"Throw the garlic bread in the oven before we get home and we have a deal."

"Deal. I've been wracking my brain about what to do with the blog."

We took off, leaving Cora in the house with the tablet. The guys zipped from street to street and scampered up roofs like monkeys on sugar rushes. Now I understood why Andris hadn't wanted to be tied to his tablet. They were having way too much fun. Who was the fastest? How many houses and building could they mark? It wouldn't have been so bad if they didn't brag.

***

It was dark by the time we finished. The guys were still on runic energy rushes.

"Who won?" Echo asked when they got back to the mansion.

"Dude, you shouldn't even be asking that," Andris said. "You were eating my dust most of the time."

"Andy, you didn't stand a chance. Did I win?" Echo tried to see the tablet.

"Was I supposed to keep a tally? Oops." Cora turned off the tablet. "Hungry anyone? The garlic bread is ready and your housekeeper is an amazing cook." She went to the oven and removed the bread.

Everyone crowded around the food. I just wanted to go home and figure out what to do about Eirik. Alone. After a long shower. All that running had left me tired. Maybe I should contact the Norns. They reluctantly answered my questions whenever I asked, and I needed some answers now. I shrugged off Torin's jacket. He'd let me borrow it when it got cold.

"I'll see you guys tomorrow," I said to the room and gave Torin his jacket. I saw the question in his eyes. "I'm just tired."

"But dinner..." He pointed at the tray the others were attacking.

"I'm not hungry."

Wrong thing to say, because he got that look on his face. The one that said he wouldn't stop until he fixed whatever problem was bothering me. He couldn't fix everything, but try telling him that.

He walked me out of the kitchen into the wide hallway connecting the foyer and the two downstairs bedrooms. My eyes found the door to the room that used to be Eirik's.

"Is anyone using Eirik's old room?"

"No." Torin studied my face then glanced at the door. As though he could read my mind, he added, "Do you want to see it?"

I nodded. He didn't ask why I wanted to see the room and I didn't explain. I wouldn't know where to start. Sure I was taking the coward's way out by not telling him about my visions of Eirik, but I would once I figured out why I was having them and how. He still felt threatened by my relationship with Eirik. He tried to hide it though.

Eirik's room was so far from the main part of the house it might have been meant for a housekeeper. Or maybe it was once part of the pool house and the original owners decided to connect it to the main house. Might explain why the kitchen's back door opened into a hallway instead of the pool deck.

Funny I hadn't really thought about all that until now. But then again, Eirik had spent most of his time at my house, so we rarely hanged out here for me to notice or care.

Torin and I didn't speak again until I was inside Eirik's room. Nothing had changed; even his bed was unmade. "Looks like someone slept in here."

Torin's eyes narrowed. "We told Mrs. Willow not to disturb this room."

"Where does Blaine sleep?"

"Next door, but his room is smaller. I don't think he'd sneak in here. That's just not his style."

Eirik's cameras were on the table, and I found myself counting them. One was missing. Had he taken it with him to Asgard? He didn't have a camera when he'd come back and helped us fight Grimnirs. Maybe he'd taken it to Hel. I'd been too distraught to notice anything that day. He might have come back in here and taken it before leaving.

I studied the pictures on the walls. Most of them were of nature, but he had quite a few of me and Cora.

"You miss him," Torin said in a subdued voice.

"Yes." I glanced at him, and for the first time I didn't see the flicker of annoyance. "But I worry about him more. I can't help it. He was a part of my life for so long." *Tell him about the visions*, urged a voice at the back of my mind. I ignored it and studied the room, noticing things that didn't make sense.

What to tell him and what to ignore?

Should I find a way to contact Eirik first? If he was the one working with Torin's father, he might need help. When his dark side took over, reasoning went out the window. On the other hand, look at what hiding my visions about Torin's father brought us. Nothing. Instead, I had doubted Torin and he'd spent days searching for his mother and hoping she was an Immortal.

Torin took my arms and turned me around. His eyes were shadowed as he lifted my chin and stroked my face. "Today has been rough on you, hasn't it?"

Just like that, everything was clear. This was Torin. The man I was madly, truly, and insanely in love with. Keeping secrets from him was beyond stupid. I tried to swallow, but my throat was tight with guilt and anger at myself.

"Eirik is back," I said in a voice barely above a whisper.

Torin glanced around the room and smiled. "Because of the unmade bed?"

"That's part of it. I saw him in my visions, Torin. He's working with your father."

Torin frowned. "But the visions were fake."

"Some were, but others were real." I sighed. "It's hard to explain. Trust me. Eirik is back, and this just confirms it. His closet door is open and there are clothes on the floor. Unless someone slept in here, his room shouldn't be this messy. His mother—the Immortal who raised him was a neat freak. She couldn't have left his room like this. And a camera is missing. A Nikon. It was his favorite."

Torin walked to the closet and looked around. He picked up a shirt from the floor, sniffed it, and then dropped it. He pivoted on his feet and entered the bathroom. When he reappeared, he was holding a towel.

"It's wet. How could he have been here without me knowing?" he asked.

Of course he shouldered all the blame. I was sure there was a name for people like him, but someone needed to tell him he wasn't a god.

"You don't live here, Torin, so of course you missed him. You've also been busy chasing your father."

He dropped the towel and closed the gap between us. "And missed something right under my nose. You're really not helping."

"Ego check, Valkyrie. Eirik could have come in and out during the day while you and the others are at school or in the middle of the night while they slept and you are at your place. This house is huge and his rooms is way over here."

"Mrs. Willow would know if he's been here. Come on." He caught my wrist.

I dug in my heels. "You can't go to her place now."

"Why not? We need answers." He tugged at my arm.

"Quit manhandling me, you Neanderthal. People just don't fall in line and do your bidding because you demand it."

He smirked. "Actually, they do."

"Not this time. One, it's late to be paying Mrs. Willow a visit. Second, it's her home and I'm sure she values her privacy. Third, you don't need proof. You already have my word that I saw him in my visions." His eyes narrowed. "He might also be the one making messes in the kitchen."

Torin let go of my arm, his eyebrows disappearing under the curly mass of hair on his forehead. "Explain."

"You really need a haircut." I reached up to touch his hair.

He trapped my hand and growled. "Are you deliberately trying to drive me insane?"

I grinned. The fatigue I'd felt earlier was gone. Fighting with him often energized me. "Ingrid told me someone's been making messes in the kitchen with leftovers and the others deny they did it. I also heard weird noises in the kitchen the other day, but when Ingrid checked, there was no one there. Eirik is here." I bet he was the one watching me before I used the portal.

Torin made a face. "No one tells me anything."

"That's because you intimidate people. Especially poor Ingrid."

"What's your excuse? Why didn't you tell me about Eirik when we talked earlier? It's obvious he's the one feeding my father information about you. The traitor."

"Eirik would never betray me."

"Then why is he working with my father?"

"I don't know. I just know he wouldn't betray me."

He made a derisive sound, somewhere between a chuckle and a snort. "Back to you keeping secrets. Why didn't you tell me?"

"I, uh... He looked different in my visions. Buff."

"So he's been bench pressing in Hel; that's not an excuse." He tilted his head to the side and studied me as though weighing my words. "What is really going on, Freckles?"

I started to shake my head then sighed. "I was hoping for proof first because I don't trust my visions."

"So far you've been spot on," he said. He cupped the back of my head and pressed his forehead against mine. "Okay. It's been a long day and I'm sure you're exhausted. I know I am. So let's do this the right way. Whatever is going on, we can deal with it together. I promise not to get mad."

"I was making out with Eirik."

Torin's eyebrows flattened. I expected a vow to snap Eirik's neck. Instead he laughed, his breath fanning my face.

"You and Eirik? Not going to happen."

I frowned. "I saw it, Torin. Three times. One time he was in the shower asking me to join him."

Torin stopped smiling and lifted his head from mine. "That's impossible. Someone is messing with your head."

He was so arrogant he believed he knew everything. "Listen, Einstein. I know what I saw, and it bugs me. If you're not going to believe me, I'm going home." I walked away.

"Whoa. Stop."

I glanced back. "Why?"

"When I found out you were a Seeress, I talked to Lavania to find out about Seeresses, to learn what you can and can't do. I figured I couldn't help you if I didn't know what you're facing."

He really was the best boyfriend ever. I walked back and took his arm. "Thank you."

He flashed his I-know-I'm-awesome grin. "Lavania told me over and over again that Seeresses can't see their own futures. It's just the way things are. Someone planted those scenes in your head, Raine. A witch. Told you—"

I covered his mouth. "Don't say it. One more mention about how right you were will get you kneed hard."

"I wasn't going to. Do you remember the first time you saw Eirik?"

"At the shop. The witches were crowding me. Some wanted to shake my hand while others just wanted to touch me."

"And you didn't see Eirik among them?"

I wrinkled my nose. "No. You think Eirik is doing this? He's not a witch."

"It's in his blood. Both Odin and Frigga practice Seidr. And Loki is just like them, too. All bloody witches." He placed his arm around my shoulder and led me out of Eirik's room. We could hear the others arguing in the kitchen as we approached. The hallway portal was to the left of the kitchen.

"Told you so... told you so..." Torin sang softly.

"Shut up." I bumped him with my shoulder.

The portal responded to us and opened into my living room. Voices reached us first, but a familiar laugh had me looking at Torin with wide eyes. I ran into the kitchen.

18. THE TRUTH HURTS

"MOM!"

She turned, pitch-black curtain of hair flowing down her back. Her green eyes grew shiny with tears. "Sweetheart."

Fighting tears, I ran to her and would have knocked her over if she weren't so tall and fit, and, of course, a Valkyrie.

She threw her arms around me. "I've missed you."

I squeezed her back. I'd missed her and worried about her and even gotten a little angry with her. Just a little because I'd tried to understand. "I heard the gods were deliberately delaying your return."

She leaned back and studied my face "Where did you hear such nonsense?"

"Norns."

"She can hear them by wishing it," Torin said.

"Really?" I couldn't tell whether she was pleased or not. She planted a kiss on each of my cheeks, leaned back, and studied my face. "I'm back now, honey. We'll deal with them together."

Just hearing her say that made me feel better. Did that mean she was officially back as a Valkyrie? Before I could ask, her gaze shifted to Torin.

"Come here, you wonderful man." She enveloped him in a hug. "Thank you for watching over them while I was gone."

Mom mothered everyone. Flamboyant. Generous. She had a big heart and an even bigger personality. Looking at her, you'd think she was a throwback from Woodstock instead of a powerful Valkyrie with Norn abilities.

Torin wore a weird expression on his face, like he was surprised and wasn't sure what to do. For nine centuries he hadn't had a family, except Andris as a companion and annoying younger brother, and had closed himself to love. Mom was welcoming him into ours, and he didn't know how to deal.

I crossed my arms and mouthed, "Hug her back."

He did, but tentatively as though he expected Mom to push him away. If only he knew. She was a hugger. A rock-sideways-squeeze-tighter hugger. A spasm crossed Torin's face as his arms wrapped around her.

Smiling, I turned and hugged Lavania. "I'm so happy you're back."

She chuckled. "When I left you were getting tired of learning about runes."

I'd been eager to see visions. If only I'd known. "That was before the witches and the mayhem."

"That bad?"

"Oh yes."

"Then we'd better start working tomorrow." Like Mom, she liked long flowing dresses, although she could rock some high-end designers. Unlike Mom, she looked about twenty-two despite being several centuries older than Torin.

Mom was still thanking Torin when I turned around.

"FYI, Mom. I took care of myself with very little help from him," I teased, joining them.

Mom arched her eyebrows. "I know you did, honey. Come here. I want to hear everything." I took her hand. It was nice to have her home. She had a way of making big things appear insignificant.

Lavania joined us, and we told them everything that had happened since they'd left. When we stopped, Mom was staring at Lavania with lips pressed into a pinched line.

"Tell them, Lavania," she said.

My eyes volleyed between them. Confusion flickered in Torin's eyes. Femi nursed her cup of tea as though she wasn't listening, but I was sure she didn't miss a thing.

"Tell us what?" Torin asked.

"Is this about Eirik?" I asked, a little scared of what they might say.

Mom frowned. "No, honey. We don't know why he would side with that odious man." She glanced at Torin. "Sorry, dear. But I'm sure he didn't do it willingly. Eirik would never hurt or betray you. Something else is going on here. Come on, Lavania."

Lavania uncrossed her legs and leaned forward. Reaching up, she tucked a lock of hair behind her ears as though nervous, but her eyes were direct when they met Torin's. "This concerns your father, or the man I only knew as the Earl. I prayed this day would never come, Torin. I'm so sorry. What do you know about him?"

"He was the illegitimate son of an Anglo-Saxon nobleman," Torin said in a tone that made it clear he didn't want to discuss his father. This conversation was going to reopen deeper wounds.

"That was his way of re-inventing himself. Femi can tell you how often and industrious Immortals have to be every few decades."

Torin's jaw flexed. "Did you turn him?"

"No. My mentor did, and she's the one he contacted when you and your brother went to war. He wanted both of you turned, but your brother chose death." She chugged water from a bottle before continuing. "William was an Immortal way before he met your mother, Torin. He was born in Hellenistic Greece and fought in more wars than I can name." She smiled. "He had quite a reputation even among Valkyries. Tough. Unstoppable. A force of nature other Immortals revered and—"

Mom cleared her throat and gave Lavania a piercing glance. It was obvious Lavania might have had a thing for the Earl.

"I'm regressing," she said, her cheeks pink. "When he met your mother, William needed to become a new man and enter the British society. Marrying your mother made that possible. The Normans had defeated the Anglo-Saxons and were revitalizing England, building monuments and pouring in money. Not that your father needed that. He'd accumulated enough wealth over the centuries, but as an Immortal, that was not the kind of thing you advertised. He had his group of Immortal friends, some of the clergymen, but they continued to help Valkyries whenever their services were needed. When your father 'died' in the fire and left no heirs, the king gave the title 'Earl of Worthington' and all the earldom to your uncle, your mother's only brother. Most of your relatives you see now are from your mother's side of the family."

No wonder none of the Earls of Worthington looked like Torin or his father. I glanced at Torin, but I doubted he was making that connection. Rage brewed in the depth of his eyes.

"So marrying my mother, a Norman, was the perfect cover," Torin said.

"Not just any Norman. A Norman *noblewoman*, King Richard's third or fourth cousin twice removed. Your noble blood comes from your mother's side, not your father's."

Torin leaned forward, his voice harsh. "I don't care about my noble blood. Why did he kill her? Another cover?"

Hearing the pain in his voice, I got up from my seat on the other side of Mom, walked around to the armchair of his seat, and reached for his hand. At first, he didn't respond, but soon he was gripping my hand so tight it hurt. I engaged pain runes, but my insides knotted with anxiety and I felt his emotional pain as though it was mine.

"No, it wasn't," Lavania said. "William is an ambitious man, but we didn't know how far he was willing to go until he killed her. All the years he fought and defended humanity, he believed, had earned him the right to be a Valkyrie, to meet and live in the halls of the gods. It became an obsession."

"He doesn't have the temperament to become a Valkyrie," Femi added.

I stared at her with wide eyes. A quick glance at Torin showed him staring at Femi with narrowed eyes. I could just imagine his thoughts. He should have vetted her thoroughly.

"You've met him?" I asked.

"Our paths crossed," Femi said. "You don't live as long as we have without our paths crossing."

Did that mean William de Clare had deliberately stayed out of Torin's radius? The tension in Torin's jaw and the increased grip on my hand said he had reached that same conclusion.

"The Valkyrie Council decided he must remain an Immortal and protect humanity, but the Earl thought he'd found a way to leave this realm and get close to the gods. He believed he needed a new soul to escort to Asgard and then he'd be able to access the Bifrost."

The implication hit me hard, and I sucked in air. That bastard had killed his own wife to get a soul. The silence that followed was heavy, but I felt Torin's pain in every breath he took and every pound of his racing heart. I wasn't sure how much he could take. I looked at Mom and begged her with my eyes to make Lavania stop, but she shook her head.

"About a century ago, he started talking to other Immortals who felt they had the right to move through the realms like the Valkyries. He has acquired quite a following."

"Where's her soul?" Torin asked in a low voice.

"Torin, please don't—"

"Stop lying to me," he spoke so calmly, which was worse than if he'd yelled. "I can forgive all the crap about who my father is and the fact that he's an Immortal, but you refused to let me escort my mother's soul to Asgard or say my goodbye, Lavania. Why? There are no laws that say you can't escort a family member. You made that up and I need to know now."

What the hell? I'd assumed his mother and brother were both in Asgard. Lavania stared at her hands, and Mom couldn't meet my gaze. As for Torin, I thought I had seen him furious. Not like this. Runes appeared on his skin. So many of them I couldn't tell what kind they were.

"Mom?" I begged.

"Sweetheart, there are some things—"

"Just tell him. Where is she?"

"He used a spell to bind her to him."

My ears started ringing as blood drained from my head. Torin jumped up and stormed off. I ran after him, engaging my runes. When he took off, I was right behind him. He cut through the residential area like a hurricane, so angry, so out of control nothing in his way stayed standing. His bellow of rage filled me with anguish.

When I caught up with him, he was headed north. It was too dark for him to run through the damn forest, glowing runes or not. He could fall and seriously hurt himself. Even a Valkyrie wouldn't recover from a mashed-up brain.

"Stop, Torin."

He glanced back as though surprised, then plunged into the forest like some wood-chopping machine, flattening everything in his path. The sound of trees snapping and crashing echoed in the dark.

I stopped and wiped my forehead with the back of my hand, tears blocking my throat. So scared I wanted to scream, I stomped my feet. "TORIN!"

The ground shook. Did I do that? I looked up and down the street. No cars. Raising my foot, I brought it down. A tremor radiated from where I stood.

Okay, that wasn't a good thing to do. I peered into the trees, debating whether to go after him. Of course I had to. From the looks of things, this must be his place for releasing steam. I just didn't remember seeing any fallen trees during our previous runs.

Carefully, I made my way past the rocks and trench bordering the road and studied the fallen trees. Torin was gone, his glow hidden by the thick forest despite the line of fallen trees.

Tomorrow the rangers would have a theory for this. Trees being uprooted from the ground without a trace of tires weren't common. If Torin left footprints, and I was sure he did, another alien story would surface in *Kayville Daily*. Cora's father, a sci-fi writer, had already started an alien invasion book series after the Grimnirs destroyed a vineyard. That had baffled local and state reporters. Then there were the people going crazy and turning on each other at The Hub and an indoor playground because of Eirik. Kayville was starting to turn into a little town of horrors.

The poor fallen trees. I touched one uprooted root, wishing we didn't leave so much supernatural evidence behind every time a soul reaper threw a hissy fit and vented.

A movement came from my left, and I jumped back. It came from the fallen tree on my left. The leaves rustled and moved as though something was crawling from under the tree. A black bear was my first thought. Torin had crashed the tree on top of a freaking sleeping bear.

The tree lifted.

It wasn't just any black bear. It was huge enough to lift the tree. My heart hurtling to my throat, I stepped back, not realizing how close I was to the manmade slope bordering the road. I lost my footing and fell backwards.

Rocks and sticks dug into my skin as I rolled toward the road. I tried to break my fall, tendrils of panic coiling around me.

I scrambled to my feet at the edge of the road, expecting the bear to come lumbering after me. Instead, the tree that had fallen was now upright. And there was no bear under it.

No, it couldn't be. Echo had said people of the Old Religion like the Druids could control elements. Did I cause the tree to lift up and replant itself by reattaching its root?

Blood pounding past my ears, I stood there undecided. Where was Torin? I needed him. I peered past the now standing tree, but there was no glowing being anywhere. Mastering some courage, I pulled myself back up to the fallen trees and touched another root. As it moved and struggled to lift itself, the roots sank into the ground.

Laughing, I touched the next root and another. Then I splayed my hands like some all-powerful witch and yelled, "Stand and let your roots sink into the earth. Live and be the giver of life and shelter."

Okay, so I got carried away, but it seemed to be working. The trees rose, creaks and rustles filling the air, the earth shaking as roots disappeared into the ground. Where was Torin? He should see this. It was really awesome.

Pleased with myself, I ran down to the middle of the road, spun around at a super speed with my hand held up, and woo-hooed. This could be the start of a trend. A pissed-of Torin hell bent on destroying everything in his path and me following him and cleaning up his mess.

Nah, that sounded exactly like what Norns did. Cleaned up after Valkyries.

This was different. He was hurting deep inside. Somewhere even I couldn't reach. His father was the devil incarnate. To do something so despicable to his own wife took a special kind of evil.

A flash of light came from deep inside the trees and pulled me to the present. It was so bright the glow kissed the treetops. Within seconds, Torin screeched to a stop beside me. His eyes burned under the glowing runes.

"What are you doing?" His voice whipped through the night, and I winced.

"Trying to get your attention," I said. "See, I fixed all the trees you destroyed. Cool, right?"

"You do not want to be around me right now, Freckles."

"I disagree. I plan to be around you when you are happy, sad, pissed off, hurting, acting like a jackass, goofing off, or showing off. Whatever and whenever. You and I are a package deal, pal. Equal partners and all that jazz." I pointed at a nearby tree and moved my finger left and right. The tree swayed. "Any time you want to destroy nature, get me first."

He leaned in until we were eye level. "Go home, Raine." His voice was mean.

"Only if you come with me. You want to stay out here, then I'm staying, too. You want pull a Flash move and sprint to Portland and back, then I'll either run with you or wait out here until you come back. But I'm not going anywhere without you, Torin St. James."

My words only seemed to infuriate him. He stepped back and thrust his fingers through his hair. "You know I don't take crap from little girls."

"I know, but that's so six months ago. You didn't scare me then and you don't scare me now." I walked to the edge of the road and sat. He remained standing. "Did you hear Ingrid's news? She's going to intern for some fashion editor at a fancy magazine in New York."

"And I care about this why?" he snarled.

"She's your ward or Immortal companion to your little brother. Do you think Andris will go ballistic?" A car was coming and he was still standing in the middle of the road. Anxiety twisted my insides, but I engaged my speed runes just in case I had to snatch him out of the way. "Or maybe he'll realize how much he loves her and go after her. Carry her out of the newsroom and bring her home. That would be so romantic." Dang it. He wasn't moving. "Ouch! That hurt. I think a snake bit me."

He was by my side in a fraction of a second. "Where?"

The car drove passed. "It's nothing. Just a stick. Can we go home now?"

He sat without saying a word. Usually he'd make a scathing comment about how I'd manipulated him. He rested his elbows on his knees and bowed his head. "She's been attached to him for over nine hundred years, Raine. Nine centuries of watching that bastard do all sorts of despicable things."

"I know." I rubbed his back. His muscles were tight, but the sparks caused by the runes on both of us seemed to relax him.

"I'm going to kill him."

He spoke so calmly a chill shot up my spine. I swallowed and tried to act nonchalant. I pushed my fingers through his hair and massaged his scalp. "I know."

"It's what he deserves. His head severed clean. Heart ripped out of his chest. I would not have been a Valkyrie if it weren't for him."

I almost reminded him that Lavania had given him a choice and he'd chosen Immortality. His brother hadn't. "Do you see James often?"

"Once in a while. Valhalla is huge, and they're always busy." He sighed. "We'd assumed Mom went to Hel's Hall. When Andris and I were assigned to Goddess Hel, I searched for her, but the place is even bigger than Asgard."

The cold was slipping under my pants despite the runes, but it must be worse for him. Unlike my long-sleeved shirt, he'd left his jacket at the mansion and only wore a T-shirt. I rested my head on his back and tried to warm him.

What was he going to do with his mother's soul? Take her to Asgard? I didn't get a chance to ask Mom if she'd been granted Valkyrie status. The thought of Dad going to Hel instead of Asgard filled me with dread. It wasn't that the place was bad. According to Echo, the Halls had plenty of rooms. The worst place was Corpus Strand, the island for the criminals.

A few more cars zipped past us, definitely speeding. I watched their taillights disappear toward town and wondered how long it would be before my ass went completely numb. Someone should come up with warmth runes for moments like this.

"I wonder if she's the reason he's never tried to find me," Torin said. "He knows I'm a Valkyrie and might see her."

"And don't forget. He wants to be you." That was it. I'd reached my limit. I stood and pulled him up. Or he allowed me to pull him up. "We are going home. I'm going to make us hot chocolate. Then you're going to hold me until we fall asleep, because tomorrow we have to come up with a plan."

"What plan?"

"How to go after the original Earl of Worthington so *I* can decapitate him."

Torin frowned. "I would never allow you to take a life."

"I would to save you or any one of our basketball-team children."

He laughed. The sound started deep in his chest and built up until he doubled over. Then he reached down, wrapped his arms around my thighs, and lifted me up. "You say the craziest things."

"But you love me anyway."

He studied my face. "I don't know. Let me think about it."

"Jackass." I thumped his head with the heel of my palm, then pushed his hair out of the way and kissed the spot. His eyes glowed. "Let's go home."

"As long as we agree on one thing. You are a healer, not a killer. Even the trees whispered it tonight as they lifted themselves from the ground. It was beautiful to watch and humbling that you did it."

"I guess I'm kind of awesome," I said.

"You've always been." He lowered me down and planted one on my lips. With our runes engaged, I could swear I felt every feeling flowing through him. The good, the bad, and the ugly.

***

I woke up with a smile on my face and was still grinning when I left the shower. Mom was home and a cup of coffee waited on my bedside table. I picked it up and walked to the window.

A shirtless Torin raised his mug. For the first time in months, I'd slept and woken up in his arms. My life was a total mess, but little things like that made it bearable.

I lifted my coffee and saluted Torin. Then I went to my closet to find something to wear. Ten minutes later, I hummed and skipped my way downstairs.

Mom was in the kitchen with Femi. I got another tight hug I couldn't escape. Didn't want to. I'd missed her hugs. "Morning, sweetheart. Happy you're still leaving your door open."

"I follow house rules whether you are here or not," I lied and slipped out of her arms.

"Happy to hear that." Then she and Femi exchanged a glance and chuckles.

My face grew warm. I'd broken it a few times. "Going to check on Dad. See you after school."

"I don't think you should work at the store anymore, honey. Lavania is back, and you two should get back to your studies."

Until the incident with the witches, I'd actually enjoyed working at the shop. "I'll talk to her today and see if we can work out a schedule or something. I mean, I don't mind helping at the store a couple times a week, Mom."

She shook her head. "Not a good idea. I don't like that the witches know where to find you. Torin can take care of the ones at school because he knows them. The ones out there are too many and we don't know who they are. Some of them could be working with Torin's father."

Home one day and already changing the rules. Great. I sighed. "Fine."

"Then we'll talk about your prom and what you're going to wear." Her voice rose with excitement.

I groaned. She was going to butt in and force me to wear something *she* liked and I absolutely loathed. "I already know what I'm going to wear, Mom. Saw it online." I caught a flash of sadness in her eyes. "Don't worry, you'll like it."

"Is that for the junior or senior prom?"

"Senior." I kissed her cheek. "Bye. Later, Femi."

"Can I choose your junior one?" Mom asked.

"No." What I wore was the one thing I had control over. I slipped inside the den. Dad looked much better and was actually sitting up. "Morning, Daddy."

"Why are you giving your mother such a hard time, pumpkin?"

Here comes the guilt trip. "If I let her help, she'll take over."

"You've grown up fast, and she misses helping you choose clothes."

I'd had no say on what I wore growing up. "Nice try, Daddy." I kissed his temple. "Not even you can convince me to work with her. Love you. Gotta run."

She was outside the door with a tray and a longsuffering look. The "why is my daughter being so difficult when all I want to do is help?" look. She'd perfected it over the years, but I was an expert at pretending not to notice.

I planted a kiss on her cheek. "Love you."

I grabbed my stuff and headed to my car. Torin was already waiting. "What's wrong?"

I turned the key and started whining. "She's back one day and she's already micromanaging my life. I can't work at the shop because of the witches, have to start studying with Lavania, and she wants to choose my prom dress. Can you believe it? Maybe we should just forget it."

"Wow, slow down," Torin warned.

I frowned. I'd left the cul-de-sac without even realizing it. "I was enjoying working at the store."

"But after last night, don't you think you should work on your witchy powers?"

I shot death rays his way with my eyes. "Don't you dare take her side. Besides, all Lavania and I worked on before we left were bind runes and we weren't done." I stopped at the stoplight. I peered out the windscreen and studied one of the trees lining the road. I pointed at it and tried to make it move like last night. Nothing.

"Green means go, not try to control trees," Torin said.

"I lost my mojo already," I said in my saddest voice ever.

"No, you haven't. You need to focus. Just like you do with your visions. Last night you were pissed. Anger takes a lot of energy. You directed all that energy into causing mini quakes. Bad witchy stuff. Then you became a tree hugger because I knocked down a few. You made them reconnect with Mother Earth.

Good witchy stuff. Tell Lavania you want to focus on harnessing that. Not the bad stuff."

I refused to let him bait me, found a parking spot, and switched off the engine. For a moment, I stared at the students hurrying past us with unseeing eyes.

I just treated Mom like crap. It didn't matter that she started running my life in less than twenty-four hours after she returned. She was home after months of uncertainties and scares.

"Freckles?"

I glanced at Torin. "I'm a bad daughter." His brow shot up. I closed my eyes and pressed my forehead on the steering wheel. "Worst. Daughter. Ever."

"No, you're not." He cupped the base of my neck and massaged it. His hand was so warm, and his fingers brushing behind my ears made me want to purr.

"I think I'm still angry with her. You know, for not telling me Dad was sick for so long. For not telling me she was a Valkyrie. For being gone the past two months. On some subliminal level, I'm really furious with her." Whoa, that sounded so grown-up for me. Hanging with Valkyries must be good for my gray matter. "Echo told Cora the Norns might have made Dad ill to punish Mom, so I think I might also be blaming her—"

"Whoa, stop. Echo is a moron, and Cora needs to shut her mouth instead of repeating stupid things like that," Torin snapped.

He was probably right. I sighed.

He tilted my head, so he could look into my eyes. "It is not your mother's fault your father is ill. You can be angry with her for other things, but not that. I've seen your parents together and what they have is amazing. Sets the bar for the rest of us." His eyebrows shot up. "Would you give up everything for me?"

"Sure." He was the reason I wanted to be a Valkyrie. I might be a Seeress, but I refused to let it define me or determine how I lived my life. Wow, another grown-up insight. "On the day you stop being a douche."

He chuckled. That sexy sound would never get old. I grinned.

I pulled out my phone when we got out of the car and made the call. Mom picked it up after a few rings. "Let's make a deal, Mom. You choose my junior prom dress and that's it. You don't do my makeup or hair."

"Ooh, I'm going to start looking right now. That includes shoes and accessories, right?"

I give her an inch, and she wants a mile. "Yes. Just don't make me look like a sixties love child. *You* rock that look. I don't."

She laughed. "Promise, but you've just given me an idea. *The Great Gatsby* outfits would look fabulous on you."

"*The Great Gatsby?*" I couldn't get through the book and I hadn't watched the movie. I had to before she turned me into the laughing stock of Kayville High. "Okay. Um, in the all the excitement of last night and this morning, I completely forgot to ask about the verdict." I tensed.

"I didn't tell you? We won, honey. I'm back," she squealed.

Wincing, I pulled the phone away from my ear and pressed on the speaker button. "That's great news. I'm happy for you."

"Happy for *us*. I can keep an eye on you and Torin for as long as I want."

Scary thought. "I gotta go, Mom. Bye." I glanced at Torin. "Don't say a word. I caved and I'm already regretting it. I'll be the one wearing flowers in my hair."

"*The Great Gatsby* was set in the twenties." He grabbed our backpacks, and we started for the building. His expression said he was remembering being there. "Aah, the jazz age. The music was amazing, the women dazzling."

I hated it when he went all nostalgic on me. "If you're trying to make me jealous, it's not working." *Liar.* I wished I'd been with him.

He smirked and put an arm around my shoulders. "Don't worry, luv. You have the next several centuries to dazzle me. Maybe I'll stop being a douche and you'll give up everything for me."

Did that really bother him? "But I love your douchebaggedness. It defines who you are."

My words appeared to please him. "Love your pain-in-the-ass-ness, too. You'd be boring otherwise."

We were joined by his friends and conversation became less private. As usual, he tucked me to his side and shielded me from their roughhousing.

Just before we entered the building, a prickly feeling had me looking back and searching the parking lot and the students crossing the street. Someone was watching us. I didn't see Gina, Rita, Bash, or his sidekicks, but the feeling persisted.

***

The prickly feeling returned during lunch. I paused in the process of shoving my books in my locker and glanced around. Rita and Gina were trying to catch my attention. I gave them a tiny smile that I hoped said "leave me alone."

My attention drifted from them.

Students were everywhere putting their books away before heading to lunch, the buzz of their conversation in the air. It didn't distract from the feeling of being watched. And it wasn't the two witches. Bash and his boys perhaps? They always gave weird vibes.

A flash of light and movement at the end of the left hallway made my Valkyrie radar go off. I squinted and searched. A broad shoulder and long Chex Mix hair disappeared around the corner. My pulsed kicked up. No, not a Valkyrie. A certain god. I took off after him, determined to confirm it. He was going toward the front of the school.

The dirty blond hair was unmistakably Eirik's. I careened around the corner, almost bumping into two girls walking backwards.

"Who's he?" one said.

"I don't know, but he's hot."

"Why are there so many new students at the end of the school year?"

"I know. Totally weird."

Totally normal in my world. I picked up speed, but the hallway split. The right headed toward the cafeteria and had a serious traffic jam. I engaged sight runes and scanned heads. No male dirty blonds. Too many female ones, most of them fake. Eirik's hair was natural.

The left hallway was empty, but chances were he'd taken it. I took off in that direction and hit the front hall running, attracting the attention of students from first lunch, who were hanging around waiting for the bell, and the second lunch students leaving. Eirik wasn't there. I went to the window and scanned the front entrance of the school and the parking lot across from it.

He was gone. Dang it! I wanted to talk. Maybe slap some sense into him.

I turned to go to the cafeteria, and another flash appeared in the corner of my eyes. He was still in the building. Why was he screwing with me? I shivered as I felt a strong supernatural energy.

"Hey, Raine," Sebastian said.

Of course, the annoying witches. The twins looked like they didn't want to be anywhere near me. That made three of us. I ignored them and hurried away.

The hallway was nearly empty, and I was aware of the three witches talking in low tones behind me. Still, I kept an eye out for Eirik. I knew I'd seen him. I couldn't have been mistaken.

I entered the cafeteria and froze, the air getting trapped in my lungs.

Eirik was waiting in line for food as though he had never left. No one appeared to be staring or pointing at him. His gaming buddies and swim teammates should be flocking around him now and asking questions. He'd been gone for half the school year and most of the swim team members knew he'd moved away.

Dizziness washed over me, and I realized I was holding my breath. My eyes found our table. At least Cora had seen him. Sondra and Kicker didn't seem to care. I found Torin. He was having a bro moment with Andris and Blaine, but he hadn't seen Eirik yet either.

Instead of going to the line, I joined Cora. She made a face and jerked her head toward Eirik. "Why aren't you rushing to give him a hug? He looked right through me and I really don't blame him. I broke his heart," she added.

"You broke whose heart?" Kicker asked, cutting a piece of her gravy-covered burrito with the side of her fork.

"No one," Cora said.

"Look, Kicker. It's the blond eye candy from our bio class." Sondra nodded at Eirik's broad back. "All the girls spent the hour staring at him and wondering who he was."

I blinked. "You, uh, don't recognize Eirik?"

"Oh, is that his name?" Kicker asked. "Eirik. It suits him."

"Recognize him from where?" Sondra added.

My eyes met Cora's. No way. The Norns couldn't have. They most definitely could. As though aware of our scrutiny, he turned and stared at us with narrowed eyes. No smile. No expression.

"Oh, crap," I whispered.

"What's wrong with him? Did you know he was back?"

I got up without answering Cora, my heart pounding so hard it drowned out other voices. I went to stand in line, my eyes on Eirik's back.

Hel must have one serious gym because he was ripped. The Eirik I'd known had the body of a swimmer—broad shoulders and narrow hips, but a bit on the skinny side. His hip-hugging jeans and chest-molding T-shirt said skinny was no longer in his vocabulary. He could pass for a surfer dude now. And I was so wrong about no one staring at him. The girls were. The two in front of me kept giggling and checking him out.

He got his pizza and started toward me. My entire body tensed, and a ringing started in my ear. Dang it, I wasn't breathing again. I struggled to control my swirling emotions as he drew closer. He walked by without slowing down or making eye contact.

I stared after him along with every girl in line. The Norns must have erased his memories, too. That didn't explain his sneaking into his bedroom at the mansion.

My eyes found Torin. He was staring at me and frowning. He had uncanny way of know when I was upset. In seconds, he was by my side. "What is it?"

"Eirik is here."

He followed my gaze and went rigid. Blue flames leaped in his eyes. "He's got some nerve."

"Torin, don't confront him." He was already striding toward Eirik. Things were about to get ugly. I caught up with him and placed my hand on his chest. His heart was racing. "Not here."

"He knows where my father is," he hissed.

"We don't know that. This could all be Norns' tricks. They've hit the erase button again. No one remembers Eirik but us. Just now, he walked right past me without recognizing me. Same with Cora. The Norns might have erased his memory, too."

Torin angled his body, his eyes going to Eirik. "He's an Asgardian. Why would they do that?"

"Because they can."

Andris and Blaine joined us. "While you two are pow-wowing, we're taking Loki Jr. out for a little chat."

His hand shot out and blocked Andris. "No. Not yet."

I glanced over my shoulder and caught the blank look on Eirik's face. He was staring at us without recognition. "Sit with us, guys," I begged.

"Can't I just tell him one thing? You know, about the mess in the kitchen and cleaning up after himself," Andris said.

I shook my head. Only Andris would create a half-baked joke during a serious situation. We moved as a group to our table. Kicker and Sondra watched the guys with wide eyes, their food forgotten. It wasn't often they all shared our table.

Across the room, Sabastian and the twins carried their trays and made a beeline for Eirik's table. They knew him. Nausea hit me hard. When they started talking like best buddies, white-hot anger spiked through me and replaced the shock. Eirik and the witches were working with the Earl.

Torin placed a tray in front of me. He'd gone and gotten my lunch. How sweet. Too bad my palate didn't appreciate it. The conversation at the table focused on anything but the identity of the four people across from us.

When they got up to leave, Eirik glanced over and, this time, he smirked. The smile was mocking. But what I saw in his eyes chilled me. He was enjoying this. The Norns hadn't erased his memories. He knew exactly who we were. He said something, and the other three witches glanced at us and laughed.

I wanted to engage my runes and go invisible just so I could slug him. My hand balled and runes appeared on my arms. Torin reached out and gripped my arm.

"Easy, Freckles."

From the runes on my arms, I must have started to fade. I focused on calming down. Trying to understand why. Remembering the old Eirik. He wasn't evil. Not all of him. For some reason, his dark side had taken over. Probably Hel's doing. I had to find a way to undo it.

I looked up and blinked. The guys were gone. "Where did they go?"

"After Eirik," Cora said.

I jumped up and raced after them before Torin started World War III.

I found Torin, Blaine, and Andris at the front hall of the school. The frustration hung in the air and wreathed their faces. I didn't need to ask to know that Eirik was gone.

"Did he say anything?" I asked.

"He didn't stick around to say much." Torin pushed his fingers through his hair, his body coiled tight. "The three guys with him are the witches who were giving you a hard time?"

I nodded reluctantly, shooting him a nervous glance. "Yes."

"They were also the shitheads at the club," Andris mumbled, and I wanted to deck him. Torin was close to his boiling point and Andris just amped up the heat.

Torin spun around, eyes fierce as they volleyed between me and Andris. "Are they?" His voice had gone low, lethal.

"You don't want to go there, Torin. Bash's father is powerful. He came to the store *before* I met Rita and Gina, which means he knew who I was. The entire family must be working with your father."

"Good." The smile that accompanied that single word sent a chill down my spine. "We can take them out after they give us my father's location."

"And Eirik?" Andris asked.

I shot him a mean look. "I don't believe he's doing it willingly. Something made him switch from good to bad. His dark side's taken over. You three stay away from him until I talk to him." They stared at me as though I'd told them I was marrying Eirik. "I mean it. Back off."

"*We* talk to him together," Torin said. His expression said he wasn't compromising. I opened my mouth to argue and his eyebrows flattened. He could be so intimidating, but that didn't bother me. I backed down though. This was about his parents, a very touchy and personal thing.

"Okay," I said.

19. EVIL SON OF A GOD

But catching up with Eirik proved easier said than done. He disappeared. He wasn't at school.

"Mr. Eirik just left," Mrs. Willow said, confirming he'd been around.

For the next two days, we watched Sebastian and the twins. Blaine and Andris took turns sleeping in Eirik's room. As though he knew they were waiting for him, he didn't come home at night. When we went on our runs, I had a feeling we were being watched.

On Thursday during band performance, I thought I saw him in the audience, but by the time we finished our pieces and the lights were turned on, he was gone. By Friday, I knew exactly what to do. I just couldn't bring myself to tell Torin.

He was a ticking bomb.

I chose history for my plan. Mr. Finney was my favorite teacher, but he was also too lenient with students. He accepted my lame excuse and sent me to the nurse's office. Hopefully, Torin would make him forget.

I headed to the band room. Band was my last class of the day, so I knew the room was empty the hour before. I locked the door, put my books on my desk, and let the need to connect with the Norns fill me.

Here goes nothing. I closed my eyes and took a deep breath. "Catie! Marj! Jeannette! I need to talk to you." I opened one eye and glanced around. No one was there. "CATIE! MARJ! JEANNETTE!"

Still no response.

Please, I need help.

A chill filled the room, and a voice said from behind me, "A little humility goes a long way, Lorraine Cooper."

For once, I was actually happy to hear Marj's grating voice. I glanced over my shoulder and shock sent my jaw tumbling down.

Marjorie "Marj" LeBlanc was *Bash?*

Sebastian Reyes grinned. My mouth turned into the Sahara Desert, and when I tried to swallow, it was all sand. No wonder I'd hated him on sight. On the other hand, I'd danced with him at the club and he'd tried to hit on me.

Ew, wrong thing to think about. How low were these three willing to sink?

Beside Sebastian stood the twins, or should I say Catie Vivanco and Jeannette Wilkes. Never in a million years would I have guessed the three witches were my Norns. They stood inside the door, and they didn't look too happy.

"Or would you prefer me looking like this?" Marj said.

I shoved my hands in the pockets of my hoodie and braced myself, expecting them to assume their true form. Hags with translucent skins. Eyes of infinite wisdom. Hair so gray they looked like rivets of smoke. After my dealings with the witches at the Mirage, I'd reached my quota of wizened people.

Blood rushed back to my head as their faces, bodies, and clothes became normal. Normal meant Marj had her smooth brown complexion and curly hair wrapped up in a bun. She still wore a disapproving look.

The blond, Jeannette, had perfected the condescending attitude. I could tell that my school was the last place she wanted to be and I didn't blame her. I'd thwarted their plans to lure me to eternal Norn servitude right here when I made them an offer they couldn't refuse. Catie, brunette, curvaceous, the last of the trio, was my favorite. She was the kindest, nicest Norn ever.

"What have you three done to Eirik?" I asked in a voice that wasn't so steady. I hated that. They'd blindside me, dang it. Again.

"We're trying to save him," Marj snapped. "You failed to do so when you let him go to his mother."

I shrugged. "Eirik's not a child. He, not I, decided he was going to visit his parents."

"Don't you mean he covered for you and your friends after you killed a few Grimnirs?" Jeannette said, a derision curling her lips.

Crap, they knew. Of course they knew. Anxiety churned my insides. Somehow, I had to bullshit my way out of this. "You mean the ones who attacked us with Maliina so we had to defend ourselves? If you hadn't recruited Maliina to do your dirty work, she wouldn't have made a deal with the goddess and come after us, prompting Eirik to come to our defense. The way I see it, you owe us for getting rid of that little piece of work. She was your mistake, and we covered for you."

Marj's eyes narrowed menacingly and my stomach dipped. Maybe I'd gone too far. Jeannette shook her head while Catie's lips twitched as though she was trying hard not to smile.

"And I'm here to collect," I added. "Where is Torin's father?"

"Are you trying to blackmail us?" Marj asked, her voice rising.

I shook my head. These three made my skin tight with goose bumps and my blood boil—a real bad combo when a girl wanted to keep her cool. I could feel sweat dripping down my back. "No, just saying we helped you out and now you can help us out. We want to know where the Earl is hiding."

"We don't make deals with renegade Norns," Marj snapped. "We…"

"Control fates of Mortals and gods, I know. But you have no problem using us to recruit new Norns."

"How do we do that?" Marj asked.

"By using Torin's father. And FYI, I'm not a Norn."

Marj chuckled darkly. "Really? Considering the number of destinies you've changed in the last couple of days alone, I think you're in denial. You are a Norn whether you like it or not."

"I can use my powers as a Seeress to help people without being slapped with that title." I sat on a desk and crossed my arms. They stayed standing. In fact, they spread out as though trying to surround me. I'd watched enough TV to recognize a pattern of attack. Surround the victim; then grab her.

My stomach churning, I stood and moved toward the back of the class. They followed. I really didn't like the way they were stalking me. At the club, they'd also tried to make me leave with them. They weren't thinking of kidnapping me, were they?

My back touched the wall, and I wished I was closer to the door. Much easier to open it and join the students in the hallway than etch runes on a wall. I hated wall portals. But I hated feeling vulnerable more. Like now.

"Back to Torin's father," I said, faking a bravado I didn't have. "First, you knew what he was going to do before he started targeting Seeresses. Instead of stopping him, you decided to put death on hold. Not all deaths. Just those bound for Asgard, so you can cherry pick future Norns from the Seeresses he willingly sacrificed."

How does she know these things? Jeanette asked.

Marj smirked. *She's guessing.*

I was. Every freaking time I was in their presence, my gray matter zipped from ordinary to super genius. Ideas just popped into my head and connections I hadn't thought of appeared. I had no idea how I did it, but I was always spot on. My confidence returned.

"What was the plan? Let him continue until he attacked me too, so you can replace me with a dead body and let my mother bury her entire family?" This time they didn't mask their surprise. "That is cold and heartless even for you," I continued, finally finding my footing. "What I don't understand is why. Why is Eirik working with him? Why are you allowing it? Why is the Earl after me?"

"Why don't you tell us? You seem to have all the answers," Jeannette said, and Marj chuckled.

Catie cut them a side-glance. "Stop toying with her."

"You always were soft when dealing with her," Marj said.

"I am compassionate when dealing with *all* our charges," Catie corrected her. "Haven't we learned anything from our dealings with this one? Being combatant gets us nowhere. We also know that no matter how often we try, *we* cannot shape her destiny. She's one of us and will choose her own. Now…" She pinned me down with serious, gray eyes. "What do you want to know?"

"Why is Torin's father after me?"

"He wants to go to Asgard, and he sees you as the means to accomplish that."

That confirmed Lavania's story, but… "Why me? I can't even see souls?"

"Of course you can," Catie said, smiling. "All you have to do is will it, but you don't need to be bothered with the dead, not when you can talk directly to us. Somehow the word is out about you, Lorraine. The supernatural world knows you can change destinies, cross realms without being a Valkyrie, and visit Asgard or Hel without escorting a soul. They didn't know *who* you were until you summoned the witches to Kayville to defend you."

Cross realms? So Echo was right. Then the last thing she said registered.

"I did not summon anyone." They glanced at each other and started their telepathic communication. I let my need to listen in fill me until I heard them. So they didn't know who called the witches either, but their main suspect was Eirik.

"Why would Eirik make the Call?" I asked.

Catie shot me a disapproving glance. "You should not listen to private conversations, Lorraine. It is rude."

My cheeks warmed. She sounded so much like Mom. Except she wasn't Mom. "And you should not go around stalking me and interfering in my life. Why would Eirik send the witches here if he's working with Torin's father?"

"Has it ever crossed your mind that maybe the witches are not here to help you?" Marj finally spoke and she did it with some serious glee. "Maybe they're part of the Earl's army."

My stomach dropped. The protection runes in the town covered all homes. Could we be protecting the very people out to get me? "You've infiltrated them, so why haven't you found out anything. At least you must know why Eirik is with the Earl."

"We don't," Catie said. "We thought he was with his parents in Hel's Hall. We are trying to find out what's going on and, if possible, help him find his way."

"Then get rid of Torin's father. You're powerful. Change his destiny. Kill him. Create an accident and chop off his head."

"We're not in the business of killing people," Marj retorted.

Yeah, yours is to screw up people's lives. "What can we do to help Eirik? His dark side has taken over. and if we don't do something, people are going to get hurt."

"We?" Marj asked.

"Yes, Marj. We. Eirik means a lot to us. To me, my mother, my father." My eyes watered. "I will not let him disappear into a black hole if I can help it. And if you try to use him to get to me again—"

"Eirik is just as important as you are to Ragnarok," Lorraine," Catie said.

Marj and Jeannette exchanged a horrified look. Marj shook her head. "She doesn't need to know all that now, Catie."

Catie smiled. "Actually, Marj, she does. It's time to stop this senseless cat and mouse game and work with her. I'm taking the lead from now on."

Whoa. I'd never heard her sound so badass. The others blinked and nodded. Way to go, Catie. She just kicked Marj to the curb and hijacked leadership. I loved it.

"Good. Let's get comfortable." She waited until they sat before she took the seat in front of me and smiled. "What do you know about Ragnarok?"

Seriously? "You want to discuss that now?"

"Yes, dear. Your next class is in," she checked her watch, "fifteen minutes. You have enough time to understand a few useful but painful facts. Now tell us about Ragnarok."

"It is the battle between the forces of good and evil and the end of this world," I said and almost rolled my eyes when they nodded. This was stupid.

"Go on," Catie said calmly.

"There will be signs of course: three years of nonstop war, chaos, and lawlessness followed by snow covering the entire world and blizzards. Finally darkness will be everywhere, as the sun, the moon, and the stars will be swallowed by the wolves. Scientifically, that doesn't make sense unless the earth goes off tangent instead of following its orbit and ends up floating in space where there are no stars, until it finds a new star to revolve around."

Catie chuckled. "Nice theory, but you forget that your science doesn't explain everything. Go on."

"But that's where theories come in."

She sighed. "Focus on Ragnarok, Lorraine. You can regale me with your theories later."

I could work with her. She was nice. "Three roosters will crow and call people to war. One will call the gods, another will call the giants, and the third will wake up the dead," I said.

They all groaned.

"What? I Googled it."

Catie jumped up and paced. "Why are you reading half-truths we left behind to placate Mortals? What is the name of your teacher?"

Did she have to ask it like Lavania was the village idiot? "She is very good, but she's been gone for a while. You know because of Mom's hearing. Maybe if you guys hadn't fought so hard to make Mom a Norn when it was obvious she wanted to be a Valkyrie, I would have gotten info from my tutor instead of Wikipedia."

"Who is this Wikipedia?" Marj demanded.

"She is right," Jeannette said at the same time, her animosity down several notches. "At least tell us you know what happens after Ragnarok."

"Some gods and goddesses survive. I'm hoping Eirik takes over for Odin, of course. There are perks to having your best friend as the main god." If Torin didn't kill him first for betraying me. Then there was the kiss he and I would share. Probably a planted vision by these three hags.

Catie shot me a pointed look, and I realize I'd stopped talking.

"Yeah, uh, the next Adam and Eve will be sheltered in the hollow space in the Yig... Ig..." I could never pronounce Yggdrasil like Ingrid. "The Eternal Tree of Life." Catie scowled. "The World Tree? The Tree of Knowledge?" Now all of them were scowling. "Are you saying the books and website are wrong about that, too?"

"The tree, *Ihg-drah-sill,* will not only house the new human couple who will repopulate the earth," Catie said slowly with her infinite patience, "there will be couples from the other realms, three Norns to continue taking care of *Yggdrasil* and weaving new destinies, Valkyries to see to the future dead, and gods too young to fight."

"Oh, so technically the tree is Noah's Ark?" I asked.

Marj cocked her eyebrows in question.

"New religion," Catie said before continuing. "A lot of the things you've mentioned are metaphors. Real wolves will not swallow the sun, and the roosters crowing at the start of Ragnarok are not really roosters. They are metaphors for *Völur.* You, as the main Seeress, will awaken the gods in Asgard. Eirik will awaken the dead in Hel's Hall. And a third *Völva* will awaken the giants. We are still searching for her."

"Or him," Marj corrected.

I had developed selective listening as soon as she'd mentioned Eirik and Hel's Hall. Torin was right. "Eirik is really a seer?"

Catie frowned as though surprised by my question. "Of course. He inherited the ability from his grandparents. You do know that Odin and Frigga both—"

"Practice Seidr," I finished. *Thank you, Ingrid.*

Rattling came from the door as someone tried to turn the handle. My watch said I still had seven minutes. I pushed against the wall and started for the door.

"We'd hoped to have the three of you in Asgard to signal Ragnarok and give us the upper hand," Catie continued as they followed me again. "We'd attack the giants while they sleep and stop the fire giant Surtr before he leaves Muspell. Catch Loki and Hel's army before they leave Hel. This way more gods and our people would survive, not just those hidden in the Yggrasil.

Now their actions made sense. They were stacking the odds in their favor. Attempting to alter destinies. Basically doing their job. Unfortunately, they needed me and Eirik, and the third Seer or Seeress to make it work. I already ruined their plans by falling in love with Torin. Eirik did when he went to visit his parents. This is their chance to get him on their side. The problem was they weren't able to control my destiny like they did average people. The Eirik I knew would never let them control his either.

I engaged my runes, unlocked the door, and turned to face them. The familiar faces were gone and, once again, Sabastian and the twins were having a mini conference. Students trickled in, but we were cloaked so they couldn't see us.

"Where is Eirik?" I asked.

They looked up, but Catie was the one who spoke. She sounded like the twins. "We don't know. He is not our charge anymore, so we don't monitor his movements. The two of you share a strong bond so you might find him faster than we. When you do, bring him to us and we'll stop William's shenanigans."

Right. Like I'd ever betray Eirik. "So you know where the Earl is?"

"Yes. We don't usually monitor Immortals, Valkyries, or those fulfilling their destinies. The Earl hasn't needed monitoring for centuries, until now."

Footsteps and voices approached. The band room was at the end of the hallway, near a side entrance students rarely used, so I knew the students' destination was here. I engaged my invisibility runes and unlocked the door.

"Which one of you planted images of Eirik in my head at the store?" I asked, heading for my oboe.

"What do you mean?" Marj asked.

"What images?" Catie added.

Their confusion appeared genuine, which meant evil Eirik had done it. What game was he playing? By the time I removed my oboe from its case, the three Norns were gone and more students were pouring into the room. If anyone noticed that I appeared suddenly by my oboe, they didn't say anything.

***

I hardly paid attention during band, my mind going over what the Norns had said. Mr. Zakowsky, my band teacher, had Vulcan hearing and usually never missed a wrong note or whispers. I made a gazillion errors, but he must have decided to give me a free pass after my performance last night.

As soon as I left the class, I searched for the Norns among the students hurrying past. I still couldn't believe I'd failed to realize they were Norns. The music must have dulled my senses at the club. When we'd met in the hallway and they'd called me a witch, I thought I'd felt their witchy powers. I should have paid more attention.

Rita and Gina stared at me as I crossed to the parking lot, but I focused on Torin and Andris. The two were conferencing by my car.

Torin looked up as I drew closer, his eyebrows lowering until they were dark slashes. "What happened?"

I must have my emotions plastered on my face for the whole world to see or he was really in tune with my feelings. He'd said he could tell when I needed him, but I'd chalked that up to male ego.

"Nothing. I'm okay. Really."

He was by my side, lifting my chin, searching for… proof? "You're not okay."

A sudden urge to cry washed over me. It was stupid really. I could stand up to anyone, but the minute he asked me what was wrong and gave me his "I'll rip apart the person responsible for making you unhappy" look, the waterworks started. Totally pathetic.

"Let's talk at the mansion," I said in an unsteady voice.

Andris watched me with worried eyes. For him to be worried, I must look like roadkill.

"It's about the Norns," I said, removing my car keys.

Torin's eyes sharpened. "Gather the troops," he instructed Andris. Then he scooped me up before I realized his intentions.

Students walking by stared and grinned. My cheeks burned. "Put me down."

"You look like crap, Freckles."

"Doesn't mean I can't walk." I wiggled, but the ground seemed too far away and I was too tired to engage my runes or fight him. The fight in me died a quiet death. I just wanted to go home and pig out on spicy chips and soda. I really should have waited until I analyzed everything the Norns told me, again, before mentioning the talk at the mansion.

The purr of the engine forced me to focus. I must have spaced out because I hadn't noticed Torin put me in the car or buckle me up.

How had I morphed from the girl who stood up to the Norns to this helpless wimp? No, that shouldn't even be important now. How was Torin going to react when he learned about the Norns? He'd probably flatten something.

Thank goodness we were going home. He didn't deal well with the Norns. Every time our paths crossed, he got caught in the middle. They'd love nothing better than to get rid of him, but so far, we'd escaped their little traps. They'd gone too far this time.

Torin took my hand and threaded our fingers as he drove. "Talk to me."

I swallowed past the knot in my throat. "When we get to the mansion."

"Not about that. About anything. Do you want to do something special this weekend? We could use a portal and go to a beach somewhere far from here. Just the two of us."

I would love nothing better than to run away and never look back, but our problems would either come with us or be waiting for us when we got back. "After we help Eirik."

He sighed. "Why is he always your problem?"

"Because our destinies are linked."

"That's the Norns' bullcrap. He's making you unhappy again, dragging you down with him." He slanted me a look, lifted my locked hands to his lips, and pressed a kiss on my knuckles. "I know. I'm an ass. We'll help him. Hopefully for the last time."

If he only knew.

Instead of branching off to our cul-de-sac, he continued up Orchard Drive to the mansion. The last two days I'd gone straight there after school for lessons, so I knew Lavania was waiting with more. We were finally working on my witch abilities, but the last thing I wanted to do this evening was work on focusing my powers and getting in touch with my inner witch or Seeress. I'd rather run with Torin and the others.

Using love as the focal point for my witch powers wasn't hard. Until Dad's accident, my life had been filled with sunshine. My childhood could even be called perfect. I had a loving mother and a doting father. Finding happy memories to draw from wasn't hard. Eirik had been part of that life. It was impossible to visualize my happy memories without him in them. Maybe that was why I couldn't see him as evil or bad.

We headed straight to the kitchen for drinks. They didn't have soda. Just bottled water. Torin opened a drawer and removed a large bag of spicy chips.

He knew me too well. He disappeared into the hallway. By the time I opened the bag and took out a chip, he was back with two sodas, ginger ale for me and root beer for him.

"I keep a stash at my place." He gave me mine and took my arm.

"Where are we going?"

"Living room."

We rarely used the room. Most of our conferences were held in the kitchen or at my place. He pulled me down to sit with him, but I ended up on his lap. I chugged my drink and dug inside the chip bag.

"When this is over, I'm definitely taking you away for the weekend," Torin said, nuzzling my neck.

I grinned. It was a nice fantasy. "Mom won't allow it."

"We'll take Andris as a chaperone."

I choked on my drink. "You're kidding. He'll fill his room with women and not come out the entire weekend. What about Lavania?"

His lips pinched. He focused on his drink, guzzling most of it.

"You have to forgive her sometime, Torin."

"We could take Cora and Echo," he suggested, sliding his fingers through my hair.

Preferring those two over Lavania? I turned my head and studied his hooded eyes. "She was following orders."

"She's had over eight *hundred* years to tell me that my mother needed my help. How can you justify that?"

I couldn't. "If you don't forgive her, you'll never be happy."

"Are you kidding? I have you." He angled my head and took possession of my senses with a single kiss. When he lifted his head, he chuckled at my response. I elbowed him. "And soon I'll have the satisfaction of setting my mother free," he added.

Did he realize he kept saying his mother instead of his mother's soul? I tried to focus on something else other than him. He lifted my hair out of the way, dropped a kiss on my shoulder, and trailed a line to my neck. I started to sweat and wished I had removed my hoodie.

The SUV pulled into the driveway. The gang had arrived. I tried to get off Torin's lap, but his arms tightened around my waist.

"Where are you going?" he breathed in my ear, and I shivered as his warm breath fanned my skin. Chuckling, he nipped my ear lobe and soothed the sting. I was a goner.

It was a wonder I heard the voices coming from the foyer. I recognized Mom's. My struggle to get off his lap was earnest this time. I smacked his arm. "Stop it. I can't talk while we cuddle."

"We do it all the time." He buried his face in my neck.

"When we are alone, not with a room full of people." He let me go, and I scooted to the other end of the couch.

He laughed. "They can tell we've been making out."

"No, they can't." Then I saw the orange patches of powder from the chips on his cheek. Yep, that will confirm it. I reached out and swiped at them. Dang it. "They're not coming off."

His lips curled some more, eyes twinkling. "Lick your finger and clean them off."

"Ew. That's gross." I used the sleeve of my sweater. "There. Clean."

"You missed the one telltale sign." He touched my lips.

Nothing I could do about that. I sucked on my lower lip, and another chuckle escaped Torin. He could be such a douche sometimes.

His smile disappeared when Lavania entered the room. I focused on the problem of their new relationship. He avoided her like the plague. Walked out whenever she walked in. Ignored her when they were in the same room. I sighed, wishing I could help him cope with the betrayal. Even I didn't understand why she never told him about his parents.

Mom and Femi entered the room. Mom's eyes sharpened on me as though checking to make sure I was unhurt.

"I'm fine, Mom," I reassured her.

She still came where I sat and rubbed my back before grabbing a seat. Andris, Blaine, and Ingrid arrived last. Ingrid's eyes were bruised as though she'd been crying, and Andris looked worried. They sat as far away from each other as possible. I'd stopped trying to figure Ingrid out.

Torin gave me a nod, but I could feel his tension. It settled on his shoulders, his clenched hands, and taut jaw.

"The three witches at our school, Bash, Alejandro, and Mattias, are really my usual three Norns."

The shock on their faces was clear.

Andris laughed, until Torin silenced him with a look. As I continued talking, rage built in his eyes. Now I wish I'd talked to him first. He turned his head and pinned Lavania with a glare.

"Did you know Eirik would signal with her?" he asked in a low voice.

Lavania shook her head, making the end of her ponytail sweep her back. Her eyes begged him for forgiveness, but all she said was, "No. I knew that Raine and two other *Völur* would give the signal, but I had no idea who the other two were. Even the fact that they wanted all them in Asgard is news to me."

"The Norns know a lot more than we Valkyries do, Torin," Mom said, leaning forward, legs crossed under her Bohemian skirt. "I wouldn't be surprised if the gods themselves don't know what the Norns have been plotting. Remember, the gods are going to be killed by the very monsters they're keeping prisoners right now. They easily could have killed Loki to stop him from joining his children and the giants during Ragnarok. Loki's son, the wolf Fenrir, is bound by the gods instead of being killed, yet the prophecy says Fenrir will kill Odin and the people on earth by the millions. The gods know death is coming and are ready for it. They understand that the world must renew itself and their sons and grandsons will replace them in the new world. It takes courage to know that and not try to change it. The Norns are cowards for attempting it."

It was a long-winded speech, but Mom nailed it. "Does that mean they really knew about Torin's f—" Torin's eyes flashed and I went with, "the Earl?"

"Yes, and they let him start this foolhardy quest of his because he'd help them get what they want. The Earl gets them Torin, which gets them you and Eirik."

"Then we should just kill him," Andris said with relish.

Ingrid made a sound that drew everyone's attention, but her eyes were on Andris. "Maybe you need to stop and look at the entire picture before you reach a conclusion." The look she shot Andris said they were no longer talking about the Earl.

"What is there to look at? He made a bad decision and must live with the consequences."

Ingrid jumped to her feet. "You're an idiot. You kill him and his soul stays linked to his wife's. I need a drink." She stormed off.

Okay, that was unexpected. This could not be about Ingrid and New York. Andris watched her leave with hard eyes, but he didn't go after her. Lavania did. Now I was really confused. Lavania barely tolerated Ingrid.

"Ingrid is right," Femi said. "The two must be unlinked before the Earl is sent to Corpus Strand. You'll need a powerful spell to do that." She glanced at me.

Torin stiffened. "Raine doesn't do spells. I don't want her anywhere near the Earl."

"Actually I was going to suggest using a certain powerful, young witch Raine helped. She was trained by one of the Earl's friends."

At least Torin stop glowering. "But the Norns said the witches might be on the Earl's side."

"Don't believe anything those hags tell you," Mom said. "Especially when they play Bad Cop slash Good Cop. You know they've anted up their attack when the nice one who always seems to fight the others takes the lead. That's when your guard should go up. She lulls you into a false sense of security, and by the time you realize she was the leader all along, you are completely under her spell."

Holy crap. *I'm such an idiot.*

Torin had closed the space between us and was searching my face before I looked up. "What is it?"

"Catie, the nice Norn, did that to me this afternoon. She acted like she was usurping Marj's position as their leader, and I bought it. I bet they planted those visions in my head, too." Worse, they'd even made me suspect Eirik. Horrified, I glanced at Mom. "What does this mean?"

"It means they probably lied to you so you would do exactly what they want," Mom said. "They probably know who called the witches here and why."

I shivered, still trying to wrap my head around what I was hearing. Those three hags played me. Torin rubbed my back. His warmth wrapped around me, slowly chasing away the shivers.

"There must be a reason they want her to focus on finding Eirik, and not the Earl," he said.

"They're probably whispering instructions in his ear," Andris said. He looked toward the doorway as Lavania entered the room, her hand gripping Ingrid's arm. She nodded briefly, and Andris responded with a brief smile.

I stopped trying to understand the drama playing out between the three of them. "So do we go after the Earl?"

"Yes, except I don't want him dead," Torin said.

I gaped at him. "What? After all he's done—"

Torin shot me a brief smile that didn't reach his eyes. "Once we release my mother's soul, I want him to spend eternity knowing that *I* deprived him of the one thing he desperately wants. If he chooses to kill himself, he'll end up like all Immortals and Valkyries who choose death, a dark soul roaming this world until he dissipates into nothing."

His words sent a chill down my spine. Choosing immortality did have some serious consequences. Ragnarok must definitely be a welcome event for them. No wonder the gods weren't trying to stop it. They might live for thousands of years, but at least they died. Immortals didn't, unless they offed themselves or stopped using runes. I wondered whether they needed permission to stop using runes and how long they lived afterwards.

"Let me see if I understand you," Blaine said slowly. "You don't plan to kill him?"

Torin shook his head. "No."

"Damn, bro. That is very noble of you," Andris said.

Noble? His plan was diabolical. Made me count myself lucky I wasn't his enemy. What would he do to Eirik if he found out he was the one who might have projected images of us into my head? I'd omitted that part in my narration because of the Norns' reaction. Now, I wasn't so sure they hadn't done it and just chosen to deny it. Bitter old hags.

Torin shrugged. "Death is too good for him. He deserves to suffer."

There was no way his father would live for eternity in defeat knowing the person responsible was living his life to the fullest. "What if he comes after us again? He won't accept this quietly."

Mom nodded. "I agree. He's not going to let this go."

"Then I will defeat him again and again until he crawls under some rock to lick his wounds."

"That's bullshit." Mom's eyes widened at my choice of word, but I didn't give her time to lecture me. "If he's as stubborn as you are, he won't give up. Are you willing to put me through this again and again, watching you suffer sleepless nights because of him?"

He glanced at me then away, his jaws clenched. "Stand down, Freckles."

"I won't. You know I'm right. He has to go." The last two nights, he'd tossed and turned, messing with both our REM cycles.

"You want me to kill him?" he asked, shutting me up. "Because I have no problem whatsoever doing it."

There was not a flicker of doubt in his eyes, but could he live with himself after killing him in the name of revenge? To protect me or Andris or someone he loved? Yes. In cold blood? I didn't think so.

"And shit happens during a battle," Andris said, earning him a glare from Mom. "Beggin' your pardon, Mrs. Cooper," he added with a perfect imitation of a southern accent. "Bad things hap'n to bad people, so maybe his goose is cooked this time."

Mom smiled. "Okay, let's take this one step at a time. What do we do first?"

Once again, everyone looked at Torin. What was wrong with them? He was struggling with some major, life-changing decisions here and they were heaping more stuff on his shoulders. I jumped in.

"I need Eirik's camera to try to locate him and Torin's seal to find the Earl. Andris, did you guys bring back the Seeresses' personal items after our globetrotting evening?"

He looked at Torin before nodding.

"Good. I'll need to get visions from them to see if I can locate Lady Adelaide's soul and, if we're lucky, hear some of the Earl's plans. Femi, we're going to need Rita and her mother. Whether they are part of the Earl's death squad or not, they owe me and I'm collecting. We need a spell to break the bond the Earl used to tether the soul to him."

Femi nodded.

"I'll go with her to watch her back," Blaine said.

"Good idea. Mom, you have no idea how clearly I can see the Norns' motives because of you. I'm going to need your help with Eirik. He considers you his mother, too, and I know what happens to me when you use your Tiger Mom voice."

She grinned. "Thank you."

"It is your worst voice ever," I reminded her. "It makes me feel this puny." I indicated with my forefinger and thumb. Torin chuckled. The look in his eyes sent heat rushing to my face. "Sorry I kind of hijacked your meeting again. You ready to take over?"

He crossed his arms and leaned back against the sofa. "Oh, no. Don't stop now."

Femi, Blaine, and Mom had already left. Andris was staring at Ingrid and Lavania. The two were talking in whispers, but Lavania kept glancing at Torin.

"Make nice with her," I whispered.

Torin shot me a warning glance.

"For me." Maybe if I kept Ingrid busy, Torin could talk to Lavania. I left his side and joined the two women. "Sorry to intrude. Is everything okay?"

Ingrid gave me a wobbly smile. "I'm not going to New York yet."

My eyes flew to Andris. What did he do? He got up and mumbled something about getting the Seeresses' amulets. I focused on Ingrid. "Why not?"

Ingrid gave me a wobbly smile. "I'm not going to New York yet."

My eyes flew to Andris. What did he do? He got up and mumbled something about getting the Seeresses' amulets. I focused on Ingrid. "Why not?"

She glanced at Lavania and smiled. "When Andris runed me, he used his personal artavus. I'm aging fast. I have wrinkles…" She touched the corner of her eye, her chin trembling. There were hardly any wrinkles. "Lavania brought back artavo for me and Cora, so I must stay here until I bond with mine and have the right runes."

"Oh. That's terrible new. What about the Internship?"

"I'll start in the fall." She gripped my hand. "I'm so sorry about the way I attacked you a few days ago, Raine. I'd just found out that I was aging and I panicked. I shouldn't have taken it out on you. The things I said were terrible and not true."

I grimaced. "Some were, so don't feel bad about it. In fact, forget about it you. When are you going to start adding new runes?"

"Lavania said the sooner..." her eyes widened as they focused on something behind me.

I whipped around and blood drained from my face. Mom stood in the doorway with Eirik's camera, but standing behind her with an artavus pressed across her throat was Eirik. Not just any artavus. It was the one the Norns had given me to kill Eirik with. It killed everything—Immortals, Valkyries, even the gods.

20. A FREED SOUL

"Eirik, what…?" Tentacles of panic coiled around me. "What are you doing?"

"I'm here for you, Raine," he said calmly. His voice had grown deeper and colder. "The Earl would like to see you."

Torin shielded me before I could respond, his runes blazing. He had them all out: strength, speed, endurance, wisdom, protection… I engaged mine too, my heart pounding hard.

Torin's runes seemed to glow brighter, like his rage fed their energy. "If you think for one moment I'd let her go anywhere with you, think again." His voice was low, vicious, and so cold I shivered. "What in Hel's Mist is wrong with you, man? She protected you. Fought the Norns for you."

Eirik growled. "Don't talk to me of Hel's Mist. I lived there and survived it by means you couldn't possibly understand. Andris, I wouldn't do that if I were you."

Andris stood to his right with the amulets he'd gone to get, his runes engaged. Lavania and Ingrid also had their runes ablaze, Ingrid's dimmer than everyone else's. She definitely needed new runes. Such an inane thing to focus on, but I needed to slow down the wave of panic threatening to down me. My ears were beginning to ring.

"No one moves or she dies," Eirik said. "I don't even have to decapitate her. Just a nick will do the trick. This blade, specially forged by the dwarves, kills everything. Interestingly, the Norns are the ones who told me where I could find it, Torin. Hidden in your house. Were you hoping to use it on me after all?"

I tried to peer around Torin, but he shifted and blocked me. He used the movement to whip his artavo from the inner pockets of his jacket.

"Raine comes with me, Torin, or many people are going to die," Eirik warned.

"The town is secure," Torin snarled.

Eirik grinned. "We can draw the Mortals out. Mortals are naturally curious. All we have to do is give them a reason to come out. Then annihilate them."

"Go ahead." Torin's body tensed. "You won't hurt Mrs. Cooper despite your threat. I don't care how much of the dark venom is flowing through your veins; you know her."

"Yes, I do." I could tell he was smiling. "Aren't you wondering why she's just standing here and letting me control the situation? I stopped by her house first before I came here, and the den is empty now."

Gasps filled the room. Dad. I found my voice again. "Eirik, don't. Don't do anything you'll regret. I'm here for you. We can fix whatever is going on."

His lips curled into a sneer. "Don't use that condescending tone with me, Raine. Do you really think I haven't had time to control my demons? I have done nothing but. Your father is at our camp. Don't worry, I'll return him as soon as you join us. I will leave your *boyfriend* instructions."

"Torin," I whispered and tried to push him out of my way. He growled. Boulders had nothing on him when he had his runes going. Would I break my bones if I body slammed him?

"Walk around him and come to me, Raine. Slowly."

"NO!" Torin growled.

I wrapped my arms around his waist and closed my eyes, focusing hard. I let the will to stop him fill me. I needed him to think of nothing but sleep and bed. He hadn't slept properly in days, so this should be easy. Our runes touching also helped. I projected the images and thoughts into his head.

Sleep. Bed. You're exhausted. This is just a bad dream. It is not happening.

"No, not real," he whispered, his eyes closing.

Eirik is not here. It's just a bad dream. I'm waiting for you. I need you to hold me while I sleep, Torin. Keep me safe.

His body shuddered as he fought the images. His knees gave away. Body grew heavy. I supported it. I used my body and knee to break his fall and lower him to the ground.

"What are you doing to him, you bastard?" Andris bellowed. From the corner of my eyes, I saw him charge toward Eirik and Mom.

"Stay back, Andris." I thrust my hand toward him. His body lifted off the floor as though hit by a gale. He slammed against the wall, leaving a huge dent. I wasn't sure whether the force of my witch attack or his runes caused the damage, but the surprised look in his eyes mirrored mine. "*I'm* doing this to Torin, not Eirik."

My focus returned to Torin, who was fast asleep at my feet, his body twisted at a weird angle. He started to snore. He was going to be in a murderous rage when he woke up.

Keeping an eye on Andris, who was staring at me as though I had gone crazy, I adjusted Torin's arms and legs. Tears rushed to my eyes. Weird. The runes still glowed on his body. Must be how he'd remained hidden in the hospital while staying with me. The thought was random, but it helped me control my tears.

"I don't know how long this will last, Andris. Move him somewhere comfortable." Torin looked so vulnerable. I touched his cheek one last time and stepped back. "Tell him not to try to find me until Mom and Dad are safe. Tell him I had to do it and that I—"

"You're wasting time, Raine," Eirik snapped.

I ignored him and locked eyes with Andris. "Tell him I love him and will always love him. Forever."

Andris nodded. I didn't look at Lavania or Ingrid. Mom had tears in her eyes when I turned to face them. "Let her go, Eirik. I'll go with you."

"Move closer," Eirik ordered.

I tried to catch his eyes, but he refused to look at me directly. "Look at me, Eirik. You're better than this. This is not—"

"Shut up, Raine," he snapped. "Andris come here and catch her."

I didn't understand, my mind still reeling from his harsh tone. He did something to Mom and her body dropped. I could have caught her if he hadn't grabbed my arm. Andris caught her before she landed on the floor.

"You're a dead man, golden boy," Andris vowed. "You have no idea who you are messing with. As long as you have her,

Torin won't care that you are a god. He will tear this world apart to find her, and I'll be right there with him."

Eirik smirked, the blade now pressed against my throat. "I look forward to meeting both of you in the battlefield. Oh, make sure you bring the Grimnir, too. I owe him a one-way ticket to Corpus Strand. Let's see how he likes it. The instructions on when and where you can get Mr. Cooper are in the wife's pocket." His runes flared and a portal appeared in the air.

I could see trees, lots of trees, and the sunrays slicing through the foliage. He pushed me ahead, the portal closing behind us. I caught a glimpse of the mansion's foyer and Andris reading a piece of paper. He looked up just before the portal closed and grinned.

Why would he be so happy when moments ago he was ready to rip into Eirik? He couldn't be relishing fighting Eirik. Andris hated to fight, and Eirik was the proud owner of a spiked flail, which I was sure he was hiding somewhere on his body, and now the Norns' artavus.

The portal closed, cool mountain air rushing on my skin and replacing the warmth of the mansion. I shivered. Birds chirped, and animal sounds came from the thickets and the trees. I turned, expecting to see the Earl and his minions, but there was no one around except Eirik and me. A prickly feeling told me we were being watched.

Part of me expected Eirik to laugh and yell "Bazinga!" Another wanted to punch him and tell him to snap out of it. I wasn't sure what had happened in Hel, but this couldn't be the result. He couldn't be this broken.

"Where are we?" I asked.

"Disengage your runes," he ordered, not bothering to answer me.

I glanced around at the fir trees and the undergrowth. There was something familiar about the woods. Could we be in Tillamook Forest? The very same forest Torin and I used for speed and reflex training?

"Why did you bring me here? I don't see the Earl or his followers."

"Turn around and follow the trail behind you," he barked.

Now I wanted to dig my heels in and refuse to obey him, but one look into his cold eyes and I turned and went down the narrow path. His amber eyes used to be warm and full of mischief. Ahead, I could see an opening in the trees. "What happened to you, Eirik?"

"You happened."

Barbed tips of hurt spiked through me. "What did I ever..." my breath caught, "do to you?"

"Everything and nothing," he mumbled.

"That's a lame and stupid answer," I retorted.

He chuckled dryly. "You taught me it was okay to be vulnerable and let others in, to see the good in people and give them a second chance. You lied. People are selfish, and when they don't get their way, they turn into monsters and screw you up good." His voice was gruff, as though he was reliving something really awful.

My anger disappeared, my heart aching for him. I wanted to turn around and hug him. "I'm so sorry. Was it that bad?"

"Stop talking and keep walking," he snarled.

I clammed up for about... two seconds. "Whatever happens here today, I love you, Eirik. I always have and always will. You are part of my family. Remember that."

He gave a derisive chuckle. "And remember this, Raine Cooper. I always have a reason for everything I do."

I stumbled on a root, and he reached out to steady me. When I touched his hand, he yanked it away from me. "Don't," he snarled.

I reigned in the anger and forced myself to focus on the positive. "There was a time you loved to hang out with me, Eirik. You held me when I cried and slayed imaginary monsters under my bed. Do you remember when we'd crawl under the blanket and read with flashlights until Mom or Dad—"

"Shut up, Raine. Just... shut it. I don't remember any of that crap."

Chuckles came from the bushes around us and my heart hurtled to my throat. My eyes darted around until I spied faces behind trees and bushes. My feet faltered. Eirik prodded me from behind with the dagger. I stumbled forward, almost twisting my ankle. This time he didn't try to help me.

We entered the clearing. Now I recognized where we were. It was the same clearing Torin and I had used during our picnic. More people came from behind the trees. At first, I counted them, but they kept popping up all around us and I lost count.

Familiar faces appeared among them, the witches who'd come to my store in the name of friendship. They were back in their witchy robes and traditional shamanic hats and cloaks. Even the old man who'd wanted to thank me for helping his son stood there with his crooked stick.

Traitors.

Bash's uncle didn't seem too happy. Bet his sons and nephew were missing and he didn't know why. Served him right. Gina and Rita didn't smile when our eyes met.

I helped you, you ungrateful shitheads.

The next faces had me gasping. Femi and Blaine. They stared back at me without showing any emotions. Mom had trusted her. *I* had defended her to Torin. As for Blaine, he'd made it obvious ever since he came back that he hated Valkyries and he wanted to go to Asgard to be with his dead girlfriend. What better way to get there than by hitching his wagon to a psycho Immortal's?

Their betrayal cut deep. I couldn't look at them anymore without cursing them out.

Everyone's eyes shifted to somewhere behind me, and I turned just as a tall guy with black hair and brilliant blue eyes entered the clearing. William de Clare, the original Earl of Worthington. Torin's father. That he looked so much like Torin was bitter sweet.

I blew out a breath, nervous energy churning my stomach. Beside him was an equally tall woman with straight medium-brown hair. I recognized her from my vision. Madam Bosvilles. They could pass for forty-somethings.

I searched behind them for the soul of Torin's mother.

How had Catie put it? I had to will it. That meant wanting it so much the need filled me. Should be easy. Freeing her was the only thing stopping me from engaging my runes and attacking the Earl.

"You delivered her, Eirik," the Earl said, and my eyes flew to him.

He sounded so much like Torin a shiver shot up my spine. And not in a nice way. He was like an older version of Torin, except his eyes were cold, nothing like Torin's warm ones.

Stupid tears rushed to my eyes, and I wanted to slap myself silly. This man should never see me in tears. I focused on seeing the soul attached to him.

"You've definitely impressed us," I heard the woman say. "You can now join us in Asgard."

"Thank you, my lady," Eirik said.

Distracted, I glanced at Eirik. He did all this to get into Asgard? Were his memories partially gone or had going to Hel turned him into a pariah in Asgard? I tried to catch his eyes, but he kept staring down.

"And you, my dear," the Earl of Worthington said, and I knew he was talking to me. "It is a pleasure to finally meet the girl who moves between the realms and talks to the Norns."

"Want to switch places?" I almost snapped, but I couldn't give him the satisfaction of knowing how I felt about my gifts, the very things he craved. Instead, I focused on the air behind him. Where was her soul?

I shifted to selective listening when the Earl started gabbing.

"My friends, we have fought and protected humanity for centuries without so much as a thank you or a handshake from the gods," he started.

The air behind him shimmered like heat rising from heated cement.

"Civilization after civilization, we've watched them begin one senseless war after another, killing each other and destroying everything only to rebuild it again."

The mirage took the shape of a woman in a long, flowing white dress with long, wide sleeves that were fitted around her wrists. The collar and the sleeves of the dress were beautifully embroidered, and she wore a cloak held in place by a cord and a belt around her waist. At first I thought she had ash-blond hair like Ingrid, until I realized her hair was covered by a white, silk scarf that flowed to her back.

"It is time we were rewarded, recognized, and given our dues," the Earl continued. "Time we sat at the table with our fallen brothers and sisters, shook hands with the gods, and drank ale served by beautiful Valkyries."

"YEAH!" the crowd yelled.

"It is our right as Immortals, our destiny..."

More screams came from his followers, more rhetoric from him about winning Ragnarok and becoming gods and goddesses. Lofty dreams, pal. Good luck with that.

The soul was now clearer, but I could still see through her. Cora had told me they looked like regular people. Maybe I was only meant to see them this way. Translucent. Apparitions of themselves. She was beautiful, her skin flawless, but her eyes... They were lifeless. Like a doll's. Totally spooky.

Did all souls look like that?

"This young Seeress will lead us to the Bifrost. We'll cross it and enter Valhalla like the heroes we are. The witches, wizards, and shamans are welcomed to join us. Your young leader has proven himself."

What? My eyes shifted from Torin's mother to Eirik. Eirik was the leader of the witches? Did that mean he'd made the Call and led the Earl to us?

"Now, Lorraine Cooper," the Earl said. "We are ready. Show us the way to the gods. Open the portal to the Bifrost."

Seriously? Did he really think it would be that simple? "No. No one is going anywhere until you release her." I pointed at the soul.

The Earl looked behind him and scowled. "Release who?"

"The poor soul you've been dragging around for centuries. Your wife. Let her go."

He laughed. "I don't know what you're talking about. There's no one there."

"Then you better look harder. You've kept her around for so long she has withered to nothing." The soul looked at me with such hope my heart ached for her. "But I can see her. Yes, Lady Adelaide, I can see you. Please, show yourself. Let them see what he's done to you."

She was struggling to maintain her human form, but she was too weak. I could see it in her eyes and the way her body dimmed. Centuries of hanging around her husband had probably drained her energy.

The Earl's eyes grew fierce. "Focus on why we came here, my friends," he yelled. "The girl is trying to confuse you. There's nothing here, nothing holding us back. She promised to lead us to Asgard."

Promised who? Eirik? Where did he go? "No, I will not," I called out.

"Look here, you silly girl," the Earl snarled. "The only reason I didn't storm into your puny town and reduce it to rubble was because Eirik said you were willing to help us. That you've wanted to go to Asgard, too, but the Norns refused you. This is a chance to show them they don't control you or your future."

"They already know that, just like they know I'd never associate with Immortals like you and her." I indicated his companion, Madam Bosvilles.

"Listen here, you brat. If you refuse, your little town will be nothing but a ghost town."

I stared at him, but my mind was on Torin's mother and freeing her. "Go ahead and torch it, and see who becomes a ghost. Lady Adelaide?" I called out. She looked up, her eyes widening. She had pale blue eyes like the present Earl of Worthington.

The Earl reached out to grab my arm, but something weird happened. The vine from a nearby tree whipped out, wrapped around his wrist, and pulled.

People moved back with gasps. Some pointed.

"Which one of you witches is doing this?" the Earl yelled, struggling. He engaged his runes. But the more he struggled, the tighter and higher the vine pulled his arm. The Immortals looked at the witches, and I knew if the Earl gave the order, they'd turn on them.

"I did it," I yelled. "Touch me again and they'll go for your neck," I threatened. "Now promise to behave until I finish here."

He tried to grab me with his other hand, but another vine shot down and snatched it. Idiot. He just had to try to prove he was Mr. Tough Guy, didn't he? Mother Nature is a witch with a capital B when it fought back.

I focused on Adelaide, who was staring at the Earl. "Focus on me, Lady Adelaide. I know who you are. You were Lady Adelaide from Normandy. You had two sons, Torin and James."

Her face crumbled. Could a soul cry?

"They loved you very much. James is waiting for you in Asgard." Torin had better escort her there. "Torin will be here shortly to take you to him. Please, fight and show yourself. Don't you want to see your children?"

Tears filled my eyes as I watched her struggle. She seemed to grow stronger. Finally, she came into existence. The witches and the Immortals were staring at her, not the Earl.

I shot the Earl a triumphant look. A few of his men must have tried to help him because they were wrapped up like mummies by the grass. Only their eyes blinked at me from thatches of green. The others, his girlfriend included, had distanced themselves from him.

"You've tortured your wife's soul for centuries, William de Clare. Release her soul now, and then we can talk about Asgard."

He sneered. "I will not be dictated to by a child."

"Yet you come to me for help?" I asked, raising my voice. A few snickers followed.

He glanced around, so sure of his place as the leader of these people. "Do you care that my wife chose to stay with me, so she and I could go to Asgard together?"

"NO!"

"We do," one lone voice rang out. A familiar female voice.

Femi? I craned my neck to find her, but the witches were pointing their staffs at us while murmuring something. Their voices rose, each speaking in a different language. But the loudest one was Femi's. Blaine was also yelling.

Then I realized what they were doing. They were chanting a spell. My eyes met Eirik's. He was chanting, too. And smiling. He winked and patted his side. I shook my head, not understanding. He pointed to his side. I patted my side and felt it.

The dagger he'd been holding was in the pocket of my hoodie. He must have slipped it there while we were walking to the clearing.

Was this his plan all along? Bringing me here to help release Lady Adelaide and save the town? What was in the note he'd left with Andris? He had some serious explaining to do after this.

Gina and Rita grinned at me at the front of the line. Blaine and Femi moved to the ends of the group, flanking them in case the Immortals attacked. Even the old witch with the crooked staff flash his stained teeth as he nodded at me, his staff pointed at the Earl.

By the third chant, I had picked up parts of it and joined in.

"We ask the Gods to break this bond
That binds Lady Adelaide to the Earl of Worthington.
He holds her soul from time gone by
Though no longer in his arms does she lie.
Gods of Old Religion release her soul.
This spell is cast and the Earl has no more hold."

The look on the Earl's face was priceless. He bellowed something, but the witches drowned him. I knew the moment the spell was broken.

A portal appeared right by Adelaide, and Torin arrived, his runes glowing. The others followed—Andris, Echo, Lavania, Ingrid, and Hawk. Even Mom was there.

His mother's soul stared at them and moved back as though afraid. Didn't she recognize Torin? "It is Torin, Lady Adelaide," I said. "Your son."

Her eyes volleyed between Torin and me as though not sure of herself. She moved toward me. Somehow, she'd decided I could be trusted.

"Take her to the mansion, Raine," Torin growled in a voice raw with emotions. Gratitude simmered in the depth of his eyes, which quickly turned to rage when he saw his father.

I didn't want to leave. What if they needed me? The Immortals outnumbered them five to one, and that was assuming all the witches were on our side.

"Go, Raine," Torin yelled. "Take her to safety."

"Follow me, Lady Adelaide. You will be safe with me." I started to lead her through the portal, but the Earl bellowed.

"No, she stays."

"Untie him, Raine," Torin ordered in a voice that said he couldn't wait to kick his father's old butt from here to Asgard and back.

I waited until Lady Adelaide was by my side and pointed at the vine. It started to unravel. This link I had with Mother Earth was surreal, but then again, everything about my life was way out there.

I disappeared through the portal with the soul of Lady Adelaide right behind me. The portal closed as soon as we stepped into the foyer. She looked around. I wasn't sure what to tell her. Truth be told, I wanted to go back to the forest, but I was stuck babysitting her.

Souls didn't exactly communicate with people verbally, but according to Torin, they understood things. "Do you remember Torin, Lady Adelaide?"

She stared at me as though I was speaking a foreign language. Maybe she didn't understand English. She spoke French when she was alive, and I didn't speak French.

She nodded.

I grinned. "Was that a yes?"

She nodded, tears welling in her eyes. Okay, Torin was not a good subject. "Please, don't cry, okay? He's okay. He's a loving and amazing guy, and you should be totally proud of him. He's a Valkyrie. That means he escorts souls to Asgard."

She nodded again.

Then inspiration hit. Cora. She could help big time here. "Lady Adelaide, I'm about to introduce you to my friend Cora. She helps souls communicate with the living. I think Torin will need her services." I pulled out my cell phone, and she watched me curiously as I texted Cora. "She can also watch you while I..."

Panic flashed in Lady Adelaide's eyes.

"No, don't be afraid. I'm going to help Torin." I peered at her. On a good day, I'd be freaking out talking to a soul. Today, anything was possible. "You want me to help Torin defeat the Earl, don't you? They need me back there in the woods because the forest listens to me." She still looked doubtful. "Please. I'd take you with me, but Torin won't be happy. He has a temper and can be quite melodramatic." She smiled and nodded. I sighed with relief. "Thank you. Cora's nice. She's a friend of mine and Torin's. She helps souls."

"At home going crazy. What's going on?" Cora texted.

"I'm opening the portal," I texted back, engaged my runes, and watched the portal form.

Cora practically raced into the room. She was a hot mess, her hair rolled up at the back of her head and eyes red as though she'd been crying. "What do you mean you want me to watch over a soul? Are they okay? Echo refused to let me go with him."

"I don't know if they're okay. I need to find out, and you can't come with me. Echo would focus on keeping you safe and not teaching the Immortals a lesson."

"Torin would, too…" Her voice trailed off when she saw Lady Adelaide. "Is that the soul I'm supposed to help? Who is she?"

"Cora, Lady Adelaide, Torin's mother. Lady Adelaide, Cora Jemison, my best friend. Explain to her what you do, Cora. I have to go." I created a portal into the forest just like Torin had taught me the last few days.

The scene was worse than I'd imagined. I almost twisted my ankle in the huge cracks criss-crossing the ground. Immortals littered the forest floor, their heads twisted at weird angles. Some witches with bruises were still fighting, but a few had joined the Immortals, including the poor old man with a crooked staff. I had seen the vision of his death, so I was happy I'd missed that.

But the trees… So many of them were on the ground. After this, I was going to have my work cut out for me. I engaged my runes, going for strength, speed, and endurance. The healing and pain runes dotted my skin automatically whenever I was in danger.

Torin was easy to spot, with his brilliant runes and his gravity-defying moves. He matched his father's moves. The body slams. The slugging. Their clothes were in tatters, their faces bloody and muddy, and their hair tangled with leaves and twigs.

"Come on, old man," Torin bellowed. "Is that all you got?"

His father dragged himself from the ground, his face red with rage. "You would not be a Valkyrie if it weren't for me, *boy*."

They charged. I winced as they collided, the force throwing them in the air. I should do something. So far no one had noticed me. Hawk made up for two men, his movements precise as he mowed down Immortals. Femi's laughter rang out with each kick and punch. The Earl's Immortals didn't stand a chance, not with the witches involved.

A witch pointed his staff at an Immortal and sent him flying across the forest, taking down several trees with him. Several Immortals were on the ground holding their heads. I was sure the images the witches projected were gruesome.

A scream came from my left. Rita, Gina, and their mother had the Earl's girlfriend trapped. She was begging them to spare her.

I hoped they drove her insane. Yeah, I know. Super bloodthirsty of me, but she deserved it. Where was Mom?

My eyes returned to Torin. He and his father were back to trading insults. Torin enjoyed a good fight, but for the first time, he wasn't having fun. Their rage was still not spent.

I sighed. Five more minutes and I was going to do something. After all, Mother Earth was on my side.

"Do we take these two or those three?" Echo yelled. I turned to caught him and Andris messing around with several Immortals.

"All of them," Andris said, and they went after the Immortals with moves any pro wrestler would be proud of.

"Raine, behind you," Lavania warned.

I turned in time to see a blurry Immortal sprinting toward me. A flicker of my hand and a fallen tree lifted and knocked him across the clearing. He landed and vines did the rest, wrapping him up like a mummy.

Someone laughed, and I whipped around. Torin gave me a thumbs up, and then he scowled. "What are you doing here?"

"Helping. Who said you're the only one who can have fun?"

"Where's my mother's soul?"

"With Cora. On your right!" I yelled.

He whipped around, going from calm breeze to a twister in a fraction of a second. He caught his attacker in the ribs with a roundhouse kick. The sound of bones cracking filled the air. Nice move.

I pointed a finger and vines wrapped him up. *Gentle, please. He has broken ribs.*

That became my job, wrapping up Immortals and keeping them down. The ones that were down kept healing and getting up, but I caught them one by one. I wasn't sure what we'd do with the witches once this craziness was done. They shouldn't remember fighting Valkyries or Immortals. Maybe Mom would come up with something.

A blur raced toward me and I braced myself for an impact, but Torin tackled her and snapped both her legs.

"No one touches her," he snarled. He looked up and called out, "You hear that?" A few people stopped pounding each other and glanced toward him. He stepped in front of me, hands on his hips. "You touch Raine Cooper and this stops being a game."

Oh, the arrogant son of… an evil Immortal. He just made me appear weak and defenseless in front of these people. I kicked him in the butt. Hard.

Because of my runes, the force flipped him over his head and he landed on his ass. Now that should make him act right. Someone laughed. I knew that laugh. I turned and my eyes met Eirik's. He saluted me and went back to fighting.

Torin glanced over his shoulder and shot me a mean look. "Stop horsing around and tie them up. If you haven't noticed, the vines are the only things keeping them down."

I stuck out my tongue. "Then stop playing around with your father and break something already," I said, twirling the vine around the woman he'd just injured.

"I already did. Several times." He jumped to his feet and took off to help Lavania who'd been ambushed. His laughter reached me, and I smiled. He was enjoying himself now.

Unbelievable. Fighting must be in their blood. Not so much in mine.

Part of me was happy the Immortals avoided me like the plague, thanks to Torin's threat. Still, I used trees to knock them out and then tied them up with vines. I was like a child poking helpless ants at a picnic.

"What do you think you're doing?" Catie asked, and I looked up.

They finally showed their faces. And they weren't Bash and the twins. "Fixing the mess you made."

"The mess we made?" Marj asked.

"Oh yes. You set the Earl on this road, hoping to use him to manipulate Torin and get me exactly where you wanted me. However, you forgot one thing."

They stepped back without answering.

"She's not alone," my mother said, coming to stand beside me. "And I know how you think."

Torin dumped his father's unconscious body at the feet of the Norns. "He's all yours. And it will be my pleasure to take out anyone you send to hurt or manipulate Raine."

Andris cleared his throat. "I have her back, too. She's the annoying younger sister I never had." He winked at me. "Or wanted."

We were slowly forming a circle around them.

Echo laughed. "This has been fun. Nice family reunion and all. Call me next time you have another." He opened a portal and disappeared.

"Stop trying to feed my student false information," Lavania snapped. "I will give her the information she needs when she's ready."

"And the rest of us," Femi said, indicating Blaine, Hawk, and Ingrid, "will always stand by the Cooper family."

I waited for Eirik to say something, but silence followed. I turned to search for him. Eirik and the witches were gone. Even the dead bodies. "Where's Eirik?"

Everyone looked around. I wasn't the only one surprised by his disappearance. Did he just stop by to save the day again? It was becoming a nasty habit. Where did he go this time and how was he going to erase the memories of all those witches?

"He took the witches with him," Mom said with a smile. "Run along and make sure they forget what happened here. It is your job to clean up after us, so fix the forest, too."

"We will take the Immortals, but Eirik will erase the witches' memories and Lorraine will fix the forest," Marj said and grinned.

I didn't understand why the three Norns wore triumphant smiles. They'd failed again. Unless everything that happened today had been part of their plan. But to what end?

They were never going to give up. Torin reached for my hand. As usual, he knew when I needed him.

"As always, it's been a pleasure. Good luck next time. Let's go home." He glanced at Mom and the others. "All of us."

He opened a portal, and we all filed in. I saw the faces of the Norns just before the portal closed. They waved and looked so pleased with themselves. I needed to find out what the other Norns had meant when they said I had to choose a side and make it official. Now that Lavania and Mom were back, they should know what that meant.

EPILOGUE

"So no one saw Eirik leave?" I asked.

"Nope." Andris planted his feet on the footstool of my chair. "I have to give it to our young god. His plan was brilliant. He called the witches, pretended he was with the Earl, and flipped the script the last minute. Sheer genius."

Yeah, it was. Without the witches' help, we might not have defeated the Immortals or released Torin's mother. Torin was catching up with his mother with Cora's help, and the older crew—Mom, Femi, Hawk, and Lavania—were at my house. I wondered what they were talking about. Probably rehashing what had happened. We had staked the mansion's kitchen while we waited for Torin to finish.

"I don't understand why he had to be so mean when he came to get Raine," Ingrid said.

"He was being watched," Blaine said. "Bosvilles is a powerful Seeress. When we left to talk to the witches, Eirik was telling them what he expected from them and it wasn't what they did. He talked about going to Asgard after joining the Immortals. Then he slipped Femi the real instructions. The spell. Supporting us. The whole nine yards."

I studied the instructions Eirik had left behind. He'd told them where my father was and where to find us and to wait until the witches did the spell and released Lady Adelaide. I wished he'd stayed.

"Do you think he went back to Hel?" Ingrid asked.

I couldn't tell them what he'd told me. There was no way he went back there.

Andris shrugged. "Possibly."

"Or Asgard," Blaine said and, for the first time, I didn't hear a yearning in his voice. He'd just seen how that need to go to Asgard could eat at someone until they were mad with it.

I checked my watch. Torin was still not done. Should I start worrying?

"We should go out and party," Blaine said.

"I'm in," Ingrid said. "This is the most fun I've had in years."

Andris jumped up and pulled her to her feet. "Then let's not stop. We'll use a portal and go anywhere—" He glanced back at me and frowned. "Coming?"

I got up. "No. I'm heading home." To wait for Torin.

Andris tilted his head. "You sure? Torin is going to escort his mother to Asgard."

"I know. You guys have fun." I followed them, waited until they used the portal, and then used it to go home. Voices came from downstairs. I heard Mom's. Femi's. Even Hawk's. What were they discussing?

I was just about to open the door when the portal opened and Torin walked in with Cora. I studied his face for signs of stress, anger, or bitterness. There was none. He was calm, happy.

"Hey," I said. Totally lame, but I couldn't think of anything else.

He chuckled, took my hand, and pulled me closer to Cora. It was strange listening to him introduce me to his mother and hearing her thoughts. When I hugged Cora, I knew I was really hugging Lady Adelaide. She was smiling when she separated from Cora, her eyes no longer glassy and lifeless.

Torin cupped my face and planted a fast one on me. "I'll be back as soon as I can. We are taking that weekend vacation together. Not a word," he said, pressing his finger to my lips. "We'll take Lavania and Ingrid."

"Great! Andris, too."

His eyebrows came down fast. "Why?"

"Because the more the merrier. And Blaine."

"Oh, I'm so going to regret this." He pressed a kiss on my forehead and turned to face his mother, who was watching us with an indulgent expression. "Come on, mother. James is waiting." He engaged his special runes and, when a portal appeared, flashing rainbow lights were visible at the other end. As soon as they reached the other side, something happened to her. She seemed more solid and less ethereal. When Torin took her hand, I grinned.

"Do you want to hear what Torin told his mother about you?" Cora asked from behind, and I turned.

I knew exactly how Torin felt about me. "Uh, I don't know. Why?"

"Because I hope Echo feels about me the way Torin feels about you." She grabbed my hand and pulled me to the bed. "Otherwise, I'm going to be green with jealousy. Let's start with the day he saw you."

As Cora talked, I found myself worrying about the forest. Had the Norns rescued the trees yet? Should I check? No, not without Torin. I wouldn't put it past the Norns to be waiting for me. I forced myself to sit still, listen to my best friend talk about our boyfriends, and pretend everything was perfect.

THE END

BIOGRAPHY

Ednah is the author of The Guardian Legacy series, a YA fantasy series about children of the fallen angels, who fight demons and protect mankind. AWAKENED, the prequel was released in September 2010 with rave reviews. BETRAYED, book one in the series was released by her new publisher Spencer Hill Press in June 2012 and HUNTED, the third installment, was released April 2013. FORGOTTEN, the next book will be released early 2015. She's presently working on the last book in the series, tentatively titled, VINDICATED.

Ednah also writes New Adult paranormal romance. RUNES is the first book in her new series. IMMORTALS (book 2) was released three months later. GRIMNIRS (book 2.5) is the bridge between book 2 and 3. Ednah is presently working on book 4, tentatively titled, WITCHES.

Under the pseudonym E. B. Walters, Ednah writes contemporary romance. SLOW BURN, the first contemporary romance with suspense, was released in April 2011. It is the first book in the Fitzgerald family series. Since then she has published six more books in this series. She's presently working on book seven.

You can visit her online at www.ednahwalters.com or www.runestheseries.com. She's also on Facebook, twitter, Google-plus, and blogger.